Pra

THE INDOMIT
& THE HAI

"I really enjoyed this book. I connected with each character and appreciated each one and how they added to the story."

– Thomas Thompson, *VolcanoEbook*

"I loved every second reading the book and can't wait for the 4th book. Thank you so much for writing such excellent stories."

– Javeria Khan, *iReader*

"I'm not ready for it to be overrrrrr"

– Jernail Radford, *iReader*

"The series so far is awesome! All three books have action, romance, and humor. The descriptions give the reader enough material that you can use your imagination and picture the scenes and characters vividly in your mind."

– Barbara Vodenik, *iReader*

"I love the scene when he asked her to please stay in the car. She replied, "Sure". Yet, she came right out. But because she is as concerned about him, as he is for her. Or later, when he is asking himself who was supposed to be guarding her. That was genius. I am absolutely looking forward to the 4th book."

– Emperess, *iReader*

"I am so in love with this series. This author has the ability to pull you into the lives of her characters so effortlessly. All her books are a must-read."

– Sallie Brown-Vinson, *GoodNovel*

"I really enjoyed this book but most of all I LOVE this series. I like the characters, the storyline, and the overall feelings when reading this book. I would recommend to everyone looking for a good book and series."

– Chenoa Abbott, *GoodNovel*

"The author is amazing, each of her characters are unique and I love how Greg's character has grown through each book!"

– Lei Sickles, *GoodNovel*

"One of my favorite books! I enjoyed it so much. Thank you, author! Will re-read it sometime."

– Jesse, *Moboreader*

"I love this series of books! The transition from one main character's story to the next is flawless."

– C. Ker, *Moboreader*

"Like your other two books, [I] love this one and [it's] nice to see a different side of Greg. Thank you for a gripping story. Can't wait for [the] next book."

– Michelle Wright, *NovelCat*

"Loved the story, loved the sass of the characters. Had me laughing in the middle of the night. Will stick around for the following books."

– Joselyn, *NovelCat*

"Done. Now the pain of waiting for [the] next book."

– Andu Lavy, *NovelCat*

THE INDOMITABLE HUNTRESS & THE HARDENED DUKE

Book Three

of Coalescence of the Five

STINA'S PEN

This is a work of fiction. Names, characters, organizations, places, events, and incidents are either products of the author's imagination or are used fictitiously.

For those who feel shackled by their past

PROLOGUE

FOURTEEN YEARS AGO

"Over here, Sush," the old man said from the hospital bed, his voice hoarse and weak. The words came out in barely a whisper.

Seventeen-year-old Sushmita Alagumalai had come home to find her uncle on the floor next to a broken mug, a pool of spilled-over coffee puddled by his side.

Her scream exerted her vocal cords like never before, making the neighbors rush over. They then called the emergency helpline as Sushmita tried to wake her uncle.

An ambulance arrived God knows how long later, and Sushmita was held back as the medical team checked the old man's vitals—another heart attack—strapped him on a stretcher, and hauled him into the ambulance, letting Sush sit with him and hold his hand. In a journey that seemed to be taking too long, all she could think of was, "Please help him. Please make him wake up. I'll be good. I'll do anything. Don't let him go too. Please."

She didn't know who or what she was praying to. She'd just lost her aunt two years ago, and she and her uncle had been grieving her death ever since. They were happy that they still had each other, until the first heart attack a year ago planted a seed of worry in her. A gnawing feeling grew as the seed sprouted, like it was telling her the last person she had wasn't going to be there for much longer. When she walked in on his fallen body, it was like her worst nightmare had come true.

At the hospital, once the ambulance doors flew open, everything that happened next was a blur. She didn't know how she got off, nor did she remember which corridors they passed through or whether she'd knocked into anyone. All she knew was that the operating room seemed too far away when it was—in fact—just right down the first hallway.

She stayed outside alone, sunk into one of the plastic chairs that were stained yellow from its original white, blind to her surroundings, deaf to any chatter, screaming, and medical staff yelling orders. Her back was bent over, elbows on her knees, mouth to her interlaced fingers that had already turned cold. Her mind was blank, and it only knew one word—please.

When the doors next to her cracked open, she shot up from her seat, eyes fixed on the two nurses and a doctor who emerged. The nurses went the other way while the doctor met her gaze, a flash of sympathy marring his face. "He wants to see you," was all he said, holding the door open for her.

She sprinted in, wasting no time, halting only when the sight before her created a force from the ground that was so strong it threatened to bring her to her knees.

Her uncle pushed a reassuring smile, asking her to come closer. She drew strength from his voice, as she always did, battling against the pull of the ground and letting his eyes guide her. By the time she had reached his side, her hands had to clench around the rail of the bed, no longer able to support herself. How could a man she once knew to be strong and invincible—one who fought for her and her aunt, one who taught her to fight for herself—now find himself in this state, unable to speak as loudly as he used to and hardly able to move?

"Sush," he drew her prying eyes from the daunting sight of machines and blood back to him. His throat bobbed. "Your aunt has always been with us. And I will always be with you."

She knew what that meant, and the tears of fear turned into those of anger. Her mouth opened, but before she could say anything, his hand raised ever so slightly as his forehead creased, knowing what she wanted to say but stopping the words right before they spilled out. "It won't be easy," he continued, "but you will do well. Your aunt and I . . . have never done anything that surpassed our pride in raising you."

Sushmita didn't know how, but her hand found his, her thumb brushing across the back, feeling the wrinkles. His grip was still strong, and she let herself hope, hope that this was a phase, that he would get better, that everything would go back to normal, as much as his exhausted eyes were telling her he'd lost the will to fight.

He swallowed a lump in his throat, and she watched the wave the movement created in case she never got to see it again. "Your aunt . . . never wanted to tell you this, but I think you have a right to know. Your mother . . . she didn't pass away from a road accident."

Her eyes grew wide, a hunger for the truth now rivaled the devastation of her uncle's state. The old man went on for a few minutes, and when he'd told her everything, he said, "We had hoped it would surface one day—the truth—but maybe you're the one who's destined to hear it. And when you do, Sush, tread wisely, choose carefully. Choose peace. Choose happiness. Choose what's best for yourself."

The corner of his lips lifted as he gave her hand a firm squeeze for a moment before his eyelids fell, his grip lost strength, and the beeping that Sush didn't hear before was now a flat monotone.

As the medical team spilled in and ushered her toward the corner, an endless supply of tears trailed down her cheeks that no number of tissues could absorb.

It was hours before the tears stopped, days before she fully processed the events of that day, and months before she accepted that she'd lost everyone she held close.

Every time she replayed her uncle's last words, a fire blossomed in the middle of her chest, and one day she decided that what was best for herself was to get to the bottom of things, to hunt down the ones who had killed her mother, and she was going to make them suffer, down to the very last creature.

CHAPTER 1

PRESENT DAY

The duke of L'ouest, Greg Claw, remained pensive as his darkened eyes examined the pictures and screenshots for what was probably the twentieth time. The report his top hacker had curated for him—behind his back—would normally warrant praise, a raise, a pat on the back for the initiative taken, but this changed everything he thought he knew, everything he thought he believed in the last three months, everything he thought he could have. This was why he had simply accepted the stack as the glow of his complexion dimmed, leaving Jade—his hacker—without a word.

The decision was supposed to be an easy one, and Greg felt ashamed to admit that he had hesitated and—for a brief moment—considered looking the other way, asking the subject why she was doing this before doing anything rash himself.

But he knew why.

It was written in the evidence. Asking wouldn't just waste more time and make him vulnerable; it'd make everyone he knew vulnerable.

What had changed his mind within microseconds? What made him just *know* that he had to do what he was going to do? Enora. Seeing his four-year-old little sweetheart in his mind was enough to steer him back onto the path which, he hoped, was the right one to embark on.

The way his little niece clung onto his pants and shirt, hid behind him, and refused to speak whenever the subject was around should have alerted Greg, but it didn't. And it made the duke feel even more idiotic that it didn't. It should have. He was Greg Claw. Something as glaring as the pup's aversion *should* have alerted him or—at the very least—made him suspicious. And Greg felt like he had failed when he didn't even instinctively feel that something was wrong.

Greg had developed doubts over time, but these little thorns hadn't grown on their own. They came about when his nieces and nephew—who normally took meeting strangers moderately well—didn't seem to take to the subject at all.

Hiding. Avoiding eye contact. Using potty breaks as an excuse to avoid having to answer the subject's questions. And the list went on.

Looking back at the way he had tried so hard, believing that the trust was real, made him feel used, naive. And he hated feeling naive. In other words, slow, slow to catch on. This was an insult that he reserved only for the truly slow, and he knew karma was a bitch when he was handed this stack of papers printed in black and white, now in a neat bundle settled against his steering wheel.

The red Sharpie—which was among Enora's things in his glove compartment—now rested in his hand as he flicked it over and over to kill time, rereading the texts and decoding the messages again even though everything was already etched into his brain.

One of the screenshot messages read:

> "Keep fucking him to keep him blind. We should be able to wrap this up in a couple of months. Then you're done."
> "Relax. He's not as sharp as they say. It'll be a loooong time before he suspects a damn thing."
> "He still thinks you're a porn star in bed?"
> "The fact that you have to ask is insulting."
> "Just checking. Do you . . . cum with him?'
> "I have to. It's part of the job. Logan, we've been through this—I think of you to come."
> "God, I'm getting a hard-on just by reading that."

The words burned Greg's eyes, and he squeezed them shut.

Once they reopened, he steadily underlined "not as sharp" and "a loooong time" in red, as if to carve it to memory and let those words deliver a blow to his soul and leave its mark there, so that he'd never be this stupid or blind again.

Three months. He'd admit it really was "a loooong time."

What these people didn't know was that anyone who crossed him couldn't even hope to survive. It was one thing to toy with his reputation and skills, but it was another to undermine his intelligence, and a completely separate ball game to play with his heart.

He checked the time on the dashboard. Two more minutes.

Greg closed his eyes once more and pressed the back of his head against the headrest, linking Alissa, *'In position?'*

'Yes, Boss.'

Greg appreciated that Alissa had filtered out the sympathy from her reply. He then checked in with Ivory and Desmond, who had been ready for a good ten minutes, just as he was.

Like the biological clock in Greg's body was in sync with the digital clock on the dashboard, his eyes opened the second the white number against the blue backdrop changed.

Peering out the window, he hoped he was wrong. He hoped his hacker was wrong. He hoped the evidence and this whole thing was an array of misunderstanding that would be brushed away as a well-executed prank.

But his people wouldn't do that to him, and he knew in his bones this was happening. He had started this mess, and Greg Claw never created any messes he couldn't clean up—advertently or inadvertently.

On cue, the five-foot-six brunette with curls covering half her back, fair skin, and an hourglass figure appeared from around the corner, just like the screenshots said she would. Her signature leather jacket that was two sizes too big covered the sunny yellow dress underneath with a crimson belt that matched her lips. Greg tried not to think of her lips or her eyes and focused on the blue velvet bag hanging loosely from her right shoulder.

When she came close to the cluster of parents, her razor-edged lips—which his most-hated cousin subtly cringed at during their encounters—curled into a smile. The way she nodded and mingled was as beautiful as it was fake. A show.

The duke's held breath was only broken when Hailey, the kindergarten teacher and one of his highest-skilled followers, linked, *'I don't care if you're going to kill me for asking this, but honestly, Your Grace . . . is this the only way? These are the pups we're risking! Among them, Enora.'*

'I'm well aware.' Greg's voice was a deep, uncompromising baritone. *'If we play this right, everyone here will be none the wiser.'*

'If she decides to deviate today, she'll still be here when the pups are released!'

'She won't deviate. The pups can be released. Everyone will be safe . . . Well, everyone except her.'

Hailey exhaled hard, her frustration and justified worry blasting through the link. *'At least tell the queen!'*

'Already have.' Silence hummed, until Greg cleared his throat. *'Which is why, as I understand, the bloodsucking empress's consort is now in her invisible form, one step away from our target. And the empress herself is at the gate. Also invisible.'*

'It's still risky,' Hailey adamantly argued.

'What we've been doing for years has been risky, Hailey. We will succeed in this just as we've succeeded in every other assignment prior to this mess. It will go smoothly. Because we—me, in particular—have a lot to lose if I screw up. I've screwed up enough in this lifetime. And I have had enough of losing.'

Ending the link in a brusquely imperious manner and stepping out of the car, Greg crossed the clear road and headed straight to the woman in her oversized leather jacket, bracing himself.

Her high-pitched laughter brought back great memories, all of which he now marked as lies. The thundercloud brewing inside him was controlled and calmed with the image of his niece in mind, returning his eyes to their original lilac shade, which he'd have to hold onto for at least another two minutes.

When he was several steps away, the parents that the subject was speaking to spotted him and made her aware of his presence.

Izabella Delilah turned, the same coy smile plastered across her face—a smile which Greg returned as she stepped forward and their lips touched. The familiar sparks traveled from their lips to his entire body, disorienting his animal, especially when her tongue demanded entrance, which he allowed only briefly.

Parting their mouths and smirking at her as naturally as he could, he murmured, "Hey, baby."

"My roguish duke," she whispered his pet name almost hungrily, invitingly, as she always did. Her hand crawled up his chest and rested on the side of his neck.

The corner of his lip tugged higher, which would have been a dead giveaway for creatures who actually paid attention, who actually knew him. Izabella Delilah clearly didn't, despite being his bonded mate whom he'd spent hundreds of hours with and slept with more times than he'd like to admit.

What a disappointment, he thought. It was at this moment that he conveyed a silent thanks that they weren't marked.

"Can I steal you away for a moment?" he asked in a gentlemanly but suggestive manner that had some of the listening ladies swooning.

Izabella's hand ran down his hard chest, stopping above his heart when her lips pursed into a pout. "Will there be enough time? Aren't the pups coming out soon?"

Stepping closer and tucking a stray piece of hair behind her ear, tracing the lobe, he muttered, "If we're quick, we can still make it."

She feigned contemplation, then resigned with an alluring smile. As usual, she tugged him by his hand and led him around the corner from where she had appeared earlier, then a second corner into the empty back alley.

The vandalized walls brought back such fond memories of him pushing her up against them as they made out like teenagers. The way their mouths devoured each other, the sounds that came from their efforts. But they never took things too far, Greg being mindful about who might appear out of the blue.

When they reached this spot today, Izabella's hands found their place on his wrists, seductively moving up his arms like they always did when they were bound to begin. She brought herself nearer to the wall and pulled him in, expecting Greg's hands to go for her ass like before.

However, instead of going for her bum, one of his hands pinned her at her collarbones as his other hand extracted a syringe from his back pocket containing a serum, which he injected into her voice box.

It was a move that she clearly hadn't seen coming, judging by those widened eyes.

CHAPTER 2

Izabella opened her mouth to speak but found herself muted. She tried to scream but realized she was only forcing air out of her lungs.

Before her brain computed what was happening, vines appeared from the concrete against her back and bound her limbs and body to the wall. Flowers of transparent petals grew within seconds on the tendrils, exuding a scent that she didn't think much of when two women she'd never seen before seemed to magically appear behind Greg, both dressed in black.

Izabella screamed Greg's name, trying to tell him about the two women, who she perceived as imposters, not knowing that they were the empress and consort of the vampire community, whose presence Greg had requested.

Greg, his eyes now a deep onyx, began, "Izabella Delilah." The fact that he had used her full name and that his eyes were a shade that she'd never seen told her everything she needed to know.

Her neck stiffened. Her wrists tried to break free, but the tendrils only tightened around them.

The duke smirked. "Did you really think I wouldn't find out?"

Her breathing shallowed. But her eyes maintained their adamant ferocity.

Greg took one step closer, making sure they looked each other eye to eye. "I have to say, the misguided confidence you and your hunter boyfriend have in me choosing you over my family, my queen, my niece really is the cherry on top of the cake of foolishness."

She said nothing but merely smiled—the most sinister smile he'd ever seen her show. He didn't even know she *had* a sinister smile. She was always sweet and flirty, but never vicious. Fierce, maybe. But never wicked. And the worst part was that they both knew it didn't take any words for the message to be conveyed: for three months, Greg Claw had been the foolish one.

"We'll see who's smiling by the end of this," Greg mused.

His rough hands trailed up her butt to her jacket, and then—without warning—he tore the garment and took satisfaction in the way her eyes widened in horror as she tried to scream, "NO!"

Casually, he instructed, "Nod for yes. Shake for no. Did this belong to your so-called ex?"

Izabella's plan was to keep her head still, hoping to minimize the threat posed to her lover now that the cat was out of the bag. But the scent from the transparent flowers contained an element that compelled her to tell the truth—to nod, just as Greg suspected she would.

He scoffed darkly, not knowing whether it was contempt or hurt that engulfed every cell and filled every last vessel in his body.

So much for believing that she ended things with her lover the day the mate bond with Greg was discovered—when they met at a hunter-lycan mediation that he had instinctively wanted to join even though he never cared about lawful politics. Some shit about her love-at-first-sight declaration and habitual repetition to anyone who'd listen.

In a zipped compartment of the torn portion of the jacket, he extracted a recording device that she'd been carrying around, a device disguised as her crimson lipstick, and crushed it with his bare hand. Tugging the blue handbag from her shoulder with force, he broke the gold-colored chain strap, creating a small wound on her shoulder.

Trying his best to ignore the twist in his chest when she winced in pain, Greg tossed the bag to Ivory, who Izabella hadn't even seen appear from the side.

Greg relished the way her eyes were incinerating his own because she knew she was losing, admitting to herself that there was no way out, unfiltered detestation now on full display.

She'd never loved him. He doubted she even liked him. Then again, she had an unfair advantage: humans, unlike wolves or lycans, didn't feel the mate bond until they were marked.

Damn the so-called sacred gift.

To minimize the pain for himself, Greg knew what he had to do first. Even his animal admitted there was no turning back, as reluctant as they were for what was to come.

In a voice he barely recognized, one that seemed soulless and dead, he recited, "I, Greg Claw, reject you, Izabella Delilah . . . as my mate."

It was as if a dagger had been struck into his heart, eliciting the most anguishing howl from his animal—a yowl of loss so piercing that Greg felt he was breaking for them both. His human, however, pressed his lips together and refused to show any pain. The agony came in waves, gnawing at his chest, shooting into his heart, weakening his being.

His fingers then spread across Izabella's chest, feeling the vibration of her beating heart, a rhythm that he once fell asleep to now becoming one that would haunt him forever. His claws extended slowly, entering her flesh leisurely as she gritted her teeth, adamantly trying not to express her affliction, but the tears escaping the corners of her eyes discredited her.

Red smears blossomed on her shirt, giving the sunny yellow a new color, and when her first cry of pain came out in a puff of air, he forced himself to smirk more darkly, reminding himself not to let what he felt for her get in the way of relishing in her suffering.

Her tensed body was loosening, and her face was decolorizing. Right before she passed out, Greg extended his claws all the way, jolting her body when he reached for her heart and tore it out. He dropped it onto the ground like the organ was just sloshy trash as he conveyed her lifeless body hanging there into memory.

The original plan was to crush her heart, but he couldn't bring himself to do it. This was as far as he could go.

Seeing this—the creature he thought was his to trust, to protect, to love, who had ended up fooling him—made him release a shaky breath as the first of his tears fell.

"Greg."

He knew that voice anywhere. Anyone knew that voice anywhere—the one that he and the rest of the kingdom instinctively bowed to. Firm with the occasional softness. Normally authoritative, now solemn.

She had insisted on coming and stayed far enough not to be seen but near enough to watch things unfold and be ready to get involved if necessary.

Greg appreciated that she hadn't interfered, that she—as always—understood that he wanted to do this: to clean up his own mess.

After a hasty wipe of the tears, he exhaled hard, wondering if this was what it felt like to be free from the mate bond—like everything in him was hollowed out. His eyes remained on the ground as he turned in her direction and fell on one knee, from his obedience to her or from the heartache of losing his mate, he wasn't sure. "My queen," he acknowledged.

He couldn't even bring himself to look at her shoes, let alone her face. And he could imagine the larger pair next to hers—her husband's—kicking his face for his failure to uncover the threat sooner, for putting his children in danger.

Greg didn't know what to expect. He wasn't even scared anymore. Enora was safe from Izabella now, and that was all he needed.

A small pair of arms wrapped around his shoulders. The queen's scent surrounded him, and the lilac color of her dress came into his peripheral vision as he knelt there, immobilized by shock.

In a sorrowful but grateful whisper, she said, "Thank you."

His arms came around her, briefly squeezing her in return, appreciating that she didn't say, "I'm sorry," or anything that reeked sympathy. He got enough of that from half his people, and he felt that energy radiating off the king's being. It was getting suffocating.

Hoisting himself up and pulling the queen to a standing position in the process, his eyes went to the bush on the opposite side of the road just to avoid making eye contact with anyone. "You two should head back. It's my turn today. Your pups will know something's up if they see us all here. Enora will definitely know something's up."

From the blurred corner of his eye, he saw his cousin—the king—nod in agreement, and the queen muttered, "We'll see you later." Only after his cousin offered him a brief squeeze on his right shoulder did they leave with the empress and consort.

Alissa and Ivory dealt with the corpse and brought the handbag to the Den. They intended to assess all her makeup and accessories, even the bag itself, since they were suspected to be well-disguised weapons.

At the kindergarten, Hailey had remained more alert than she'd ever been in her entire career and kept a close eye on her surroundings, holding the two princesses and the prince close. She now gazed at the trio with a smile, relief washing over her when she received Alissa's update.

Greg washed his hands with bottled water and disinfected them with sanitizer. The last thing he needed was for one of the pups to smell blood on him. He checked his clothes, making sure there weren't any bloodstains, and exhaled impatiently when he had to change everything. It was a good thing Ivory had his spare clothes in a bag.

After throwing the clothes into the trash, he brisk-walked to the kindergarten, avoiding everyone's glances filled with questions that he was not going to entertain as he searched for the only creatures who mattered.

"There! He's here!" the prince, Ken, exclaimed.

The smallest girl in her violet dress behind Ken looked up, then gazed to Greg's left and right. When she discovered he had come alone, her cute little lips parted to display the grin that melted her uncle's heart as she dashed toward him, almost tripping twice in her matching violet shoes before she leaped into his open arms and screamed, "Uncle Gweg!"

Squeezing her, mentally conveying apologies that weren't spoken and taking comfort in her safety, he pulled himself together, acted casual, and asked the usual question, "How's my little sweetheart?"

"I shot three cups at bweaktime!"

"Did you now?"

She nodded proudly, making Greg smile.

"That's two cups up from yesterday. Want ice cream to celebrate?"

Pressing her lips and shaking her head, she placed her little hand on his nose, something she did when she was going to ask for something. "I want to feed duckies again."

Greg's brows raised in comprehension, seeing the mischief in her lilac eyes. "We'll have to go home and ask your mommy and daddy first. And if they say yes, remember, this time we're throwing the bread *near* the ducks, not *at* them. Alright, sweetheart?"

Enora chuckled but didn't give an answer.

Instructing the elder princess, Reida, and the prince, Ken, to grip onto his pants, they crossed the road together. The doors of the driver and passenger seat flipped upward like wings ready for take-off, and Ken could finally reach the button on the driver's side specifically placed at the highest region so that it was out of reach of the pups.

Greg had always allowed Ken three seconds to try to reach for the button before doing it himself and telling the pup he might get it the next time.

To both the duke's and prince's surprise, Ken managed to reach it today, and Reida gaped at the opening door to the backseat she'd seen hundreds of times, then back at her grinning brother.

Greg began the usual headcount, despite there being only three of them. "Alright, let's go. Backseat headcount: Princess. Check. Cousin look-alike. Check." He watched the two climb into the booster seats, sit upright, and then methodically buckle themselves. He then leaned over to make the final adjustments for both pups, double-checked, and then jabbed the button for the door to close. Finally, he brought Enora to the passenger's seat and buckled her himself.

When he was done, he left a kiss on Enora's forehead and said, "Special seat headcount: my little sweetheart. Check." Enora giggled and paddled her feet before Greg shut the door and got into the driver's side.

On the way back, Greg tried not to think about the emptiness in his chest. He listened to how Ken and Reida went on their usual conversation of why only Enora could ever sit in front, which the elder princess answered—probably for the hundredth time—was because their youngest sibling was their uncle's favorite, which the prince found unfair.

Grow up, you little shit. Life isn't fair, Greg thought to himself. No, he didn't care that Ken was only four.

CHAPTER 3

At the Paw-Claw residence—the king changed his last name to include his mate's a few years back as a birthday gift to himself—Greg extracted a white envelope from under his seat. Meanwhile the two pups behind raced to unbuckle themselves before getting out as soon as the car doors were opened and racing to the front door. Enora waited patiently for Greg to unbuckle her, carry her out, and set her on her feet. Her hand reached for his as they took their time traipsing to the entrance.

Enora was filling him in with her classmates' profiles and quirks, and he listened attentively, enjoying the momentary distraction despite having already memorized every single profile of the pups and their families in that kindergarten.

It wasn't as if he knew everything either, he admitted. He didn't know which ones threw watercolors and painted their classmates' faces and clothes during art, demanded a potty break twenty times a day, or vandalized the tables and chairs and subsequently got detention. All this nitty-gritty, Greg learned from Enora. He particularly liked the one who screamed and cried in history lessons because the pup found historical pictures and ancient writings spooky.

King Alexandar and Queen Lucianne greeted their pups with hugs that lasted longer than usual and kisses that spoke their relief before sending them to the kitchen, where Empress Pellethia and Empress-Consort Octavia would keep them distracted while the king and queen spoke to the duke.

Enora, after being embraced and kissed by her parents, stood between them and her uncle, refusing to leave. Greg asked the king and queen if he could take her to the pond later that evening, emphasizing that Enora had promised not to assault the ducks this time, even though she'd said no such thing.

Enora blinked her wide lilac eyes—her secret weapon to raise the chances of getting what she wanted.

Her father still wondered how—of all the skills his youngest could have inherited from her mother—she had inherited this one.

Enora had grown to learn that blinking innocently bagged her father, and persuading her mother was the real challenge, so she was elated when Lucy said yes so quickly this time. She wrapped her mother's leg in a grateful hug, but then something came to her mind.

Facing her uncle with a faltered smile, she asked, "Uncle Gweg, will Aunty Izabella be coming too?"

Lucy and Xandar stiffened. Lucy's mouth opened, but Greg beat her in offering an explanation, "No, sweetheart. It's just you and me. Is that okay?"

"Yay!" Enora wrapped her uncle's leg before obediently disappearing to the kitchen to join her brother and sister. The faster she ate and finished her mundane homework, the quicker she'd be throwing bread at the ducks to vent her frustration of being trapped with coloring and repetitive scribbling of the same word just to learn the spelling.

The three adults at the front door exchanged relieved but awkward looks. Greg exhaled hard and began their murmured conversation. "I honestly don't know where to start, so why don't one of you deliver the first blow and we'll take things from there."

"Greg," Xandar began, his hand falling on his mate's waist as he chose his words carefully, "we'll deal with things with the hunters. If you want to keep the corpse or require anything that can be traced to their territory, just say the word. We'll handle the politics from our end."

"I'm half surprise you're not strangling me right now, Cousin." For once, the way Greg addressed him contained no hatred. The tone came out flat and neutral, hiding the exhaustion and defeat that his soul was drowning in.

Lucy uttered, "There's no need to strangle you, Greg. You put our pups first. You put the entire kingdom first."

That sounded really nice and noble, but Greg knew he'd only put Enora first. Reida second. Ken? Maybe somewhere on the same level as his followers, so that'd be fourth or fifth. The rest of the kingdom? Well, unless they had a scarred past and could potentially qualify as a maverick, they technically weren't his problem. The large chunk of that population was left in the very safe hands of his cousins and cousins-in-law.

Anyway, here was the point: Even with a shorter list of creatures to protect, he had screwed up when he trusted something as vague and unreliable as feelings from the fucking mate bond!

Shaking his head at his blindness with a self-deprecating smile, Greg murmured, "And to think someone like me deserved love." He scoffed. "Pathetic."

The queen interjected, "It's not pathetic, Greg. It's not pathetic to want to be wanted. This was a terrible experience . . . No, terrible isn't a strong enough word. The word I'm looking for probably hasn't been invented yet. Anyway, the fact is none of this devalues you as a creature. You were so many things before she showed up, and you are still those things now that she's gone. You have us. You have your people. You have Enora."

"Thankfully," Greg muttered. "If there isn't anything else at the moment, I'll come by later. To take her to the pond."

"Have you eaten? You could join us for lunch."

"No, my queen. I need to . . . get some shit out of my head."

Lucy understood that better than anyone. After a rejection, one normally wanted to be alone. She nodded in comprehension, and her brows pinched together when she reiterated Xandar's words, "Let us know if you have any specific request about the hunters involved, Greg. And whether you need anything else."

"Duly noted. Thank you, my queen. Cousin."

Trotting to his car without looking back, Greg sped out of the residence for the forest where he used to spend a lot of time with his now-dead mate.

###

Striding along the familiar path that he once moseyed through with Izabella—hand in hand—like an actual couple, he had to fight off the sudden urge to burn down the entire forest to erase every lie created here.

He reached the tree—their tree.

Greg brought Enora along once and she hated it. Not the forest. She hated having to spend time with his mate. Izabella actually glowed brighter, but in hindsight, Greg now knew that her giddy flamboyance was for her own motives, not because she was interested in getting to know the family member he held closest to his heart.

Looking at the dried-up leaves on the ground now, Greg recalled how Enora would put herself at least three feet away from the woman, despite being repeatedly told that she wasn't going to be harmed, despite being shown that the huntress carried no weapon, despite Izabella bringing a teddy bear to coax her.

By the way, Enora accepted the teddy bear to appease her uncle, but the moment Izabella left in a separate car after the date and Greg was bringing Enora home, she asked for a potty break midway. After parking in front of a thrift store, Greg thought Enora was warming up to the stuffed animal when she brought it out from the car with her.

As they approached the store where there was a bin outside, she feigned surprise and pointed at a tree to Greg's right. He held her hand on his left. The moment he turned, Enora flung the plush toy into the trash. His swift sight caught her doing it. He would have asked if it was an accident, but it clearly wasn't. And the girl had the audacity to turn back to him with a satisfied smile and said, "I don't need to potty anymore, Uncle Gweg."

Greg lowered himself into a squat to level their gaze, and when she told him why she'd pretended to look accepting of the toy, her uncle brushed a kiss on her forehead and apologized for making her feel the need to accept Izabella's gift just to make him happy. Greg promised that he'd never put her in a position where she had to appease him again. She could do or say anything, as long as she wasn't hurting anyone.

Enora blinked in a way like an idea came to her. Her eyes went to the trash can that was far too tall for her to see the contents inside. At the end of her contemplation, she asked innocently, "Does that mean I can buwn the teddy now, Uncle Gweg?"

"No," Greg said, and hoisted her into her arms, carrying her back to the car before she got any other ideas. "Weaver would freak out with the open burning, your mother would slaughter me, and your Uncle Blackfur would laugh while she did it. And you would be grounded until you turn eighteen. Maybe longer."

Greg now chuckled at the memory. He never told Izabella about it, keeping his lips sealed even when she suspected Enora might have given the teddy away "because she didn't look very happy with it."

It was interesting . . .

Of all the things a pup could do with a toy they didn't like—leave it in the corner of the room and never play with it, torture it for the hell of it, take out the insides—Izabella had settled on the reason Enora might have given it away.

Pups were territorial with their toys, even the ones they didn't like. It was about having more than it was about liking. Why would an adult think that a pup had disposed of the toy unless they knew the toy wasn't in the child's playroom?

At least his niece was sharper than he was. It was a good thing Enora had gotten rid of it.

Upon coming out of memory lane, Greg stripped and shifted. His brown-furred animal flexed its shoulders and growled at the tree. Then, with its bare hands on both sides of the trunk, it hauled the tree toward the sky with all its might. The muscles in his body tightened, his veins popped, and his jaw tensed, and when the sound of the first snap of roots entered his ears, a surge of strength motivated him to tug further. More snaps followed until the entire tree was uprooted.

Greg lifted the tree above his head like it was just a barbell, and his chest rose and fell as his eyes searched for a suitable position before he threw it in the direction of the coursing river, forming a diagonal bridge across the stream.

Shifting back and getting out a lighter, he set the tree ablaze and watched the billowing smoke engulfing the space. He kept an eye on the grass, splashing water or stepping on the flames if any chunk caught fire. When the tree was about eighty percent burned through and could fit into the river, he kicked it in, and the crisp structure submerged for a moment before coming back to the surface, letting the water take it downstream.

If this was ever reported, Weaver would freak out. The queen would kill him. And Blackfur would have a good laugh.

CHAPTER 4

In the evening, with Enora in the space on his crossed legs, they tore stale bread, and the girl clearly hadn't gotten the memo when she aimed the first chunk at the mother duck of purple feathers, a turquoise beak, and yellow eyes. She only missed because Greg lifted her and turned her away right on time, so the bread was hurled neatly in front of the animal, who quacked in appreciation. And so it became a game, for Enora to estimate how far off she should aim to get the ducks while her uncle deflected her point of focus.

Her giggles showed that she was having more fun than during their previous duck-feeding exercise. When the last of the bread was gone, some of which injured two ducklings and most of which scattered around the flock, Enora pulled out a strand of leaf next to Greg's leg and tried to reach the dragonfly minding its own business above an empty lily pad.

Before the insect got away, a gray elastic structure came from underwater at the edge of the lily pad, and the dragonfly disappeared into a gray frog's mouth as it hopped onto the lily pad. Enora flung the leaf in her hand at the frog, who ate her newfound live toy, not that the amphibian cared as it plopped back into the water, blending in with the stones at the bottom.

Greg chuckled, his chin gently rested on the crown of her head. "Hey, sweetheart, can I ask you something?"

"Mm-hm."

"Did you . . . hate Izabella?"

Enora pursed her lips for a second before muttering, "Maybe."

"And your brother and sister?"

"Maybe."

"Sweetheart—" he turned her to face him "—you know what I love most about you?"

Her head swung side to side.

"That you are honest. You tell me the truth no matter what. That's what I love most about you."

She blinked twice, then avoided his gaze, murmuring, "I don't like Aunty Iza."

"There we go."

Greg's tone and small smile sounded so encouraging that Enora continued, "Her lips are too wed. Her fingers are always cold. Her smwile is like those bad guys on TV. Weida says her laugh is skeawy. Ken says Aunty Iza makes him feel icky. He always hides behind Mommy. Weida always gets Daddy to help wash her hands and face if Aunty Iza touches her."

Wow, Greg thought: that was a lot of information. "Were you ever . . . scared of her?"

Enora shook her head. "I'm skeawd when my teacher calls Mommy."

Fair, Greg thought. He'd be scared too. "Thank you, sweetheart. I just had to know."

Pulling out another blade of grass, Enora leaned into his warmth and articulated, "I'm not skeawd of Aunty Iza. I'm skeawd that . . . if I don't like Aunty Iza, I don't get to feed duckies with you anymore. And I don't get my special seat when I go to school. And you won't bwing me and Weida and Ken to school anymore. And you won't bwing us home."

Greg didn't think his heart could break any further. It was then he realized Izabella's death didn't leave it hollow. He could feel the organ enduring a sharp twist from Enora's words. "Sweetheart, that would never happen. Why would you think that? Did Mommy or Daddy tell you that?"

It was his cousin. It *had* to be his cousin. Goddess, he hated his cousin. Or was it the distant cousin? Maybe his distant cousin-in-law?

With a shake of her little head, Enora said, "Mommy and Daddy say you will love me no matter what."

"They're right." Oh, so it wasn't his cousin.

Mindlessly tearing the grass into strips, she explained, "After I wanted to buwn Aunty Iza's teddy, you didn't come for two weeks. Mommy and Daddy said you had work. But you never work for two weeks, Uncle Gweg." Technically, he worked every day, but he refrained from correcting her when her eyes watered as she looked up at him and asked, "Were you angwy with me for hating Aunty Iza's teddy, Uncle Gweg?"

Oh. So it was *him*. This was all on him.

"Sweetheart, I was never angry with you. In fact, I should have let you burn the teddy. And I really was working. I was helping your Aunt Pelly set up a security system in her empire. But you're right, I should have called." Rubbing her arms to soothe her, he vouched, "If I have to work that long again, I'll call, okay?"

"Mm-kay." The glistening eyes cleared as she snuggled into him.

"And, sweetheart, you don't have to call Izabella 'Aunty' anymore. She's not your aunt. She's never going to be your aunt, alright? She's gone." He kept his head up so she didn't see the way his eyes watered and his Adam's apple bobbed.

A ghost of a smile curled Enora's lips, and she simply played with her grass and nodded like it wasn't news. "Mommy said she left to pay for something. Weida asked what she forgot to pay. Mommy said it's a few things. All very expwensive."

The edge of Greg's lips tugged upward.

Left—yes, left the universe.

Pay for something—her sins, her betrayal, for breaking his trust and his heart.

All very expensive. He preferred priceless, but this worked too.

"Your mommy's right," Greg mused. "And let's not say Izabella's name even if we have to, okay?"

Enora's brows pinched in confusion. "You mean . . . give her another name, Uncle Gweg?"

"Yes. Like a nickname. A secret code. One that only we both know. You pick."

Her lilac eyes were on the ducks, but her mind was far away, brows creased as she pondered hard. Her fingers on the grass were so still it looked like she was posing for a portrait.

When she finally moved, her lips parted, and a toothy grin lit up her face when she suggested, "Ugly Deli?"

Greg's brows rose in surprise. Izabella Delilah was hot. Smoking hot. When they went public, the media described her as a rare beauty with an enviable body and a charismatic smile, which Greg wholeheartedly agreed with. Then again, he was slightly blinded by the mate bond. Slightly.

At present, Greg matched his niece's smile. "Ugly Deli it is."

"Yay!"

###

When Lucy asked Enora how duck-feeding went, the fact that her pup leaped in jubilance with twinkling eyes and began rambling about the ducklings, dragonflies, frogs, and grass showed that she'd had fun. But when her mother questioned whether she hurt any ducks with askance, Enora pressed her lips tightly and shook her head, refusing to look her mother in the eye.

After giving Greg a hasty hug and the usual goodbye kiss on his cheek, Enora bypassed her mother and scampered into the villa toward her room.

When they heard the door shut with a thud, Xandar uttered, "Getting into trouble seems to be good practice for her speed. She didn't even trip this time."

Lucy exhaled hard. She really didn't want to ask. "How many did she assault today, Greg?"

The duke shrugged like it wasn't a big deal. "Two. Ducklings."

"This girl," Lucy reproached with knitted brows, glancing in the direction her daughter had disappeared in.

"It's just a phase, my queen. The ducks will bore her one day. Besides, there were six ducks in the pond, so the majority were safe. Just as we can't realistically be expected to protect everyone in the kingdom, we can't realistically be expected to protect every duck in the pond."

Lucy pinched her nose bridge, exhaling hard as Xandar's strong hands came to her shoulders, his thumb rubbing soothing circles while he pressed his lips together, trying to contain his amusement.

Unbeknownst to him, his simple gesture set a heaviness in Greg's heart, reminding the duke of how close he had been to having what they had—a relationship, a bond that was destined to last a lifetime. And Greg had to remind himself that—unlike his cousin and queen—the bond with Izabella was anything but authentic.

He harrumphed and, out of curiosity, asked, "How long have you both known your pups hated my mate?"

Their eyes snapped to him, both flabbergasted. A quick glance flickered between them before Lucy said, "Since the first time they met her, so a little over two months?"

His thick brows pulled together. "And no one ever mentioned this to me because?"

Xandar remarked, "Because we thought you knew." His brows dipped lower. "The pups weren't even subtle. Reida and Ken tried to be, but Enora definitely wasn't. Besides, you always seem to know everything."

"What a flattering explanation," Greg replied numbly with as much sarcasm as he could muster.

Xandar wasn't done. "And honestly, Greg, even if we wanted to tell you, how do you expect us to do it? Just walk up to you and ask our kids to spill every insult—"

"That'll do, darling. He gets it." Lucy's hand on her husband's chest made him drop the rest of the sentence before she turned her attention back to the duke. "Greg . . . we, as adults, understand that . . . in a family . . . there will be creatures that we click with and creatures that we don't and perhaps never will get along with. But that doesn't mean the latter can't be part of the family, especially if she's good for her mate, more so if she makes him happy. The thing is, Greg . . . your happiness triumphed over the . . . intolerance our pups have for Izabella."

"It shouldn't triumph over their safety, my queen."

"And it didn't. It never did," she firmly replied.

That was when it hit him—how Lucy and Xandar always insisted he carried his poison detector around, especially when they knew Izabella was in town. They made a point to ask whether the detector ever detected anything: it didn't. And whether it was switched on: it was. And whether it was under constant maintenance and improvement: again, yes, it was.

Greg had assumed their paranoia was because mavericks, new and old, now roamed the streets and posed a threat to their pups. He thought they were particularly concerned about the newer recruits.

Only now did Greg realize it was never the mavericks they were skeptical about; it was her—Izabella.

In the two times Greg had come to get Enora for a bonding session with Izabella, Lucy reminded him that Enora was never to be left with anyone but him, not even with his mate, meaning if Enora needed a potty break, Greg was to accompany her, not Izabella. The queen couldn't even stop herself from asking Greg and her daughter to be careful during those times.

"You always knew something was off," Greg murmured, looking into her lilac-and-onyx eyes.

Biting her bottom lip, Lucy nodded curtly and guiltily. "The issue was I didn't know what I was worried about. I wanted to trust her. I liked how happy you were with her. But something about her felt amiss. I didn't say anything because I didn't have hard proof. I didn't even have a proper reason, to be honest. She was . . . trying to be approachable, trying to be nice, trying to . . . belong.

And I didn't want to take away someone who meant so much to you based on my own groundless distrust."

"Your instinct," Greg interjected, "should have been a good enough reason to distrust, my queen." He added her title to sound a little less rude.

Quietly, she admitted, "I don't disagree. With hindsight, I knew I should have said something, no matter how baseless it was. At least it would have hinted to you in some way. I . . . there's no excuse. I'm sorry."

Greg took in a lungful of the evening air, mindlessly gazing at the water feature, watching parts of the water scintillating under the last light of day, forming little stars that danced with the endless ripples. "Just so we're clear, I'm not blaming either of you for this. I just . . . had to know what everyone was thinking when I was rendered blind."

He didn't join them for dinner, saying he still needed time alone, driving home and running through a few messages from his followers—the mavericks—before plopping into his home office chair.

The twins' birthday was the following week, and Greg settled on getting Enora a toy crossbow she'd been eyeing. He wanted to get her another archery set—the biggest one in the best store—but Hailey had called dibs on it in the mavericks' group link, so Greg had to find something else.

For Ken, he'd be getting a boring 500-piece puzzle set. The child seemed obsessed with working on those after school, to the point the queen had to confiscate them a few times just to make him finish his homework. Greg then wondered what pup even did puzzles these days when virtual games were so much more exciting with their vibrant colors, vivid animation, and exhilarating sound effects.

When the duke deduced that the prince had probably gotten the boring gene from the king, who had gotten it from the Blackfurs, he began mentally combing through the things he'd like his cousin and cousin-in-law to demand from the hunters.

CHAPTER 5

Four months later, Greg found himself in an elevator headed for the sixteenth floor alongside his cousins and the queen, along with the ministers and a few warriors.

The metal doors parted, and they trooped down the well-lit corridor with glass-walled meeting rooms on each side, indifferent to the humans peering at them. Only the room at the end had opaque walls and doors, bookended by a guard on each side. At the sight of the neighboring species, the guards instinctively blocked the entrance, forbidding entry.

It was their presence that told Lucy where to go. She knew who they guarded anyway. "Lowell. Harlow. Is Valor in there?"

Lowell, blond with a diamond face, replied with crossed arms, "He's in a meeting, a matter of great urgency that just arose. You have been notified about the postponement of the treaty execution, I believe, Your Majesty."

Lucy's head tilted to the side as her lips lifted into a smirk. "We have a meeting with him. Now. It was scheduled last week, and it's a matter of interspecies urgency. Unless his matter concerns the vampires—which I doubt it does—whatever came up last minute on his end can wait."

"I'm afraid I'm not authorized to let you enter," Lowell responded with resistance.

"I didn't ask if you're authorized," Lucy said. "I'm *informing* you that I'm going in there and will have you thrown aside if need be."

By his side, Harlow—who had dark hair and a broader frame—pulled out his pistol and aimed at Lucy. That barely lasted a second when a stone-faced Tobias Tristan, the kingdom's minister of defense—who was right in front of

Harlow—broke the pistol with one hand. The weapon shattered into pieces, and its pieces scattered across the terrazzo floor.

Xandar stepped forward, towering over Harlow, blocking his view of Lucy. He reached for the front placket of the man's uniform, lifting him off the ground, making the guard do a 180 when his hands tried to get Xandar's hand to loosen as the human began apologizing and begging for mercy.

Onyx-eyed and inundated by homicidal rage, the king warned, "The next time you even think of disrespecting my wife, I will crush your limbs, tear out your balls and your dick, and make the smallest incision in your throat through which I will take out your ribs one by one. In that order. Do you understand me?"

The guard nodded hastily as Lowell subconsciously stepped away from the door, his hand frozen by his side, reluctant to draw his weapon from the holster.

The queen offered a meek, apologetic smile. "I'm sorry that your irresponsible coward of a boss put you and your colleague in the middle of this, Lowell. Thank you for your cooperation."

Lucy's small hand made the gentlest contact with her husband's bicep as she stood on her toes to peck a kiss on his jaw, whispering, "That's very sweet of you, darling. Please put him down. Gently. We don't want to be late."

Xandar mm-ed and lowered the man who—once his feet touched the ground once more—sprinted out of the king's grip.

Greg couldn't help the scoff that left his lips when the guy almost tripped while making his escape. Even Enora ran better.

The lycan warriors pushed the doors that opened into the room of officials, all of whom were hunters. A projection of a map flickered on the white wall.

"Out," Xandar ordered the room, then pointed at the beer-bellied man at the head of the table and stipulated, "Except you."

"Your Majesty." Commander Valor, the leader of hunters with salt-and-pepper hair, stood, stunned. "We're in the middle of a discussion about . . ."

"Oh, good." Lucy's perky voice bloomed before she strode to the front, eyed the presentation with an empty smile, and said, "We're here for a discussion too. And we're ready to start."

Chairs scraped against the floor as everyone hung their heads low and scurried out without being instructed.

After the king pulled out a chair for his mate and she sat, he sank into the seat between her and Valor as the remaining lycan and werewolf ministers and warriors took their places in the still-warm seats.

Valor exhaled. Frustration and reluctance hung in the expelled air before he hollered, "Alagumalai, Patterson, Abbott."

One woman and two men pivoted their gazes to him when their boss added, "Get your asses back in here."

They strode back in without a word.

Greg, like everyone else, studied them as they took their seats opposite Xandar, Lucy, and himself.

Hunters didn't necessarily choose their profession. They might have been human, but they were a class of their own. One could dream about being one of them, but if he didn't possess the birthmark on his nape in one of the three categories of their kind, there was no way he'd qualify—let alone be welcomed—to be a professional hunter.

There were one of three types a hunter could be born into: First was the archers—even though no hunter used bows and arrows nowadays—also known as the defenders, those who were said to be the best in combat and anything involving physical attacks or defenses. Second was the octopuses—the brains on strategy and tactics not solely in battles and wars, but also in mediating between species. Finally was the chameleons or—put simply—undercover agents, which was what Izabella was despite her once saying that she "loved not having to work whenever she visited lycan territory."

While the archers, octopuses, and chameleons had a birthmark on their napes to signify the category they were destined for, the leader—when chosen by the majority—had his or her birthmark changed into a crown, which was the mark Valor had on his nape, one he wore with pride.

Unlike vampires with an exclusive skill, a hunter possessed skills across each category, though their proficiency in ones they weren't born with may be lower. For example, they may have been born octopuses, but that didn't mean they weren't good in combat; they were just generally less skillful than the archers.

The man furthest from Valor, seated directly opposite Greg, was Giovanni Patterson—a six-foot-two blond with a defined jawline, thin lips, and a narrow frame. His muscles bulged from the baby-blue short-sleeved shirt, and his complementary blue eyes had already been stuck on Lucy the moment he was called back in.

He had recently been appointed chief chameleon when the former chief and deputy were found to have "accidentally" woven themselves into the conspiracy with Delilah. Patterson had always been apt at getting what he wanted when he wanted. Ask him for advice, and he'd tell you that looks would only get you so far. Or not far at all. What mattered was what came out of your mouth, your eyes, and the tone you used to persuade. Which was why he was so drawn to Lucy.

Unlike so many he had had the displeasure of working with, the little gamma just got it. She knew how to act and when and how to react. And when he said she knew how to act, she *really* knew how to act. Act calm, act happy, act amicable, act harmless—she had it all. It was no surprise to Patterson that she hooked the king. Sure, he would give her points for her beauty and the mate bond, but that wolf—well, now lycan—could talk, could present, could impress, and could make people kneel, metaphorically when she was a gamma and literally now that she was queen.

They were very alike, Patterson thought. He could easily bend people to his will too. The trick was to be aware of the unaware and use these as the weak links to seize the prize.

On his second meeting with her in attendance as gamma many years ago, Patterson used his chameleon skills on Lucy—flattering and flirting with her, even saying that she "must" have an after-meeting coffee chat with him and maybe they could "do something more . . . enticing later tonight"—all to get her to go easier on them during the mediation.

Lucy offered almost no response, giving one-sentence answers. Patterson didn't think much of it, figuring she was playing hard to get. She did smile, after all. Funny how he didn't see it was an empty smile. Little did he know he'd successfully pissed her off, though she didn't show it at that time. Her alpha brother was pissed, too, and that should have been a sign, but Patterson didn't take it as an indication that things wouldn't go as he wanted. Overconfidence had been his downfall.

The repercussions of his actions came out when the mediation began and Lucy demanded the hunters trade more than the original bargain due to Patterson's "inappropriate mannerism and repugnant behavior to a partner species, which insults not only me but my species as a whole."

Sure, Patterson had a tough few months after that as the octopuses constantly reminded him about how stupid he'd been, but being the sweet talker he was, he managed to get back into Valor's good books and climb to the top of his kind while those know-it-alls remained exactly where they were—below him. Well, except for one know-it-all, the one seated two chairs away, but, eh . . . they were on equal standing now as far as hierarchy was concerned—him being chief chameleon and her—of all people—becoming chief octopus.

Forgetting about Chief Know-It-All, Patterson's blue eyes scanned the gamma-turned-queen from her head to those bare arms. Still as smooth as ever. He'd bet they tasted good too. Her sleeveless maroon dress that accentuated her assets was really turni—

"Watch the way you look at her or you'll have trouble seeing for the next few days. Or weeks." The warning came in a whisper beside him. The whisper—though soft—carried a firm warning. Patterson didn't have to turn to know that it was the queen's best friend who was, annoyingly, always around.

"Relax, Minister," Patterson muttered, tearing his lustful gaze off Lucy and only stealing glances now and looking away when the king's murderous gaze scorched his eyes.

The hunter to his right was Axel Abbott—chief archer. He was a broad-framed six-footer with short black hair that stood like small spikes, though his personality was anything but spiky. His arms remained crossed over a forest-green shirt as he leaned back into his chair, but his shaking left leg under the table gave away his anxiety, which he hoped only his colleagues could see, not realizing the faint sound that every werewolf and lycan could hear.

The constant thud, thud, thud was already driving Greg mad, and his animal asked whether they could just rip off the hunter's leg already.

Axel Abbott had never been much of a talker as far as Lucy, Toby, and their fellow gammas recalled. He just stood there like a loyal guard, nodding curtly or giving one-sentence responses when asked a question. Some even labeled him as being discriminatory when he shelled up with wolves but opened up with his fellow hunters and huntresses. Axel was careful about who he mingled with, never saying more than he thought was necessary. "Do more, talk less," was his motto. Fitting for an archer, as Valor always put it.

Finally, the only woman among the three who had to drag their asses back in was the leader of the octopuses—Sushmita Alagumalai. She was a six-footer with brown skin, dark brown eyes, a square face, and raven hair bunched into a low ponytail that reached her upper back, where the strands curled in all directions. A bright pink, worn-out headband sat on her head, tucking in the smaller curls that threatened to spring free. On her neck sat a gold chain necklace weighted by a locket of the same color.

About time, Lucy thought. She knew Sushmita from her days as gamma and always felt this huntress had the most sense. Sushmita fought for the benefit of hunters, but she was the only octopus who refrained from disregarding the interests of wolves during mediations. She'd been in the shadows for some time when less worthy octopuses took the helm and snatched credit for her ideas, solutions, and responses.

More than once while Lucy was in a heated discussion with the chief octopus and he or she went speechless, feigning a look of contemplation with furrowed brows, she'd seen Sushmita scribble something on her notepad before pushing it to her superior, who'd then glance over it and reply in accordance to the contents of the note. More than once, the chief read the scribbles without understanding what it meant, which made the reply come out nonsensical. This was when Lucy and her fellow gammas would turn their attention to the actual person she was debating with as the gamma of gammas asked in utter confusion, "What?"

Sushmita would try to hide a smile—secretly taunting her own head of division—and would continue the discussion on behalf of her superior from there, only stopping when she didn't have the authority to decide for their side, reluctantly turning to her leader for the okay.

Toby used to say Sushmita was the only brain the hunters had and joked that if they were to abduct her, it'd crumble the hunters' operations overnight. It was an exaggeration, of course, but he and Lucy would begin fantasizing about plucking Sushmita out—just temporarily—whenever they wanted an easy win against the hunters. There were times they were mad at Sushmita for her rebuttals and propositions, but—more often than not—they could live with the middle ground she'd eventually reach with the wolves.

Greg's eyes trailed from Sushmita's unruly curls to the over-conspicuous pink headband, taking note of the way she leaned forward just slightly, her arms folded inward at her elbows that were anchored on the table. Her eyes were a dark wall, giving away nothing. And unlike her archer colleague's, her leg was definitely not fidgeting. Thank goddess.

Sushmita was studying him as well, knowing that the duke was the main reason for this meeting the king and queen had fought tooth and nail for. Taking in his partially onyx eyes on his sharp face and pitch-black hair, a concave nose above the full set of lips—a look that broke hearts—she wondered if he'd broken that many hearts to deserve this one hell of a heartbreak.

Sushmita had seen him only once when he came to surprise Izabella with a visit. The chief octopus and many others had a hard time guessing what Izabella had accomplished to deserve the undivided attention of such a powerful figure that was known to be closed-off and practically allergic to commitment.

Izabella was not a hustler. She'd do the bare minimum and sweet-talk her way through the rest of any given task. Nobility was an intangible idea that she fancied, not a trait she possessed. And whether the now-dead chameleon was smart was up for debate.

It was an odd fit with the duke, but—as one of Sushmita's colleagues chimed like a broken record—the mate bond triumphed over all logic. Many had been secretly happy that Izabella was killed because . . . well, not many liked her to begin with, especially not the octopuses, whom Izabella had little, if any, respect for.

In Izabella's defense, some octopuses called her a beauty with no brains, which was not objectively accurate. So her hatred toward their group could be seen as a justified response.

Sushmita felt neither happy nor sad when the news of the chameleon's death reached them, thinking that Valor would have to filter the rest of the chameleons. But the moment most of the former chiefs and deputy chiefs were found to be involved in what was later termed as the Delilah Conspiracy, thus were suspended with immediate effect, Sushmita was called up to handle all correspondence and public statements regarding the issue.

And she cursed. Day and night. And she didn't care when the rest of the hunters gave her disapproving looks. Half of them thought her outbursts were justified, so who *fucking* cared what the other half thought?

Sushmita had never spent so many hours scrutinizing her own drafts and replies to emails that were signed by both Xandar and Lucy, though at least sixty percent of them sounded exactly like Lucy, who had an eye as sharp as an arrow and a brain as crafty as a fox.

The threats within those lines were new, so the huntress wagered that was the king's doing. And she was right. It was.

Sushmita had long thought Lucy was actually born a fox rather than a wolf and hated every fucking chameleon, archer, and octopus involved in the fucking shit with Izabella that Sushmita now had to clean up. The huntress respected the gamma turned queen, but this woman really had to start contributing to the cost of coffee she had to down to stay more alert than usual these past four months.

She felt Greg's gaze sear into her skin and guessed that he'd been briefed about who had really been carrying this clusterfuck of an issue. Valor was just the one with the final say, who Sushmita had been constantly arguing with about solutions and corresponding consequences.

When Valor said he'd sent word to the lycans and werewolves that the meeting would be postponed and he used "an urgent matter" as an excuse, Sushmita blew up, telling him to be ready to watch his family slaughtered and his house burned to the ground and prepare himself for when the lycans' and wolves' wrath spread until no hunter was safe. Needless to say, she was the least surprised when the lycans and wolves barged in.

But she *was* surprised that the guards outside remained alive and that nothing and no one was burned to the ground. Yet.

Maybe they'll burn something later, she thought.

The dark circles under her eyes didn't bother her. But what was coming next strained her—mentally and psychologically. She was on her second cup of coffee before noon and had only Izabella and her pals to blame for the predicament she was now ordered to defend. Defend fucking idiots. One of whom had the easy way out—death.

At times like these, Sushmita would wonder why she even became a huntress in the first place. Sigh.

But she knew exactly why she was here. There was only one reason holding her from leaving, and after seeing that through, she'd be out the door, and these bozos could deal with their own shitshow.

CHAPTER 6

Greg felt something when he looked at Sushmita: immense distrust—an involuntary response that oozed from Izabella's betrayal. Every huntress was an enemy, he was sure. This one was no exception. She may be an octopus, but for all anyone knew, she was probably also a part-time chameleon, given how attractive she was. And chameleons were the most ruthless of the bunch.

He knew she'd been the brains behind Correspondence, the queen had told him so, but he imagined her to be more . . . defensive, like Patterson; or anxious, like Abbott.

If Greg's facial reading wasn't off, the huntress just looked tired. And enraged. Yes, definitely enraged. And she had no right to be! It was her fellow huntress who'd started this whole thing.

Sushmita exhaled as she scribbled one word on her notepad and pushed it to Valor, who took one look and his eyebrows shot to his hair before he pushed back the notepad. Facing the royals, he began, "Like we said before, Izabella Delilah's crime . . ."

Lucy interrupted. "I think the chief octopus's recommendation on how you should start this meeting would make us want to kill you less, Valor." She'd seen the scribble given how big and clear the handwriting was, and it said *apologize*. When the commander discarded her advice like trash instead of treating it as gold, the lycan rulers could feel the huntress's frustration from across the table.

Valor checked his cards. The odds were definitely stacked against him, against all of them—as Sushmita had been drilling into his head so hard for months on end that he'd begun having nightmares about the way her nostrils flared when she said it.

The leader swallowed the lump of ego in his throat, clenched his teeth, and tried again, "I apologize for attempting to postpone our meeting."

"For lying," Lucy pressed mercilessly.

"The matter was urgent, Your Majesty." He tried not to spit at her title, as much as he wanted to, but the way he despised being spoken to by someone who was decades younger than him *and* a woman slipped off in a subtle way.

Lucy's brows raised. She'd seen the projection on the white screen earlier. "A discussion of your people's ranking and stations for next term is *not* more important than the threat several of yours posed to our people, my family. Wouldn't you agree?"

It was a dare. It'd take a fool not to see it. Valor didn't have to look to Sushmita to know the right move was to concede. "Yes, Your Majesty," he uttered grudgingly, fingers digging into the flesh on his lap to cope with the bruised ego. Fucking lycans. Fucking wolves. Fuck them all! This one, though small, caused the biggest problems! If times were different, he'd shove a dagger down her throat or put a clean bullet through her skull.

One of Lucy's hands was on Xandar's lap since they sat with his hand over hers, more to keep him from exploding than to keep her calm. The king began, "Now that we've laid your lies on the table and gotten that out of the way—" Xandar accepted the document Lucy handed to him and placed it in front of Valor "—let's go through this one more time, then sign it off, and you can get back to that very urgent matter of yours."

"With much respect, Your Majesty," Valor began, putting Sushmita on higher alert. *What is he doing?* she thought. "We need more time to assess the feasibility of your demands."

Toby pointedly noted, "You had four months."

"Minister, the treaty—which practically demands we give your species physical access to our operations and security systems for the next three months and virtual access for the next decade—is, I'm not sorry to say, too steep a price for the . . . incident that the duke had the misfortune of suffering."

Sushmita's head tilted back, closing her eyes so no one would see what she was thinking, which was her boss being yet another fucking idiot.

God help her.

Greg would admit that when he put that particular item in his list of demands, he'd expected a firm and flat no from his cousin if not from the queen first. He was surprised when they fully supported it.

"Misfortune," Lucy began with a voice of frost, "is a condition brought about by nature, something none of us can control. What happened to the duke was *not* a misfortune. It was a conspiracy designed to compromise our species. A scheme to get close to the duke to take my daughter's blood, and you call that an *incident*? Which the duke had the *misfortune of suffering*?"

She scoffed, and an upward tug at the right corner of her lips did nothing to take away the deathliness on her face when she added with feigned understanding, "Well, I suppose everyone has a different way of assessing the gravity of a situation. I would say more, always being big on words, but my Nouvelan's resolution is to speak less. So let's try something new."

Lucy turned to Greg as he extracted a black velvet box from his inner coat and opened the lid as if he was offering the queen jewelry, when it was to reveal a multi-needle syringe disguised as a hairbrush. Lucy's eyes darkened to a deep onyx as she took it from the extravagant casing.

The queen continued, "Fortunately, the substance inside remains functional. It was tested on several rats, all of which died within weeks, as you well know, since you've been given the report and a sample of the substance, which your own people have returned with similar reports. It's very creative, using malleable needles to pass it off as a common brush, only this brush can subtly extract the victim's blood while injecting the suppressants inside to numb the victim's receptors so she would be none the wiser. It's extremely clever, using needles that hold the substance in so its scent and danger remain undetectable."

Her chair scraped against the floor as she stood. "Now, Valor, to help you better understand the gravity of the situation, I'm going to use this brush on you. We'll see if anything happens. If it does—if you drop dead—it'll simply be an incident that you'd have the misfortune of suffering. Let's start, shall we?"

Valor was about to shoot up from his seat, but the lycan warriors stepped forward and held him down. His face turned white as Lucy's heels clicked toward him, and his paling lips quivered as Abbott attempted to get off his seat only to be stopped by another lycan warrior.

When the tips of the brush touched the first strands of hair, Valor leaned away and yelled, "Alright! Alright! Just . . . remove that thing!"

Holding it in place, Lucy prompted, "Was it just an incident?"

"N-No," Valor gritted.

"That the duke had the misfortune of suffering?" she pressed.

Valor's eyes inadvertently met Greg's cold ones before the commander looked away, muttering, "No."

"Glad to know we're finally on the same page," Lucy replied with a cocky smile, freeing him from the brush and hearing him release a relieved sigh as she turned to her warriors. "That'll do, Fiona, Simon. Thank you." The warriors bowed and released their hold of Valor, stepping back into their positions.

Patterson's dick twitched at Lucy's speech and the show that followed. Something about her made everything that had just happened hot as fuck. He had to cross his legs to hide the erection as one hand went over his mouth to hide the smile underneath.

His arousal hit the noses of many, and all raging eyes turned to him when Lucy threatened with a growl, "Turn off the damn thing or I will tear off the structure myself and feed it to Valor's dog."

"It's harder than it seems," he muttered to himself, only realizing his poor choice of words after they left his lips, and the pun that was clearly not intended made Xandar shoot up from his chair, pulling Patterson from across the table, earning a groan from the hunter when his knees hit the edge.

Greg turned to Lucy while watching the show. "Should I help tear off the structure, my queen?"

"No, Greg. Not today."

"Another day, then," Greg muttered.

Xandar's claws from his thumb and index finger at Patterson's jawline sunk into his skin. Patterson grunted, desperate to refrain from screaming and cursing at his own body's response to the brute's mate. Red fluid trickled from the wounds, and everyone smelled Patterson's blood.

Although most had their eyes either on Xandar or the struggling Patterson, Sushmita's eyes stuck to her notepad, her hand holding her head like it was too heavy. *I'm surrounded by idiots*, she thought for probably the hundredth time.

A loud crash followed when Xandar threw Patterson's body back into his seat and the hunter fell with the chair upon the impact, groaning again as his hand rushed to feel his wounds.

With a hand on Lucy's back, Xandar warned, "That should remind you about control. And if it doesn't, I'm more than happy to make adjustments to help you remember. But that would involve the permanent removal my wife suggested, and it would not be fed to a dog. It would be shoved down your throat."

That made Patterson's structure shrivel as his chest rose and fell in exhausted breaths. He refused Abbott's outstretched hand and pushed himself up, setting the chair back in place, avoiding looking at Lucy in case he lost it again.

Sushmita scribbled something and pushed the notepad to Valor, who—this time—covered it with his palm and leaned back before reading it from his hand. The note read:

> If you don't sign the damn thing now, the list will only get longer. You and Patterson just made it longer.

Putting the notepad facedown, Valor exhaled sharply. "Let's get this over with."

CHAPTER 7

After illegible signatures were slashed across dotted lines, Lucy demanded, "Where are they?"

"Well," Valor began, "seeing that I initially sought a postponement, the ones behind the conspiracy aren't her—"

Lucy and Xandar growled, shooting up from their seats once more as their thunderous rumble echoed through the room, at which time every other wolf and lycan stood. The strength of their snarls reverberated through everyone's eardrums, making Abbott and Valor shudder internally.

Their glacial onyx eyes drained the color out of Valor, and Xandar's voice turned deeper and more threatening than anyone had ever heard when he ordered, "You fucking get them here. In this room. In thirty minutes. Or we *will* invoke Clause 4."

Valor didn't need reminding what Clause 4 was: "In the event of a breach, the kingdom may hold the commander of hunters hostage until the breach is remedied, subjecting him to any form of treatment the kingdom deemed appropriate. Where the breach remains unremedied within the first month, the defense minister will subsequently be taken hostage."

Valor turned to Sushmita, who shot him a what-are-you-waiting-for look, and Lucy prompted in a tone that was no less menacing than her mate's, "Twenty. Nine. Minutes."

Valor's hand shot to his trouser pocket and entered a number on his speed dial. He concentrated on hiding his fidgeting hands and quivering lips as his eyes wandered anywhere but at the primitive monsters in the room, the smallest one now pulled to sit on her husband's lap as they both watched Valor like a hawk.

The standard ring-back tone going *doop-doop* sounded morbid for the first time, like it was prophesying that Valor's pulse on the electrocardiogram would match the cycle of a double beat and then nothing for a few times before the line went flat.

God, he hoped the line wouldn't go dead. It was such a bad omen.

Two cycles passed before the recipient picked up, at which time Valor barked for him to round up those under suspension and bring them to the headquarters within twenty minutes. Although aggression was evident in his voice, the slither of fear and panic coiled in his order was equally apparent. And it pleased Greg, Toby, and Lovelace the most.

Uncomfortable silence unfurled in the room as sweat beaded Valor's forehead and drenched his armpits.

Christian leisurely sipped the bottled water like it was just another break between meeting sessions, though creases of impatience marred his smooth brows and spoke for his resentment at the hunters' feeble attempt to break away from the agreement.

At the twenty-ninth minute, the elevator doors had still not opened. The crippling silence was made worse when Greg conveniently chose this time to crack his knuckles, relishing the way Valor jerked as the commander stood and called the same number, almost turning into a ghost now, even wishing he was a ghost so he could float out of the room.

The line went dead.

Valor muttered a curse and dialed again.

Toby casually mentioned they were down to ten seconds.

At that moment, the bell of the elevator chimed, sounding like the extension of Valor's life pass had been approved when the metal doors parted and the suspended ones were brought in with hands bound behind their backs, each held by two escorts.

The commander released a puff of air and sunk back into his chair. Abbott appeared relieved, too, looking less stoned. Patterson didn't show much, like it didn't matter if Valor was taken. Sushmita showed close to nothing.

Greg rose from his seat like he was welcoming royalty when—in fact—he was more than ready to kill. Lucy got onto her feet as well as the warriors held the doors open while the hunters brought in their four suspended colleagues.

By his side, Lucy asked, "Any alterations to your request, Greg?" Her voice was softened, encouraging, and harmless. Nothing like the way she spoke to Valor. Greg assumed it marked the difference between an ally and a foe. It'd take him a few more years to realize that the tone she'd just used was actually reserved for family.

His onyx eyes never left the six-foot-two hunter with light brown hair when he responded in a respectful murmur, "No, my queen. No alterations necessary."

She gave a nod of acknowledgment, took three steps to the wall, and knocked twice on it with her knuckles, satisfied with the solid sound that came out before saying, "Line them up here, please. Three feet apart."

One of the escorts took one step forward. "Your Majesty, I thought it was agreed this was to be dealt with in the w—"

Valor cut him off, "Zip it, Johnson. Line them."

Shocked at the hostility, the hunter apologized, "Pardon me, Commander."

Johnson was about to move when Xandar uttered, "If you don't say the words I want to hear in the next twenty seconds, you'll be added to this lineup."

Words he wanted to hear? Johnson was a hunter, not a mind-reader. How on earth would he know what the lycan king wanted him to say?

It was only when Johnson's dilated pupils and frantic mind began searching that he noticed Xandar's hand covering the queen's small shoulder, the king's thumb stroking it leisurely, lovingly. Only those closest to the royal couple knew Xandar's hand was also to restrict his queen's movement. She may not have wanted or needed an apology, but he did.

Johnson cleared his throat and uttered, "I'm sorry for questioning you, Your Majesty."

"No hard feelings," Lucy replied with a cordial smile.

"As long as it doesn't happen again," Xandar warned with the same scowl, which prompted Johnson to nod and bow low in response.

The escorts placed their mouth-taped colleagues against the wall, pinning their wrists and ankles with portable metal holders that dug into the concrete.

The first in the line-up was the former chief octopus, Zasper Zavier, now placed before Xandar; the second was the former deputy chief archer, Sofia Zelasko, now before Christian; the third, the former chief chameleon, Seni Intitulada, placed before Lucy; and finally, the one Greg had been waiting patiently to end since the day he killed his mate—the former deputy chief chameleon, Logan Larson.

Larson was a green-eyed six-foot-two broad frame with dark hair, a square face, and thin lips—a more-than-suitable chameleon. As Greg assessed him, he glowered. Since the hostages' mouths were taped, Larson could only channel the depth of acrimony he had for the duke through his eyes: for fucking his girlfriend then killing her; for turning his colleagues and boss against him; for keeping him isolated from the world in the past four months only to slaughter him now.

As Xandar, Lucy, and Christian took their positions, Greg interjected, "Wait." Pivoting to Lucy, he said, "I'd actually prefer to use the glass wall for him."

Ignoring Larson's muffled protests, Lucy asked, "And for the other three?"

"I really don't give a fuck as long as they're dead, my queen."

"Okay." Facing her prey, her claws extended like a sword from a scabbard when she coolly said, "We'll be done in a bit and meet you outside."

"Take your time, my queen. I'm sure Larson and I would love to see this venture to the end."

"Hm," Lucy snickered, knowing Greg just wanted to watch his prey suffer and tremble in fear before ultimately killing him. She would too.

Turning back to their own prey, Christian and Xandar delivered swift kills, through the victims' throats and stomachs before breaking their necks, letting the lifeless bodies sag.

Lucy's claws were about to plunge through Seni's abdomen when the woman's muffled "please" and stream of tears made Lucy sigh in impatience. Pulling the tape off with force as Seni yelped, Lucy didn't even register the redness around the huntress's mouth when the queen asked in exasperation, "What?"

Seni's frantic plea came out rushed like she was catching a train, "Please, Your Majesty. Please. We weren't lying. There really is someone else, someone calling the shots. Only Izabella knew them. Whoever they are, they must have removed all evidence somehow and . . ."

Lucy cut her off, "What a convenient incident you've had the misfortune of suffering."

The stupid excuse Seni was spurting had been used by every conspirator for months, yet no evidence could be recovered to prove it. The monarchy had decided that whether there was someone else or not didn't erase the fact that these people were involved in attempting to steal Enora's blood to be sold in the black market because of its speculated healing abilities that she is suspected to have inherited from her mother.

Before Lucy's claws went through, Seni exclaimed, "No! I have a child. She's just turned three. My daughter and husband need me."

"Oh, I know about your family," Lucy replied, cold and callous. "And I'm quite sure your daughter would grow up just fine without having you as a role model. The last thing I need is for you to teach the next generation to inject and extract things from our future generation without caring whether they'll live or die."

With that, Lucy's claws dug into the former chief chameleon's abdomen. Seni's screams were cut short when Lucy's claws swiftly swiped all the way up through her chest, throat, and head, making this the bloodiest execution thus far. And due to Lucy's lack of height, some blood splattered on her dress and more got on her face.

Before she could turn to Greg and his victim, Xandar spun her around, a bottled water from the table ready in one hand and a tissue tucked in the other as he gently cleaned the dots and streaks of blood off her cheeks, forehead, nose, and jaw. He then pecked a kiss on her nose to indicate that he was done and was rewarded with her soft smile and a hushed, '*Thank you,*' through their link.

Greg got busy, dragging Larson out by his hair that had grown long enough to be tugged. The warriors held the door open for the duke as he hauled the red-faced, muffled chameleon until the first glass wall came into view and he slammed the hunter against it.

Larson groaned as Greg held him up by jabbing his claws through the hunter's collar, feeling the tips meeting the glass surface while Larson screamed a muffled line of curses. Deciding to improvise instead of going ahead with the initial method to end the bastard, Greg made their eyes fuse before smirking darkly, relishing in the hunter's weakened state.

Without warning, the duke crushed Larson's elbows and ankles, broke his limbs, and watched him take bated breaths and turn pale, about to pass out. Right before he did, Greg's hand went low, sliding his claws through his penis and testicles, earning another cry.

Rage fueled the duke as he struck Larson's head against the glass, sending his victim into a daze and breaking the glass that dug into Larson's nape. Taking a broken shard, Greg stabbed it into Larson's throat, watching blood ooze like juice from a fruit. Finally, he tore out the chameleon's ribs. One by one. Larson was already dead by the second rib, but Greg didn't care. He went on until the last bone was out and snapped. Only then did he let go of the body.

Taking lungfuls of air, he appraised his handiwork while everyone around him remained silent.

Christian found the sequence of his slaughter bizarrely familiar. Toby and Lucy—when they realized where the steps had come from—turned to Xandar, who was equally stupefied.

When Greg was done and locked eyes with his cousin, he uttered, "Inspiration can come from the most unlikely of places."

His claws retracted, and—for some reason—his eyes locked with Sushmita's. He didn't know why, but for a brief moment, he felt like they were the only two creatures in the room. Then her voice permeated through the silence when she asked, "The agreement doesn't state that the kingdom wants the corpses, but are they required, Your Graces, Your Majesties?"

Her voice. Smooth. Silky. Cool and collected. Why hadn't he heard anything like this before? The tone was meant to be flat, he knew. But how did something flat carry its own melody?

"Greg?" the queen's voice tore his mind out of oblivion.

Greg felt stares on him. Knowing he was given the choice, he muttered, "No need. We don't need these bodies polluting the kingdom."

Sushmita pushed a polite smile and asked Lucy and Xandar whether there was anything else they wanted to discuss. There wasn't, so they thanked her—ignoring Valor—and called it a day.

On their way back in Xandar's jet, Lucy sank into the seat facing Greg and asked if he was alright—he'd had better days—and whether he could tell Enora about the change in his work schedule starting the following week—of course, how hard could it be?

CHAPTER 8

"You're going away again?" Enora asked, a film of water glossing over her lilac eyes threatening to spill over.

Greg hesitated. So this was why the queen had asked him to tell Enora. Having this conversation was harder than he'd thought. "Yes, sweetheart. We're going to see each other a little less, but only for the next three months. I'll still pick you up from school on Fridays, and we can go to the pond or the park on Saturdays. After three months, everything will be back to normal. And I'll pick you three times a week again, as usual."

Enora's gaze lowered to the grass around her shoes. Then a sniffle escaped her, sending a crack into her uncle's heart as he hoisted her into his arms. "I'll still be here, Enora. This isn't like the one with your Aunt Pelly where I disappeared completely for two weeks. I'll meet you two days every week and I'll call every day."

"You pwomise?"

"I promise."

She sniffled again, her arms around his neck tightened. After some time, she asked, "Are you going to see Ugly Deli?"

"No, Enora. She's gone. For good."

He spared her the details of how—after the mavericks had gotten everything from Izabella, he ordered his people to burn the body, with the monarchy's seal of approval, of course. Izabella then stayed in a mason jar of ash in his office desk drawer. And every time he thought about her ashes, he couldn't help the gnawing feeling in his stomach. He felt like he was lying to Enora about never seeing his former mate again. He was technically still seeing her, though in a different form.

Two months after the cremation, he and his animal decided it was time to let go completely. They brought the jar to the same street Enora had asked for a potty break with the teddy bear, and he threw it into the same bin, swiftly turning away before he had second thoughts.

Coaxing her now, he said, "This is purely for work, I promise."

"Can I come with you, Uncle Gweg?"

That warranted a big, fat, undebatable NO. He was infiltrating a circle that had almost put her in danger. There was no way he'd bring her, even if she begged. "I'm sorry, sweetheart. I can't do that. Maybe . . . when you're older, you can come with me to these things. But not now, not this time."

After a quiet moment, she asked sadly, "Is it because I'm too shwort?"

Not wanting to tell her the dangers she'd be exposed to, he clicked his tongue and fibbed, "Yes, that's exactly it. When you're as tall as . . ." He had to give her something which seemed reachable in the near future—though it realistically wasn't—and settled with ". . . your mother, I'll take you. It'll be easier for you to see and touch everything then."

"Mm-kay," she murmured, resigned.

Setting her on her feet, Enora threw one last crumb into the pond, which fell nowhere near the ducks as it floated a short throw away, a further testament to her sorrow.

"I'll be back before you know it. Don't shoot anyone while I'm gone, okay? We might not get to go anywhere on weekends if any of your teachers call your mother."

"He startwed it," she complained, albeit meekly, kicking a pebble nearby, which fell into the water and created a ripple.

It was about a classmate who pulled her ponytail before she got out her birthday crossbow—which should not have been in her bag to begin with—and shot the rubber bullet at the guy's nape. A perfect shot. It left no mark or injury, but the boy cried and whined for fifteen minutes, so the teacher had to call Lucy.

Enora's weapon was confiscated by her mother for three full days, which surprised the pup. She thought she'd lose it for a week or longer. As it turned out, her parents placed part of the blame on the one who pulled her hair.

Greg thought the confiscation was a little excessive. Enora acted in self-defense . . . sort of. It was good to start defending oneself at a young age. "You could always tell Aunty Hailey, you know? Say your head hurts after the basta—after your classmate pulled your hair."

"Will Aunty Hailey give me a cwossbow?"

"I doubt it. You could try asking." He then made a mental note to tell Hailey to make sure there weren't any crossbows within Enora's reach in kindergarten, and to have someone watch this pup during her daily archery playtimes in case Enora got the idea to use those instead.

CHAPTER 9

The following week, Greg and thirty mavericks trooped into hunters headquarters.

Each division of hunters would have ten mavericks breathing down their necks in the coming months, who would rotate at month's end. Greg himself would turn up in any department at any time he deemed fit. Bless his cousin-in-law . . . fine, and cousin, for materializing this big-shot request he'd made.

The archers, chameleons, and octopuses crammed in the welcome lounge to greet them. Valor's idea was to start with an introduction session "to break the ice."

A frustrated exhale left Greg when he replied, "I break necks and limbs, sometimes ribs, but never ice." Taking one step closer, towering over Valor, who swallowed and tried not to squirm, Greg declared, "I'm not here to make friends, Valor. My people and I have memorized every face, name, and background of every hunter months before today. If you and your people have not conveyed the thirty-one names and faces here to memory, I'd recommend you step down. I don't appreciate being slowed down by inefficiency and incompetence."

The air turned cold. The rays of morning sun penetrating through the glass became an illusion of warmth as the air-conditioner blasting arctic breeze offered a better representation of reality. The only heat present was that radiating off the duke, which ranged from anything between impatient and infuriated to downright murderous.

Valor cleared his throat. "Your Grace, we are simply extending common courtesy. We can always skip over the introductions if—"

"If we're not in the control rooms in the next minute, I'll be extending my version of common courtesy."

Several hunters jolted as Valor turned to his people and gave them a nod to disperse and lead the mavericks to the respective departments.

"Right this way, Your Grace," Sushmita's voice, cool and collected, echoed into his ears. Her hand gestured to the left when a ghost of a smile played on her lips. It wasn't a coy one like Izabella used to wear, nor a seductive one that he was used to getting from females who were either fishing for a duchess position or looking for a good fuck.

Sushmita's smile was one of amusement. And it wasn't for him. It was for herself. The upward curl might have been mild, but it was significant.

Greg recalled seeing her when he had come for Izabella, but Sushmita's face was as hard as granite at that time, as she studied the papers in her hands, which he felt suited her. Oddly enough, this lighter smile suited her just as well.

She'd make a top-notch chameleon. In other words, she was a grade A danger.

As Sushmita and the other octopuses led them down the hallway, she couldn't resist replaying Greg's words to Valor.

Finally, someone to call him out, someone who could safely do so without suffering any repercussions, someone who could make him yield and squirm like an insect. She began wondering whether it was a wolf/lycan gene to have a way with words, because Greg's threat was epically phrased.

She wasn't surprised that he himself had opted to start with the octopuses. It was where she would've started. He'd sync all their data with his own—she assumed—new device. From there, he and the mavericks would look for suspicious patterns to sniff out possible moles and threats.

He'd probably move on to the chameleons next, and Sushmita pictured him arguing with Patterson, who'd be forced to give in. Man, what she'd give to watch that unfold. That one was another hunter who needed a telling-off, though a tearing-off would work equally fine for her.

In the elevator that held five mavericks, Greg, Sushmita, and two of her own, she tapped on LG 2 and waited as the metal structure brought them to a steady descent.

"Something funny?" Greg questioned, unamused. His partial onyx eyes fixated on her.

The two with her—an orange-haired huntress and bald hunter—stiffened. Were they going to die already? They knew they should have taken the elevator without the duke.

Even the mavericks got edgy, but Sushmita simply responded, "Oh, you have no idea, Your Grace. If you'd been here for as long as we have, you'd enjoy Valor's subtle squirming as much as I did." There was a pause as she considered her words, then added, "Actually, now that I think about it, the squirming wasn't subtle enough."

She chuckled briefly, unconcerned that no one had joined her. The laugh was never for anyone but herself anyway.

Caught off guard by her directness and lack of hostility, Greg took a moment, then answered, "Blandishments will do you and your colleagues no favors, Alagumalai." This was the first time he had said her name out loud, and the way it rolled off his tongue was surprisingly smooth, like a blade sliding over thawed butter.

The metal doors opened, and Sushmita was the first to step out, responding, "Then this is probably the first time in my life I feel blessed for not having that skill in my repertoire."

The trenches were made up of dark walls and cement floors, cubicles grouped according to departments, the brightest thing in the room being a partitioned section that sat right in the middle, which had glass walls and white tables, and the kingdom's forces recognized—from the floor plans that they obtained through hacking—that it was the room where the octopuses ran tests on their equipment and devices.

Raising her voice, Sushmita instructed her people to turn on every computer and open the programs as instructed the previous day. Twisting back to Greg, she completed their conversation at her normal volume, "Just so we're clear, Your Grace, flattery is only available upstairs—on the seventh, eighth, and ninth floor. You won't find a lot of it down here in our trenches. Anyway—" the orange-head reappeared and handed the tablet in her hand to the chief as she took a closer look at the duke, scanning him from head to toe, which he ignored, his own eyes still pinned on the chief, who swiped through the device with knitted brows before handing it to Greg "—Valor said to 'guide' you, but after unintentionally and successfully flattering you for the day, I'd rather not push my luck and insult you by going through something you'd probably figure out on your own."

Dropping the tablet into his hand, she added, "Have fun. If you have complaints to file, I'll either be on this floor or one floor above. Valor would be on the tenth floor if not with the chameleons on the seventh, eighth, and ninth."

Before Greg uttered a word in reply, her peripheral vision caught something behind him. Her brows dipped low as displeasure took over her face. She strode past him and hollered, "I said THREE screens! Why are there only two? Great, now one. What are you two doing?"

There was something about the way she shouted, the way she fumed, that turned heads. Well, Greg's head, at least. He wondered if she knew she'd unintentionally and successfully flattered him the second time in less than five minutes when she simply handed him the tablet without offering Valor's instructed guidance.

Guidance. Ha. Idiot.

Though clearly, the same could not be said about the head of the trenches.

Allowing himself a moment to watch Sushmita check the program while the two junior octopuses muttered frantic explanations, Greg then forcefully drew his attention to the device in hand, extracted his thumbnail, and inserted it into the port, copying the contents within seconds and syncing it to his and the mavericks' own devices.

He'd had Jade and a few others hack the hunters' files and systems before today, but they reported back that some required authentication mechanisms that they didn't have and couldn't create.

The mavericks browsed through the files and split up, scattering amongst the hunters.

Greg knew exactly where he wanted to start—with Human Resources, the most seemingly obscure part of the headquarters. He had every name, face, and background. But he needed everything they had on file. Every award, hobby, and unrelated degree qualification. Everything.

A screen was vacated for him, and he took his time scrutinizing. The five octopuses in the department tried to ignore his daunting presence, yet it was undoubted that their work was slowed down, and their breaths hitched whenever Greg moved just the slightest inch—be it to stretch his legs or lean back into his seat.

It was unnerving. And they thought having Sushmita lingering around them was bad.

None of the octopuses knew nor noticed the duke's gaze subconsciously flickered to their chief every few minutes before he had to consciously tear his eyes away. There was something about her, something that drew him in and made him look. He didn't know what it was, though he was sure it wasn't just the pink headband.

CHAPTER 10

"He's hot, isn't he?" whispered the orange-hair huntress, Hazel Robinson. Hazel was deputy chief with a personality that was in direct contrast with her superior's. She was the approachable one, the friendly one, the one you'd want at a party because she'd light up the room.

Sushmita, on the other hand, would just dim everything down. At least, that was how she felt.

It was surprising to them both that Sushmita was appointed chief when Hazel was already deputy under their former chief, Zasper Zavier. Sushmita tried to change the defense ministry's minds, but they saw no merit in "she'd already been deputy for years," so the position went to Sushmita, who the ministry knew would handle the publicity and mediation with the kingdom well enough that they would remain alive at the end of things.

Hazel and Abbott had been under close scrutiny when their respective chief and deputy had been found to be involved in the conspiracy. It took several weeks before they were cleared.

Abbott immediately screened his archers, and even offered his superiors every form of cooperation needed to ensure they got to the bottom of things so that no other hunter was wrongfully blamed.

Hazel went into shock at the magnitude of crime, finding it hard to believe that a person she'd been shadowing for so long had been keeping something that even she—as deputy—didn't know, using the duration of time of her suspension pending full investigation to seek therapy. She came back only to find out Sushmita had taken over as chief and that she'd be reporting to her.

Thankfully, Hazel bore no grudge and had no hard feelings, having befriended Sushmita long before the latter was nominated and appointed, even admitting that Sushmita had been spoon-feeding their predecessors anyway.

"Huh?" Sushmita now questioned flatly and mindlessly; ninety-nine percent of her attention was given to the list of weapon inventory while generously offering Hazel her final one percent.

"The duke," Hazel whispered. "He's hot."

Taking a pencil to tick through the numbers, Sushmita uttered monotonously, "You could always get him one of your ice lattes to cool him down."

Ignoring the disinterest in her monotonous tone, Hazel asked, "You think I could?" She actually sounded excited. "I mean, I'm not as catchy as Izabella, but he'd go for me regardless, right? I've got a brain, and we both know she didn't have much of it, unless his type is one without much gray matter, which can't be true. They did say he fell for their queen once. She's not exactly brainless."

"That fox is definitely *not* brainless," Sushmita mumbled, already feeling a throb in her head from thinking of having to deal with Lucy.

"I know! I'm not brainless either! I have a shot, right?"

"Hazel, you're given a head to use, not to fish. It's working hours. How are the lists in your hand coming along?"

"How can you concentrate with him in the room? Look at him."

Sushmita didn't. The next list took precedence—one on border patrol.

Why was Monica Upshaw pulled out of the agreed station to stand guard—again? This was beginning to reek of the Catrine Carter pattern.

"Yo, Sush. You listening?" Hazel snapped her fingers by Sush's two o'clock, waving in her face for better measure. She was rambling about how brooding Greg was when she noticed Sush had zoned out, probably when she was talking about the bulges of his biceps.

Blinking, Sush asked, "Did Valor sneak in any last-minute notice about archers being reassigned for something that I don't know about?" She hoped there was something on paper. She'd love to skip meeting her boss.

Hazel's brows raised, seriousness taking over. "Not that I know of. Let me go check with Correspondence."

"That'd be great. Thank you."

Lingering for another brief moment, Hazel confessed in a whisper, "I'll pass Human Resources on the way. Might flash him a smile. Wish me luck."

Setting the lists aside and drawing up the field plans on the hologram, she replied indifferently, "Good luck on not getting on his nerves."

"Thanks!"

Hazel skipped away as Sushmita perched on her chair, double-checking whether any other archers' names had gone missing. They hadn't. It was only Monica Upshaw.

Sushmita then checked the chameleons. None were missing either. Even Catrine Carter was placed back on duty, though her post was a little too remote if Sushmita was being honest—a small town with terrible internet access and a civilization that seemed to be decades behind theirs. Valor and Patterson insisted it was fine and—as a non-chameleon—Sushmita gave in. One thing she'd learned was to pick her battles.

But a thought lingered at the back of her mind: Was this a battle she should take up or pass up?

Catrine Carter was excused from many chameleon duties for months before things went back to normal. Sushmita and several others had asked her about needing to skip duties so often. Catrine Carter would've had everyone's sympathy had she not simpered and spat "personal reasons" in their faces like she had a weapon under her sleeve and would use it before even considering telling the truth. The pattern lasted eight months, ending just two months back.

Sushmita thought the shady matter was over. Now, Monica Upshaw, an archer, seemed to be following in Catrine Carter's footsteps.

So where was Monica supposed to guard now? Her name was nowhere on the map.

Sushmita fired a text to Abbott, and the chief archer's reply was that Valor cleared it. He wasn't given a reason.

Sigh. Sushmita would have to ask Valor about it later. For once, could she just go one day without having to see her boss? She'd already seen enough of him in the four months of trying to clean up Delilah's manure. The stench of fatigue probably still lingered on her. And the job was clearly far from done, seeing that the duke and his forces had just begun their infiltration today.

Fuck her job. Fuck her life.

CHAPTER 11

Greg was reading Sush's profile.

The first part, he already knew: only child, orphaned at age ten, stayed with maternal relatives until a few days shy of her eighteen birthday before the last of them—her uncle, passed on. After high school, she took up mechanical engineering with a full scholarship in her first year, partial scholarship in subsequent years while taking up jobs at restaurants, malls, and two-day events that paid a lot. She graduated with a Second Class (Upper) Division and secured a job at a moderately reputable company but quit two years later and joined the hunters.

Here was what he didn't know: she took multiple courses in hacking; her parents were what they called *liabilities*—non-hunters. Both died in road accidents, albeit separate ones. It was rare for a hunter to be born out of two liabilities, but history did prove this was possible.

In the midst of working, he heard a shriek, followed by a crash and an overdramatic, "Ouch! Ooooh! Help!" coming from somewhere near him as the Human Resources folks dashed to the source.

Greg reclined his chair and witnessed Hazel with palms pressed against the floor and papers scattered around her, yet she made no effort to push herself up while her colleagues offered her hands and asked if she was alright.

His animal's eyes rolled. Enora could get up quicker than that and never made such a fuss from a simple fall. If anything, the adults around her made a bigger fuss, him included. Greg didn't care if Hazel wasn't a lycan and didn't possess the healing abilities of one.

Sighing at the loss of two precious seconds of being nosy, he drew his attention back to the computer, narrowly missing eye contact with Hazel.

The deputy's shoulders fell when he didn't come to help her like her colleagues did. Finally pushing herself off the ground, she shambled toward his cubicle yet still got no response. Coming up with an immediate plan B, Hazel then leaned against the cubicle next to his, chatting with Aaron about their last time out at a bar and how so many of them had to decode Izabella's messages, intentionally leading Aaron to mention that Hazel had been instrumental in the effort.

When Greg reached the end of Sushmita's profile, he moved on to the next, which—coincidentally—was Hazel's. There was a "Strengths" section, and the duke thought she left out a few attributes: inconsiderate, loud, vexing. Or did those fit under a "Weaknesses" section that—for some reason—wasn't included here?

In his peripheral vision, he caught sight of Sushmita. "Chief?" The word escaped his lips before going through his brain, which didn't often happen.

Sushmita had just extracted one ring folder and was reaching for another when their eyes locked and she questioned, "Already? It hasn't even been an hour."

A corner of his lips tipped up just slightly. "I like to work in peace. If you could keep your traffic cone of a deputy a little busier and away from this area, I'd really appreciate it."

Sushmita's eyes flickered to Hazel's embarrassed ones, uttering, "Haze, go check the correspondence."

Under his breath, Greg muttered, "And maybe don't trip on purpose this time."

Sushmita didn't hear it, given the distance and her focus back on the files in hand, but Aaron and Hazel did. A brighter flush of crimson rose to the deputy's cheeks as she subconsciously ran her fingers down her orange, traffic-cone-colored hair and scurried away.

Even with the welcomed silence, Greg just couldn't keep his eyes on Hazel's picture-perfect profile for more than a few seconds as the creature to his right continued intriguing him.

It bothered him that Sushmita seemed to be able to pull off any look. The pondering one now was a little different from the hard look on his only visit to this place: Her brow was not as arched, her lips flat rather than frowned.

Slamming the files shut and shoving them back into place, she heaved a sigh and turned, which was when their eyes locked again. Her brows raised. "Another complaint?"

His lips twitched almost imperceptibly. "Not yet."

She nodded in acknowledgment and strode back to her station, where her fingers tapped furiously on her tablet.

Only then did Greg get back to Hazel's profile. Perfect upbringing. Goldmine parents: a former chief octopus and former deputy chief octopus, now retired and living their days in a quiet countryside. Hazel had good grades. Joined the hunters fresh out of high school while finishing college in civil engineering and graduating as valedictorian. Goddess, this was mind-numbing. Might as well add that she was hunter royalty after her name.

"Boss?" Ella Tristan, one of his mavericks, stood by his cubicle. "Is this a good time?"

Swiveling his chair to face her, eager for an escape, he said, "There has never been a better time, Tristan. Show me."

Ella handed him the blueprints and sketches, explaining, "Amara—the huntress I've been working with—said these were retrieved from Delilah's and Larson's private abode. We don't have a copy. Should I ask to borrow the originals, or would scanning them do?"

Skimming through each page, he instructed, "Scan. Front and back, even if it's empty. Use Jade's version for the scanner. I want them to be near original."

Ella retrieved the papers from him, nodded, and left.

Turning back to his screen, Greg's animal groaned. Telling himself that the sooner he finished this silver spoon garbage, the quicker he could move on, he went through it in one painful minute before heaving a sigh of relieved accomplishment and proceeding to the next person.

CHAPTER 12

Sushmita made her way to the lunch lounge built exclusively for the chameleons, while the octopuses and archers spent their lunch hour on a separate floor. The chameleons' lounge had posh furniture and high-tier lighting, floors that shone, and air-conditioners that were all fully functional.

Sushmita breezed past the food stations and chameleons queuing to form a millipede, and headed straight to the VIP section where the salt-and-pepper hair of her boss came into view.

Patterson was there too. As expected.

The chief chameleon sat leaning back with one leg over the other, an arm casually resting on the empty chair next to him, chatting with Valor with the confident, easy smile that gave him such a big boost in climbing up the ranks.

Sushmita wasn't sure whether it was the pattering of her sneakers or her radiating annoyance that alerted Patterson's senses, who held onto his smile with more effort like weights had been attached on both ends of his lips when she barged over. His lips moved, saying something to Valor, making the commander's shoulders sag.

Valor blasted out a gust of frustration, murmuring under his breath when Sushmita appeared with her mouth curved into a scowl. Not bothering with a greeting or a smile, she began, "Monica Upshaw. When? Why? How much more of the same thing am I going to see?"

"Isn't she an archer? As in, within Abbott's jurisdiction?" Patterson's irritating voice rang through the air.

Pivoting her glare to him, she replied, "Why, yes. Congratulations, Patterson. I must have mistook our boss for Abbott. Promotion looks great on you. Aren't you a smart little boy now?"

Patterson's throat convulsed with a choking swallow, feeling her tone putting him in a gradually shrinking box. Attempting to mask the intimidation by putting on a victimized smile he'd long mastered, he said, "We're all adults here, Sush. Let's just calm down and discuss this."

Taking one step toward the chameleon, Sush uttered, "What a mature suggestion from you. Funny how you can recite something like that yet not have the aptitude to tell when your presence and opinions are neither asked for nor required. Unless you have something useful to say, save your little chameleon tongue for an actual assignment."

Turning to Valor, Sush continued, "I take it that you've been ignoring my messages and emails since this morning?"

Valor harrumphed and defended, "I was busy with th—"

"So it's a yes. Since I can't get you to face me any other way, we're back to the four months of me hunting you down at lunch hour again." She moved his empty bowl away, the broth inside almost flew out, and Patterson jerked when he thought his new suit was going to be ruined.

She spread out the map on the table, before the commander's eyes. "This damn thing had been revised and approved *with* Monica Upshaw's name in Team E. What happened? Why doesn't Abbott know anything either?"

Valor's hard gaze told her to stand down and show more respect as he remarked, "I'm certain it's because he knows when to ask questions and when to take orders as they are."

"Unfortunately for you, I'm an octopus. Not asking questions is not my thing, especially after the Delilah fiasco that my people and I had to clean up. I swear, Boss, if Upshaw is part of yet another ploy that's going to explode in our faces . . ."

Valor's fist hit the table, bringing the buzzing lounge into a dead silence. The sizzling from a pan at one of the stations resonated beautifully with the fuming Valor. *Insolent woman*, he thought. In a tone that left no room for argument, he uttered through clenched teeth, "We will discuss this after lunch. In my office."

The thing about Sush was that—for every tone that left no room for argument—she'd inevitably find a way to impale her argument into that very room. Lowering her voice, her palms pressed on the edge of the table when she leaned in with eyes of flames that rivaled Valor's. "You had the whole morning to discuss this in your office. Either give me my answers now or I'll send her name to the defense ministry and let them decide if she should remain a hunter. I don't need to tell you what my recommendation would be."

A hunter at the next table choked on his potatoes, and a few others bit the inner walls of their mouths, awaiting their boss's response.

As quickly as shards of shock intruded Valor's eyes, they left, leaving the anger that was simmering before raging even stronger. "Are you threatening me, Alagumalai?"

"I'm extending the courtesy of informing you about my next move if you choose not to cooperate, Valor. You may like the apprehensive feeling every time we get an email from the kingdom, but I don't."

"Then maybe you're not cut out for the job."

Unfazed, Sush said sardonically, "Yes, a suitable replacement should be nominated and sworn in immediately, even though I got eight out of ten votes from the defense ministry when I was elected chief. Wouldn't recommending my dismissal now look good on you?"

Valor's jaw clenched taut, forehead crimped. "Monica Upshaw's case was ordered by a higher-up. You'd have to ask them if you're fixated on answers."

"Which department?"

"Defense."

She tried not to look too exasperated, but her tone failed before her face did. "I know. Which Department of Defense? Do you have a name?"

"All I received was an email."

"Forward it to me."

"Mm."

Straightening her back, she folded her arms across her chest as she waited.

Valor was dragging back his coffee that Patterson had moved away when voices were raised, but the shadow of the octopus blocking the sun from the windows continued blocking his peace of mind. His brows knitted like he was asking what else she wanted, her right brow raised like she was asking what he was waiting for.

Muttering a grumble under his breath, he fished out his phone from his pocket and—in less than ten seconds—forwarded her the email.

Sush remained rooted until she received it on her phone. Without a word of thanks, she turned, which was when Valor said, "Be careful where you step,

Alagumalai. Hierarchy and power exist for a reason, and they stretch further than you may think."

Offering him the minimum amount of attention she could spare, she replied, "Enlightening. Thanks for the input, Boss."

Even with all that hierarchy and power, they still needed *her* to handle the Delilah conspiracy aftermath. Whatever the stretch of power was, it clearly didn't stretch far enough.

Marching out of the lounge that sounded more like a library, the chatters only regained their vigor when Sush disappeared into the elevator and returned to her trenches.

CHAPTER 13

Exiting the elevator, Sush drew in a greedy lungful of air. She loved the smell of the trenches, and she wasn't sure whether that was odd. Even before she was chief, her senses loved it here.

She didn't like the politics, the gossip, the need to please the higher-ups, but the work? God, she *loved* the work. She especially loved inventing things and tweaking inventions, drawing immense satisfaction from bringing her imagination to life, running tests, finding solutions to problems, improving designs, and modifying structures. This was her place, her escape. Sure, there were bad days, but even those days had good stuff in them.

It was sad that she'd have to leave once she'd avenged her mother. It was the main reason she stayed, she felt—to linger around long enough to be entrusted with every piece of information within the headquarters. Deep down, she knew she'd love to stay forever if she could. But she couldn't have it both ways. It wouldn't be wise or feasible to stay by the end of her plan, unless she wanted multiple bullets to her head.

Turning her attention to the email for the Monica Upshaw issue, she found that orders came from the Administrative Division of the defense ministry.

Valor wasn't kidding. This was very high up.

Sush worded a draft and chose not to hit the Send button just yet, knowing from experience that sending something unretractable when she was fit with rage would do her no favors. She only leaned back into her swivel chair for two peaceful seconds before a deep voice came from her side, "Chief?"

Good God, she thought in frustration.

Her eyes snapped open. Greg held a brown paper bag and a cup of iced latte, setting both on her desk. "Are you a latte person?"

Eyes trailing to the cup with condensed vapor lining the exterior, she curtly said, "No."

Taking the cup away, he said, "Good. I'll just dump this in the trash."

"Is the latte supposed to be a bribe?"

Visibly annoyed, he replied, "I don't know. Ask Traffic Cone."

It took her exhausted brain a moment to realize he meant Hazel. Her turned-down lips now crept upward, and she had to press them into a line so she didn't smile and burst out laughing.

Greg's gaze went to her moving lips, a rush of . . . something overtaking him. Shutting his eyes to refocus, he then uttered, "I admire your ability to find humor in any situation, Alagumalai. But I really don't see any in this one. Tell her to fucking do her job and stop."

"I already have. You can always issue a formal complaint with HR. Oh wait, you're in their department today. Maybe you could file your own complaint."

"Will she be suspended, then fired?"

"Well, not necessarily. It still has to go through the discipl—"

"Fucking dammit," he murmured.

She knew he was pissed. She knew she shouldn't find any of this amusing. But here she was. Struggling not to laugh. The duke could make Valor shrivel so well yet found Hazel insurmountable.

Her sights went to the paper bag. Pushing herself up and placing it on her lap, she opened it and asked, "What did she get you? Oh, two bagels and cream cheese. Hm. Strange. It's not what she usually eats."

"I was told it's what *you* usually eat," Greg clarified. She paused, stunned. His lilac eyes met her inky ones. In the pocket of silence, his brows converged when he added, "If the barista in the cafeteria named Nancy lied to me, she's going to be my second complaint for the day. And I'll be demanding a full refund of my money."

Coming out of the brain freeze, Sush glanced at the bagels, cleared her throat, and uttered, "She didn't lie to you. And Nancy is a sweetheart. Leave her out of your agenda." Looking at the bagels again like they might disappear and affirm the version of reality that she was used to—one where no one bought her food—she then questioned, "Why are you bribing me with bagels? What do you want?"

"Consider this a thank-you for the smooth access to just about everything in your trenches thus far. If you can keep Traffic Cone out of my zone, your lunch is on me for the next three months."

Not one to say no to free food, especially not her favorite food. She got out a bagel and bit into it when she said, "Hazel's not that bad."

"Her hair itself is a warning sign." His arms folded as he leaned against her desk.

Sush scoffed, the corner of her lip tilting up. "I should let her know you don't like iced lattes. What did you drink at lunch today?"

Greg's eyes snapped to her, suspicion written all over his face. Voice deep and serious, he uttered, "Don't you dare give her any ideas."

She shrugged. "Maybe I just want to bribe you back? You look like the type to take your coffee black."

"So what's your point? If it matches my soul, I take it."

"Same here," Sush mumbled between chews, her attention stolen by her lit-up screen, which was when Greg took the opportunity to let his face soften, observing her face, watching her jaw move in a rhythm.

When she was done typing whatever, his expressionless exterior came back up. "Traffic Cone said you were meeting Valor for lunch."

"Your Grace," she began between mouthfuls of the second bagel, hand held up and forefinger raising to make a point. "When you put it that way, it sounds like I was having a meal and a good chat with my boss."

"I take it that it didn't go well?" He tried to sound monotonous, but concern slithered into his voice and snuck into their conversation.

Sush didn't see the significance, figuring he could be as tolerable and respectable as the queen, so she responded, "Oh, it went well, alright. For me, at least. The thing about this place is you have to make things go well for it to go well. Sway just once and the current will take you. And you'll drown yourself serving them if they don't drown you first."

"How ominously inspiring."

"Thank you."

He chuckled briefly—his first real laugh in months with someone other than his favorite niece. He felt lighter, more liberated.

Sush didn't warm up to many people upon a first meeting, but Greg's presence encouraged her to ramble on, "The fight—I mean, the 'discussion' with Valor was about an archer who's being put off duty without reason, so I invaded the chameleon lounge for answers."

Unblinking, Greg demanded, "Why haven't I seen that?"

Setting down the bagel, her eyes grew wide in feigned shock, a hand lifted in a hyperbolized gesture when she said, "I know! Can you believe it? Sure sucks to be you, Your Grace."

Noting the sarcasm, Greg inhaled, reluctant to cut off this newly built bridge. "Apologies, Alagumalai. Why didn't you know? Why weren't you informed?" She may not have known, but Greg drew some placidity from saying her name.

Resuming the munching of her bagel, she said, "My guess? The one behind it probably didn't want a nuisance like me blocking the way."

"And you'd block the way for a whole cluster of reasons, I gather?"

"Of course. The last thing I need is another interspecies debacle to deal with."

There was a pause. Greg's relaxed posture stiffened. His pupils dilated, and adrenaline rushed through his bloodstream as his fight-or-flight response activated, readying him to fight since Greg Claw didn't take flight. Ever.

Swallowing a snarl, he questioned, "This poses a threat to the kingdom?"

Taking a glimpse around, Sush lowered her voice, admitting, "That's the thing, Your Grace—I don't know. That's why I cornered Valor. Just so you know, the four months dealing with the Delilah fiasco haven't been easy for us either. I'm sure you bore the brunt of the whole thing, but the octopuses around you haven't had a restful night since—through no fault of our own. If it makes things any easier, I'll keep you in the loop. You're not the only one demanding answers."

The certainty in her eyes brought his animal to a sit, despite its zest to pounce, threaten, and kill. He didn't just have a lot to lose. He had *everything* to lose now that Enora was in the picture. His beast was as protective of the pup as his human was, whose onyx eyes faded in intensity when Sush mentioned keeping him in the loop.

Drawing a breath to make sure he didn't say something offensive, he asked, "Where's the loop at now?"

Shaking her head in disapprobation, she said, "Valor claims to be acting on orders from the defense ministry. He gave me a copy of the email leading to the Administrative Division." Seeing his eyes leave her face and venture to the table, staring into space, Sush promptly added, "Do me a favor and don't get involved, Your Grace. This is *my* job scope. *My* jurisdiction. Let me handle it."

A faint smile of guilt pushed the corner of his lips at getting caught for what he really wanted to do. The emotion stitched a thread of humor into his fury, his animal growling quietly in respectful concurrence.

But was it just that—respectful concurrence and nothing more?

Greg was a creature known to never concur without a fight. His animal was no different. If he decided to get involved, he got involved. And he'd go all the way. No half-baked attempts. No loose ends. Either perfection or nothing at all.

Yet right now, even after he'd decided to squeeze every piece of intelligence out of the hunters before he came today, he couldn't find it in himself to encroach on Sush's turf, especially after she'd spelled it out to him. It was a strange, unnerving feeling. There was something about this octopus that just made him listen.

No. Not strange. And definitely not unnerving. He was Greg Claw. Nothing unnerved him.

There was only one word to describe the chief octopus—*dangerous*, probably like a siren. Maybe worse. She wasn't even singing, and he was already being cordial.

When his cousin and cousin-in-law reminded him never to give the hunters a reason to rescind the agreement—in other words, not to be rude and offensive—Greg knew it'd be challenging. For better measure, the queen even whispered to Enora—with him present—that Uncle Greg had promised "to be nice" on his work trip.

He hadn't. If he made any promises, it would be to rain fire. Every single day. For the next three months.

But when Lucy emphasized it'd do him a favor in the long run, he agreed to exercise control.

Sush—oddly—wasn't making things difficult. At all.

Not odd.

Dangerous.

Goddess, he'd have to drill that word into his and his animal's shared head.

CHAPTER 14

Sushmita reached her one-bedroom apartment after midnight. Lying in bed and staring into the darkness that jeeringly matched her life, she kept telling her body to go to sleep. But it couldn't. Her energy levels would normally be wiped out by now, and she may not even remember her head touching the pillow or whether she pulled up the blankets. But tonight, she even had the mental and physical strength to charge her phone.

Yes, she knew it wasn't good for the battery. No, she didn't care.

Her brain was still buzzing, nerves still firing. From Delilah to Valor to Catrine Carter to Monica Upshaw, and to . . . Greg.

Why Greg though? She delved deeper into that.

Unlike the catastrophe of a person she'd imagined, he actually seemed . . . decent. Not the choice of word she'd go for from the little she knew about him before today, especially not after the way he'd ended Logan Larson. She should be terrified from witnessing the kill, but she actually felt envious that Greg was granted permission to do something she'd wanted to do but couldn't without breaking hunter codes and the law. Larson was one of the five people who'd started the shit and given her and the other octopuses hell anyway. The duke hadn't had the best composure during the execution, but Sushmita didn't assume the worst of him just from that one day.

From the unflattering articles that mushroomed about his past when he went public with Delilah, Greg Claw was presented to be ruthless and temperamental, dangerous and unreliable.

The number of such articles didn't dwindle even when the king and queen were asked to comment. Their joint reply was brief, stating that the duke's misdeeds may have left a mark, but the fact that His Grace had been instrumental in eradicating threats in recent years had left an equal, if not more impactful, legacy.

Reporters began writing about the cousins' animus, even questioning whether the kingdom was stable now that they purported to be working together. This was when several reached out to the more popular ruler—the queen—for her comment, asking specifically about the friction between her mate and cousin-in-law, and the fox left a few words on her normally-uneventful social media account, "It's enlightening to know that a significant segment of today's precocious journalists have impliedly welcomed others to judge them based on their pasts, just as their work does for others. The unjustified derisive narrative on outdated facts brings such clarity to each writer's own character, exemplifies their finesse in staying stuck in bygone times, and speaks volumes about their future in journalism."

That burn didn't just drive up shares and reactions; it scalded many rising journalists. And the queen's statement escalated to a degree that no one had expected, not even the queen herself. Former classmates and acquaintances who shared animosity with those journalists dug into the past and shared embarrassing tales that any reasonable creature would rather keep buried.

One journalist was reported to have suffered a nervous breakdown after pictures of her cozying up with her professor resurfaced and went viral, the caption unhelpfully adding that she scored a distinction in the subject, but the grade was later revoked when the matter came to light. Another journalist—who was married with a pup—was suspended pending an investigation when someone disclosed she'd been sexually harassed by him back in college, as were many of her female classmates. And no less than twenty editors were demoted for green-lighting stories with an "unjustified derisive narrative" that—the news agencies claimed—was not what they stood for.

The human instinct—not their animals, who were genetically programmed to bow to their rulers—was to get back at the queen, but everyone knew better than to do that, especially when the king's threat to one of their own several years back marked the profession like a permanent tattoo. The consequences would be more lethal professionally and swifter than a few lines going viral on social media. So the matter was put to rest, and only objective, well-balanced articles survived, which wasn't many of them.

There were only three, if Sush wasn't mistaken. Out of hundreds.

When the saga made headlines in the human world, almost everyone got invested—Sush included, raising her to-go coffee cup to Lucy's statement when she read it over lunch, finding humor in those words since she wasn't at the receiving end.

Sush sensed then—just as she was sure now—the duke's character wasn't fully captured by the media. She may not know the duke, but she knew the queen. That woman may be nice to anyone in general—provided one didn't piss her off—but she was highly selective of her inner circle. If the duke was in her inner circle now, it only meant he was—at the very least—tolerable.

And Sush had to admit he was. Better than tolerable, in fact. She enjoyed their conversation after lunch, as dead as his tone was. The thing about tone was that one's choice of words could set an entire sentence ablaze without minding intonation. He was living proof of that.

Sush was brought up in an expressive household. Voices were raised when there was either excitement, anger, or distance between the ones speaking and listening; tone was lowered to express guilt or tell a secret. Even their hands and arms did a litany of exercises when they spoke: the forefinger was used when a point was being made; the lowering of one's head with one hand inches from their face meant the situation being told was dire; a wave of a hand at a roughly forty-five-degree angle over a surface was most likely accompanied by a *no*; both hands directed toward something meant, "This!" And the list went on.

Sush was considered the least expressive in her family, having been to schools and met people who gawked awkwardly at her if her hands flew out of the cultural circumference per individual and moved beyond the unspoken quota for the day or on an occasion that didn't customarily invoke such a reaction.

She still used her hands and arms, but her movements were more controlled than her late mother's and deceased relatives'. Being older now, she didn't care if people gawked at her. A part of her even felt she was honoring them by simply letting her forelimbs fly.

Greg was so different. So stiff. So controlled. Any movement he made—so far—seemed minimal and calculated. The most impactful hand exercise he had was probably pinching his forehead or nose bridge.

It was astounding that he hadn't filed a complaint against her just for her excessive hand gestures yet.

Maybe he would. Tomorrow. Or another day.

He had three months anyway. There was no rush.

For a reason not yet clear to Sush, she replayed their after-lunch conversation, and—halfway through—her mind was finally put to rest.

CHAPTER 15

"Did you know he threw the iced latte right down the sink?" Hazel whispered like a flood had just swept away an entire village.

"Really? I didn't think someone like him would drain a cup before throwing it into the trash. Ow! Haze!" Sush flinched when her deputy struck her arm with a thick ring folder.

Sulking in her chair and tucking the folder back under her tablet on her lap, Hazel said, "You're usually funny when you're mean, but not this time."

Rubbing away the sensation from the blow, Sush said, "Maybe the duke's just here to work, Haze. How about you give him a pass? It's not like you don't have other offers. And pull up B-12 for me, please."

Tapping on her keyboard, she complained, "No offers or prospects can beat him."

"You just met him. Yesterday," Sush noted pointedly.

"Exactly! And he's already ticked all my boxes!"

Brows furrowing like a judgmental mother, Sush uttered, "I'm rather concerned about what those boxes entail if they can all be ticked in one day, Hazel."

"He has to have a handsome face, a Greek god body, a panty-dropping voice, and a job with enough money. Oh, and he has to be someone I could make pretty babies with," Hazel listed casually. Too casually.

For the first time in years, Sush had no idea how to respond. Her mind shut down for half a minute before it rebooted. "You did not just tell me that."

Hazel shrugged. "I want pretty babies. And a job with enough money is important. I have a job with enough money. I don't see why my future partner shouldn't be the same."

"I agree." Sush then lowered her voice into a hush like they were sharing nuclear codes. "But the rest of the list could be left out by hitting me with two words—it's private."

Hazel shrugged again, this time with a gleam in her eye. "You asked, Boss."

Sush sighed and murmured, "Oh my god. I am never asking you any personal questions again."

"C'mon, friends talk about these things. What's on your list?"

"Wh— No."

"I told you mine."

"Honestly, it was a test. And you failed. Horribly. You shouldn't be that specific. While we're on it, your list should be longer, with more desired personality traits. Maybe with a dash of common ground. Now, where's my B-12?"

"Ugh," Hazel groaned.

While waiting, Sush couldn't help but mentally review Hazel's list again. God, why did Hazel have to tell her that? Why did she ask in the first place? The frank answers were now etched into the walls of her mind, and Sush didn't know how to scrub them off. It was easy to see Hazel wanting those things.

In another time, one before Sush knew about the hunters, before she became one and learned its secrets—buried and unburied—she'd desired those things in a partner, too, save for the pretty babies part. She'd never been particularly keen on having children. She didn't hate kids, but she never saw herself as needing to have them, never saw herself as a mother—a personal preference and choice that, unfortunately, some people still thought they had a say in.

Hazel's mind was no longer on her list as she thought of Greg's lack of reciprocity again, still mourning the thrown-out latte. "I can't believe he did that. He could've just told me he didn't like it."

Blinking out of her thoughts, Sush replied, "I thought he did."

"I mean, yeah, he did. But I thought he was just being nice and shy about accepting a drink from a stranger he met on the first day. He could have told me he *actually* didn't like it, you know? I could've ordered something else for him. What do you think he likes?"

The previous day's conversation with Greg flashed into Sush's mind like a thunderbolt, and she had to bite the inner corners of her lips to feign contemplation and force down a smile. Greg said not to give Hazel any ideas, but there was an itch to do just that, just to see how he'd react.

Then again, Sush herself wouldn't appreciate it if an admirer she wasn't interested in got inside information from people she trusted with the small details of her life—not that she had any admirers to begin with, or people she trusted with the small details of her life, but the logic still applied.

In the end, Sush said, "Maybe you can just ask him?" Yes, that was a safe answer, she thought.

But as the thought came, so did something else—something in her gut telling her that it felt wrong, though Sush couldn't yet comprehend how. She didn't divulge anything, so she wasn't betraying Greg per se, nor was she discouraging her friend from pursuing the person she seemed to be genuinely interested in, despite the questionable boxes she had drawn up. She was being supportive of her friend and keeping Greg's petty secret.

Which part of that was even wrong? And why did she feel a slight, uncomfortable heat at the pit of her stomach at the thought of Hazel going after Greg?

Catching her thoughts drifting like wood to the crest of a waterfall, her sudden awareness halted the current and reined in her focus, directing it to the hologram finally set before her eyes.

Hazel drew up B-12: the territory where Monica Upshaw was supposed to guard with fourteen others. Sushmita was wondering if the shortage of one would require an immediate replacement. The perimeter was considerably large, but the rate of danger was low, so her tentative plan was to leave it at fourteen. If she wanted fifteen, it'd give rise to another problem of where to get another archer from. This site hadn't had an issue in three years. It should be safe.

"Morning, Chief." The voice—deep and sure—reverberated into her eardrums. And it did something to her heart. It moved? No, that wasn't the correct word. The heart was held by vessels. It couldn't just move. So it... what? Vibrated? Jumped? Whatever he did, it was strange that she reacted that way.

Hazel, who was slumped lazily like she had no reason left to live, was jostled by Greg's voice and became fully ready to spread her contagious light to the rest of the world. With starry eyes, she chirped, "Good morning, Your Grace. Beautiful day, isn't it? There was even a rainbow earlier this morning. I got a picture. Wanna see?"

Greg's throat worked before he delivered a curt, "No."

"Oh," Hazel's swift swiping came to an abrupt pause. "You don't like rainbows?"

Sush snorted. She couldn't help it. She'd been holding onto that since Hazel wondered about what he liked to drink. When she realized Hazel's eyes were on her, she cleared her throat. "Sorry, something in my throat. I think we can leave B-12 as it is. Let's review Abbott's proposals that came in yesterday."

Hazel reluctantly turned her attention back to the tablet, sighing like she'd been working hard all day when it had only been twenty minutes, tops.

Her gaze pivoting to Greg, Sush began, "Good morning, Your Grace. What is it about rainbows that bothers you?"

His eyes narrowed, and his head shook slightly like he was saying, "Don't you dare go there."

Swallowing a chuckle but unable to hold back a smile that lit up her face, she got to the point, "What do you need?"

His brows raised ever so slightly, confusion marring them. "What makes you think I need something?"

"Well, you don't strike me as the type to enjoy small talk."

"Perceptive. And true." A hint of a smile threatened to tear down the facade he was holding up. "So am I correct to assume it's not customary for hunters to greet each other in the morning?"

Without missing a beat, Sush's sardonic switch came on. "Yeah, we prefer to do it at night."

A hunter, whose seat wasn't far from where they were, spurted his water and choked, turning around to cough and block out the laughter, droplets drizzling onto the cement floor. While most eyes, including Hazel's, remained on the choking hunter, Greg closed in on Sush's ear, his scent of musk and sandalwood invading her nostrils when he whispered, "We do *it* at night, too, some better than others."

His breath skated over her skin, the warmth doing something to her senses, permeating through the shell of her ear and traveling to other parts of her body.

Her head spun, meeting the glint in his eyes. She recognized that look—one that issued a challenge, one that wasn't going to back down. Since she had been genetically programmed to hate losing, her arms folded across her chest and her posture straightened as she mocked ignorance of the innuendo, asking, "And how would some convey a morning greeting better than others, Your Grace? I'm afraid I'm not familiar with deviations. It's quite standard in the human world."

As hard as Greg tried to keep his exterior stiff with crossed arms and a straightened spine, unintentionally mimicking her stance, his lips became increasingly difficult to flatten. Something in her words tickled his lycan, and his amusement was getting out of hand.

But it was as if they were having too much fun too soon.

From the side, Hazel chimed, "Maybe they just howl to each other?"

In an instant, his humor was snatched, his face hardened again. Ignoring Hazel, he unilaterally decided to change the subject, asking Sush, "Do you have a lunch date with your noble leader today?"

Sush tried not to smile. She didn't want to jinx it. "No, so don't do or ask him anything that'll require me to."

"Hm," Greg hummed. "I'll see you at the cafeteria later then."

"Really?" Hazel's eyes bulged, shining so much that they held several stars. "We get to sit with you?"

Greg's brows arched like Hazel was going mad, until Sush explained, "Hazel and I normally eat together, so congratulations, Your Grace. You just scored yourself the most entertaining lunch partner the octopuses have to offer."

Turning to Hazel with immense difficulty like the screws on his neck had suddenly turned rusty, Greg said, "Apologies, Deputy. I was only speaking to the chief."

"But I'm great company! Right, Sush?"

"Oh yeah," Sush replied nonchalantly, tapping on her tablet, then added more enthusiastically, "She's really great company. She might even be generous enough to buy you lunch." Greg threw her a *not-helping* look.

"Oh, yes! That reminds me: what's your choice of beverage, Your Grace?"

Greg clicked his tongue. "I'm going to pretend you didn't ask that. Excuse me, I should head back to work." Turning to Sush, he speedily murmured, "If she shows up at my lunch table, you owe me bagels *and* coffee."

"I don't recall that clause being in the treaty," she muttered back.

"I'll submit a formal application to the queen to work something out, if need be."

It was a joke. They both knew it was a joke, and yet the mere mention of Lucy made Sush flinch and spew out in a frustrated whisper, "Don't make the mother of your kingdom keep me awake even more. Do you have *any* idea how little sleep I get having to deal with her and her husband?"

His heart constricted for a moment, and a modicum of guilt made its way into him, but he still managed to say, "I look forward to hearing it over lunch without any . . ." Greg glanced at Hazel and continued, ". . . warning signals present."

Striding away before Hazel got the cheerful, "See you later," greeting out, Greg invaded the correspondence circle and reached for a random file, pulled a chair, and began flipping through, disregarding the sudden jerks and subsequent silence of fear circulating around the department.

They'd get used to him.

Eventually.

Half of his brain was replaying his conversation with Sush, convincing itself that she was a potential ally. He'd asked her to join him for lunch without thinking, which had never happened before.

Yes, he'd asked for a brief, private meeting with potential allies and followers, but it was always done *with* thought. Sush was the first exception.

The plan this morning was simply to greet her and walk away, yet when it was time to move, he didn't. His legs just didn't carry him. He didn't understand why. He wasn't even like this with Izabella. Come to think of it, he'd found it harder to walk away from Enora than Izabella, even when the bond was still intact.

Sush was a different case though. He couldn't even walk away when he thought he should. It was her deputy that made leaving the section easy.

Setting the incongruence of his action aside, Greg talked himself into believing that he'd scouted talents of all sorts for decades, so the thing with the chief back there was simply him acting on instinct. Spotting an ally became second nature to him, so he didn't have to think before asking for the routine brief meeting. With that, he diverted most of his attention to the next file.

Most.

A part of him reserved his remaining attention for a certain huntress that his eyes seemed to find every few minutes.

CHAPTER 16

At lunch, Hazel asked Sush about why she had to get Greg bagels and coffee. Sush lied eloquently on the spot, saying that she lost a bet against the duke about his age, to which Hazel reprimanded, "How could you not know that? Everyone knows it's a hundred and ninety! Five years older than the king! Last I checked, you're thirty-five, so aren't you supposed to have the memory of a thirty-five-year-old?"

"Unlike you, my brain cells are limited, and I have to be selective about what I store in them. His age seemed too trivial to warrant a space in my mental archive." The truth was that she knew. Like Greg, she'd memorized his and the mavericks' profiles and faces before they showed up, down to the most trivial detail of their ages.

"So . . . he just happened to tell you he took coffee?" Suspicion crawled onto Hazel's face.

"Nope. He just said whoever lost the bet would buy the other bagels and coffee."

"You two sure are getting along," Hazel remarked, not even trying to hide her indignation.

Hoping that this wouldn't start a stir because Hazel really was one of the best brains and kindest hearts in the trenches, Sush said, "Well, the mavericks are getting along with some of our own. It'd be wrong for us not to do the same with their leader."

Hazel sighed, resigned, seeing Sush's point without much effort. "Why isn't he like that with me though?" she questioned, getting lost in thought for a moment. Then her eyes snapped wide in horror when she whispered, "Is it because I look like Izabella? Is that why he's allergic to me? Wait, do I even *look* like Izabella?"

"Hazel," Sush took the tray, paid, and led them to the lunch table. "Give yourself more credit. You look nothing like that bitch."

"Oh," Hazel heaved a relieved breath. "For a minute there I thought . . . but then why . . ." She dropped the conversation when they had reached their spot.

Sush placed the tray containing a plate of bagels and a mug of steaming coffee in front of Greg before she plopped into the seat facing him and next to Hazel, who began dividing the pizza that she and Sush were going to share.

Greg took one glance at the deputy splitting the crust before his eyes flickered to the chief, giving her a slight shake of his head like he was disappointed she couldn't take care of such a simple task.

Sush's head angled a little to her right, a smug smile plastered her face, silently conveying, "I don't work for you."

His brows raised to acknowledge her defiance before his eyes glazed over, linking Jade and Ella to join him with specific instructions to keep Traffic Cone busy if she started talking, which he was positive would happen soon.

"So you're a coffee person, Your Grace?" Hazel began.

Oh, Goddess. I have been atoning for my sins for years. Please spare me from this torment.

The Goddess must have heard him. Before he needed to articulate a response, an extra chirpy Ella appeared and slid in next to Greg, smiling radiantly, though inauthentically for those who really knew her and had seen her smile before. "Hi, mind if Jade and I join you guys? Oh, I've been meaning to tell you this since yesterday, Hazel—you pull off that hair color really well. It really brings out your personality. Lights up the trenches in a way."

Ella genuinely liked the color on Hazel but hadn't brushed past the deputy to tell her yet. And she intentionally brought it up now despite knowing Greg didn't like it because he'd just made her work during lunch break when she'd normally spend time linking Toby. This was her small way of getting back at her boss, which seemed to be working since she could hear his sharp exhale that spoke for his exasperation.

Hazel had just split the pizza and handed Sush her share when she met Ella's blue eyes smiling back at her, which was contagious, and the deputy's lips curled up. "You really think so? Thank you. I like to switch things up and keep people on their toes." Eyes shifting to Jade, she offered a bright smile.

Jade didn't even know why he was there and merely lifted his chin and uttered a brief, "'Sup." He then sank next to Ella, hoping she'd be able to do most of the talking. He was in tech for a reason—he didn't like being on the field where he'd have to smile and pretend. He could do it, but he hated it. It wasted so much energy that could be used to actually build something: a code, an algorithm, a freaking system! It was beyond him why he was asked to join them.

As Ella listened attentively to Hazel telling her about how being a huntress was her calling, Greg's eyes, which were darting to the chief more often than usual, did not escape Ella, nor did their eye signals, which persisted even when he was biting into the bagel. It looked as if her boss and the chief were having a conversation without saying anything.

She knew the look well, and a modicum of worry for Greg set in her stomach. The last thing they needed was Izabella 2.0.

When the crowd dispersed at the end of lunch hour, Ella linked Toby, telling him she'd be working late, wanting to do an extensive background dig through the physical and digital archives in the trenches with Jade and a few others on the chief octopus, expressing her concern that Greg may have been treading into dangerous waters without knowing again.

Her normally supportive husband's response was, *'Right. Right. That makes sense. Babe, remind me: bosses and employees—who's supposed to take care of who again?'*

CHAPTER 17

Back in the trenches, Greg popped from correspondence to system maintenance to weaponry maintenance when he heard her sigh. It was as if his auditory nerves had been programmed to listen for that sound. His ears perked, his skimming of the inventory list paused, his chin lifted. He watched as Sush dumped the clipboard next to the keyboard as she slumped into her swivel chair, brows furrowed and mouth downturned in a frown as she scrolled through her phone.

Setting the list in his hand onto his chair, he strode across the space, toward the elevator, jabbed the number six, tapped his foot impatiently against the ground as he waited for the elevator bell to chime faintly, stepped onto the cafeteria floor, and made a beeline for the coffee bar.

Nancy looked up from her phone when Greg asked, "What does the chief octopus normally take when she looks like she's about to yell at someone?"

Nancy's curious expression turned apprehensive. "What did you do?"

"I highly doubt it's me. If it were, she would've said it to my face as she does with everyone. Do you know what she takes when she's like that? Just coffee, something ice-blended, something sweet?"

"Uh, so she's frustrated, right?"

"Seems like it."

"Alrighty." Nancy moved to the display case and placed two cream puffs into a white paper box. Folding the lid inward, she explained, "Sush doesn't take more caffeine when she's stressed like that. In the last few months when she looked like she was losing it, I normally treated her to one of these babies or matcha cupcakes. Since the cupcakes are sold out, this is our only option." As Nancy jabbed the numbers on the cash register, she asked, "She sent you to get them?"

"No," Greg replied curtly, placing a note on the counter and saying, "Keep the change."

Nancy took the cash. The corner of her lips twitched up. "Thank you. For taking care of her. She needs it, as much as she denies it."

Taking care of her. Those four words did something to his mind, his heart. Was he taking care of her?

Not knowing how to respond, he merely offered a firm nod and left at a brisk pace. In the elevator, he thought about what Nancy had said: "She needs it, as much as she denies it." The barista weaved his simple gesture in such an inappropriately intimate way. This was just a snack, something to . . . to what? To make sure she was alright? Because if she wasn't, then the smooth-sailing extraction of hunter intelligence would be compromised?

Yes, yes. He couldn't have that. That was the point of the cream puffs. It wasn't anything more. It *couldn't* be anything more. His last encounter with a huntress did not go well, and he'd made it a point to draw a very clear line that he'd never cross again.

But that didn't mean he should close off professional prospects in this world. He'd seen the systems and inventories, and it was promising. Just because one huntress had finagled him, it didn't mean he should eradicate learning from them, especially not from her—the most luminous one of all.

Greg hadn't noticed the slight tug of his lips until he noticed his reflection when the elevator bell chimed. Pulling the corner back down to form a flat line, he cleared his throat and exited, heading straight for the chief, who didn't look like she was going to yell at someone anymore. Now, she looked like she was going to execute the murders of more than one creature as she continued scrolling on her phone. And she wore that look so damn well that it was getting more difficult not to smile from witnessing the sight.

Settling the box on the only empty spot he could find in her paper-filled space, he said, "Eat first, then kill. It's more effective. I speak from experience."

Sush's brows were still arched deep when her eyes rose to meet his. The ocean of frustration in her orbs welcomed a fragment of relief. Noting the familiar box, she reached for it and set it on her lap. "Oh, good. Another bribe. I really need this right now. Did Nancy help you again?"

"She did." He leaned against the desk, conveying her movements to memory: the way she took her time looking for the end of the tape sealing the box, the manner with which her fingernail scratched at the corner when she found it, the spark of excitement in her eyes as the tape came loose and she opened the lid.

Observing her was therapeutic, almost as therapeutic as . . . oh no.

No, no, no.

He forbade himself from thinking about Izabella. Observing her and finding that therapeutic had been a big mistake, one he did not intend to repeat.

His eyes tore away right before Sush beamed at the sight of the cream puffs. He forcefully curled his tongue inward to stop himself from speaking until he'd run his sentences through his brain at least three times. Pushing himself off her desk, he said, "I'm headed back to the inventory section."

"Mm, wait." The force of her voice, though there was actually no force to the normal creature, pulled him to a halt. Getting her phone, Sush unlocked, swiped, and handed her device and the box with the second cream puff to him. "You'll need this more than I do after reading that."

As she pushed herself off her seat to wash her hands, Greg held her phone in one hand and the paper box in the other. The email was about the Monica Upshaw query. Sush sent an email the previous day and had just asked for a follow-up. The response she got was that Upshaw had been exempted for a reason that couldn't be disclosed in the interest of national security, which the hunters had no jurisdiction to question.

"Told you you'd need the puff." Sush's taunting voice pulled his onyx gaze from the screen, and she smirked as she sank back into her chair, bringing some lilac shades back into his eyes.

"National security? Aren't all of you here the ones steering the wheels of national security?" he snapped.

Her index finger came up. "That's flattering, Your Grace. You're forgetting the soldiers."

"Not. Funny."

Her lips pressed down, and her head slowly swung side to side. "Wasn't a joke to begin with."

Heaving a deep sigh, reining his anger, he then asked, "The face-to-face meeting you're demanding in your response to the email—what are the odds of them granting it?"

"Zero point one percent."

"Excuse me?"

"I honestly don't know, Your Grace. I've never done anything like this. The last time something like this happened, my predecessor did nothing. I have no precedent to follow here, so expect a lot of trials and errors as this moves forward. Have you seen my noble leader's separate email to me, by the way?"

He hadn't. Tapping the Back button and finding the first correspondence on top, Greg seethed when Valor essentially told her to stop pursuing the matter, adding that it wouldn't end well for her. "Is this a threat?" he questioned.

"Yes. Another empty one. He can't get rid of me that easily. I got in without his vote anyway. The tricky part now is to get what I want without pissing off the rest who did vote for me."

"I suppose that means I can't get involved."

"You can." A glint in her eye appeared when she went on, "If they fire me, you'll have a new chief to correspond with, which would most likely be Haz—"

"Don't," Greg interjected like she was reciting a curse. "Stop there. I fully comprehend the direness of this situation."

Sush chuckled briefly. His revulsion to her deputy was comical. Eyeing the paper box, she asked, "You *are* going to eat that, right?"

Handing her the box and phone, he replied, "It'll take more than a pastry ball to cool me off."

Reaccepting the puff, she bit into the second puff, and her eyes darted back to the computer screen when she said through the mouthful, "Mm. Maybe what you need to cool off is something that is actually cold, like an iced latt—"

She felt a gust of wind, and when she turned, Greg had already disappeared. Her head craned and spun around the trenches, scouring, and found him back at the inventory section, a folder already in his hands.

Their eyes met briefly, and Sush's lips tugged upward in a knowing smile, a gesture that Greg's lips matched as he shook his head.

Hazel witnessed the exchange, growing conflicted, wondering if this changed things.

CHAPTER 18

In the dark room of Sush's apartment, the red strips displaying the time on her bedside alarm clock showed 3:16 a.m. when the sound of her ringtone blared through the room, jostling her awake. Phones were never turned off in this profession, especially those of chiefs or deputies. They were paid a laughable wage to work fixed hours and be reachable at all hours.

Swiping to answer the call without checking the caller identification, she hid under the covers with her eyes closed while the caller spoke.

A security breach. In the east. EAST.

She didn't choose to stay in the west because she'd enjoy taking a hell of a long flight to the other side of the globe, especially not when it was still dark, her bed still warm, and her eyelids still heavy. She tried wriggling her way out of the assignment, saying that she'd send Hazel and two more octopuses, but when the representative from the east said Valor ordered her and Abbott to be there, she checked her messages and—for longer than a brief moment—considered deleting the commander's message and claiming she'd received no such instruction.

Dragging her exhausted bones out of bed and getting some shuteye in the Uber on the way to the airport, Sushmita dropped Hazel a text saying that she'd have to take charge until she'd settled things in the east. The two octopuses she asked for were already there—one groggy and the other awake. Wide awake. She wished she had that level of energy, not minding the dark circles beneath those alert eyes. When Abbott joined them, they boarded the plane.

During take-off, they sat facing each other, flipping open their laptops to view the documents and pictures in the files they downloaded beforehand as

Sush began scrutinizing the reason she pulled her ass out of bed and quickly concluded that—for once—this was a justified emergency.

How the hell did something like this happen?

"What the . . ." the hunter seated next to her murmured under his breath, then—instead of enlarging the picture using the plus icon accessibly placed at the bottom right corner—he brought the screen closer to his face like he was pouring the light into his eyes. Sush wondered if that was what he did to look awake.

The huntress seated opposite her was as sleepy as she was until her green eyes bulged at the first picture, enlarging it with the touchpad, too stunned to consider lifting her laptop like her colleague.

Abbott wasn't doing any better, face paling in dismay before closing his eyes to convey a silent prayer.

###

In the evening when the pinks and yellows surrounding the descending crimson sun were pressed back by the darker blue and purple, Kenji Suzuki, the representative from the east who'd called, met them outside the taped perimeter. He greeted his colleagues from the west with formal handshakes but said hi to Sushmita with a hug that even shocked the chief octopus herself, whispering, "It's good to see you again, Sush."

Sush promptly pushed him away, using just the right amount of force so it didn't look like any drama was about to unfold.

Kenji smiled broadly and was about to say something when an impatient, grim rumble came from behind the westerners. "If you invited us for small talk, I suggest a video call. Otherwise, make yourself useful and lead us to the crime scene."

All eyes fell on Greg, an impassive Ella and Jade right behind him. A heated sensation crawled up his chest, painting a deathliness in his eyes when Kenji held Sush. Greg's bodily instincts brought him to her side, the space between them narrower than one would expect. Despite his lethal energy, Sush remained unafraid.

Wary, maybe. But not afraid.

Sush would normally prized personal space, but at this time, she didn't even think to move as her sleepy brain computed how Greg knew about this emergency.

Kenji's friendliness wavered as apprehensiveness grew. He skimmed the duke and offered a curt nod, acknowledging, "Your Grace. This is a surprise."

"How so?"

Keeping the fidgeting leg to himself, Kenji said, "Well, for one, I only called my colleagues. I didn't make any calls to the mavericks."

"How very heartbreaking," Greg replied monotonously with crossed arms.

On a normal day, Sush would've found that funny. But given the circumstances they were in, she decided this wasn't the best time to laugh, thus ending up thinning her lips to suppress a smile. She'd normally have no issues keeping a straight face, but the lack of sleep must have been getting to her brain's control centers.

Kenji's eyes found their way to her, and she harrumphed before replying, "It's in the treaty, Kenji. His Grace has full access to the ins and outs of our systems, including sudden breaches like the one here. How about we reduce the likelihood of the duke flying off the handle by heading to the crime scene?"

Skipping over the fact that Greg had already flown off the handle, Kenji muttered, "Sure." Perhaps there were other handles that would fly off. Kenji took another sideways glance at Greg, having so many questions for Sush about the duke but knowing these were questions for another day.

The police and archers let them through the black-and-yellow tape. They stood on a plain field with a thick forest up ahead. The innocuous site was misleading enough to overlook the fact that it was the most heavily monitored part of the east, where the octopus's eastern lair was right underneath. Today, thanks to the tape, the field that could have passed as a manicured lawn seemed like a cleaned-up murder site, which it was.

The stench of blood hung in the air, despite its faded odor, leading Greg and the mavericks right to where six archers had been killed.

Just like the reports said: The deceased archers had surrounded their assailant before dropping like flies. Their blood now stained the grass brown. The kill was swift. And odd.

One minute the archers surrounded a figure in a beanie whose face was fully covered save for a set of eyes. The archers bellowed in rage, demanding the intruder stand down and raise both hands.

The intruder looked around at the guns pointed neatly at him, and an object fell from his hand. The object was later found to be the murder weapon—a knife.

An archer ordered the intruder to raise both hands, and it was done slowly. The hands that hung on his sides, near his trouser pockets, slid up, and when his hand reached the pocket and slid over the fabric, a sound of water from sprinklers made the archers look around, and—seconds later—they began screaming. The intruder picked up the knife and slashed each of their necks, making each one collapse to the ground before he disappeared into the thick trees.

Several questions arose: Who was the intruder, what was he after, who turned on the sprinklers, and what made the archers scream?

CHAPTER 19

The latter two questions had been answered by an autopsy report and affirmed by the eastern octopuses: The sprinklers were not turned on from the control room, meaning they could've only been switched on by an external source. They traced it to an unauthorized wireless device, suspecting that the intruder had a remote in his trousers pocket that managed the feat.

As for the screaming, the sprinklers sprayed not water, but zahar: an airborne substance that tampered with its victim's neurons. They'd feel as if a million needles were being pierced through their skin, causing momentary paralysis while their assailant struck. Zahar wasn't lethal in open spaces, but it did buy time.

Why wasn't the assailant himself affected? The octopuses concluded he either had already ingested an antidote or wasn't human to begin with. Zahar didn't affect lycans, werewolves, or vampires, so no one ruled out that the intruder could be one of their neighboring species.

When a five-foot-two eastern octopus made this suggestion, she warily glanced at the three lycans, which triggered Greg to say, "Of course. Why wouldn't we want to kill six archers when the conspiracy against our kind was led by two chameleons? And of course we'd resort to attacking the east when our problems stemmed from the west. Who knows what we'd do next? Detonate the eastern trenches, perhaps."

His sardonic response at the illogicality of the eastern hunters' suspicions was not well received. Sush was the only human who wasn't fearful of their safety in the duke's presence by then. Despite her fatigue, she could still tell when he was and wasn't serious. If he was serious, he'd just do it—like how he killed Izabella. He wouldn't bother making an announcement.

Sush's firm voice permeated through the skeptical silence, speaking directly to Kenji and the five eastern octopuses, "There was an extensive, four-month investigation and back-and-forth negotiation before the execution of our western members was passed, and punishment was confined to them. If you suspect the imposter may be a lycan, it is unlikely that he or she was sent by the kingdom. They wouldn't skip through the procedure."

"Wasn't Delilah executed prior to any procedure, Sush?" Kenji reminded, drawing a snarl from Greg's lycan for two reasons: One, this dickhead probably spearheaded the thought that lycans were behind the assassination, and two, he had the gall to call the chief by name.

And the tone he used. Goddess, Greg could tear out the hunter's voice box for just that.

Sush eyed Kenji, a warning glint evident in her eyes when she replied, "Yes, and—for your sake—I hope you know why."

A lump followed the wave-like muscle contractions of his throat, headed downward. Every hunter knew the execution of Izabella Delilah had been legal. There was long-established legislation that allowed foreign species to execute an imposter the moment irrefutable evidence surfaced. It was created to secure one's territory and was neither amended nor repealed. It was deplorable for any hunter not to know this.

Kenji was the Head Octopus of the east. He definitely knew it.

"That aside," Sush moved on, "has anything been taken from the headquarters or inventory?"

The five-foot-two octopus, Mei Ling, reported, "Our team detected an intrusion on PC 3A. Seven folders were opened. However, they contain very different content. We failed to find a connection, Chief."

"Flag them. I'll check from my end. For now, report to the government that their water sources have been compromised, seeing the water from the sprinklers comes from their source. Ask for footage to see if there has been tampering. I want a list of employees overlooking the water system in the past month. And go through the list of thugs, especially the latest ones."

Thugs were hunters who were either dismissed or had resigned and gone rogue. They weren't as common as rogues and proditors, but existed nonetheless.

"How did the intruder get in to reach the computer, by the way?" Sush asked.

Mei Ling explained, "One of our colleague's access cards was used, Chief.

He reported it being stolen six minutes before the incident and recalled someone knocking into him on his walk home, so we suspect it was picked out of his pocket during the collision."

"Any footage verifying that?"

She shook her head solemnly.

"Alright. I need one more thing." Sush's eyes skidded across the row of monitors. "The clock in and out data of the eastern hunters—sync it with the west."

Mei Ling was jotting down the demands before her stylus pen halted.

Kenji's brows knitted, his voice laced with a hint of anger, taking umbrage at the chief's suggestion. "With respect, Sush, I doubt it's one of our own. No access cards needed to be stolen if it was. And there clearly haven't been traces of our files being hacked into, seeing it was opened directly. Our security system is the most sophisticated and thorough one to date, even better than—forgive me for saying this—the one in the west."

Greg scoffed. "Funny how the sophistication couldn't prevent six deaths and an intrusion."

Sush released a sigh and turned to Greg. "Your Grace, I know you don't care if I say this, but I'm really tired. If you could make things easier by not trying to start a stir that I'll have to mellow out, I'd appreciate it."

Uneasiness curbed the remaining disparaging comments the duke had for the eastern octopuses. His stomach coiled when she said he wouldn't care. It sounded so wrong that it was eating him alive. How could he not care? It was as difficult to see her tired as it was to see her being questioned by her fucking subordinates.

Sush diverted her attention back to Kenji and noted, "I didn't ask you whether it was one of yours, Kenji. And I didn't ask about the advancement of your systems. As chief, I'm *instructing* you to have the data I need synced. I hope that won't be an issue."

Swallowing another lump in his throat, he responded meekly, "It won't be. You'll have everything within the next twenty-four hours."

"Two hours. Not more. You're just transferring and flagging data. Any longer and it'd raise suspicions of fabrication. Not with me, but with the higher-ups if this escalates to them. I'm not taking any chances." With that, Sush strode off before further negotiations began. The westerners were at her heels, leaving the lair with her.

Mei Ling and her colleagues delegated the tasks and got to work while Greg threw one final scowl at Kenji before he left.

CHAPTER 20

The following day, Sush was scrutinizing each flagged file. Frustration filled her when formatting issues disturbed her flow. These were very old files overseen by Kenji's predecessor, who wasn't exactly the most efficient or thorough octopus, so Sush supposed she should have expected half-baked work like this.

It really bothered her, but since the retired hunter was not within her vicinity to be yelled at, all she could do was sigh to herself as she perfected the documents by correcting each formatting issue that didn't conform to their standards.

These old-timers, she thought to herself in dismay.

Her flow got better after each rectification, until one broke her momentum—an archive from over a decade ago about the remnants of a victim suspected to have been bombed. Her eyes trailed along each line, each photo. Her heart raced, sweat beaded on her forehead, the rise and fall of her chest grew more fervent as her breathing shallowed.

"Sush?" The voice, careful and gentle, pulled her back to reality.

This wasn't the first time something like this had happened. The first time was when she learned about this method of killing.

Over the years, when she thought about the incident, her stability would waver, the dauntlessness in her would vanish, her heart would pump faster to cause a stampede within her blood vessels. Over the years, someone would catch her in this panic. Her eyes would swing to them, vulnerable and afraid. They would comfort her, sympathize with her, or use this against her. Over the years, she taught herself to wait before looking anywhere, to close her eyes, inhale, count to ten, remember who she was, how far she'd come, where she'd planned to go. Only then would she face the witness to her panic.

"Sush, are you okay? Hey." The gentle voice drew closer, and so did his hand.

Sush's reflexes made her lean away. Her swivel chair created a distance that the hand was closing. She met a set of triangular eyes staring back at her, and the first words that spilled from her mouth were, "What are you doing here?"

Kenji's brows rose. "Nice to see you too. Are you okay? You look like you were having a panic attack."

"Nah," she fibbed, waving a hand to substantiate the lie. "Was just thinking about a nightmare I had before I woke up on the floor this morning."

The valley between Kenji's brows narrowed, his posture curved, leaning toward her, and his whisper emanated concern when he asked, "You still get nightmares?"

Her right shoulder lifted and fell. "Everyone does, Kenji. Don't make a big deal out of it. Now, back to my question: Why are you here? I don't recall approving your transfer from the east."

That drew a short chuckle out of him. Straightening his spine, he set a brown paper bag Sush hadn't seen him holding on her desk. "I, uh . . . felt really bad about yesterday. I didn't mean to question your order. It just . . ." He sighed. "I suppose we're all under a lot of pressure after what happened. Valor is already questioning my competence, so I got defensive when you asked for the clock in and out data. I overreacted. And I'm sorry." Pushing the bag toward her, he spoke with visible anxiety, "I hope you still like the matcha cupcakes from upstairs."

Pulling the bag inches toward herself as an expression of forgiveness, she replied, "I do. Thanks, Kenji. How are the rest in the east?"

His face crumpled in uneasiness. "Pretty shaken, to be honest. The archers are already admonishing us. I just had a row with Asahi this morning. He's panicking. I've never seen him panic."

"Well, as the head of the eastern archers, those were his people."

Somberness deluged his eyes in a way that was impossible to miss. The frown only added to show how hard the murders had been on him as well. "They were our people, too, Sush. I don't take this lightly. I doubt you do either. Asahi had no right to think the octopuses didn't give their all. And then there's Valor—" he checked his watch "—who I have to see in five minutes, so I'd better make a move. Again, I'm sorry for yesterday. Won't happen again. Have a good day, and let me know if there are any updates on your end."

"Good luck," Sush uttered ominously, knowing that if there was one thing that Valor could do, it was make them feel worse when they already felt bad.

He offered a meek smile. "Thank you. I'll need it."

Her eyes followed him until he entered the elevator. When the metal doors closed, they gave each other a brief wave before Kenji disappeared from view.

"So why didn't it work?" Greg's cold voice made Sush jump in her seat.

Her hand flew to her heart at his sudden presence, and she sighed before remarking, "Jeez, you should wear a bell, Your Grace."

"Hm." He placed a bag similar to Kenji's on her desk, and Sush oddly forgot about the one Kenji had brought and set Greg's bag on her lap, opening it. "Oh, I could get used to this. What's the bribe today?"

"The same as your ex-boyfriend's, I gather," he answered, hoping she'd correct him on the label he'd just assigned to the eastern octopus.

But she didn't. Which meant that they *were* an item once.

Sush opened the box and found that Greg was right about the snack being the same as what Kenji had bought. Well, almost. Kenji's box was smaller, which would only fit one cupcake this size. Greg got her two.

He entered the trenches with the treats, when he saw Kenji speaking to her, so he stayed within their vicinity and eavesdropped like the gentleman he wasn't.

As Sush licked the green frosting, she said, "You know, I don't think you made a very good deal. Hazel seems to have given up, so it'll be easier to keep her away from you now. You practically have to treat me for nothing in return."

"I'm not taking any chances," Greg uttered, more relaxed, now leaning against her desk with his arms crossed.

It was the first time Sush noticed his arms. The way they filled out his sleeves and looked like they were going to rupture the seams caught her eye, even though this wasn't the first time he stood this close.

Why hadn't she noticed it before? Hazel was right, the bulges were distinct. It was hard not to look.

"So why didn't it work?" he demanded, less icily.

"Why didn't what work?" Sush questioned, lost and flustered.

A thread of humor weaved into him, evident from the smile he was suppressing. "The thing you had with Mr. Sophisticated. Why didn't it work?"

"Oh. Didn't take you for being nosy." Sush took a bite of the cupcake because licking the frosting seemed inappropriate now. "Long distance. Kenji was from here before his promotion sent him to the east. I thought of applying for a transfer, but I preferred the environment here, so I stayed. The work demands and distance didn't offer the luxury of quality time, so we decided the relationship had run its course. If you were hoping for a dramatic breakup story, I'll have to disappoint you. We parted on good terms."

That was only half the truth. Although she and Kenji had parted on good terms, long distance wasn't the only reason or the main reason.

Sush had seen things as a huntress, learned things—things she wished she never knew, never dwelled on. She wished she had it in her to forgive, accept, and move on. But she didn't and couldn't.

She didn't want Kenji to catch her doing what she'd set out to do, nor did she want him to get involved. So she ended things. She wanted to see through her plan more than she wanted a future with him. The decision was thoroughly thought through, and to this day, she had no regrets.

"Hm," Greg mused, replaying the previous day's events—how Kenji held her like she was his—and a splinter of anger returned. "So Mr. Sophisticated came today to rekindle an old flame?"

The words kindled a different flame within him—a less romantic kind, a raging kind. His jaw clenched taut as he waited for her answer.

"The only flames Kenji is concerned about are Valor's. The shit in the east yesterday was enough for him to be summoned. I hope the sprinklers in Valor's office work. I'm pretty sure my boss is up there with a flamethrower right now."

Greg's jaw loosened, and the onyx in his eyes lessened. He didn't mind the sprinklers not working, actually. It'd kill two hunters in one arson. The situation was so naturally perfect that no intervention was necessary for it to unfold. Shaking himself out of Sush's metaphor of her boss's anger, he watched her push the last chunk of the first cupcake into her mouth when he decided he should say something, just so it didn't look like he was watching her over-attentively.

"I still fail to comprehend how you're able to inject humor into any situation, Chief," he said, picturing Valor with a flamethrower that he probably couldn't even hold, let alone use efficiently.

Sush's forefinger lifted, and his animal sat, recognizing the cue that she was about to make a point. "I don't inject, Your Grace. I extract. Humor is always there. The ones who can't find it are either lacking in creativity, mindful about not offending someone, or are mourning a loss. Otherwise, like happiness and sadness, amusement can be found in everything. It's just a matter of perspective."

After reading her file, she was the last person he'd expected to be able to find humor in any—let alone every—situation.

"Mm," Sush added, "I should mention I couldn't find humor in the four months cleaning the sewer that my predecessor, Delilah, and the other three left behind. There was no humor in that situation. It was exhausting."

Greg's lips twitched. "You were probably mourning a huge loss."

Her eyes narrowed. She doubted he didn't know the animosity she had for the conspirators. Green frosting dotted her upper lip when she said, "Hah. Funny. Loss of what?"

His eyes dropped to the green dot on her lip, fighting the urge to wipe it off with his thumb as he listed flatly, "Sleep. Routine. Peace of mind." He truly believed Sush was suffering in that duration since he'd even heard it from Nancy.

Her chewing halted. She blinked, digesting his reasoning, and then her jaw moved again as she nodded. "That's actually true. See, the point stands: There's humor in everything."

"In that case, I look forward to hearing what comes out of your mouth after Mr. Sophisticated and the noble leader set each other on fire."

Licking up the last bit of icing off her thumb and closing the empty box, she mocked suspicion when she questioned, "You didn't tamper with the sprinklers in Valor's office, did you?"

Greg's lips curled into a smirk. Pushing himself to stand straight, he replied, "Wouldn't that make humor extraction easy."

She scoffed. The sound brought a twinkle into her eyes, one that he'd never noticed before—because they were never there. Sush could find humor in many situations, but most of it was insensitive humor—things she kept to herself. Sometimes it was self-deprecating humor, thinking back to how naive she was when she thought engineering was the only thing she was going to do until retirement, or when she thought her mother died of a simple road accident. Such humor simply kept her sane and entertained. It never brought the shine that Greg was witnessing.

Sush would be the first to admit that she was prepared for a chaotic three months with the duke and mavericks infiltrating their circle, but it was pleasantly surprising that they seemed to be getting along. She might even say he was better company than most of the people she'd met in her life. Whenever she said something, he never seemed to find it insensitive, disrespectful, or inappropriate. She'd gotten a shit ton of people telling her—through their judgmental gazes—that her comments could come off as offensive.

Oversensitive paper towels, she thought. Only Hazel seemed amused with her comebacks, unless the comment was for her.

There was something different about Greg. She couldn't put her finger on it but beneath the stony exterior who'd delivered the most brutal execution in hunter history, he was someone she . . . clicked with.

The hum of Greg's phone stole their gazes from each other. The duke scanned the name on the screen, and his eyes widened like he was caught doing something he shouldn't. He checked his watch, his brows rose at the time, and he hastily swiped to answer. "Hey, sweetheart. How was your day?"

And just like that, Sush's moment of lightheartedness came to an end. Heat radiated from the center of her chest, and sourness developed in her stomach as her intestines coiled. And it only got worse when Greg covered the mouthpiece and curtly said to her, "See you tomorrow."

Forcing a meek smile as he strode away, she tossed the empty box into the wastepaper basket under her desk with more force than necessary. As she furiously scrolled through the flagged documents, her mind questioned why she was angry in the first place.

Greg Claw was a duke, now in the good books of the kingdom. He was a bachelor with wealth, status, connections, and vicious charm.

How was it a surprise that he'd already moved on from Izabella and now had someone else?

If it wasn't a surprise, why did Sush feel something akin to betrayal?

CHAPTER 21

"Uncle Gweg! Why didn't you call?"

He was just two minutes late. Even so, heaviness settled in his being. "I'm sorry, sweetheart. I lost track of time. Had a good day today?"

A moment of silence passed before Enora's whisper rang through the line, "I shot Lionel MacDonald today and ran. He doesn't know who did it."

Although Greg could hear the smile in her voice and his animal howled in pride, his human's eyes snapped shut.

Shit.

As an afterthought, she added, "Don't tell Mommy."

"Sweetheart," Greg exhaled, pinching the bridge of his nose, "this call is recorded."

"What's recworded?"

"It means everything we're saying now will be on your mommy's phone and she can replay what we're saying like how you watch cartoons over and over again."

A stretch of silence followed before Enora innocently asked, "So I should thwow away Mommy's phone, Uncle Gweg?"

"What? No! Just . . ." How was he going to resolve this? "Alright, Enora. Lesson one: Never tell secrets through a phone, a computer, or anything that's not a mind-link or the actual person, got it?"

Giving her time to digest as he got into his car, slotted in the key, and started the engine, his niece carefully combed through the memories of the day and spoke again when he started driving, "Mm . . . Ken peed in class today."

Greg chuckled. "What was that like?"

Enora described in detail—with repetitive words due to her limited vocabulary—how a puddle formed below her brother's seat because he couldn't hold it in while waiting for the previous student to return from using the restroom, how it stank, and how Ken almost cried when some of the others started making fun of him, the loudest being Lionel MacDonald.

"Is that why you shot him, sweetheart?"

"Mm-hm. And he stole Lisa's wed crayon once. And . . . and he took Jack's doll. He pulled out the doll's head and threw it at 'em. Jack cwied and his mommy came to get 'em. And . . . and he bwoke an a-whow Aunty Hailey gave me for my bwirthday."

"Yeah, I remember the birthday arrow. Aunty Hailey did get you new ones, didn't she?"

"Yeah, but he bwoke the old one!"

"Lionel MacDonald is definitely a pain in the a—is definitely an immature classmate. How's your brother?"

"He said he doesn't want to go to school anymore, but Mommy and Daddy said he'll still go tomowwow."

"He'll be fine. Here's a tip: Ask him to pee into Lionel MacDonald's bag next time." Greg regretted his words as soon as he said them. To a phone. On a call. That was recorded. Clearing his throat, he uttered, "Enora, just so we're clear, that was a joke. I wasn't serious, okay? Don't tell your brother to do that, and don't think of doing that yourself either, got it?"

"How do I pee in a bag, Uncle Gweg?" Enora's voice came in contemplative curiosity.

"You can't. It's not possible." Why wasn't it possible? Damn him. "You'll hurt yourself. Don't do it. Hey, how's that archery practice coming along? Signed up for the competition yet?" He prayed Enora's precociousness with bows, arrows, and crossbows didn't include an advanced ability to detect a deflection in subject.

It was as if his prayers were answered when Enora's excited voice blared through the speaker, "Yeah! And I almost hit the wed dot today!"

"Atta girl! When I come home this weekend, we'll go to the pond to celebrate, okay?"

"Yay!"

Greg heard some muffles in the background before Enora sadly said, "Mommy says it's my bedtime now. Bye-bye, Uncle Gweg. I love you."

I love you—three powerful words that weren't said to him for over a century; three syllables that he never said to anyone after his mother passed away.

When this niece of his said it the first time, Greg was so shocked that he froze and the smile he had faltered in an instant. Enora beamed and waited for him to say it back, and when his shock didn't thaw for the next five seconds, a shadow of doubt entered her eyes and moisture formed in her eyes. "You don't love me, Uncle Gweg?" He scooped her up and brought her back into his embrace, held her tight, and whispered that he loved her more than anything in the world.

It took him some time and practice to be able to say the words to her naturally, but he eventually got the hang of it, and now, whenever Enora used those words, his automatic response flowed out like current down a waterfall. "I love you, too, sweetheart. Sweet dreams."

The call dropped, and Greg knew for a fact the next connection would come was via mind-link. He checked the time on the dashboard and counted down the minutes as he arrived at the diplomatic residence.

Within thirty minutes or so, her link came through, *'Is there something I should know, Greg?'*

'I doubt it's something you don't already know, my queen. And good evening to you too. The sky's pretty clear on this side today, in case you were wondering.'

'Lesson one? Should I be given a copy of the syllabus?'

'You've already graduated. Giving you a copy would be a waste of paper. Weaver would never forgive you. My cousins, on the other hand, may need it. Since we're on that issue, I have a question: What weapon was it and where did she get it?' He remembered Lucy checking her pups' bags right before they left the house every morning since Enora shot a classmate with her crossbow, so whatever she used today couldn't be her own toy.

A frustrated sigh came from Lucy's end. *'A crossbow, coincidentally. And it was her classmate's—Colin's. There was a search, and it was found in his bag. But one of the teachers saw Colin when Lionel was hurt, so they dropped him from the suspect list.'*

'Is Enora on it?'

'Surprisingly, no. It seems she was on a potty break.'

Greg's smile of pride couldn't have been wider. This was one of the many reasons she was his favorite. What other pup would know how to lie, shoot the target, and make sure she had an alibi at the same time? And at the tender age of *five*?

'This isn't something to be proud of, Greg.'

Trying to sound monotonously indifferent but failing miserably, he merely responded, *'I didn't say anything, my queen.'*

His smile was evident even from his link, making Lucy respond, *'Your silence pretty much said it all. And your cousin seems more impressed than angered too. Do you know he just got Enora out of bed and is now feeding her ice cream in the kitchen, telling her it's because she's working hard in archery practice? We know that's a lie. He enjoyed her undercover adventure a little too much. What's in the Claw gene that's hardwired you two to find any of this okay?'*

'The fact that she shot the one who laughed at her brother, broke her toy, and bullied countless other classmates is something to be celebrated, my queen. It's practically self-defense.'

There was another sigh—an exasperated one. *'Exactly what Xandar said. You two should really look up the definition of self-defense because the law would disagree.'*

'You're not going to ground or restrict her from anything, are you? Swap the classroom setting for a battlefield and she'd be a heroine.'

'Honestly, I don't know what I'm going to do. And my mate, his second-in-command, and now the leader of the Secret Service ARE OF NO HELP!'

Greg nodded to himself, impressed. *'Got to hand it to Blackfur. Didn't think he'd have it in him to approve such barbarism.'*

'It seems Ianne had a hand in it too. She helps water the plants in kindergarten. But today, she distracted Colin with a watering can when Enora "borrowed" the crossbow.'

Greg was so stunned that he froze while taking out leftovers from the fridge, half bent over with the chilly air blasting at his face and refrigerator light shining on his forehead. It took him a moment to defrost and let the door shut as he strode toward the microwave. *'Blackfur must be proud.'*

'But Annie is annoyed. So am I.'

'Well then, I'm sure you and the duchess can sort things out. Get the Lionel pup expelled and restore peace in the kindergarten. The other pups would appreciate it, I'm sure.'

'I'm not saying what Lionel did was okay. Frankly, it's wrong. I'd restrict him from all leisure if I was his mother. But I'm not. And these are pups. They don't know any better yet.'

'A rubber bullet to the eye would speed up the learning process fairly quickly.'

'You know what? Forget it. I'll just continue ranting to your cousin about this until I've calmed down enough to speak to the teachers about talking to the MacDonalds. As for Enora's curriculum with you—legal lessons only, Greg. And no teachings or tutorials of peeing in someone else's bag!'

Pressing back a guilty smile as the microwave buzzed in the background, he replied, *'Duly noted, my queen. And since we're already speaking, let me update you on the hunters' debacle thus far.'*

Greg informed her about the eastern intrusion and the western issue about an archer being pulled out of station without reason. Lucy asked whether he'd gone through the eastern files. He had. *'There isn't a pattern. Whoever breached the system got what he wanted and opened the other files to throw us off. Jade traced the duration each file had been open, and the longest is the one with the explosion.'*

Lucy's voice came out concerned and ominous when she linked, *'There are so many other ways to kill a creature. Why use bombs?'*

'Erase traceability would be my best guess, but I'll have to look further into it, my queen. Something tells me there's more than what's written on those pages. I'll keep you posted.'

'Thank you, Greg. And send my regards to Sush.'

The link ended, and the first question Greg asked himself was, "What the fuck did that mean?"

CHAPTER 22

Sush was in a simulator on the archer's floor, versatile earplugs stuck into each ear, a twelve-gauge shotgun in hand, and eyewear that brought out the simulation and protected her sight painted a shade of violet over her eyes. The archer behind the control panel, Millicent, gave her a thumbs-up from behind the glass partition, signaling that the simulation was about to begin.

Millicent faded away, as did the control room.

Darkness sunk, and for a moment, there was nothing. As Sush's eyes adjusted, her surroundings welcomed her in strides. Leaves rustled from the high trees with branches flung wide, branches that seemed to nearly touch yet ultimately grew parallel to their neighboring limb, almost as if nature forbade them from ever meeting. Breezy fingers of the forest grazed her cheek as the crickets serenaded like a hectic first rehearsal rather than a ready performance.

A steady burble of running water became Sush's due north, and her head swung like a slow pendulum from side to side before she picked up her feet, the grass susurrating underfoot as she padded beneath the trees until the sound of the water became too loud to ignore. There, she used a tree trunk as cover, then another, and another, growing more vigilant with each step.

The last time she did this, a lycan came growling from the high branches, so her eyes instinctively scanned not just the ground, but the trees, especially the one she was under.

When there was nothing, her neck craned to study the river. The bushes fizzled and moved, and it wasn't by the wind. Sush lowered herself into a squat, gun held to her side. Then, a brown wolf that couldn't be older than twenty-five emerged. It was cautious, face popping from the leaves before its whole body came through. It didn't spot Sush, whose muzzle now steadied into an aim.

This was the hunters' territory. Any wolf who trespassed was a rogue, and the hunters were given full liberty to shoot, as agreed with the kingdom years ago.

Sush's fingers at the trigger tightened, and just as the animal's tongue took the first lap of water, she fired. A clean shot. A quick death. The creature didn't even howl. Several archers had taught her to shoot at a certain part for a certain type of howl. Some even took the pleasure of hearing each one. But she had always aimed for silence. A smile gleamed on her lips when she got it.

But then, her ears caught something.

A snap, some rustling, both sounds caught in a repetitive cycle that was getting louder.

Her head turned, her gaze pivoted, and she came face-to-face with a seven-foot lycan that hadn't growled until now. Its hand swung high from the back, claws extended in a sleek motion, and flew at Sush, who dodged the attack by rolling away. Far away. On her abdomen, she didn't bother getting up before aiming at the lycan and delivering her shot. Its howl pierced through her ears, gnawing at her chest as she fired another shot, but she missed as it dug out the bullet.

She swapped the silver bullets for oleander ones, and the lycan lunged at her when she had just loaded the magazine. Her overall posture and fingers counted on muscle memory and fired. The creature whimpered before falling on top of her with a thud.

Dragging herself from under the dead creature and reloading, her senses jolted when she heard a scream—a human's scream. Her body gravitated toward the concerning voice before her mind could keep up. Her heart thumped faster when multiple growls came from the same direction as her feet hit the ground in quicker paces.

"Help! Help! SomeBODY help! AhHhhh!" The voice, distorted somewhere in the middle, came, and Sush continued sprinting as she made a mental note to have the earplugs taken back to the trenches for repairs.

The moment Sush was within range, she took less than a second to aim and fire, dismissing the howl and firing again until the first wolf was dead, then the second one, which was running away. The third one had begun tearing through the flesh of its prey when Sush fired a clean shot. Then there was nothing but silence.

Sush waited two whole seconds before sprinting to the victim. She was probably in her early twenties, her dark hair sprawled on the ground, face filled with red scratches and eyes wide, staring into emptiness. A blotch of red blossomed from her chest where parts of her flesh and ribs were exposed, and the sight had Sush kneeling, tears stinging her eyes.

The dead girl faded into darkness, as did everything else.

Sush hoisted herself to her feet, waiting for the familiar walls to emerge, and the first thing that welcomed her back to reality wasn't the blue eyes of Millicent, but the mystifying lilac ones of Greg, which didn't feel like they were looking at her, but looking *into* her.

"Round four or break for the day, Sush?" Millicent's familiar voice came through the versatile earplugs that simulated the sounds in her weekly practice and conveyed messages from the control room.

"Break," Sush said, tearing her gaze away from Greg like it never fell on him.

Exiting through the door, handing the gun to the next person and taking off the protective gear, she sank onto the bench and swapped hunting shoes for her sneakers, readying herself for a cordial conversation with the person approaching her in strides that boasted his confidence, the click of his shoes enunciating his domineering presence.

"Morning, Chief," Greg began.

"Morning, Duke."

Greg would've cackled if she didn't sound so . . . withdrawn, maybe even a little dismissive. "Are you alright?"

"I just failed to save a civilian, so, yeah, I'm doing swell."

"It was a simulation, Sush," Greg noted pointedly. The sound of her name from his lips sounded smooth. Too smooth. Like caramel flowing down ice cream. She liked it a little too much. Receiving no response, he added, "And Millicent said you beat your own record from last week. Shouldn't that warrant a celebration?"

Her head swung to him. "You know Millicent?"

"She was controlling the simulation, and we spoke briefly, so we're acquainted."

She scoffed. "Would've thought you'd give her an offensive nickname like you do everyone else."

His hands went to his pockets, and it made him look more attractive in a way that should be illegal. "Not everyone is vexing enough to qualify for a nickname. And don't change the subject: Why are you upset? It was fake. You know it was fake. I would've understood frustration but not exactly distress."

"How about this, Your Grace?" She stood, handed the shoes to the archer on duty, and strode down the corridor, Greg keeping up with ease as she questioned, "Why is it so important for you to know?"

His tongue rolled in his mouth. The words were at the back of his throat, demanding they be set free. His brain was customs, checking the contents and forbidding their exit. Ultimately, he swallowed and said, "I thought we'd be allies by now."

Allies? Her brows rose at his choice of word. "And allies tell each other if something upsets them? Really?"

"Yes," Greg noted, not saying more, not trusting himself to say more. He didn't want to create a loophole he couldn't cover on time.

Sush uttered, "Well, it might be like that in your circle back in the kingdom. But here, unless our emotions get in the way of the work, we neither talk nor ask about it. And the hunters who qualify already passed the test of emotional control. Which means I have too. I'm fine."

"I just thought you needed to get something off your chest. My apologies if there was a misinterpretation."

He was hoping she'd open up to him, tell him the reason for the tears he saw behind her eyes when their gaze locked. He assumed it had something to do with a real-life experience, or something within the simulation that brought back memories of a trauma, or something about her mother, perhaps. She seemed close to her maternal side of the family until they were gone. He almost brought up her mother but held back when it felt like she was guarding that door with her life. If this was what she wanted, he wouldn't push her. He wouldn't force her to say or do anything. He doubted he could ever.

An awkward silence unfurled between them until Greg's voice permeated, uttering, "I'll be around here with the archers for half the day. See you in the trenches later." He turned on his heels, but before taking the first step, he said, "I almost forgot: The queen sends her regards."

Then, he left, and Sush was left discombobulated as she watched his retreating figure, an irritating want spiraling through her before she forced herself to look the other way and leave, not knowing that Greg stole a glance at her as he turned around the corner.

Back in the trenches, at her desk, she found a familiar brown paper bag in its usual spot. The waft of bagels made her mouth water, and there was something new—a grilled chicken sandwich in a transparent, rectangular plastic box. The scrawl in black marker read: "In case you're getting sick of bagels."

She hated it. She hated that it made her soften when it shouldn't, mellowed her anger and annoyance when it wasn't supposed to, and made her heart melt and soar at the same time.

How was his sweetheart back home okay with him buying lunch for another woman every other day?

Opening up to allies about one's feelings was still a plausible step, but this? Uh-uh. There was no way. Those animals were possessive by nature. There was no way any woman would be okay when her man offered a gesture like this to another female. Sush herself wasn't an animal, and even she wouldn't be okay with it.

Sighing to herself, she plopped into her chair and shot Greg a text, asking for his banking details to transfer the day's lunch expenditure to him. Sush didn't know whether to feel elated or exasperated when he replied, "Just buy me a coffee in about an hour. A big one."

CHAPTER 23

Greg locked his phone after replying to her message, sighing to himself, wondering why she was suddenly shutting him out. He thought they were getting along well. Better than well, even. Why the sudden change of behavior? Where was the playful sass, the ease that was there whenever they were together? How did something like that get flushed out overnight?

And honestly, why did he care?

In his defense, it would've been easier not to care if she didn't draw him in like a fucking magnet with everything she did: the way she talked, walked, ate, drank, puzzled over a task. Goddess, especially the way she puzzled over a task—the way her brows arched, the manner in which her body stilled, the way her eyes got lost on the page or on the screen. It was mind-consuming.

Letting Sush linger at the back of his mind, then diverting—or rather forcing—his concentration back to the chief archer showing him the room with their inventory labeled in a perfectly organized manner, he chose to refrain from asking whose idea it was to label things in bright colored markers since he recognized that handwriting from going through the octopuses' records and notes.

Abbott possessed limited vocabulary during their walk down inventory aisles, answering questions with, "Yes," "No," "Last week," "Indeed," and, "As authorized." For a moment, Greg began to wonder whether Abbott was just a puppet and the real chief archer was hidden among the rest.

"And the explosives? Where were they kept the last time hunters used them?" Greg questioned.

Finally, the emotion that was absent from Abbott's face embraced a flicker of surprise and some offense. "Never in the history of this humble profession have any explosives been stored, Your Grace."

Wow. Greg didn't know Abbott had that many words in his arsenal. Maybe he wasn't a puppet after all.

Abbott mistook Greg's surprise for disbelief and went on, "I'm certain you haven't come across any records of explosives in the octopuses' archives. If there are none there, there are none here. We don't bypass them. In fact, everything you see around you runs through them before they have a place on the shelves and on these floors."

Give this man a trophy because that was *a lot* of words, so many that it drew an impressed nod out of Greg. Taking another look around just to see if Abbott would fill the silence with more information, Greg came to terms with the fact that the chief had probably maxed out his quota for the day, and he began, "So how do you explain the Sakura Kondo case?"

Abbott stiffened. "That case involved a death that was not connected to this profession, Your Grace."

"Was not connected, or was not supposed to be connected, Chief?" A pocket of silence followed before Greg continued, "Because the facts are uncanny: a twenty-five-year-old octopus, fresh out on the field for one year, and on one unfaithful night, she was simply lured out into a jungle and had explosives tied to her and—quoting the records—disappeared and was presumed dead." He scoffed. "Funny how her remains were confirmed to be scattered at the murder site, yet the records still leave her death as a presumption and not a fact."

"Procedures may have been different back then, Your Grace," Abbott said, speaking through gritted teeth.

"I'm sure they were. But that isn't the point, Chief." He stopped inspecting the rows of ammunition, turning to face Abbott. "Are you certain you don't have the slightest suspicion that the hunters' system might have been involved in that explosion?"

Abbott's throat bobbed. Still, he managed a straight face. "I am in no position to speak for those who came before me, Your Grace. But I can say there has never been evidence linking them to Kondo's death."

"I know. There's no evidence linking anything or anyone to her death. No jealous exes, no beneficiaries, no enemies. It wouldn't seem strange if it wasn't so . . . clean," Greg mused.

They took another few steps before Abbott had enough courage to ask his first question, "If I may, Your Grace, what is the significance of the Kondo case?"

Greg's gaze pivoted to him, judgment for Abbott's indifference on full display. "After the six deaths in the east, you don't think this is something to be concerned about, Chief?"

"I thought the attack in the east involved zahar and a knife."

"Systems change. Methods can change too. A different modus operandi doesn't equate to a different culprit."

"You're certain they're the same party? From the Kondo murder?"

"I'm not certain of anything. Evidence is limited. Hypotheses vary with each variable. And this . . . must be the poison chamber." They came to the very end of the room, at a door painted black with a white sign that had the red words "CAUTION" nailed to the door.

As Greg flung it open, Abbott made it a point to note, "Like everything out here, everything in there has passed the octopuses' assessments before sitting on those shelves."

"I don't doubt it," Greg murmured, gingerly running his fingers over the black-and-white labels that were in a different handwriting, one he'd been seeing a lot in recent days as well, one that had a different effect on him than the colorful ones outside. The ones in here were works of art; the way each curlicue swayed, curled, and twisted offered a peek into the writer's soul, a glimpse into her personality. And he found himself melting, smiling.

It was Abbott's throat-clearing and voice that pulled Greg out of his thoughts, pulling his lips back into a straight line as the chief archer asserted, "We don't store zahar in our inventories, Your Grace. Not here in the west nor in the east. The culprit who used it couldn't have gotten it from us."

Greg mm-ed and then asked when Monica Upshaw was due to return, to which Abbott sheepishly admitted that even he didn't have that information. Deciding that he'd seen enough, Greg thanked the chief for his time and left.

In the elevator on the way down to the trenches, he linked someone from his network: Nash Beaufort, the rogue he'd asked to take over Ruby Lyworth's poison-production factory after throwing Lyworth into prison for treason and—off the record—for crossing him personally.

'Your Grace, how can I be of assistance?'

'Has anyone bought zahar from you in the past . . . I don't know. How long does zahar last?'

'Two years. Five if left unopened.'

'Noted. Have there been purchases?'

'Yes. It's an affordable form of pest control among our kind, so it's a product that sells on its own. Should I curate the list of purchasers and send them over?'

'Yes. Any human buyers?'

'Not that I recall. I'll look through them again and let you know.'

'Looking forward to it.'

'Always a pleasure to serve, Your Grace.'

Greg's eyes cleared when the metal doors opened, and he made a beeline to his desk, huffing an exhausted exhale until he saw a large to-go cup that pushed the corners of his lips upward. He looked across the space, finding her at her computer, hand pressing her pink headband like she was trying to fuse it into her head, dark eyes focused on the screen, tipping the edge of his lips even higher.

Beautiful.

He sank into the chair, and that was when he noticed the same calligraphic scrawl he'd seen in the poison chamber, which read, "Just so you know: You don't have to keep buying me lunch."

He frowned, wondering if he was making her uncomfortable.

He liked buying her lunch. It gave him an excuse to talk to her and learn about the things she liked. He made a mental note to ask her about this later, not wanting to stop immediately. He'd be back in the kingdom the next day, so the talk could be postponed to the following work week.

The coffee was still warm, and the first bitter sip tasted better than it normally did. He savored each drop, hoping that this cup wouldn't be his last from her.

CHAPTER 24

In the kingdom the next day, Enora held a yellow sheet of paper as she leaped into her uncle's ready arms that hoisted her up. Her tiny arms wrapped around his neck and squeezed tightly as his other niece and nephew gave him hello hugs at his legs. Gently patting Reida on her head and ruffling Ken's hair, he then turned his attention to his favorite. "What do you have here, sweetheart?"

He reached for the sheet blocking his peripheral view. His thumb smoothened the crumpled side where Enora's fist was, holding the flyer further from his face to make out the big, black words.

Enora's grip loosened when she asked with doe eyes, "Will you come, Uncle Gweg?"

It was about the archery competition she'd signed up for.

Leaving a quick kiss on her temple, he conveyed the date and time to memory. "Of course, sweetheart. Wouldn't miss it for the world."

"Yay!" Her arms shot to the sky as her uncle beamed brighter than the afternoon sun. So much energy and life inside such a small creature.

On the drive back, the three pups filled him in on their week almost all at once.

There was a time when he and his animal would growl to silence a room, but this was not such a time, despite it being a little challenging to drive while listening to all three—sometimes varying versions—of a tale. His animal "offered" to listen to Enora, asking his human to take the other two. It was a good thing pups were repetitive. By the time they reached the villa, Greg had heard their top tales of the week at least twice.

As the pups in the backseat went on their usual race to the front door, Greg unbuckled Enora and got her out as she rambled on about Lionel MacDonald being kept a close eye on by every teacher and almost stealing another pup's paintbrush but being caught by Hailey before he even left their classmate's desk.

At the door, Greg set Enora on her feet, but she held onto his sleeve and asked whether they could go to the park. It was not an innocent request. If trips to ponds meant assaulting ducks, those to the park meant shooting nests out of trees with a slingshot. Greg had had a few nests made and planted in the trees on their last playdate just so she wouldn't go after the real ones. They were still in a box in the boot of his car.

Greg looked to his cousin and cousin-in-law for an answer.

Doe eyes on her mother, despite knowing its ineffectiveness, the pup begged, "Mommy, pweez?"

Enora had been explicitly informed that she would only have one playdate a week instead of two—on a Saturday—with Uncle Greg if she misbehaved in school while he was gone. Only now did the pup regret the shot to Lionel MacDonald's nape. She knew her father wasn't mad at her for doing it. But her mother was a different story.

Enora didn't get a lecture, only being told by Lucy—in controlled calmness—to tell her teachers or parents these things instead of taking matters into her own hands. But the pup was convinced that it wasn't her father's warmth—but her mother's raging heat—that was melting the ice cream that night.

Lucy *was* mad, but only a small portion of the fury was toward her daughter. Some of it was frustration at her husband and his cousins, and a large chunk of it was at herself for not knowing what to do. It didn't help when her own father sided with her pup and encouraged her to use her royal prerogative to get Lionel MacDonald expelled, and she had to tell the old man that that wasn't what the prerogative was for.

Looking at Enora now, Lucy sighed and uttered, "After lunch and homework. And only one hour this time. For dragging Ianne into your schemes this week."

Enora only understood the first half of her mother's decision, and it lit her up like a lantern as she jumped in jubilance. She and Greg normally had two hours, but an hour was better than nothing. Finally letting go of Greg's sleeve and saying she'd see him later, Enora obediently disappeared into the dining room where Mrs. Parker was with her siblings, and her parents sat her uncle in the living room. Greg declined lunch because he'd already grabbed a quick bite before picking up the pups.

Lucy began, "The first week has been . . . surprisingly eventful."

Greg scoffed. "Alagumalai would've preferred the opposite, as would the rest of the octopuses, I gather."

Lucy's brows rose at Sush's last name, and Xandar's own knitted as his wife questioned, "Are you really calling her that, or is it only because you're now with us, Greg?"

"I normally call her 'Chief.'"

"Really?" Lucy questioned with an amused smile of disbelief, her husband swallowing a chuckle as he willed his lips to stay as flat as possible.

Greg shot his cousin a glare when he responded to Lucy, "One experience with a huntress is enough, my queen. Let's not think I'm there for anything more than business." Even as he said it, he felt the nudge in his chest, then a prick, one that told the rest of him that it was not the complete truth.

A truth that even Lucy knew about. "Well, I didn't expect you to be there for anything more than that either, but things can happen in these business ventures. Besides, I can't say the glow you brought home today doesn't suit you."

"That," Greg interjected, flushing just slightly, "is because of the pups."

"Hm, sure," Lucy hummed, calling his bluff without calling his bluff.

Xandar, as if Greg wasn't still in the same room, turned to Lucy and uttered softly, "You know, they do complement each other. The temper, the brains, the stealth. Even the impatience, I think."

With a hand on his lap, Lucy corrected in an affectionate whisper, "Darling, you're forgetting their tempers simmer away when they're around each other. Ella said it's the only time Sush smiles. And we know your cousin. Who have you seen him smile around other than Enora?"

"Hold up. You planted Tristan to keep tabs on me?" Greg queried.

The royal couple's smiles faltered as their heads turned to Greg when Xandar bluntly said, "If we wanted to do that, Greg, we would've sent the warriors, not relied on someone who's pledged loyalty to the Service."

"Ella has been concerned," Lucy elaborated. "And Toby and I talk. Often."

Greg insisted, "Nothing is happening." And his insides cracked at the admission, that truth. Things were happening, and then it just stopped.

"We know," Lucy said, almost sadly, thinking back to Toby's most recent gossip report that Sush and Greg hadn't been speaking to each other before Greg returned to the kingdom. Lucy shrugged. "Letting go does take time. I just hope the one you'll eventually choose will be available when you're ready. No rush, though, Greg. Wounds take time to heal."

"I won't pursue a huntress, my queen." As much as he wanted to. "Their kind brings more trouble than they're worth."

"Do you really think that?" Lucy questioned, planting a seed of doubt in his mind. "The woman who posed a danger to our family has never been the epitome of a huntress, never even possessed the fundamental qualities that profession represents, almost as if she only qualified because of the mark on her nape. Not every huntress is like her. You've met many of them by now. Are all of them like her? Is anyone like her at all?"

Enora had told everyone at home that Greg didn't want to use Izabella's name even when they were talking about her—boasting that she and her uncle had a secret code that she refused to share, which upset Ken—so Lucy was careful to leave Izabella's name out.

"Well," Greg reflected, "there is a traffic cone that ticked me off."

Xandar defended, "Ella said Hazel seems okay though."

"For the love of Goddess, don't take a warning hazard's side, cousin!"

"Don't deflect, Greg," Xandar hit back. "Take your time coming to terms with any internal turmoil you're experiencing, and we just wanted to say that we'll be here for you and we're happy for you."

Greg narrowed his eyes at his sentimentality. His animal almost gagged. "There is literally *nothing* to be happy about. Nothing is happening, and we're not even bonded. That makes this connection, if there's even one, weaker tha—"

"Are you sure about that?" Lucy interrupted before he finished. "What if this is just a Ydaer phenomenon?"

Ydaer was a scientist who studied mate bonds and discovered that creatures who hadn't let go of the past wouldn't be able to open themselves to feel the bond of a destined mate. Ydaer argued that holding onto bygones created an emotional block that muted a creature's senses and blinded them from feeling the one they were destined for. He theorized that the Goddess implanted this internal mechanism as a way of making sure a creature was ready to meet someone better before allowing the said creature to sense the second chance—a theory that was never confirmed due to the lack of evidence.

Lucy herself disagreed with the theory for the longest time since she never considered herself "ready" for any mate bond since the first. Only when Xandar barged into her life and loved her the way no one ever had did she understand: She was ready in the sense that she'd moved on from the opinions of her past mates, moved on from the experiences enough to stop herself from thinking about them to the point that she never thought about them anymore. Sure, there were those side effects that lingered and were only alleviated gradually through conscious healing, but she'd let that baggage go—focusing on her life to remind herself of her worth, to remember who she was, what she wanted, attributes she wouldn't compromise, and a purpose that—serendipitously—complemented her indecent beast's.

Greg shifted in his seat, declaring, "I *have* moved on from that woman. But that doesn't mean I want to feel another mate bond."

Lucy nodded, comprehending—the residual anger at the injustice of the situation laced heavy in his voice, giving him away. "Anyway," Lucy offered the diversion he sought. "Tell us about the simulation with the archers. It sounds interesting. Ella said Sush designed the versatile earplugs. Is that true?"

"It is," Greg replied, letting his guard down the moment that conversation diverted from the mate bond. As he struggled to hide a smile at the mention of Sush, along with her ingenuity, he went on, "That's just one of the many things she came up with for the hunters. There's also the simulator itself, the safety features, the inventory system. And that's just the summary. She's . . . incredibly brilliant. Efficient. And anyone should see her scaring the shit out of the incompetent slackers in the trenches at least once in their lives. It really is t—"

Greg only realized he'd diverted himself to the very topic he sought to divert away from when the couple before him watched him with smiling eyes, making him harrumph and redirect his point of focus. "So, the simulator." He droned on about the details and—at one point—admitted that it might even be a good addition to the Den.

They spoke until Enora finished the last of her homework and showed it to her mother, who made no comment on the rushed handwriting that was barely legible and gave her a pass to go to the park, where the pup shot the fake nests, kicking the ground when she missed and leaping into the air when she struck.

###

That night, Greg lay awake thinking about his conversation with the king and queen, about the damn seed the queen had planted in his head. Honestly, he'd only ever watch over her and her pups. Why did she have to mess up his mind like this?

He didn't want a mate, let alone a huntress for a mate.

No discussions. That was his decision. And that was final.

But as his consciousness drifted and his subconscious was left to wander, he began asking why Sush had to be a huntress, why he hadn't met her first. She was incomparable: so raw, so real, so direct, so . . . beautiful.

He couldn't help but agree with his cousin that he and Sush were very alike in terms of work ethic and ambition. Maybe even intelligence in some respects, though there were times he'd readily admit she was better, such as the times when he had to decipher the inventions she came up with. And that made her all the more alluring.

His room suddenly felt too big, the bed too large, the place too soundless. He wanted to feel a warmth next to him, to hear a steady breathing or a snore, to reach out to put his arm over the breather, to hear her make a sound when he pulled her close.

He wanted it to be her.

CHAPTER 25

Greg walked into the headquarters the following week mentally rehearsing the way he was going to phrase the question of asking Sush whether his presence was impeding her peace of mind. The question then arose as to *when* he should ask it. Sooner would be more appropriate, more gentlemanly, more respectful.

But he knew himself.

His track record did not display a good line of appropriate or gentlemanly behavior. Respect was another matter, unless someone pushed his buttons. He decided that—unless Sush flinched, jerked, or outright said that he was making her uncomfortable—he wouldn't raise the matter.

It was a dirty way to buy time, he knew. But he only had three months with her and was not going to prematurely shorten it.

She didn't entertain him with a chat when he greeted her in the morning, merely greeting him back. That was when Greg noticed something—the smell of frangipanis and lime wafting off her seemed a little stronger than usual, making him linger there a little longer before pulling himself away and dragging his perplexity with him. Convincing himself that it may just be a higher concentration of perfume for the day, he willed his eyes back to work, not knowing that Sush never wore perfume.

The hours dragged on until around midday, when Sush appeared at Greg's station. He'd chosen to sit there more often than anywhere else that the inventory folks got him a permanent desk and chair. This part of the trenches offered him the most unobstructed view of the chief, so he'd always find himself back here no matter how far he went.

Her palm landed on his desk to get his attention when she said, "Any plans this afternoon? I'm headed to the defense ministry."

He didn't need her palm there to announce her presence. Her scent, which was still stronger than the previous week, like a perfume that didn't wear off throughout the day, was already a headline. Her hand on his desk only made his mind venture along thoughts of taking it and pulling her in, to make her stumble and fall into him before holding her on his lap.

Shutting his eyes and turning away as he heaved a sigh, disgusted with himself, he replied, "No plans. Meet you there."

Her palm left the table. But she didn't. "Did something happen?"

Not trusting his mind not to wander the way it shouldn't, he kept his eyes closed and answered, "Lots of things happened."

"Namely?"

"Things you already know. Things from the past four months."

"You're derailing."

"I know."

There was a stretch of silence as Sush checked her own attire, wondering if it was because of her that his eyes had to remain shut. She was in a pantsuit—the same thing she wore on the conspirators' execution day. He didn't seem to have any problems looking at her then. "Look, whatever it is, remove it from your system. I need your head clear and alert at the ministry."

"Will do. See you later," he uttered, feeling her leave before letting his eyes open, telling himself to think about anything but caging her in his arms.

###

When it was time to leave for the ministry, Greg stepped out of the headquarters entrance doors opening to the parking lot only to find Sush waiting by his car with arms crossed, back leaning against the wall.

His right brow rose, his way of asking, "Yes?"

In response, she straightened and uttered, "I couldn't unlock my car. Some hacker got into the system and tampered with the motion sensors. When I unhacked it, I found the tires deflated. All four of them. So I need a ride while the octopuses go through the surveillance footage of the parking lot."

Suspicion poured over Greg at the hacking *and* tire deflation. His gaze turned to her car across the parking lot, forehead creased. If she had gotten into that car and hit the road, she could've gotten hurt, or worse.

Her voice from the side chimed, “If you’re not comfortable carpooling, I’ll just call an—”

“Get in,” Greg ordered as he unlocked his vehicle, and the doors of the driver’s and passenger’s seats lifted like a pair of wings. He’d set the passenger’s side to open automatically for Enora’s sake.

It was a hassle having to go to the driver’s side, push a button, wait for the passenger’s door to open, and then buckle his sweetheart in. He tried putting her through the driver’s seat, but she’d grown up so fast that he hit her head once and never used the shortcut again, even though the pup said it only felt like a brush. He checked for bruises and bulges multiple times that day, even asking the queen whether there were any that night, and the queen had to remind him that although pups healed slower, they still healed. If there was nothing during the day, there wasn’t anything that night. And there wasn’t. Lucy and Xandar checked as soon as Greg brought Enora home and apologized to them.

Sush and Greg got in and buckled up as the doors closed. While starting the engine, Greg asked, “Who else knows you’re headed for the ministry today?” He checked his own car’s system and made sure everything remained in top shape before putting it to drive.

“Valor definitely knows. I copied him in those emails. Abbott too. Since it concerns an archer.”

“That’s it? You didn’t tell anyone else before you left? Do the octopuses know where you are right now?”

“Well, I obviously had to tell Hazel. She’s in charge until I get back.”

“And chameleons? Does Patterson know?”

“Well, I didn’t tell him, but I can’t say the same for Valor. He treats the chief chameleon like a brother, when Patterson is only interested in kissing the ass of whoever’s on top.”

“Do they know I’m joining you?”

“Nope.” That explained the soundness of his vehicle. She went on, “I didn’t want them to make me run through a bunch of diplomatic applications and approvals that’d take God knows how long to file and process. Besides, the treaty clearly states the kingdom can demand getting involved in anything concerning security in these three months.”

His lips twitched, and his teasing voice carried a hint of flirt when he uttered, “I don’t recall making this particular demand.”

Head swung to him, she snapped, “Do you want to scorch the answer out of them with me or not?”

Pressing back the curl of his lips, containing his amusement as his animal cackled, he said, "Apologies, Chief. Thank you for seeing through the demand I must have forgotten making via telepathy."

Ignoring the sarcasm, she waved a hand. "It's nothing. And it's not as if they don't expect me to drag someone along. I've already informed the ministry that another member of the team will be joining me today."

"Another member of the team." Greg contemplated her choice of words. "And am I correct to assume you didn't mention who that member is?"

"Yep."

A light chuckle left him, one that made her heart do that . . . jumping, vibrating thing.

"You're misleading them," he deduced.

"No," her point-making finger came up, the gesture reining back her control over her heart as she argued, "I'm *helping* them improve their efficiency by bypassing procedures that impair it, especially after they ghosted my email, saying they need more time to find the file pertaining to the issue. The Monica Upshaw thing just started last month. How deep can a recent file be buried? A monkey would be able to locate it in under an hour."

Beaming as brightly as the rays of light penetrating through the windshield, he asked, "Should we drop by at a zoo to pick one out then?"

"The nearest one is an hour's drive from headquarters in the opposite direction. It's too late for that."

Greg's lips curled all the way up, and it became contagious. Sush found herself looking, her eyes softening. Over the past week, she'd gradually come to terms with the fact that he was beguiling without a smile, but only now did she realize he was drop-dead gorgeous with one. It was like a gift that already looked enticing on the outside and even more so when it had been unwrapped. Where the beguiling side of him elicited the non-filtered part of her to say anything that came to mind, this gorgeous side of him silenced her and made her still, enticing her to admire the view she didn't often get to see, not wanting to miss a sight so rare.

"Sush?" he threw her a glance, concern varnishing his eyes.

She blinked. "What?" He must have caught her looking. Oh God. She was even smiling, noticing her lips curled only after she'd blinked, and the thought tinged a soft pink on her cheeks.

Greg felt her stare on him, and—even through his peripheral vision—he could tell it was the first time she looked at him that way, like nothing else around them mattered. If he didn't say something soon, he was going to stop the car and do something he'd regret—grab her hand, grope her body, kiss her lips. Goddess, the thought of kissing her did something to his groin that almost made him groan. His grip on the steering wheel tightened as he fought the urge to touch her everywhere. Thank Goddess humans couldn't smell arousals the way lycans did.

Thinking of something quickly, he'd ask if there were any updates on the surveillance footage from the parking lot yet. Her cheeks gained a certain color as she ransacked her bag for her tablet to check for emails, and he bit his inner lip knowing he wasn't the only one fighting this pull between them.

But if his reason for staying away was because of his former mate, what was hers?

CHAPTER 26

Greg had been paying more attention to her facial transmutation after hearing from the queen—through Tristan—that Sush didn't smile a lot around anyone. He was surprised to learn that it was true. For someone who claimed to be able to extract humor from anything, she didn't smile a lot. That entire morning, as she checked on each department and handed out orders, her lips either remained flat or were pulled to a frown. Yet he himself had witnessed her smile—even laugh—several times in the previous week.

"They're still running through them. Nothing out of the ordinary yet," she said, slipping her tablet back into her bag.

Thoughts of touching her took the backseat as his protective instincts kicked in. The suspect pool—in other words, the people who knew she was headed for the ministry—was enormous. As they passed streets and trees, he swallowed a lump in his throat, voice a deep baritone when he cautiously asked, "Do you know anyone who wants you dead?"

Without hesitation, she uttered, "I think it'd be easier to name people who don't want me dead."

"Why?" Greg snapped a little too loudly. The deep, protective rumble that promised vengeance ricocheted off the walls of the car and made its way into her heart, making the naive part of her swoon.

Shoving aside the way his words made her feel, she casually replied, "News flash, Your Grace. I spearheaded a negotiation that got many predecessors and top performers killed."

"Executed."

"Same difference."

Making a turn at a junction, he went on, "It wasn't your fault. They screwed up. We executed them for attempting to harm a member of the royal family. If there wasn't a negotiation, we'd wage war and kill all of you." A shot of pain launched to his heart at the thought of her dying by their hands.

"Good luck trying to win that argument," Sush responded monotonously. "The fact is, I'm a huntress. I'm supposed to side with my people."

"Mindlessly side with them?" He scoffed. "Senselessness doesn't suit you, Chief."

The edges of her lips tipped. Something about his eloquence with words made her smile without thought. "I don't think it suits me either, hence the targets on my head. I think I'm only safe now because they haven't decided on a suitable replacement yet."

"Sush," Greg exhaled. The way he said her name made her ears perk, brought her thoughts to a standstill, and made her heart stop. "Don't say that," he urged in a low murmur, almost begging, then paused, swallowing so many words, yet the loudest ones slipped through, "You're *not* replaceable."

She didn't blink, nor did she move. Her mind went blank as her heart beat louder, faster. For the next minute, there was nothing but the quiet hum of the engine, the gentle blast of the air conditioner.

Greg's compliment would've sounded flat and professional if his tone wasn't so low and . . . gentle, almost intimate, like a gentle breeze brushing across her cheek. The words rippled within her, making her feel something—special, precious, treasured.

Greg didn't know what he was doing anymore. He'd thought he'd be keeping things cordial and professional, but it was proving to be difficult.

It was Sush who broke the silence when she cleared her throat while hoping Greg couldn't hear her racing heart. "Anyway, enough about whoever did whatever to my car. Once they've gone through the cameras, I'll know the culprit. Let's just . . . talk about something else."

He could hear her thumping heart, and the rhythm—though frantic—was beautiful, like horses galloping through a meadow. "What do you want to talk about?" he asked, hoping she'd calm down, wanting—needing—her to be at ease with him.

She sighed. She had hoped he'd pick. Talking about the weather would only go so far since they both hated small talk. "Did you have a good weekend?" That was an equally stupid question, she thought, but she couldn't think of anything else. He had a family and a special someone. Of course his weekend would be good!

"I did. You?"

Shooting him a glare, she said, "You did? That's all you're going to say? At least boast about your perfect life to make me question the defective one I'm living."

An incomprehensible smile glided up his face, and he questioned, "No one's life is perfect, Sush. Mine is no exception. What did you do last weekend?"

"Sleep. Eat. Avoid checking emails and messages. Archery on Sunday."

Greg's brows shot to his hair. "You shoot?"

Turning to him somewhat offended, she said, "Why are you so surprised? I'm not ill-equipped with weapons just because I'm an octopus."

"No. I know. I've seen you use a gun, but . . . I thought your kind only deals with modern weapons these days."

With a gentle nod, she replied, "That's true to a large extent. Archery isn't a requirement. It's my leisure. There are all kinds of things to shoot at that range, not just the conventional stagnant targets. We shoot empty bottles, flying discs, balloons, those kinds of things."

"And which was it last Sunday?" he prompted, captivated by the melody in her voice that spoke for her happiness.

Sush beamed brighter. "The balloons. It was fun. They're like heads floating about. Things I can imagine as people and shoot without legal repercussions."

That drew another chuckle out of Greg. He'd never thought of that. A moving target was more realistic and would be more entertaining in terms of leisure. "Is that your target of choice? The balloons?"

"No. I prefer the crockery set upward on a moving train."

His smile faltered, eyes bulged wide, picturing it. "Pardon me, but . . . what?"

Her eyes rolled. "Not an actual train, Your Grace. A large-sized toy train. Placed at a distance. It took me a while to realize the most efficient way wasn't to aim at the crockery. Going for the rods connecting the wheels is the fastest way to win the game. I can smash ten plates with two arrows when the train turns over."

His face crumpled. "So shooting the train itself doesn't disqualify you?"

"Nope. If it did, lots of beginners would've been disqualified."

His features eased in understanding as he nodded. He then wondered if Sush was up to training his little sweetheart, if she could be trusted to do it, if

Enora would like her to do it. Greg himself knew the basics of archery, but he'd only ever practiced on immobile targets. Sush seemed to be taking it to another level.

"I hope you know this is a quid pro quo conversation, Your Grace. It's your turn to tell me what you did last weekend."

"Spent time with my family and went to the park."

"With your sweetheart?" she intended for it to come out as a tease, but a tinge of bitterness slipped through, one she couldn't take back.

CHAPTER 27

The mention of Enora got Greg on high alert. His pupils dilated, his claws underneath his nails readied, and his shoulders stiffened. It was common knowledge that the king and queen had pups, but it wasn't common knowledge that Greg shared a bond with their youngest.

"How do you know about my sweetheart?" his voice dropped to a dangerous baritone as his eyes darkened.

Trying to sound bored, Sush looked out the windshield and uttered, "You took a call last week after work and rushed out after that, like you'd been caught cheating on her."

There was one word in that sentence that smothered his defensiveness and splattered perplexity on him instead. For a brief second, he wondered if they were referring to the same person. Then, the waters of amused comprehension washed over him.

So that explained the sudden change, the swift barrier erected overnight.

Failing at swallowing the chuckles, his eyes stayed focused on the road ahead as he continued thinking about it.

Sush, on the other hand, was not amused. "I take it that the misunderstandings have been cleared?" Some part of her hoped he'd say no, but that bright smile she annoyingly found attractive had already burst her bubble. She refrained from asking how they were cleared, in case it involved acts that would scar her mind the same way Hazel's personal answers were etched there forever.

Wondering how far he could take this, Greg began, "There wasn't a misunderstanding. She just called because I didn't ring her at our usual time."

"Our usual time" made Sush's fingernails dig into her thigh, creating crescent marks through the fabric of her pants. "She didn't fire you an endless list of questions to confirm your loyalty? What an unusual reaction."

Greg had a feeling pressing his lips together wasn't going to hold back the laughter for much longer. "She knows I'm loyal to her. Her whole family does. I'm practically at their mercy. In fact, it'd be unusual for her to doubt me. She's trusted me since she was several months old."

Sush tried to smile. Usually, when people told her these things, she'd find it beautiful—something with a future that grew over time, like two seeds that met on the same tree being thrown apart before they grew into mature trees, where their branches touched, meeting once more. It made her believe that—no matter what—time brought two people together.

Today, however, she found *nothing* beautiful.

The sky was too blue. The clouds were too fluffy. The tar on the road was too faded. And why were there so many flowers there, there, and there? The petals would just fall off and litter the roads! And do you know who liked littered roads? Fucking no one!

Clearing her throat and regretting glancing at Greg as soon as she saw how much he glowed and how big his smile was, she said, "Talk about rekindling an old flame."

"The flame was never extinguished," Greg confided.

A shockwave channeled through Sush. "Not even when you were with Delilah?"

"No." Greg's head gave a slight shake, smile still broad. "Especially not then."

Sush mm-ed, taking note. Wouldn't that mean he had cheated on Izabella? No one needed to physically be with another before it amounted to cheating in Sush's dictionary. Emotional straying constituted cheating as well. Period. Greg was not the victim she'd thought he was. Delilah may have been the main villain, but Greg wasn't blameless, she deduced, somehow liking him less for it.

When they reached their destination and Greg put the car into a park, he marveled at her thinking face and felt that he'd stretched the misperception far enough. Getting his phone from the console, he offered, "Let me show you a photo of her. She's the most adorable little creature to grace our world."

Little. Ha. Sush knew it.

These big men, especially animalistic lycan men, had a penchant for little women. She knew it! Just look at the king and queen. Six footers like Sush wouldn't stand a chance, she thought. "There really is no need." She'd said it so defensively that it might as well have been, "No thank you," plus throwing his phone out the window. Sush didn't want another face on a helium balloon. There already weren't enough balloons. "I don't want to know. Really. It's your priv—"

Greg unlocked his phone and swiped to the section of the home screen with only one app for her to view the wallpaper in full, pushing his phone into her hand. Sush's eyes widened at the toddler in a white top and denim blue shorts, hair in a high, dark ponytail as she pulled back a rubber-tipped arrow fastened on a bow, lilac eyes fierce, staring ahead, sweaty streaks of hair clinging to her temple.

What am I supposed to be looking at again? Sush asked herself.

"My five-year-old niece takes archery practice very seriously," Greg mused.

Their eyes met. His twinkled in mischief and amusement, and hers burned with embarrassment and rage. "You little . . ." Sush growled, cheeks turning crimson, not sure whether it was from her anger or humiliation.

Copying her by raising his forefinger, Greg said, "I am—by no means—little. But my sweetheart is. Look at her. She's cute, isn't she? Slightly violent at times. But cute."

Eyes following his back to the screen, she stared at Enora's picture for another two whole seconds before muttering to the phone, "I'm going to teach you to shoot his balls. Both at once. With *real* arrows."

His lycan rolled over and let out a loud guffaw, hand slamming on the floor of his mind. Sush looked like she was about to kill him, and they weren't even afraid. They wanted to see her pounce and see what else she'd do.

"Now that we've cleared that up," Greg said, plucking his phone out of her hand and turning off the ignition, he continued, "let's get this Monica Upshaw mystery over with and grab a few bagels and coffee after."

He wanted to close this case? Just like that?

Since the damn phone call the previous week, Sush had been riding an ongoing cycle of rage and self-judgment, telling herself she and Greg weren't even a good fit, so the fact that he had someone didn't matter! Now he was declaring that they'd *cleared that up*? Excuse him!

Her finger jabbed at his shoulder that felt like a concrete wall, and she spoke through fiery eyes, "You just got yourself demoted. You can stay in your fucking car like an Uber driver while I do this myself. I'll just tell them the team member had an unexpected accident."

"What accident?" he asked, almost challengingly, his smile still intact.

Her fist was about to land on the part of his chest where his heart was—because he'd toyed with her emotions during their entire conversation—but Greg caught it just in time, hand wrapping around her clenched fist, his force unmatched. Her second fist sought to deliver a blow to his jaw, but Greg caught that one too.

He was unperturbed, still amused. He didn't even look like he was exerting any force when she was already perspiring from the endeavor. "Jealousy looks interesting on you, Sush. Positively interesting."

Her cheeks developed a deeper shade of red as she hissed, "Save your self-flattery for another occasion. I'm going to set you and this car on fire as soon as I get off." She didn't know how, but she was going to do it. Should've kept a lighter in her back pocket.

"How about you save that for why we actually came? And maybe we should take a minute to calm down before scorching the people in that building," he suggested, voice mellowing and imploring, his thumbs gingerly stroking her fists, feeling the width of her fingers, the hardness of her knuckles.

That was when he felt a tingle, a low voltage of current slipping into his veins from their touch.

CHAPTER 28

It wasn't the mate bond; Greg knew that much. The sparks from one would be stronger, clearer, more will-bending. This wasn't it. But the flicker warmed his skin, dilated his pupils, and made his heart beat like a pack of rogues running toward their prey.

Reluctantly releasing her hands, he uttered, "Let's go. We don't want to be late."

Both doors lifted, and Sush was forced to get out of the car when the person she wanted to scream at had already gotten out. The temptation to yell was as strong as the need to hide away for a few hours until she'd decided how best to present herself again after that debacle.

She was jealous, even though they weren't anything.

What were they, exactly?

Historically speaking, they were enemies by nature. Hunters used to have this bad habit of... well, hunting. And for the longest time, they liked a challenge, so they hunted beasts like werewolves and lycans for leisure. Hunting werewolves was doable and safe at first. Hunting lycans was safe for a short while, until the lycans rounded up the wolves and they hunted the hunters together.

To summarize history, the hunters' fun ended there—when lycans waged war and launched a surprise attack, decimating over half of the small population of hunters. Only two archers were left standing, and even they were taken hostage to ensure a "peaceful settlement" was reached. The corpses and bloodshed served as a brutal reminder of how unmatched humans were against those beasts. The hunters may have had oleander, but even that didn't help win battles or the war. The birthmarks on their napes were just that—marks. They didn't give them the boost of strength, speed, and instant healing that was desperately needed with creatures of that size and caliber.

Anyway, that was history. They weren't supposed to be enemies anymore after Greg was bonded to Delilah, but that optimistic future took a major turn, obviously. So they were probably back to square one.

And yet, Sush didn't feel like they were.

The conspiracy of Delilah et al. may have been the interspecies stir of the century, but the lycans and werewolves didn't attack. They negotiated. Forcefully, but they still did.

And there was an issue with how Greg could have pushed any and every one of her buttons since the first day yet didn't. Once he'd gotten everything stipulated in the treaty, he didn't do anything that made their lives more difficult even though he could easily rebuke them for their less-than-perfect systems, drop a snarky remark or two a day, or do something petty like steal or misplace documents on purpose. But he didn't.

Don't even get her started on the ongoing bagel purchase.

So between her and him, they clearly weren't enemies. But did that make them friends? Allies? Maybe something . . . more?

No.

The bottom line was he was a duke and she was a huntress. The last time a pairing like this happened, the huntress ended up dead—not that Sush disagreed with the outcome—and the duke ended up angry, betrayed, and heartbroken. There was no way he'd let it happen again. And there was no way she'd choose him over executing the plan she'd kept to herself for years.

They'd crossed paths at the wrong time, in the wrong circumstance, she felt. They could be friends, but she doubted either of them would consider crossing that line they'd mutually drawn to keep each other at a safe distance.

But if the distance was safe, why did she feel safer with him close? Did he feel it too? Or did he prefer her behind the line, at a distance?

"What is going on in that head of yours?" His voice, an inviting octave, drew her eyes to his. Even as they strolled through the front doors, they were trained on her. The lilac there offered so much attention and held such deep curiosity, maybe even fragments of concern.

Reminding herself to think straight, she lied, "My head's flipping through history, searching for a viable way to plot my revenge against you and your car using your niece. Fortunately for you, I can't think of anything at the moment."

The concern dissipated, curiosity traded for mirth as his lips tugged just the slightest. "I suppose it's rational to want to kill me for not being able to read your mind."

Disregarding the sarcasm for the second time that day, she uttered, "I'm glad you agree."

They had to stop the moment they reached the front desk, where the receptionist informed them that the defense minister was still in a meeting and required Sush and Greg to wait a while. On the registration form, Sush was careful to leave Greg's name out, simply labeling his presence as her team member before handing it back to the receptionist. They waited three minutes before the defense minister had the front desk send them up.

The receptionist knew who Greg was and was aware of what Sush was playing at, but made no comment and gave them a pass card to ascend.

The doors opened to the sixteenth floor, and Sush stepped out to have someone call her name from the left corridor. Her guard lowered, and her gaze pivoted as she turned to the source.

Deputy defense minister Agu Adebayo beamed broadly. He stood at six foot three with short hair and a good build. He was an octopus and used to work in the trenches, and hence had been acquainted with Sush before joining the ministry.

To Greg's surprise, and annoyance, he and Sush wrapped each other in an embrace which lasted a little too long for Greg's comfort—even though it was only two seconds, tops. A low growl rumbled under his animal's breath, and his human followed his instinct to stand next to her.

Agu's eyes trailed to the duke, holding onto his smile as best he could and stretching out his hand, greeting, "Your Grace."

"Minister," Greg addressed curtly, reluctantly. When their hands collided, it took a lot of strength to refrain from crushing all the bones there.

Sensing the coldness instantly, Agu strayed back to Sush and began, "I'd ask how everything is going, but you being here on short notice must mean bad news."

"I hope not," Sush said. "You really couldn't find anything?"

"I could," he admitted, eyes dimming, jaw clenched taut as his eyes flickered to his superior's office for a brief second. "But it's just marked as confidential. And—for some reason—I, as deputy, am not privy to matters concerning the highest level of national security. I never knew there was more than one level of national security until last week."

"Can't you appeal?" Sush pressed.

"At what cost, Sush?" His voice lowered into a murmur as he looked around, feigning a smile at his colleagues down the corridor. "You know how it is here. Ferdinand has been in this office since I was shooting hoops in high school. I've only been here for over a year."

Sush firmly insisted, "You got into office because you qualify to be here, Agu."

"We both know that, but to appeal for more power, which essentially requires me to go behind Ferdinand's back . . . it requires support—majority support. I doubt the president would veto such a thing. As much as times are changing, they haven't changed enough for people like us to make that move without being kicked out. You remember Sarauniya. She didn't just fight for people like us, she fought for everybody, and they still thought she was too rebellious to be kept in the ranks."

Sighing at that legendary lost potential, Sush uttered, "There were too many small minds in the defense ministry in her time anyway. I always saw her as president."

Agu's lips tugged high. "Me too. She was the noblest archer and hunter I've ever had the pleasure of working with in my time at the headquarters." The smile withered a bit when he continued, "It's sad having to see her stand behind Ferdinand on our visits to the troops she's training, but she told me she'd rather be somewhere she can make a difference, even if it is a slight one."

Sush shot him a look and uttered, "You're somewhere you can make a difference, too, Agu. You just have to want to do it. You've come this far. If you need support, either find it or create it."

His eyes roved warily again before he muttered, "I'll try." Seeing his secretary a few feet away about to remind him about a meeting he was already late for, Agu gave the young man a nod and turned back to Sush. "Nice talking to you, Sush, as always. Don't send my regards to Hazel. In fact, don't tell her we ran into each other at all. And you still owe me a coffee and shooting session."

"Shoot what? You?" Greg questioned.

Both pairs of eyes snapped to him as Agu released a short, awkward, lonely chuckle. "I'm pretty sure the lycans would beat her to that, Your Grace. I'll uh... leave you both to it."

Greg's onyx eyes seared into him until he was out of sight before they trailed back to a smug-looking octopus, who remarked, "Jealousy looks interesting on you, Your Grace. Positively interesting."

Sush had expected him to either deny, change the subject, or fire back with a snide comment, so nothing prepared her when he smirked, stepping so close that she could feel the heat radiating from his being as he towered over her. "Come now, Sush. We're *way* past using titles."

Those words did something to her heart. His voice sent a pleasurable trail of heat throughout her body and moistened her lower region. The manner he spoke didn't penetrate into her soul, but worse, touched her in a fingerlike caress, teasing her and tempting her to beg for more. The way he looked at her—with darkened eyes that held a type of hunger she wasn't unfamiliar with—sent a hot flush to her face.

"Alagumalai?" a voice boomed from the end of the corridor.

This was the first time—and hopefully last time—Sush was grateful to the defense minister for anything. At least he'd made a good save, even if it was unintentionally done, and the one calling her was his secretary, as the minister himself sat behind his desk, a yellow stress ball in his fist as he waited.

Sush pushed past Greg, who followed at her heels. An obnoxiously arrogant smirk tipped the corner of his lips as he subtly inhaled the remaining scent of her arousal lingering in the hallway, storing it in his lungs like the animal he was before his attention turned to the big shot they had come to see.

The defense minister had silver hair with a receding hairline on the right, but he looked fit for someone in his fifties, which shouldn't be a surprise since he was a chameleon, a type of hunter that generally looked good at any age. Those blue eyes held as much disapproval and distaste as the grim line pulling down his lips.

He should lose the yellow ball, Greg thought. It made him look like one of those kids who picked fights with people they couldn't handle.

At Ferdinand's door, where Sush greeted him and he remained leaned back in his swivel chair and stayed silent in response, the defense minister's eyes glued to Greg.

Greg didn't bother offering him a greeting first. Ferdinand was not his superior. Greg didn't even greet his own cousin every time they met. It would always depend on his mood. And his cousin was king. Ferdinand was just a minister.

If this human was waiting for one of the only two lycan dukes in the kingdom to extend the courtesy, the minister's inflated sense of self-esteem was in for a wait to eternity.

During the silent battle, Greg began finding Ferdinand familiar, though he couldn't quite put his finger on what it was yet.

CHAPTER 29

"Your Grace. This is a surprise," Ferdinand finally yielded.

"I can tell, seeing that your shock impeded your visual and auditory perception," Greg replied monotonously, still disregarding the man's title and position. The gears in his head continued to turn. They'd never met. He'd seen the man's photo, but that wasn't where Greg recognized . . . parts of him. This person—his energy and scent—were as new as they were foreign, but segments of his features reminded Greg of someone. He just couldn't figure out who.

Ferdinand's frown forced itself into a superficial smile as he straightened himself in his seat. Dropping the ball next to a paperweight, he stated, "I can see and hear you, Your Grace."

"Presumptuous and obtuse if you think I was talking about your behavior toward me."

Brows crinkled and forehead creased, Ferdinand took a moment to decipher those words before his eyes beat his brain when they ventured to Sush, who was looking at Greg like she was trying to get their gaze to lock in order to stop him.

The minister's throat bobbed, and a sliver of wariness entered his eyes before they cleared and he uttered, "Alagumalai, has His Grace been guided through our procedures before entering my office today?"

Sush's gaze left Greg. "The treaty allows for his presence without procedural compliance, Minister. Clause 7.4."

"Really?" he murmured in doubt.

Greg interjected, "You mean to say you didn't read the clauses copied to you throughout the negotiation?"

"I have, Your Grace." Ferdinand eked out that same empty smile. "And if I remember correctly, it states that procedure is only waived if it pertains to the kingdom's security, which we haven't established whether it is yet."

"You mean to say after that stunt your kind pulled off, I'm going to wait and trust *your* judgment on whether this concerns the kingdom's safety?" More importantly, on whether this concerned Enora's safety. Greg watched Ferdinand swallow; his blue eyes flickered out the window to hide a gleam of exasperation.

Sush took over, "His presence was approved when the treaty was signed. And him being here is not our biggest issue. I need to know the reason behind Monica Upshaw's off-duty schedule."

"And why is this pertinent?" Ferdinand's head swung to her as he challenged. "You're an employee of the hunters. Your question concerns issues handled by the ministry. You've been told this was confidential, yet here you are. There's a line that did not disappear just because you were appointed as the new chief, Alagumalai."

"I, of all people, am well aware of that line," Sush refuted as calmly as the cold sea, though her insides had already exploded and even an island miles away would've been able to sight the smoke brimming from her internal volcano. "If I wasn't, I would've barged through your doors when Catrine Carter was put off-duty for the very same confidential reason. But I didn't. Because that was within my predecessor's jurisdiction. Since I'm leading the brains and mechanics of the hunters now, this issue is within *my* jurisdiction because it concerns a hunter. The ministry crossed the line when it touched one of us, effectively getting me involved. Where is Upshaw now?"

"Executing a governmental task."

"Which one?"

Ferdinand leaned back into the chair like it was just another boring meeting when he answered, "Strictly confidential."

"Where?" Sush pressed.

"That's equally confidential."

A silence descended into the room, so clear one could hear the wall clock tick, so explicit the speech from the next room snuck through in muffled chomps.

Sush's insistence didn't waver, her eyes didn't tame, her will didn't bend when her voice, low and cautionary, permeated through, "For all of our sakes, I hope this isn't another Delila—"

"Watch your words, Chief." Ferdinand's voice cut her off like a blade slid across paper. "I agree the patterns between Carter and Upshaw have their similarities, but let me remind you that Carter was in no way connected to Delilah and the others. So this does not pertain to the kingdom, nor does it concern you in terms of jurisdiction. The defense ministry is *still* superior to hunters headquarters. We hold the final word in security issues, and your job is to take orders as they come, not question them to hinder efficiency."

A low snarl slipped through Greg's slightly parted lips even as Sush shot him a look. His eyes might have been onyx, but he was seeing red. Sush assumed Greg would hurl a derisive comment if she didn't stop him when—in fact—all Greg wanted to do at the moment was to go old-school and pounce. With claws. Maybe even canines. Who the fuck did this puny old man think he was, talking to her like that?

Then a soft but sharp whisper pierced through his ears, "Greg, *don't*. I'm handling this."

The order pulled his plotting for the minister's murder to a halt. The way she said his name made his anger recede and obliged his lycan to sit.

Comprehension entered the minister's eyes as quickly as it left, thinking to himself that this was an unexpected development.

Sush turned back to Ferdinand. "If anything happens to her, know that the blood is on your hands. I have exhausted every possible way to keep all hunters safe. If you insist on holding up the drawbridge, you bear the consequences."

"You're making something out of nothing, Alagumalai. She's safe."

"I thought no one on a confidential assignment for the government could ever be guaranteed their safety. When has this changed?" Sush refuted.

He had lied. He had lied and been caught. They just didn't know what the lie was. Either Monica Upshaw was not on a governmental task, or she wasn't actually safe.

Rising from his chair and jabbing a button by the paperweight, Ferdinand muttered, "We are done here. You're both dismissed."

His secretary flung the door open and showed them out even though Sush had been in the building countless times and wouldn't get lost even with her eyes closed.

She and Greg passed Agu's office. He was pacing about, phone glued to his left ear as his mouth moved. His brows rose like he was asking her how it went, and her head gave a subtle shake to say, "Not well." Agu then pressed his lips into a line and shrugged at one shoulder—the indication that they couldn't do anything at the moment. Powerless subordinates.

If there was one thing Sush hated more than Valor, it was helplessness.

Back in Ferdinand's office, the old man sank back into his chair and heaved a bone-tired sigh as Sush and Greg disappeared into the elevator. His nervous-looking secretary stood by the door, so Ferdinand nodded at him and demanded, "What?"

"A call just came in, Minister. About Catrine Carter."

The minister's brows lifted. "That woman is really filling the space in these walls today. What about her?"

Face ashen, the young man swallowed and reported, "They said she's dead."

CHAPTER 30

"WHAT?" Sush's voice blared in Greg's car, and his lycan was pushed back by the volume before he got back up and demanded his human to ask what was going on.

Sush put Hazel on speaker as the deputy reported at a frantic pace, "Autopsy said she'd been dead for ten hours before the body was found. They took a full hour to identify her before notifying us about . . ." Greg double-parked as Hazel's voice continued ringing through ". . . the cause of death—multiple stab wounds to her chest, abdomen, and face. No belongings were taken. Cash, credit cards, a five-figure watch—they all remained intact and present on the property. They weren't after money. Valor is sending four archers to retrieve her body, and the defense ministry has been notified. Did Ferdinand say anything?"

"No, but . . ." Sush sighed. "I wonder if he already knew when we were there."

"You asked about Monica Upshaw?"

"Yes."

Hazel's voice angled on a wary edge when she asked, "And what did he say?"

"That she's safe."

There was a dead pause, and then Hazel's voice came through, "Let's hope she is. Because I doubt anyone wants to follow in Catrine's footsteps after learning about her destiny. Anyway, that's the report. Is there anything else I haven't done that I should do?"

"Alert every hunter across the globe and order them to find Monica Upshaw."

Voice lowered into a whisper, her deputy asked, "Can we do that though? Do we have th—"

"Haze, I don't care! Upshaw could be next. Find her and warn her. I'll deal with Ferdinand, Valor, and the entire freaking army when the time comes. Just find her."

"Alrighty, Chief," Hazel squeaked.

After Sush hung up, Greg asked, "Should we head back to the ministry?"

Two silent minutes passed as Sush's downcast eyes roved left to right again and again like she was speed-reading a plan at the last minute when she was really just staring into space. In an almost inaudible whisper, she murmured, "No. If he doesn't want to tell us, there's nothing we can do to pursue the matter. But . . ." she sighed, leaning into the headrest, already knowing she was going to regret her next words, which she prattled through with shut eyes, "I need your hackers to get into the defense ministry's files and communications without leaving a trace." When there was nothing but silence from his end, she prompted, "Can they do it? Without leaving a trace?"

The pads of her fingers pressed on her forehead like she was getting a migraine. Then a large hand—callous and warm—cupped her jaw, imploring her eyes to open as he gingerly turned her face so she'd be looking into his lilac orbs, the warmth of his touch invoking a kind of comfort that she needed. "They can. But are you sure that's what you want, Sush?"

Sush didn't know how else to keep the rest of them safe. She didn't have the extent of information to predict a weak spot prone to attack. She might not have been with the hunters for much longer, but that didn't mean she didn't care about them at all. Firm in her decision, she muttered, "Yes."

Her orders—written and oral—normally came out loud and certain. One could hear her barking orders through her texts and emails even without any exclamation points present. All instructions were delivered with confidence that it was the right way forward.

This was the first time Greg had heard her voice filled with so much skepticism. What troubled him most was the vulnerableness in her eyes and the frailty in her voice.

His thumb trailed along her jawline, conveying the way it curved and angled to memory when her breath hitched, making him pause. His hand was about to let go. But her face—ever so slightly—leaned into his touch. The reaction was imperceptible to the eye but tangible to the touch—the gentlest pressure leaning against it like a head would a pillow.

She relaxed, his eyes following the movement of her parted lips as she slowly released the puff of air, anxiety leaving with the brief exhalation. The tip of his thumb traced the outline of her lower lip, his eyes fixated there like he was in a trance. He took his time, following the upward and downward bend of the delicate structure.

So soft. So plump. So perfect.

Neither of them knew how much time had passed before Greg uttered, "At any time you want the hacking to stop, just say the word and I'll pull the plug, okay? You have a say in this. It's your department, your people, your jurisdiction. You're not doing this alone. We'll get to the bottom of this together, you hear me?"

His voice was imbued with a sense of control, a control that Sush really wasn't feeling in herself at the moment. Everything had happened so fast. One minute she was arguing with Ferdinand about Monica Upshaw, quoting the Catrine Carter pattern, and the next minute Carter was reported dead. For ten hours. How did a huntress die without anyone knowing for ten fucking hours?

"Sush," Greg noticed her attention leaving, guilt setting its dirty foot in her eyes, and he brought her back. "One, it's not your fault. Two, it's not over. We'll handle this. We'll stop this, with or without Valor, Ferdinand, and the other imbeciles, alright?"

Mental and emotional fatigue got the better of her, and all she could do was nod, though her gratitude was channeled clearly through her eyes, accepting the certainty flowing from his gaze. The back of his hand glided across her jawline before trailing down her neck, stopping right above the golden chain of her necklace, and he tore himself away.

His eyes glazed over, linking Jade, who was happy to finally have something far more interesting to work on than scanning systems and files like a robot. There was something about the forbidden nature of hacking that gave him a shot of adrenaline and brought his soul to life.

Eyes cleared, Greg turned back to Sush, who was now looking out the window, seeing the rain droplets trickle down in tiny blobs. One hand was on her neck, between her collarbones, her slender fingers fiddling with the locket; her other hand lay on her lap in a clenched fist.

Keeping a worried exhale to himself, he cautiously reached for the fist, his hand covering it like a blanket, not expecting it to loosen like it did when he said, "Let's just get something to eat and focus on our next move."

She mm-ed, fingers letting go of the locket, fist unclasped completely, allowing his fingers to slide between hers, letting their palms meet before he began driving again.

The death was unsettling. The more Sush thought about it, the more she felt Catrine Carter had been stationed at a remote location so she could be killed.

What if the one who'd stabbed Catrine to death wasn't an external assailant, but someone sent by the defense ministry or—God forbid—hunters headquarters itself? What if it was something within the headquarters that Sush was not privy to despite being the chief octopus, something only available in a physical archive that she had no access to? What if Catrine discovered something that a higher-up didn't want found, and died before she could report it?

CHAPTER 31

Sush and Greg were the only ones in the cafeteria. Two mugs of black coffee sat between them, along with cream puffs, bagels, and a chicken sandwich—all untouched, even after Greg had spread the cream cheese for her.

"One thing, Sush," Greg urged, leaning in and bringing her attention back into the room. "Just eat one thing."

She blinked, coming out of her thoughts. She assessed her options and picked up half a bagel—the half with a more generous amount of cream cheese, biting into it without really tasting the flavors and texture.

Greg popped a cream puff into his mouth as he continued watching her, praying Jade got the archives and correspondence fast so her mind would be kept away from the whys and focused on the hows.

This must be how Kenji felt, Sush thought. Shocked. Rattled.

She didn't take the eastern deaths easy, but the western death somehow felt worse, even though Catrine Carter was as much a stranger as the archers from the east.

Why was that? she wondered.

Both murders were unexpected. Both happened beyond their control . . . or did they? Some part of Sush felt she had retained a degree of control over the one in the west, because she saw the red flags, even brought it up, but didn't argue it through, didn't fight til the end.

She *chose* not to pick a fight with Patterson and Valor about reassigning Carter to a less deserted location and one with better reception and connectivity. She could have argued, may have had a shot at pulling her out, but she didn't.

Would it have made a difference to Carter's life?

Thinking about how off-putting Catrine Carter's personality was didn't make Sush feel any better. Someone who deserved to be scratched in the face didn't necessarily deserve to be murdered. Thinking about herself, Sush would be the first to admit she was not the nicest or most accommodating person—on a team, in a room, or at a dinner—but that didn't mean she deserved to die . . . right?

The cafeteria door swung open. The click of the footsteps halted briefly before the pitter-patter charged toward the only occupied table.

Sush's back faced the door, yet she didn't have to turn to know who was approaching them. Funny thing about footsteps—each person's carried a different beat, a different click, a distinct shuffle or lack thereof.

Greg, on the other hand, trained his eyes on Patterson like it was a warning that he would attack if the chief chameleon so much as said one offensive word to his octopus.

Patterson's mouth opened, but before the words came out, Sush spoke at her usual volume and tone, "What?"

His instincts made him take an uneasy glance at Greg. The modicum of confidence that the chameleon had at the door must have ebbed away as he neared the table. The wisp of unease niggling at his stomach quickly morphed into wariness, undoubtedly affected by the lethal energy radiating off the duke.

Clearing his throat like it would boost his confidence, Patterson turned back to Sush. "Valor asked to get you to screen through the chameleons' assignment posts and let us know if anything needs ame—-"

Sush scoffed, muttering, "So that's what it takes to be heard around here. Death. Of the relevant type of hunter. Good to know."

Valor didn't even demand a screening after the six archers' deaths in the east. SIX.

Now one chameleon had died, and their commander suddenly decided to pull up his socks.

Sush and a few others had been conducting the screening after the eastern deaths though. Without being told to. They hadn't found anything awry yet. And after the assassinations, Kenji had been bound to require approvals from Sush and Valor for everything—from the biggest decisions like approving new recruits to the smallest ones like fixing a system bug, which was ridiculous. Kenji's skills were superior to Sush's when it came to bugs. There were times when *she* consulted *him* to have her bugs fixed. Sush had pointed out the absurdity, but Valor didn't give a damn even though the noble leader himself knew nothing about building and fixing systems either.

Patterson bit the inner walls of his mouth, taking her hit without thinking of hitting back for the first time. "Valor and I agree this is our fault, our oversight. You warned us. We didn't listen. And Catrine paid the price."

As Sush lifted the mug and tipped it to the left, then right, watching her drink swirl, she asked, "Did Valor's ego grow a bruise so big he couldn't move his ass and tell me this himself?"

"He's actually at LG 2 now," Patterson disclosed. "We left his office at the same time. Spent the past hour with Ferdinand on speaker. I came to grab an espresso. They ran out on our floor. And Valor was heading straight down."

"Hm," bringing the mug to her lips, Sush murmured. "How the tables have turned—him hunting me down instead."

Patterson shifted his weight from his right foot to the left, and one hand rubbed his nape. "And uh . . . I'd say take your time on the screening, but Valor and Ferdinand were hoping it could be done by th—"

"I know. Anything else?"

"Uh, no. I don't think so. I'll uh . . . let you know if there is." Turning to a stone-faced Greg, he nodded in acknowledgment. "Your Grace."

After fetching his espresso, he left, and Greg heard Patterson heave a relieved sigh when he was a few steps to the door.

Greg watched as Sush's tough, callous exterior melted away, replaced with the woman he'd seen in the car, worry and distress tainting her otherwise perfect face. Deciding to distract her from herself, he began, "Leaking Dam isn't taking the news well either. Never thought he'd have it in him to care about his subordinates that much."

Sush's brows crinkled at the nickname. Her brain cells shifted from the ways she could've prevented Catrine's death, now concentrating fully on who Greg was referring to. As she watched Greg take a sip from his mug, his eyes never leaving her, the epiphany came and her eyes narrowed, a reaction that tipped the edge of his lips as he set down his drink.

Patterson's dam of arousal had leaked the other day, and it almost welcomed a slaughter. The label was innocuous enough to be casually dropped anywhere while still capturing the essence of its origins.

Brows pinched, she questioned, "Is this why you have hundreds of followers under your command? So you'll have more time and brain power to get creative with names for everyone?"

If it'd distract her when she needed to be distracted, then, yes, he'd block out time and brain power doing it. "You have to admit, the names I come up with are better suited to them than the ones their parents gave them without even knowing them."

This miraculously pulled the smallest smile out of her as she shook her head slowly, more from amusement than disapproval. If she was being honest with herself, there'd been no disapproval at all. Though naming Hazel Traffic Cone would prove to be a problem. Her hair color changed every few months. Before orange, it was bubblegum blue. Sush chose not to bring it up, not wanting to give Greg any ideas. Yet.

Her thoughts went back to what he'd said—about Patterson not taking Catrine's death well. Bringing her mug to her lips, her smile withered when she said, "Funny how the heart works—hanging onto a person long after the relationship is over. Guess Leaking Dam still cares about the latest dead chameleon even after their breakup years ago."

CHAPTER 32

Greg's thumb fiddling the ear of the mug paused, eyes enlarged and jaw tensed, finding no humor in Sush, who simply shrugged.

Annoyance set in, and he noted, "Sush, as much as I want to, we've established that I can't read your mind. Kindly elaborate."

She was going to tell him. She just didn't know where to start. Patterson and Carter were an item for quite a while—before Sush herself joined the hunters.

Greg's impatience had put a stop to her mind that had already been slowed from the day's events. The words "as much as I want to" did most of the magic, conjuring thoughts that Sush never thought she had.

Deciding for herself that she needed something uplifting if she were to survive the remaining hours of the day, her lips tipped into a smile—one Greg instantly recognized as the one she showed before she was about to drop a tease. "I don't think any clause in the treaty obligates a disclosure of that particular information, Your Grace."

The manner in which she uttered his title was different. It carried a distinctive tune, one that was enough to threaten a leak of his own dam as he swallowed a hungry growl. Her light tone carried a level of playfulness, but her eyes held a tantalizing challenge that—for some reason—affected his groin.

Leaning in with the obnoxiously arrogant smirk that had turned her on back at the ministry, he was pleased to see that it was affecting her even before he'd begun speaking. A faint whiff of her arousal invaded the space between them as she shifted in her seat, probably trying to hide it. Using the same deep voice to keep his momentum, Greg said, "Since it's not in the treaty, I'd have to find other ways of getting that intel. Is that what you're saying, Sush?"

"Pretty much," she replied casually, hoping it'd alter the atmosphere before she heated up completely.

But Greg wasn't done just yet. She'd started this game. He wasn't letting her off the hook until he was done playing. Eyeing her like a predator, he questioned, "So you want me to choke it out of you?"

The gleam in his eye and the image she imagined solely from those words intensified her arousal, fogging her mind.

It took Greg everything to restrain himself and his animal from taking her right there in the middle of the cafeteria. Over the table, on the floor—it didn't matter.

As difficult as it was to resist him, Sush bit her lip to hide an upward curl that betrayed her, lifting the mug to her lips again to properly mask it, hoping her arousal couldn't be detected yet, when, in fact, Greg was already breathing in the delicious scent like it was oxygen to his lungs.

Pulling herself out of the dirty fantasy, she simply uttered, "If allies have to choke one another for intel, they're not really allies. All you had to say was please."

"Oh, my dear." He chuckled, brief and dark. "When we get far enough, you'll be the one using that word, again and again, heaving it like you need air. . ." His gaze dropped to her mouth. "Gasping it as you ache for more, *begging* me to give you every inch." Eyes trailing back to her increasingly flushed face, he declared, "That word will be the only one you'll know, apart from my name."

Knowing he wasn't going to back out despite her efforts, she leaned in, leveled her eyes with his, and looked into the lilac with a dare. "Are you talking about you or me?"

The dare—coupled with that voice and that fucking upward curl of her lips—did it: broke his dam, and Greg was beyond grateful that he was the only animal in the cafeteria, though the darker side of him didn't mind having an audience, more than ready to announce his claim over the creature that he was going to make his.

His momentary surprise boosted her confidence, and she continued in the same quiet tone, "Something tells me you may have used the wrong pronouns, Greg."

Greg had no idea what it was in her voice, but the way she said his name was overpowering. At the ministry, it restrained him. Now, it enticed him, and he was willing to do anything to hear her say it again and again. For the first time since they'd met, Greg allowed his searing eyes to trail from the crown of her head to her face and down her neck to the jutting collarbone that wasn't covered by her shirt. They then moved down to the curve of her breasts—practically undressing her with his eyes, all while she watched him do it.

When her breathing hitched and arousal intensified, his arrogant smirk came back into place, eyes meeting hers once more, knowing she was too deep to climb out now. "I think my linguistic proficiency remains proficient. Perhaps you'd like to look over your own."

Before Sush could respond, Greg's smile fell as his peripheral vision caught something, making him clear his throat, effectively wiping away the inappropriate atmosphere for a more professional one when he murmured, "You might want to lie about the redness of your face. Your noble leader is heading our way."

Despite frantically trying to forget the last few minutes, Sush waved a hand like it'd be no big deal in hopes of calming herself when she speedily murmured, "Sure, I'll just say you infuriated me by being an asshole in Ferdinand's office."

"That could work if you're able to adjust the way you're looking at me on time."

"What does that mean?" she asked as the heavy footsteps drew nearer.

Greg stole a glance at her before looking straight ahead once more, swallowing before stating, "You don't look infuriated. Not the mildest. You look flushed."

Thinking fast, she decided, "Then I'll just say you've been humiliating me and the hunters' competence after learning about Carter's death."

"Or I've been humiliating you about your ineptitude in pronouns. That could work. It isn't even a lie."

"Fuck you," Sush hissed in the lowest whisper she could manage at his unhelpfulness.

"Looking forward to it," Greg murmured, face dead and tone flat when Valor finally reached the table, at which time Sush's face looked a little less red and a lot more irritated.

Since Valor possessed no senses to detect the heat and arousals, he greeted Greg, who acknowledged him with a curt nod before the commander turned to the chief octopus. Valor spent the next most torturous three minutes of his life saying the things Patterson said before, and almost choked when he had to cough out the word "apologize." That caused Greg to snort, earning a quick glare from his octopus before he forced his lips into a straight line that was not going to hold for another sixty seconds.

After Valor left, Sush kicked Greg at his knee, and the duke could only look at her with the widest smile, declaring with admiration and pride, "Goddess, you are wondrous. Getting an apology from a misogynist without coercion."

Shaking his head in pure awe, he added, "I doubt another huntress in history has managed such a feat."

As much as those words became the fingers that caressed her heart, Sush gave a slight shake of her head as her forefinger came up, moving left to right like the swinging pendulum on a metronome. "He and Patterson need my help and most likely want me to go easy on them while I screen and report. Let's not forget it took a death to manage such a feat."

"Which brings us back to the topic before our . . . heated discussion." Greg leaned back with a knowing smirk, prompting, "What's the story behind Patterson and Carter?"

Sush stared into space, recalling the facts. "They were in a steady relationship, even known as the *it* couple, not just amongst the chameleons, but amongst the hunters as a whole. There were rumors that people had seen them fucking in parks and parking lots. They were even caught doing it in the printing room on the machine once. Yes, it was sanitized after that. No, no one used it again. All seemed well until Patterson returned early from a work trip in the east. He caught Carter and another hunter doing it in one of the male stalls. And they were done. Patterson never dated again. But Carter, fuh!" Sush shook her head, arms crossed as she leaned back. "Carter moved on. *Fast.* That hunter she was caught with? Logan Larson."

Greg's wide eyes grew impossibly wider. His former mate's boyfriend. How did Izabella fit into this, though?

It was as if Sush had read his mind. "Carter and Larson had a very brief fling, lasting several weeks. Delilah came into the picture as a new recruit, and Carter's status was single since."

After a short pause, at which time Greg's surprise morphed into disbelief, he questioned, "Carter never screwed anyone since? You're sure?"

"No, I am not," Sush readily admitted with a matter-of-fact shake of her head. "One thing you need to know about me, Greg, is that gossip reaches me last. Something that doesn't concern my career would have to be bigger than a wildfire to get my attention. If irrelevant scandals and tales have reached me, they have reached everyone. I'm not privy to the personal lives of the hunters if it doesn't affect their work and our systems. So, no, I'm not sure if Carter screwed another since Larson. I'd bet she did if you're asking me to speculate. She had men drooling over her everywhere she went."

Taking a few minutes to take all this in, Greg deduced, "So Patterson is a suspect, motivated by jealousy and anger."

Sush downed the last of her coffee, stood, and responded with a simple, "Yep," like she wasn't answering a heavy question.

CHAPTER 33

A day later, after taking off from work, Jade, Sush, and Hazel met at Greg's place after Greg completed his chat session with Enora. Only when Enora had to say a sad goodbye and utter the routine, "I love you," did Greg let the three in, replying, "I love you, too, sweetheart. Sweet dreams. Talk to you tomorrow."

The words drew nothing out of Jade, who—like every maverick—knew who it was at the other end of the line, so he extracted his stuff and methodically arranged everything on the kitchen counter like it was just another evening after work; it shocked Hazel, who kept up with news and gossip of *all* kinds yet didn't know Greg already had someone; and as for Sush—who knew he said those words while letting them in on purpose—she shot him an annoyed glare which earned her his taunting smile when they both recalled their conversation from his car.

As Greg strode past her, his hand made the lightest touch on her lower back—one as delicate as an ethereal brush, softening her but confusing Hazel, who blinked with furrowed brows and finally found her voice when she said, "So . . . you have someone back home, Your Grace?"

Shooting Sush another glance with an upward tip of his lips, Greg mindlessly replied, "I do."

"Someone special?"

"More than special—important," Greg noted seriously. His smile gradually ebbed, now with arms crossed as he stood next to Jade, casting a cursory glance of the evidence on white sheets of paper arranged on his countertop.

"Lucky girl," Hazel commented.

Greg remained silent, not seeing the point in elaborating further. Those who knew him and Enora would know he was the lucky one to share such a close bond with the pup. It was never the other way around. Not even close.

When the duke remained silent, Hazel shot Sush a perplexed look, one the chief didn't catch because her mind was already where Greg's was—on the evidence.

Greg and the mavericks had checked the diplomatic residence for bugs, cameras, wires, or any other devices that would pose an invasion of privacy and found none. That was good for the hunters and their government because it was a clause in the treaty that there should be no such installations. Planting anything was as unwise as it was lethal—the one who ordered it would be taken hostage, the ones who installed it would be killed, Clause 4.1.1.

The papers Jade was lying around contained all kinds of things, from redacted documents to photographic evidence to witness testimonies.

"Where did they say they got these from again?" Hazel asked Sush in a whisper.

"Defense ministry," Sush responded nonchalantly, eyes never leaving the papers.

Eyes bulging out of their sockets, Hazel whisper-yelled, "They hacked into the defense ministry?"

"Under my orders, yes." Sush refrained from telling Hazel that Greg had already hacked into it once before—prior to the months of negotiation and execution of the treaty.

Suppressing every instinct telling her to scream in pure panic, Hazel took a few breaths and made a beeline to the only two bottles of alcohol. She took a glass and opened a bottle without asking, pouring and downing the liquid in one sitting.

Sush's fingers plucked a printed picture, leaving a rectangular space between the surrounding sheets. It was a case from over a decade ago of a woman lying on grass, ginger hair sprawled but not covering her wide, empty eyes, a streak of red conspicuously trailed down her neck. The fine lines below the picture read, "Porsha Delaware, aged 28, Octopus, 1:17 a.m."

Sush's fingers dragged another sheet next to the picture, describing how Delaware was captured by street cameras coming out of her house a little after 12:30 a.m., walking down two blocks, looking over her shoulder every few steps and pausing at a corner before turning to a back alley. No one was seen coming out until Delaware's corpse was found by a neighbor throwing out the trash.

Inhabitants of nearby buildings said they heard no screams. Needless to say, no one saw Delaware's assailant.

Sush held onto both sheets in one hand longer than necessary, and her fingers from her free hand had begun fiddling with her locket again.

Greg's bone of concern for her pulled him to the other side of the counter, his right shoulder behind her left, his breath fanning her ear as he studied the piece. Delaware carried a bag when she left the house, but no bag was found with the corpse. If Jade had gotten everything there was in this case, the bag had never been retrieved.

When Sush's lips pulled into a frown in a way that was demanding answers, she dropped the sheets back onto the counter and took a few steps to the left to study everything else, at which time Greg's hand snuck in another brush—this time along her waist.

Hazel had finally toned down her anxiety enough to be the fourth set of eyes she came to be, swirling her drink and assessing the redacted documents, trying to make sense of the chronology and—hopefully—find a pattern.

The silence layered, deepened like an ocean. The ruffling and flipping papers were like the hum of the underwater current—fitting and natural. So when Jade's voice cut through the space, Hazel jumped in the high chair like there was going to be a shark attack, despite the hacker speaking at his usual volume, "This is just some of the shit I found. There's still a lot to fork through. I only picked out those with neck slashing and after-midnight murders so far. Gotta admit, I'm surprised."

"You and me both," Sush murmured.

When Hazel didn't make a sound, Greg prompted, "You've known about these, Deputy?"

Hazel cut short her sipping to answer, "Yes. Zasper . . . uh, the former chief octopus, was privy to these things, so I was too. Not many octopuses know the details though. It's not just Sush. Zasper and the other chiefs, along with Valor and Ferdinand, agreed to keep things between the higher-ups to avoid causing a panic."

Blinking at the stupidity of expecting ignorance to be bliss, Greg questioned, "And no one objected? Not one single deputy from the headquarters and the ministry?"

The judgment in his voice couldn't have been clearer. The look in his eyes made one feel like an insect struggling in a futile attempt to scurry away.

Sush's elbow gently nudged at his chest, doubting he felt anything with that solid surface when she defended Hazel, "Before the Delilah Conspiracy, no one spoke against those above them. It wasn't just Hazel. It was all of us, me included."

In a softer tone that held zero judgment, he noted, "You were *never* the deputy."

She shrugged. "I wouldn't have done it either, even if I were. Being naive, we saw it as a matter of respect, of having faith that our superiors knew best. We were told about one of our own being sacrificed and had to tighten and improve security measures, but all of us held back from asking the whys, only focused on the hows. We didn't go all out arguing that without knowing the whys, the hows we came up with would be reasonable at best and useless at worst. Whenever a final decision was made, we almost never questioned it, not until recently."

Knowing that Sush was only saying this to get him to stop attacking Hazel, Greg huffed, "Fine."

Dropping the matter, they drew the similarities they could find. All victims were young: Porsha Delaware, twenty-eight, a western octopus, from over a decade ago; Regina and Austin Chen, twenty-six, fraternal twins and western chameleons from seven years back; and Shahrul Ibrahim, twenty-nine, another octopus, though he was from the east.

The second thing found was that their laptops and phones were never retrieved. Only the Chen twins had a desktop back at their place, and the octopuses who investigated at that time didn't find anything out of the ordinary. It was just work files synced to their computer the same way every hunter would have on their personal devices.

The jarring detail was these deaths seemed targeted, unlike the one with the six archers from the east, whose communication devices remained intact and with them after the attack.

Were the after-midnight killings from the past related to the recent murders in the east? Or were they separate crimes?

Who was that person in a beanie? And did Delaware, Ibrahim, and the Chens stumble upon something that someone wanted to keep under lock and key, even if it meant shutting them up for good?

By the end of the night, they were nowhere closer to getting where they hoped to be when they started, calling it a day and hoping Jade would find something else soon, something leading them to the assailant.

CHAPTER 34

The octopuses completed the screening Valor asked for within a week. Hunters were either relocated, given more team members, or reassigned completely. They sent a formal request to the government, urging them to improve communication systems in remote areas. Once Ferdinand shared the horrors of Catrine Carter's death, the motion to see through the hunters' request received a unanimous vote.

There was some noise made by a member of the opposition party, a young woman named Joyce Clearwater, who promptly reminded the house that her party had made those recommendations several times before but was brushed aside by the leading party, using this opportunity to argue that the leading party would never take precautions seriously until the people suffered "in the most tragic manner." Despite the slurs that went on for a few minutes after that, the result was the same—improve communication systems where Catrine Carter died.

Clearwater's words were drowned out by the support that the government obtained following that motion. The media captured the story of how many civilians praised the government's effort, of how—despite the small populations—their welfare was not neglected. The president and many other government officials credited Ferdinand for the success, and only those behind the scenes knew it was hunters headquarters that deserved the commendation.

Seeing Ferdinand in a video with that empty political smile, shaking hands and saying, "Thank you," like a broken record, Greg almost tore his eyes out of their sockets. He would've marked the video as being irrelevant had something not slipped—Ferdinand's face. He was composed as the epitome of a leader at first, but as his face turned away from the cameras, Greg spotted something in the old man's eye—impatience and discomfort, maybe even a little fear.

Heaving a frustrated sigh, Greg pulled the video progress bar all the way back to the left and rewatched it—muted this time—and that was when he saw it: how Ferdinand's head swung left to right as soon as he stepped out of his chauffeured car, three bodyguards equally wary. The minister's grim line only pulled into a smile when he saw the first cameras, but faltered just slightly when he locked eyes with Clearwater, who was putting on an equally hypocritical act.

For the next few hours, Greg pulled up old videos of the minister, quickly realizing he used to only have one bodyguard and never bothered to look anywhere beyond his field of vision, less so if it required him turning his head. Greg ran through the dates of each video and found the two extra bodyguards were added several months back, sometime after he killed Izabella.

Strange.

Was the minister worried that the lycans would go after him in the course of the interspecies negotiation? Why would he be worried about that? When Jade and several other mavericks infiltrated the conspirators' communications, it was deduced that the ones involved were the ones they eventually killed, no more.

"Hey, you alright?" the world's most beautiful voice stroked his eardrums as a tall cup of coffee came near his hand.

Sush's fingers only left the cup for a brief moment when Greg swiftly grabbed them, smiling to himself as he watched his thumb tracing her finger pads. Eyes trailing the length of brown skin up to her face, he uttered, "Oddly, I'm feeling much better."

Sush's eyes narrowed, but she didn't retract her hand, so Greg held onto it, beaming brighter as Sush pointed out, "In case you haven't noticed, it's lunch hour. But you seem busy. I could grab you something. What do you want to have?"

Greg's eyes snapped to his watch, and he shot up from his seat, realizing the floor was almost empty. Taking the coffee and getting a quick sip, he then pointed at the elevator. "Let's go."

"What were you doing anyway?" Sush questioned once they were in the elevator. He handed her his phone with the screen unlocked. Sush scrolled through his search history and noted in mock ignorance, "Fanboying Ferdinand. I should have known. That whole asshole persona the other day was just your nerves talking."

With an arrogant smirk, his hand snuck around her back as he uttered in a deep rumble, "Nerves, as I understand, can go two ways—two opposing ways, either with fear or audacity." His hand on her back trailed downward, testing the waters as his fingers brushed across her butt in a slow, teasing touch. In a seductive whisper, he said, "I hope I won't have to stipulate which one of the two I'm more inclined to embrace."

His animal got increasingly cocky when they felt her inch closer into his palm while her eyes tried to focus on the list of videos she was still scrolling through, strategically avoiding making eye contact.

As his lycan released a coquettish growl, his human's lips tipped higher, and he murmured, "I'm not sure how an octopus's nerves work, but I plan to find out." When his hand covered one of her butt cheeks, holding it and feeling its softness and warmth, she released a soft sigh that quickly turned into a gasp at his sudden, rough squeeze.

Their eyes met, and the haughtiness that he wore obnoxiously well tied strings around her heart, hauling her to him with the upward crook of his lips.

Sush only broke free from his gaze when the elevator bell dinged, and she slammed his phone into his chest as his fingers brushed over hers before walking out. The chief octopus pressed back a smile and ignored the looks she was getting for the conspicuous glow on her face, a vast difference from the murderous energy she used to walk around with. Greg tailed her and kept his hands to himself, pulling the straight face a little more successfully than she did, though the mavericks could still see the difference in him.

It was easier to keep his lips in a line the moment he saw they were headed to a table with some of the mavericks and the Traffic Cone. Goddess, he wished he could mind-link his octopus, but he had a feeling she understood the meaning behind the exhausted look he was giving her, because of the way she smirked. He practically shook his head like she'd just sent him to hell.

"Oh yeah, the scandal was *huge*." Hazel was in the middle of sharing an old gossip with the mavericks—Ella, Jade, and Lexton. Another octopus, Amara, filled in gaps if Hazel left any, but mostly stayed quiet, letting Hazel expand on the tale. Hazel droned on, "There was even an actual meeting of whether cameras should be installed in the male restroom."

Jade and Lexton flinched and exchanged glances. They didn't think to check when they used the restrooms. And it had been weeks!

Hazel chuckled. "Relax, it didn't get approved, though it would've been funny."

Lexton shook his head, dragging out his reply to emphasize his, "No," almost mortified despite the long list of other less legal things he'd done that a normal creature would find more mortifying.

No one at the table—or at the cafeteria, for that matter—was blind to the way Greg and Sush were stealing glances at one another, sometimes catching each other's gaze, sometimes not, despite there being no words passed between them. It was as if their eyes spoke, speaking a language that only they could understand.

The mavericks had come to terms with the fact that their boss was now deep in with the chief octopus, and only hoped what they intended to tell him next wouldn't be seen as an attempt to crush his fantasy, but to keep him and the rest of them safe.

CHAPTER 35

The cafeteria was almost vacant. And the moment Sush stood, Greg and the others followed suit, which was when Ella said, "Boss, we have a report from the kingdom." It was practically code for, "We have information about the hunters that we cannot say in front of the hunters."

His hand instinctively went to Sush's lower back again in a light graze when he murmured, "See you later," into her ear and sank back into his seat as Sush, Hazel, and Amara left. Vix and Baxter came and slid into the empty seats, and their group link began.

Jade started, *'Boss, the defense ministry knows we're hacking.'*

Greg's gaze turned fierce, wary.

'We think someone leaked,' the main hacker added.

After a long pause, noting the faces around him that seemed to want to tell him something yet were considering holding back, Greg questioned, *'And you think it's the chief?'* His tone came out more as a warning for Jade to think carefully before answering, though it wasn't intended to be that way, so while Jade swallowed a lump in his throat, his boss added, *'Let's get one thing straight: She* asked *for those files to be hacked. It makes no sense for her to leak.'*

'Would it make sense for Hazel to leak it though? She was there that night with you and Jade,' Ella ventured.

Baxter, Vix, and Lexton were helping Jade with the bulk, so Baxter answered, *'We ain't got no proof of either of 'em leakin', but it's freaky the tops changed codes and systems one week after boss and Jade had that thing with the chief and dep.'*

'Excuse me?' Greg's brows rose. Then eyeing Jade, he said, *'You still haven't answered my question. Is there a reason to suspect the chief?'*

Jade considered his words, then harrumphed even though he was using the mind-link. *'She is not dropped from the suspect list.'*

Those words had the effect of shattering every bit of hope stitched into the broken parts of the duke's heart, his soul. It was only then he realized that he'd been hoping to mark her, claim her, make her his. Greg didn't know when this yearning began, but he was already in the middle of it. Again. He'd even shown her Enora's picture. What was he thinking? His face grew dark, serious.

'Elaborate.' It was all Greg could think of saying after pulling himself together.

Jade explained, *'If the chief isn't . . . on our side, she could be asking us to hack to enhance their own systems. She may have people with innovation skills who'll pick us up when we hack. I checked the last time the defense ministry changed their systems. Guess what? It was when they set it up. They'd never changed it. Not until last night. But . . .'* something in that last word injected hopefulness in the duke, who had to remind himself to not celebrate too soon.

If Sush was a threat, he'd have to put an end to the bullshit fantasies that seemed to be spiraling out of control in his mind and body. His wants would always come second to keeping Enora safe. This was something that was never going to change. He wouldn't let anyone hurt the pup, not even the woman he was falling for, *especially* not the woman he was falling for.

Jade continued, *'But this is wholly speculation, Boss. And I'd be lying if I didn't say my skepticism is caused by the post-traumatic event of . . . Ugly Deli.'*

Greg instructed all mavericks to use that name whenever they had to bring up Izabella. And it fit the dead chameleon perfectly, he thought.

Ugly intentions. Ugly heart. Ugly end. His little sweetheart was a true genius.

Ella turned to Jade, giving him a look of uncertainty. *'Sush isn't like that one though. Not in a lot of ways.'*

Turning to her, Jade argued, *'Don't you find it weird she looked completely fine after the six murders in the east but flipped when there was* one *death here in the west? You don't suspect her reaction to the western death could have been an act? At all?'*

'That's different!' Ella insisted. *'The ones in the east were more Kenji's responsibility than hers. The systems and correspondence show Sush only acknowledged changes and decisions. She may be his superior in name, but Kenji had a lot of leeway before the murders. It makes sense for him to have taken the deaths harder. And Sush wasn't left unscathed after returning from the east, hastening the other octopuses like she'd set them on fire if they slowed down, and reviewing*

and re-reviewing codes and systems like a maniac herself before the Catrine Carter death became a more morbid distraction.'

'She didn't look the least shaken. For six,' Jade reminded, comfortable with his own stance.

'Didn't you guys mention she looked tired but gave orders wide awake in the east?' Vix interrupted, then shrugged, *'Maybe she was shocked. Maybe the shock kept her awake.'*

'She. Wasn't. Shaken,' Jade repeated for the umpteenth time.

Greg's voice, cold and calm, cut into the discussion. *'Was the deputy shaken?'*

Everyone turned to Vix, Baxter, and Lexton, who remained at headquarters when the rest of them were in the east.

'Kinda.'

'Less chatty that morning.'

'Girl kept checkin' her phone and typin', especially after lunch.'

'Did she speak to anyone about it?' Greg questioned.

The three looked between themselves when Vix said, *'She could've. We weren't near her station to eavesdrop, Boss.'*

Exhaling in a long, disapproving sigh, Greg continued, *'Do you three at least remember who she spoke to?'*

Vix knew that. *'Amara, Liena, Teddy, and Holden.'*

'That's it?' Greg's brows rose again. *'That chatterbox spoke to only four people the whole day?'*

'The rest were our people, Boss,' Vix clarified.

Turning to Jade, Greg ordered, *'Hack into the deputy's phone. I want to know what she was checking, seeing the chief was either on the plane or too occupied with Mr. Sophisticated and the eastern octopuses to be sending Traffic Cone messages.'*

Jade nodded slowly, hoping there was another order succeeding that—one that involved the chief.

Greg read his face and stated, *'Cursory search of the chief only."* His chest constricted even while still issuing the order. His animal was getting him to retract the order already. Ignoring the beast, Greg added, *'If you find nothing from that preliminary search, drop it.* Do not *expand. For now. If something comes up in the deputy's phone connecting to the chief, we expand. But not yet.'*

'Duly noted, Boss,' Jade murmured.

Greg stood, which was when he recalled something. *'Tristan, I need you to run through Catrine Carter's background. The chief mentioned her public status was single after Larson. I want to know her private status. Pull up her accounts, email, and physical mail if there is any. I don't care how you do it—hack or ask without raising suspicions.'*

'I'll get to it.'

They were back in the trenches an hour past lunch. The moment Greg exited the elevator, his eyes locked with Sush. The tug of her lips was as beautiful as it was painful.

Could this all have been another ploy? Another lie?

As he brought himself to remember she was still a suspect and he had a role to play, his lips curled up in the coy way he'd looked at her in the elevator and at the cafeteria when they were alone the other day, tearing his eyes away and heading for his station before he lost its bearing.

Little did he know he didn't fool Sush, who instinctively felt the difference in his smile. The ones before were deep and heated—they hid something and drew her in, tempting her to explore. This one when he came out of the elevator seemed . . . hollow. Even forced. There was no tantalizing enigma, just a stone wall.

Her eyes scanned the mavericks who'd stayed past lunch hour with him, and she wondered what could've happened, not knowing that—next to her—Hazel was watching her perplexity with an equally curious face.

CHAPTER 36

Ella completed her task within thirty-six hours, reporting that Catrine Carter's bank statements and balances hadn't changed much pre- and post-Larson. Emails were clean. She didn't find anything interesting in the phone records either. But the thing that intrigued her was that even though Carter's bank statements didn't change, her outward appearance did.

Ella showed Greg before and after pictures of Carter, and the difference in the chameleon's hair, makeup, clothes, bags, and accessories was glaring. Greg checked the bank records again, at which time Ella promptly noted that Carter couldn't have afforded the change with a huntress's payroll.

"Have you traced her purchases?" Greg asked, fascinated and suspicious.

"That's where it gets weirder, Boss." Greg turned to her, and she explained, "Hair, I could find, because her name is in the salon's registry, registered post-Larson. But I couldn't find anything on the rest. I matched the timeline with the brands' purchase records, and there was a vague pattern—an unknown customer paid large amounts in cash. And the amount matches the value of the bags Carter was carrying soon after."

Cash. "Looks like not all chameleons are foolish," Greg uttered, impressed by the precaution taken. "So she had someone. Any luck finding out who it was?"

"Not at the moment, Boss. But I'm currently looking through footage of the area she used to live in before she was assigned to that remote location."

Handing her back the pictures, he instructed, "Keep me posted on the updates. Good work, Tristan."

"I'll get to it." Ella nodded. Greg smelled frangipanis when Ella beamed and greeted, "Good morning, Chief."

"Hi, Ella." The voice, usually lively, stern, sure, sounded . . . different.

What happened? Greg wondered.

Ella excused herself.

Without looking at Sush, Greg scrolled through the maverick's report even though he'd already read through it the previous night, eyes staying on the tablet when he asked, "Everything alright?"

"You tell me." The tone willed Greg to look her in the eye—commanded him to. Wow, she was pissed. "Like you, I can't read minds. What the hell is wrong?"

Thinking of deflecting was a coward's way out, but Greg couldn't think of any feasible alternative at the moment. "What makes you think something's wrong?"

Well, for one, he hadn't properly touched her or whispered inappropriate things into her ear in days. The infrequent contact his hand made with her back was fleeting and felt obligatory and dead, devoid of the playful flirtation and heated tension. Even the beautiful, obnoxious smirk he carried held a sliver of wariness and uncertainty. The creatures around her may not have noticed a shift in the duke's comportment, but she did.

Sush released an exasperated sigh, seeing right through him. She could see he understood what she meant yet was being willfully ignorant. She'd ask why but doubted he'd tell her if he didn't want to. He'd just deflect again, or worse—lie.

Curling her tongue in her mouth to roll away the words she wanted to spit, reining everything in to avoid calling him out in the middle of the trenches with all the air she had in her lungs, her lips parted. It was a move that pulled Greg's sights to her mouth as his brows knitted like he was looking at something that he couldn't have—and she uttered flatly, "If and when you decide to tell me, you know where I'll be . . . Your Grace."

The last two words hit him harder than the Izabella revelation. The disappointment in Sush's eyes wrapped its fingers around his heart, demanding answers that he couldn't give. At least not yet. The click of her shoes when she left drained his peace of mind and sapped his sanity.

Of course she didn't know it was killing him as much as it was killing her. The distance he had put between them wasn't just getting suffocating; it was escalating his need for her. She used to be able to stay put somewhere in his mind, only coming forward when he wanted her to, which—admittedly—was already quite often.

But since several days ago, it was as if she was done staying put, ransacking his head and plaguing his thoughts during the day and invading his dreams at night.

In a low, impatient murmur, Greg linked Jade, *'What have you got on the deputy so far?'*

Jade paused, which in itself wasn't a good sign. *'I'm questioning my hacking skills, Boss. I can't find shit for that timeframe.'*

'Come again?' Greg pressed, voice raised.

'The deputy only got one text in the morning—from the chief, before the flight, putting her in charge. Then nothing throughout the day when the chief was gone. Not even from Valor or anyone else. There is nothing after lunch. I asked Baxter three times whether he was sure the texting was after lunch. I think he's pissed at me now. Boss . . .' Jade sighed *'. . . I'm convinced I got the wrong device. But I can't find shit on her tablet either. She doesn't use it to communicate.'*

'What's on her activity log?'

'Socials. Haven't dug deep enough to know the details yet.'

'Step on it, Jade.'

'Doing my best, Boss. I'll update you ASAP.'

Sighing as his eyes cleared, he was about to breeze through the last inventory sheet when a distant stare made him look. His gaze locked with Sush for less than a second before she looked away, busying herself on her computer.

Once he was done with the last paragraph, he pushed himself off his seat, intending to pay the chameleons a surprise visit. He was already in a bad mood, might as well put the risk of his fury and sarcasm on the most manipulative type of hunters. Taking it out on the octopuses didn't seem right, and the archers were growing on him, so that left the chameleons to absorb his wrath.

"Your Grace, you got a minute?" Traffic Cone, normally loud and lively, was soft and cautious today.

Pushing his chair back, he said, "No, I'm not interested in coffee, lunch, or parties."

Hazel's brows crinkled. "This isn't about food or parties. It's just . . . is everything okay with you and the kingdom? Sush hasn't been herself these past couple of days. She hasn't said anything, but does it have anything to do with you?"

Blinking at her direct and prying tone, he clicked his tongue and replied, "That's between us. Stay out of it."

Hazel's eyes fumed for the first time since they met when she snapped, "I would if it wasn't affecting my friend's peace of mind!" The inventory folks paused all work and looked their way, swiftly turning away the moment Greg and Hazel skimmed over them. Heaving a quick exhale to compose herself, Hazel snapped in an angry whisper, "Whatever shit's going on with you, you shouldn't take it out on her. Man up and talk. Tell her. It's not that hard."

He only wished he *could* tell her. He only wished it wasn't that hard. "Thank you for your expert advice," Greg responded sardonically, walking around her. "Now, if you'll excuse me, I'm already late for disrupting the chameleons' peace of mind."

Hazel's mouth opened—ready to deliver another retort—when something vibrated in her pocket. Greg spotted the jutting corner of her phone when she slid the device out just slightly, leaving the rest of it in her pocket. And within a second, Hazel's rage evaporated. Letting it vibrate, she turned back to Greg and hissed, "You're lucky I have to get this right now."

"Finally. Something we can both agree on."

As she shot him a glare and trotted away, out of the trenches toward the direction of the emergency exit, Greg realized something, and his pacing to the elevator came to an awkward pause as his eyes stayed on the door Hazel had just disappeared through.

'Jade.'

'Boss, come on. It hasn't even been an hour.'

Ignoring his protest, Greg asked, *'What color is the deputy's phone?'*

'Yellow. With glitter. Is this a test of my observation skills?'

'Locate it. Where is the phone now?'

After a moment, Jade linked, *'At her desk. The impediment is a little thick, so it could be in her purse at her desk. Or in the drawer. Why?'*

Greg scoffed darkly. He knew she was a warning sign. *'She's answering another phone. Black. Just disappeared through the back corridor. Trace it and run through it.'*

CHAPTER 37

Greg stepped onto the chameleons' floor and wondered whether he'd entered the wrong place. When the mavericks mentioned the chameleons' work floor had an interior equivalent to some of the most exquisite hotels they'd seen or broken into, Greg simply assumed his followers just hadn't seen enough exquisite hotels.

Being here now, he wondered if he'd seen enough exquisite hotels. The place was a far cry from the mundane interior of the trenches.

The floor here was tiled with marble, for Goddess knew what reason. The left side opened to a huge gym partitioned from the rest of the floor by glass walls; its interior was Moroccan themed with vibrant red, orange, and yellow. Every treadmill and bike was occupied; two who were running almost lost their momentum at the sight of the duke, nearly slipping off the machines. At the far end, even though there were about twenty chameleons at the dumbbell rack that stretched across the wall, the area was spacious enough that it didn't look overcrowded.

Greg plodded past the gym and came to the adjacent section—an Iceland-themed lecture room. A hologram floated like an aurora in the middle, where an instructor was delivering what seemed to be a lecture on disguises. She was showing the class a picture of herself in two very different disguises that would make one think they were two different people if he or she didn't look carefully enough.

The next dimly lit room had flagstone flooring and plants all around the edges, with wisterias hanging from the ceiling. A small, round table was set up in the middle with a candlelight at its center and two chairs positioned facing each other. A small class of ten stood by the far side, observing and taking notes.

A pair of chameleons dressed like they were on a date sat facing each other—one looked controlled and attentive, and the other was smiley and appeared in love.

As the beaming one shifted in her seat, leaned in, blinked, smiled, and pushed her hair back and laughed in a way that reminded Greg of Izabella, he realized immediately why his former mate had never wanted to show him her work floor. He was her test subject, probably for her final exam, and she had passed with flying colors. Before she was killed, that is.

Withdrawing from the room and blinking away the sight like the Forest of Oderem had just dropped dirt into his eyes, Greg turned to the next room that offered him a source of comfort—the simulator. Finally, something logical in a workplace. Arms crossed, he waited for something to happen with more enthusiasm than he'd expected.

A male chameleon stood at the far end, wearing simulation contact lenses. Upon the signal from the control room, the chameleon was shown vastly different surroundings. There was an exterior screen not far from Greg, showing the observers the simulation, which was a crowded day market with clamorous chattering and bargaining.

In the simulation, the chameleon spotted a fictitious intelligence officer who had her phone in her side pocket shielded by a tote bag as a man selling produce showed her the day's best deals. The chameleon's eyes scanned the crowd before he bumped into the produce man, making both the vendor and customer fall. The chameleon apologized frantically and helped the grocer back onto his feet as another person helped the intelligence officer, whom he conveyed another apology to and offered a strategic hug, one that was brief enough to not raise suspicions but long enough for him to pick her device that was already jutting out.

"Your Grace, how can I help you?" Patterson called out from the end of the corridor with a smile so fake that Greg would rather he wore Ferdinand's frown or Abbott's straight face.

Patterson was only here because—when the chameleons who'd sighted Greg notified the chief—the chief and deputy had argued about who was to attend to the duke. Patterson ultimately lost the coin flip and now had to play pleasant, but not before clarifying with his deputy that it would be her turn next time around.

"Hush," Greg admonished, making Patterson instinctively hold his tongue, his senses not forgetting the injuries inflicted by the king and this duke's willingness to help the other day.

The chameleon in the simulator didn't turn back when the intelligence officer realized her phone was gone. He walked brusquely to a few clothes racks and took off the cap and wig and dumped them into his camera bag. Shrugging off the jacket and shoving it in there as well, he then casually browsed through the belt section and swiftly got out a pair of sunshades from the side pocket and slipped them on. When he reached the end of the simulator, a sound blared, and he extracted the contacts, smiling at the room beaming in green, indicating that he had passed. Red digital figures on the wall ahead showed the number nineteen.

"He's one of our best," Patterson pointed out. "A nineteen-second quick change in public places is high-tier. The majority are closer to the thirty-second mark."

"Too bad personality changes take longer than thirty seconds," Greg murmured.

Patterson bit the inner walls of his mouth and decided to stay quiet for the time being, not speak unless spoken to.

"Impressive decor," Greg noted after a quiet moment.

Patterson looked around even though he'd seen everything countless times throughout the years. "We have my predecessor to thank for that. Seni was very particular about the . . . suitability of the rooms we train in, needing them to be conducive and encouraging. And she was relatively . . . persuasive with Valor."

Greg scoffed. "I can imagine. If a graduate could pull off one of the most notable conspiracies in interspecies history, imagine the level of skill of the one who had a hand in teaching her."

Patterson didn't imagine this interaction to be easy, but this was getting harder than his final exam. "Your Grace, none of us condone the . . . subterfuge of Seni, Delilah, and the others. I hope that's an understood fact." Despite the steady tone, his right leg had begun to fidget, so he placed his full weight on it to keep it still.

"That'd better *be* a fact, or the chameleons will face sudden extinction," Greg muttered as he watched the next candidate step into the simulator. This was so much duller than the one on the archers' floor, which had more hand combat than all this game of . . . dress-up. He particularly missed seeing a certain octopus behind those walls. He wondered if he would be able to do it again: watch her, wait for her to come out, and then have a decent conversation with her with perfect restraint over his urge to kiss her.

"Anyway," Patterson interrupted his thoughts, "how about you make yourself at home and let me know if you need anything, Your Grace. No need to call or punch a button. Just give my name a shout. One of the chameleons will notify me."

The click-clack of Patterson's footsteps gave away how much he wanted to leave. For a chameleon—the chief chameleon—he wasn't putting in a lot of effort to hide his emotions, Greg thought.

Out of spite, Greg decided to burst Patterson's bubble of relief by asking, "How was the conversation with Ferdinand the other day?"

Patterson cursed internally and regretted not walking faster, then turned to the duke and admitted, "If I am to summarize, Your Grace, it was awful."

"And if you are not summarizing?" Greg pressed, more than eager to force him down the memory lane that Patterson clearly did not want to walk through.

Patterson sighed, getting more wrinkles just by recalling the defense minister's phone call. "He sounded upset. And was definitely enraged, questioning why we'd never submit requests to have soldiers stationed at her location."

The word *upset* rang alarm bells. "He knew Carter?" Greg questioned, brows drawing in.

Patterson's face crimped. "I'm not sure if he *knew* her per se. Professionally, they met once or twice on Ferdinand's annual visit to our headquarters. I wouldn't say he knew her, but she probably . . . left an impression on him."

"The groin-stimulating kind of impression?"

Patterson's lips curled into a smirk. "Perhaps."

"Were they fucking?"

The chief shook his head slightly and shrugged a shoulder. "Your Grace, I'd be slammed with a lawsuit if I answered anything but no."

The words combined with his body language was a strong maybe. "You've never cared enough to find out?" Greg asked.

"Nope."

Taking that in, Greg ventured, "You and Carter were once an item, I hear?"

Patterson snickered, knowing where he was going with things. "If I wanted to kill her, Your Grace, I wouldn't have waited this long. It's been years since things ended. And let me just say, the last time I cared enough to do anything for and with the chameleon's top seductress, I found myself used and betrayed—a sentiment you can surely relate to. I've never given a damn about what she did after our breakup."

"Did *she* care about what *you* did?"

Patterson scoffed, almost sadly. "I doubt she remembered I existed after that. She was always busy with those . . . confidential assignments, coming back looking like an upgraded version of herself after every trip."

"And no one knows where those trips sent her?"

"No, but there were clues," Patterson replied, looking at the glass walls and recalling the past. "After the first confidential assignment, she came back with her hair restyled. Nothing traceable there. The second, she returned with a six-figure phone—a model that wasn't scheduled to be released on the market for another nine months. The third assignment, she was wearing a cashmere shawl from the winter line when it was still summer. These new things aren't found just anywhere in the world. There are specific locations to source them, so the . . ." he waved at the chameleons in the gym ". . . gossipers among us began speculating."

This was the part that made it difficult to connect Carter to Ferdinand. The minister's paycheck didn't allow him to afford those luxurious purchases for himself, let alone afford those for a mistress. Greg checked the minister's accounts and those of his wife and children. They were well-kept and balanced, and conspicuously too modest to afford Catrine Carter's upgrades.

"Couldn't the gifts be flown in from the source?" Greg ventured. Perhaps there was someone amongst them who flew often and came back with those gifts.

Patterson gave a brief nod. "That was one of the speculations, yes. Others refuted by saying she was at the source itself because the other things she came back with were local to a particular location." Patterson's lips pressed in a thin line, and his brows rose and fell like he was implying that things were the way they were. "Catrine Carter never confirmed or denied any of this. No one can know for sure."

Venturing along other possible explanations, Greg uttered, "So it's safe to say she didn't go on those trips with colleagues. But she does have a sister on file."

"Estranged sister," Patterson corrected. "They hadn't spoken to one another since Catrine joined us and Claire was shunned for being a Liability."

Greg mentally skimmed through his newfound knowledge. Estranged sister. "So from your memory, the dead Carter was never seen with anyone after the fling with Delilah's co-conspirator?"

Knowing he meant Logan Larson, Patterson murmured, "Yes," then held his tongue.

Greg noticed, and his pressing gaze fixed on the chief. From Greg's experience, staying silent after a person had spoken instinctively prompted them to say more than they'd intended to. And it worked like a charm in this case as well when Patterson proceeded to add, "This may or may not mean anything, Your

Grace: Catrine Carter has a penchant for anyone she can benefit from. The only thing she'd give in return is her body, nothing more."

"Insightful."

A melancholic upward curl tipped his lips. "Make of it what you will. At least she's no longer my problem."

"Whose problem do you think she is?" Greg asked, voice deepening in warning. If Patterson said it was Sush's problem, he'd pounce.

Patterson failed to comprehend the duke's sudden defensiveness and simply replied, "The state's. They neglected the importance of communication and security in remote locations. She was murdered on their watch. Not ours."

Talk about moving on.

"You told Sush it was yours and Valor's fault," Greg reminded, taking solace in saying her name.

In distaste, Patterson disclosed, "On record, it is, unfortunately. The state doesn't take accountability very well. Ferdinand is neither willing nor ready to retire or resign."

Greg smirked. "Occupational hazard."

"Honestly, not what I thought I was signing up for. But here we are."

Greg gave a curt nod, acknowledging his reply. Turning back to the simulator to watch the next candidate, the duke assumed the chief chameleon would make his escape. Only Patterson didn't.

Coming next to the duke, the chief said, "We're alike that way, Your Grace. Despite being a chameleon myself, I'd be the first to say we are the worst bunch to get involved with. You just don't know what's real, especially when you're dealing with one of the best."

Mercilessly, Greg noted, "You were worse. I had the mate bond to blind me. You didn't."

Patterson could merely smile, couldn't argue. "It's not just the women, by the way. Many men here are like that too."

"I suspect you're going to tell me you're not one of them?"

"Mm. Depends on how you look at it," Patterson said honestly. "After my experience with Carter, I've kept my guard up and only live by the triple *F*s. I make this very clear with anyone who gets close, yet many still can't distinguish between foreplay and reality."

"And the triple *F*s stand for?"

"Find. Fuck. Forget," Patterson declared with a glow of pride. "Relatable?"

If Patterson had asked Greg that question several years ago, it would've been a sure yes. But now, Greg found himself holding the chameleon's waiting stare and replying, "Not the slightest. Not anymore, at least."

Patterson nodded as the duke turned back to the simulator; comprehension flickered through the chief's eyes. "She's a good one," he uttered in quiet concurrence. Lilac eyes snapped to Patterson's blue ones when the chameleon continued, "Don't get me wrong, I've lost count of the number of times I wanted to strangle her or bury her alive or wished she suffered from a sore throat that would last for all eternity, but . . ." he sighed in resignation, admitting, "she has been a valuable asset to the hunters. She still is. Almost indispensable. Only a handful can think like her, keep things in order as she does, not get us killed the way she does, build things with a vision that only she can see."

Greg may not have realized, but his entire being softened at the mention of her.

Patterson then added a tease, "If you're still in doubt, I'd say she's safer than your last choice. At least Sush isn't a chameleon."

Only Greg wasn't in doubt about how he felt, but he was in doubt about who she was, what her intentions were. He hadn't spoken to her long enough to truly know her yet, and he only hoped he'd have that chance. He hoped she wasn't another Izabella.

As the thought came, so did Jade's link, making Greg leave the floor without so much as a thank-you to Patterson.

CHAPTER 38

After another shitty test run of the new earplugs, Sush dragged her exhausted self to the elevator, intending to head to the archers' floor to blow off some steam at their gun range. When the elevator arrived, she already felt better that the octopuses who looked like they were waiting to ascend said they were waiting for another two of their own to return from the restrooms. Sush had the space all to herself and tried not to look too happy about not needing to share and make small talk with anyone on the ride up.

Right before the metal doors closed, a hand came between them, making both doors part before Greg stepped inside.

"Are you out of your mind?" Sush reprimanded.

"Give me a minute," he urged in his usual monotone as the doors closed and he extracted a spider-shaped device from his jacket pocket.

Sush didn't give him another second when she barged forward and reached for his hand that was sandwiched by the metal doors a few seconds ago, holding it up to the light and inspecting it.

The gesture made Greg pause—stunned. The concern lining the creases of her forehead softened his being and turned his lycan into a cooing slab of goo. For a moment, he forgot where they were, until he noticed the rising red digits of the elevator through the reflection and recalled the gadget in his free hand, quickly latching it onto the metal surface that had sent a faint green hue around the edges of the doors.

If Sush noticed what he had just done, she made no comment. She didn't even look. Her attention was still on his not-injured hand, her thumb and fingers running over his skin brusquely, scouring for—at the very least—scratches.

She didn't seem convinced he was uninjured, pulling his hand closer to the light as a lot of anger and worry dominated her eyes. There was nothing on the outside, she decided. But there were definitely more than a few broken bones from his little stunt. Fucking idiot.

His thumb stroked her hand when he uttered, "I'm fine." Their eyes locked. The connection and depth that had been gone in the past few days were now there—bare and clear as he elaborated matter-of-factly, "Lycans possess superior healing abilities."

The worry for him flitted away as she narrowed her eyes and shoved his hand back at him, slightly embarrassed that she had forgotten about that little detail of their species. "Fucking show-off."

He held onto her hand when she sought to let go, pulling her into him, holding her close. "I want to apologize for my behavior," he began, eyes already begging for forgiveness even before he got all the words out. "There was an issue that came up, one that involved you as a suspect—as absurd as that sounds now—so I had to keep my distance."

Apprehensiveness shadowed her eyes. "What issue?"

"The defense ministry reworked their systems after Jade began hacking. We didn't think it was a coincidence."

Her brows lifted, and she caught on quick. "And you thought I was the mole? Seriously?"

Shifting in uneasiness, he murmured, "There was a . . . probable suspicion that you may be . . . using us to enhance your own systems—to make us show you what you're up against and implement an upgrade to keep us out."

Sush's ears heated up when her free hand came up to chest level, and her voice turned hauntingly low when she said, "Personally, I prefer a more effective method of getting that type of information. You may have heard of it." Her voice turned up a few notches when she exclaimed, "It's called ASKING!"

His lycan covered its ears, cowering before the volume. His human stood his ground, refusing to back away. He cautiously brought her hand to his lips, leaving a featherlike kiss on the back of her fingers, cooling Sush to a degree when he continued gazing pleadingly into her eyes, uttering sheepishly but sincerely, "I really do apologize."

His lilac eyes held her captive, and her frustration gradually dissolved, rage vaporized, and incinerating eyes welcomed back a calmness that she hadn't been feeling these past couple of days. With the fury gone, her mind presented her with the main reason she was the suspect in the first place: She was probably the first octopus, or the first hunter, in history to seek help from a lycan—and not just any lycan, the lycan duke, one of the most influential and powerful figures of a species that humans had never gotten along with. And then there was the fact that Delilah had already given their entire species the license to draw the worst conclusions when it came to interspecies mingling and cooperation.

With that in mind, she drew a breath before saying, "It's fine. I understand."

She tried to take back her hand, but Greg held it tighter when he argued, "It is definitely *not* fine." His brows arched in a way that was disapproving of her quick forgiveness. "You've never given me a reason to mistrust you. I should have never thought you'd do something like that."

Blinking, her irritation returned when she asked, "Do you want us to move on from this episode or not?"

His frown faded away, replaced by a grateful smile, lighting up his whole face when he confessed, "I missed you."

It was insane how three simple words ignited an array of emotions within them both. Sush's eyes stayed in his gaze for a moment before her attention went to her hand in his. His grip was gentle yet firm.

This. This was how he held her. It carried warmth, willingness, a need to never let go. Not the empty, barren touches she'd been getting in the past day and a half.

Her heart willed her to speak, to say something to him. But her brain wasn't wired to say the words as smoothly as he did, with as much certainty and confidence as he carried. She'd only ever said them to her family, not even to friends. She couldn't even recall saying it to Kenji when they dated.

It was one thing to flirt, but to make a three-word declaration like that was taking things to a level that Sush wasn't sure she was ready for—especially when she reminded herself of why things with Kenji had to end and why she'd never gone looking for another intimate relationship. She definitely wasn't looking for Greg, but he'd barged right into her life anyway.

Right now, she was looking for an escape, a change of subject. And her senses finally picked up the metal thing with glowing green edges, making her brows furrow in curiosity and fascination.

Greg's gaze followed hers. "Ah, that. The creators call it a *stopper*. It makes any metal object stop once it's positioned onto the surface."

Sush gravitated toward the gadget, studying it with wide eyes from every possible angle, enthralled by the creation. Tapping on it to get a hint of the material used, she muttered, "So this can essentially stop a car from moving."

"It can," Greg confirmed, his free hand resting on her waist, watching her watch the stopper. "What's on your mind?" he whispered in a baritone that reverberated through her ears, making her heart pump faster and making him relieved that he still had that effect on her.

In a conspiratorial whisper, she harrumphed and said, "I could've used this to keep Valor's car in the parking lot every time he pissed me off."

Greg scoffed, amused.

It encouraged Sush to add, "I mean, someone would eventually give him a ride back, but the momentary inconvenience would feel very satisfying."

Not even trying to hide his smile, he responded, "I'll have the team make you a few if inconveniencing your noble leader means that much to you. But personally, I'd wait for the car to move before latching it on. Makes for better entertainment, more exhilarating, too, in fact."

A ghost of a smile tipped Sush's lips despite making no comment. Her hand covered the device, wanting to pull it off and see the bottom part of it, but Greg's hand came over hers, halting her from extracting the stopper because he wasn't done yet.

In nothing but annoyance, her gaze pivoted to him, which was when he uttered ominously, "We need to talk about your deputy."

CHAPTER 39

The fact that Greg didn't use Hazel's nickname was not a good sign.

"What about her?" Sush asked, though—as her mind recalled there being suspects earlier—she already had a good idea of what was coming next.

His creasing forehead was a clear indication that he wasn't enjoying having to break it to Sush that someone she saw as her friend may not be as trustworthy as she presented herself to be. "Jade found things on her encrypted phone. Sh—"

Sush drew her eyes closed and held her hand up in a stop sign. "Pause right there. Her what?"

Greg stared at her for a good second before murmuring under his breath, "Well, at least we know the encrypted phone isn't common knowledge."

"It's not," Sush stated like it was obvious. "The only one we know with such a thing is Valor. Not even the chiefs have one."

Greg's brows shot to his hair at the mention of the commander. "That is . . . insightful. Who does Valor communicate with on that thing?"

"We assume it's for receiving orders from the higher-ups in the defense ministry."

"So Ferdinand?"

"I don't know. Maybe? I don't think it's exclusively him though. Ferdinand isn't the only one privy to top-secret files."

Greg hm-ed, taking note, and thought of recruiting Vix, Baxter, and Lexton to help Jade. The pool was getting bigger.

"So what did Jade find?" she asked charily.

Offering her his full attention now, he replied, "He hasn't cracked everything just yet, but from everything he's found so far, she's communicating with someone in coded messages, though we can't pinpoint who it is. There are a few segments to it: something about Great Horned Owls being sacrificed while the Rat—with a capital *R*—is let off from above, and the plan would work because the other rats wouldn't know how to save the owls." Greg's perplexity was shared with Sush, who was getting confused *and* frustrated. He then added, "Last I checked, rats were lower down the food chain, hence are more likely to celebrate if their predators are sacrificed. Why is this going against that?"

As her brain stared at the mental wall that announced her dead end, she asked, "What is the rest of it? Maybe there's a bigger picture we're not seeing yet."

"Data leaked when the sun rose."

"What?" Her eyes squinted like the sun was piercing her eyes, when they were actually in an enclosed space with four opaque walls.

Helplessly, Greg noted, "Sush, I really should be the one to ask that question. I'm new here."

Her brows knitted in disagreement when her finger jabbed at his chest. "You've been here for almost a month. You're *not* new. Data leaked when the sun rose?" She threw her hands in the air. "Data can leak anytime! God! What else?"

Greg recalled the last bit, "The hyenas are coming for those who are left."

Sush exhaled, frustration hitting its peak that she wanted to scream so badly. *Deep breath, Sush. Deep breath,* she told herself. "Hyenas? Really? Where are we? In a desert? I must have missed the sand and the heatwaves in the years I've been here."

"Maybe it's not really the animals but a specific group of them. She did say *the* hyenas, not a pack in general."

"And that makes it so much clearer," Sush retorted, though Greg didn't take her sarcasm to heart. If anything, it made him smile. Wrapping herself with one arm because her other hand was still with Greg, she stared at the floor, contemplating, then muttering her thoughts aloud, "Asking Hazel wouldn't be the best move."

Greg considered, and then his lips quirked. "It may be. After all, you've mentioned that your preferred approach is ask—ow." He acknowledged her elbow to his chest in a monotonous tone but with an affectionate smile. The blow wasn't even a blow, more like a prompt to not rub it in her face by shoving her own words back at her.

Sush continued thinking. "And we can't ask or tell Valor in case he's on the other end of the line."

"About that—are there physical archives in his office that are not kept in the digital cloud?"

She blinked, swallowing the "no" that was at the tip of her tongue. She used to be sure it was no, but now . . . "I didn't think there were at first, but . . . I've personally never looked through the papers in his office. I'm not sure if Hazel has. But before me, Zasper Zavier did, I think. He used to joke about how losing Valor's office to a fire would be more tragic than losing Valor himself because Valor wouldn't be able to remember everything in those files passed down from one commander to the next. I used to think it was only for good humor. But Valor never really laughed. He smiled to be amiable because Ferdinand and the others from the ministry found it funny. Maybe Valor just didn't want to cause a scene."

Greg considered their options and urged, "Sush, we need to get those files. Something about the Catrine Carter death doesn't seem right. And it's not just the fact that she was murdered in a remote location. I think her death was only a piece of the puzzle."

"You're saying Hazel, Valor . . . if they're communicating, they're other pieces of the same puzzle?"

"Maybe, maybe not. Until we have more to go on, I can't be sure. None of us can."

"So what do we do with Hazel? Report her? Suspend and confine her until investigations are complete?"

"That may not be wise, Sush. The last thing we need is for our only link to the big picture to be assassinated like Carter. We don't want to bury the only lead we have for now."

Sush nodded in agreement. "No Hazel. No Valor. Definitely no Ferdinand. Abbott is loyal to a fault to authority, so to Valor and the defense ministry. And Patterson's just . . ." She sighed, already exhausted from thinking about the other chief. "So I'm basically playing detective alone."

Tugging her closer, his thick brows dipped and his eyes channeled a promise when he uttered, "You're not alone, Sush. You never will be. I'm here. You couldn't get rid of me even if you wanted to."

A quiet moment passed when she went momentarily speechless from his declaration before she found her voice again. "I was talking about the hunters, but . . ." She trailed off when his stroking of the back of her hand pulled her gaze to their joined hands and she uttered, "Thank you." Lifting her face to meet his smiling eyes, she added in a tease, "And it's nice to know the so-called black sheep of the royal family isn't all black."

Those words and that smile drew out his coquettish smirk. His hands naturally found her bum, pinning her against him as her hands steadied herself against his chest. He closed in on her ear and murmured, "I've grown out of that fleece in recent years." His voice, deep and sultry, accelerated her heart rate.

His mouth traced the shell of her ear, following the curve before the tip of his tongue glided across her earlobe, eliciting her sigh and soft moan. The faint scent of arousal entered his nostrils when he added, "The black fleece became a little too . . . tight." His crotch pushed against his zipper and was now pressed against Sush's thigh. Her arousal intensified, and he could almost picture the moisture between her folds, making his mouth water.

As his hands massaged her butt in unhurried, sensuous motions, he continued, "I'm not anything the media says anymore, my octopus." The magic of the last two words weakened her knees, making her melt into him like butter on toast.

In an alluring whisper, he continued, "I'm not a lycan in sheep's clothing. Though . . . I must admit: I'm the most morally reprehensible royal you'll meet, using deplorable methods and taking them to the very *extreme*." His emphasis on the last word was slow, seductive. His lips trailed along her jaw and reached the corner of her lips, where he declared, "I've never bothered borrowing a sheep's clothing, Sush. I've always worn everything that represents me, showing who I am. With *pride*."

It should have sounded arrogant. In a normal setting—a less confined setting with his hands not on her butt and his mouth not caressing her face—it would have sounded arrogant. But those words—especially the last words—heated Sush even further, escalating her need for him, her restraint weakening by the minute, his piercing gaze challenging her thinning walls.

Sush heard the alarm bells in her head, telling her that she needed to come clean with him about who she was and what she was up to before they took things further, but she blurred out the sirens and warnings, wanting to soak into the moment and deal with the repercussions later.

Their noses brushed and breaths mingled. The surface of his lips touched hers, and his eyes chose this time to glaze over.

He was going to kill someone.

CHAPTER 40

'B*oss!'* Ella linked in panic.

Greg heaved a frustrated sigh and pulled away from Sush, who was about to protest before noticing his glazed-over eyes, so she fell silent and waited patiently as he replied, *'You'd better make sure someone is dying, or you're going to lose an organ, Tristan. I don't care if your husband would eventually get the queen to extract one of my own later.'*

Ella's panic hit the next notch. *'SomeONE dying? Boss! The archers ARE DYING! IT'S MORE THAN ONE! THEY'RE TRAPPED! WHATEVER IS IN THERE IS MAKING OUR PEOPLE DIZZY, AND SOME ARE CLOSE TO PASSING OUT! THE HUNTERS ARE ALREADY DROPPING LIKE FLIES! JADE STILL CAN'T HACK HIMSELF IN. WHERE THE HELL IS SUSH? HAVE YOU SEEN HER?'*

Shit.

'How did it happen?' he asked, trying to remain calm, though Ella might be extracting his organs herself soon.

'Boss, with much respect, how about we save the autopsy for later and FIND THE FREAKING CHIEF!' Exactly why he'd asked how it happened—to get to the root of the problem before finding a viable solution. There clearly wasn't time to reason with Ella, especially when she continued spewing in a hurry, *'The octopuses say only Valor, Sush, and Abbott have the codes to the archers' floors that have magically locked themselves. Abbott is unconscious. Valor is unreachable. Sush can't be found! Those with the archers said even Hazel and a few octopuses have dropped unconscious from shock. We need to find Sush!'*

'Sush is with me. Give me a moment, Tristan.' One eye cleared and locked with Sush's, and his grip on her arms tightened when he said, "Codes for the archers' floors. Now."

Sush blinked, perplexed. "What? Why?"

"Something's happened. They can't get out. My people are there, but it's not looking good for both sides, much less the hunters. Codes, Sush."

He was worried she'd panic or pass out like Hazel, but Sush's perplexity morphed into worry, and eventually something in her took charge, her face coming back to the way it was whenever she was in the trenches, fierce but controlled when she calmly said, "200223."

Greg linked Ella the digits, and within the next three seconds, she reported—with more relief—that it had worked. The mavericks were getting the hunters out and the ambulances and paramedics had already been alerted and were on their way.

Ending the link, Greg recalled the way Sush's face and composure had shifted within seconds, how she didn't even crack under the pressure like Ella or—worse still—surrender consciousness like the useless Traffic Cone. He shouldn't have been surprised, given that she was the one who led negotiations years before she was appointed chief, but he was still astounded. Her control was impeccable.

Before his thoughts came to an end, she barged toward the stopper, extracted it, and waited for the elevator to take her to the archers' floor. Greg came between her and the panel, double tapping the number to undo her attempt and tapping G instead, twisting to her and sternly saying, "You are not going anywhere near there. We'll assess the damage from outside."

Right before Sush could argue, they heard a sound, and the elevator went into free fall, bringing them both to their knees as Greg growled and glued the stopper back onto the door. The deafening shriek on the external cables permeated their senses as his arm wrapped around Sush and pulled her in, locking her in his embrace to shield her from any possible impact while his free hand reached to swipe across all the lower floor buttons, hoping the system would make the elevator stop on the way down.

Within seconds that felt like forever, the metal cube they were in came to a halt. Greg wasn't sure whether it was tapping the lower floor buttons or the stopper, or both, that had managed it.

Helping Sush onto her feet, he had her wait at the inner corner when his claws dug through the metal door. Then digging his fingers through, he folded the metal in and kicked it open.

Retracting the sharp structures, he offered Sush his hand. "Time to go."

The elevator stopped between the lobby and the upper floor of the trenches, so Greg lifted her to the upper opening before she crawled her way out, after which she offered him her arm as he climbed out behind her.

"You alright?" he asked, hand reaching for her face, thumb tracing her skin, searching for scratches and wounds.

"Yeah, I'm fine. Are y— On second thought, I'm not going to ask. You've already shown off your healing abilities today."

They headed for the line of mavericks carrying two hunters at a time over their shoulders, trailing down the emergency stairs and out of the building where the ambulances were. Flashing red lights, loud orders, and numerous stretchers filled the usually deserted space outside the headquarters.

After Baxter set down two of the ones he carried with the medical teams, he dashed to Greg, picking a small, empty jar out of his pocket and placing it into his boss's ready hand. "Air sample." The maverick then disappeared back into the building, along with many others. The lycans had pretty much recovered but were cursing under their breaths, not knowing about the metal walls that would descend and trap them in.

Sush's eyes scanned the fallen archers. Some were being given time-of-death declarations, and others were being resuscitated. Hazel was nowhere in sight. Several ambulances had left, and more were leaving as the doctors on site called for backup. Sush wondered if Hazel was already being sent to the hospital.

Patterson arrived—hair disheveled, tie loose as dismay coated his features. He came over, looked Sush dead in the eye, and hissed, "Where the hell were you?"

Greg came to her side, and the chief chameleon took a step back by instinct when the duke explained, "The chief octopus was trapped in the elevator that went into free fall. We're lucky to have gotten out in one piece. Any more questions?"

Patterson's urge to blame vaporized, and his features morphed into one of shame and shock. "Wha— How?" Facing Sush, he said, "Maintenance has never been skipped, even before we took charge of the divisions."

"I don't know how," Sush admitted, equally appalled. "For now, we can only hope the deaths and damage are kept to a minimum. I'll get the octopuses to run full checks on the archers' floors to figure out why the attack was launched in the first place. Have you seen Hazel?"

Trying to maintain his composure, Patterson uttered, "No, but the ones who did said she was one of the first to leave in an ambulance."

"Any chameleons involved?"

"Six," he said grimly. "They were there for the weekly combat training. One has just been pronounced dead."

They shared a melancholic moment of silence as their eyes roamed the space. Every archer was still unconscious.

As Sush's hawk eyes scanned the field, her rage escalated with each second she couldn't find the hunter she was searching for.

Where. Was. Valor?

CHAPTER 41

"I was in a meeting with the defense ministry," Valor disclosed in his office, his voice speaking for his displeasure at Sush's tone when she demanded to know his whereabouts during the attack.

Sush and Greg had easily deciphered most of the animal code from Hazel's secret correspondence after the catastrophe.

"The Great Horned Owls" was code for "the archers, sacrificed."

"Rat with a capital *R* being let off from above"? Sush herself was let off from above when the elevator malfunctioned. She and Greg speculated that his presence in the elevator was most likely not considered since he had forced himself in at the last minute.

The next code—"other rats wouldn't know how to save the owls"—meant no other octopus knew how to save the archers. Because none of them knew the codes.

The next one—"data leaked when the sun rose"—took them a little more time, but they eventually figured it out. The sun rose from the east. Data that someone didn't want found had been leaked from the attack in the east.

The only uncrackable code left was the one with the hyenas.

They kept the codes between themselves and the mavericks, not knowing which other hunter to trust at present, especially when even the commander himself didn't seem as fazed as they expected him to be.

Patterson, for once, wasn't defending Valor either, but his voice managed to hide his anger slightly better than Sush when he questioned, "Didn't you receive the countless calls and messages from us, Commander? No one else had the codes."

Although taken aback, Valor replied, "Communication devices have never been allowed behind those doors. They don't want us to be recording the meeting in secret, nor do they want to risk having hackers listening to our discussion. Alagumalai and Abbott always had the codes. The recent mishap has taken place in an unforeseeable circumstance."

"Mishap?" Sush's whisper may have taken away the volume, but it didn't take away her infuriation. Kenji even subconsciously took a step away from her as she unleashed her wrath with the same fire in her eyes as when she barged into his office during the four-month negotiation. "Fifty-two archers are dead, Valor. Dead. Thirty-six are incapacitated. Sixteen are in a coma, including their chief *and* deputy. The inventory rooms and poison chamber were encroached into. No one even knows who brought in the zahar or how it was snuck into the headquarters and then to the archers' floors *undetected*. Cameras around the entire headquarters were clearly hacked to stop us from finding the culprit. A *mishap*? Do you even know how dire our situation is? Do you even know what this means?"

Her hands pressed on his table as she leaned in. "With no defenders left here, we'd have to call back at least half of those at the borders. The archers would be spread thin, increasing the likelihood of *more* of them dying from attacks like the one in the east. Someone is challenging our defenses, and they are succeeding. This is a *ploy*, Valor. *Not* a mishap."

After a long moment of uncomfortable silence, no one coming to the commander's rescue, Valor asked, "And what do you want me to do, hm? Stand in their place and guard the border?"

"That would be ideal," she said without showing any signs of wavering. "Except you'd lose all functionality if I chopped you up into several pieces and assigned each part of you across our borders."

Kenji bit the inner walls of his mouth at her response, knowing it wasn't an ideal time to find anything amusing, and was telling himself that Sush wasn't joking. Patterson glanced at the ceiling and then out the window, fully comprehending the consequences but not seeing a solution just yet. Greg, who stood at the far left, couldn't help his lips from tilting upward as his crossed arms loosened and thumbs hooked to his pants pockets.

Valor's patience snapped. He stood from behind his desk, forehead carrying waves of frustration. "And you think I'm not doing anything? When this reached Ferdinand, the first person he blamed was *you*."

Greg's spine straightened, prepared to engage in violence yet still trying to convince himself that Sush didn't need his help. This was her turf, her boss, her fight.

Sush's eyes widened in further fury, the control over her volume now gone with Valor's outburst. "I was trapped in a fucking elevator that chose that exact time to malfunction!"

"Exactly. Ferdinand said you may have staged it to deflect suspicions off yourself!"

"That's *incredibly* logical since I wouldn't be a suspect if I was dead!"

"The point is, Alagumalai, you didn't die. And you had a protector with you to shield you from death." Valor nodded at Greg.

The duke promptly interjected, "I barged in at the eleventh hour, right before the doors closed behind her. Getting stuck and almost dying was definitely not part of the plan."

Valor treaded more cautiously. "I understand, Your Grace, which is why—" his sights returned to Sush "—I've told Ferdinand you couldn't have been the culprit. You had nothing to gain. And His Grace's presence was most likely due to something in the treaty. The minister was going to use this instance to dismiss you, Alagumalai. Not just from the octopuses, but from the hunters entirely. I saved your ass!"

That was definitely a surprise for the chief octopus. Valor had never saved anyone's ass but his own. He didn't even try very hard to save the asses of those involved in the Delilah Conspiracy. He'd asked the lycans for better terms, better understanding—all of which were worded by Sush, of course—but he'd never asked for them to be spared. It was as if the commander simply accepted that was their fate. Sush was never one to believe a person could change overnight, which only meant Valor needed her alive and within the headquarters. If he needed her alive, he couldn't be the one behind it. If he wasn't the one behind it, he and Hazel were probably not exchanging any encrypted messages instigating the attack. Which meant Hazel was communicating with someone else.

Sush tone mellowed out when she said, "So you clearly still need me. I'm now telling you that I can't create waterproof robots to take the archers' places overnight."

Valor waved a hand and stated matter-of-factly, "We're all trained in fields that are not our own. The extra octopuses and chameleons can ta—"

Patterson's eyes widened, and he interrupted without hesitation, growing fearful for his own division. "Commander, I have to disagree."

"They're not trained well enough!" Sush exclaimed, getting straight to the point that Patterson had planned to gradually transition to. She didn't have time for a gradual transition when she went on, "Yes, they can defend themselves, but we're talking about defending a whole territory. We can get everyone to pick up practice sessions, but it'll take at least a month before they're as field ready as an archer."

"Maybe not even then," Patterson murmured, sighing and glancing at the ceiling.

Valor spat, "So what do you two suggest we do? Leave the headquarters archer-free? Compromise defenses at the borders? God forbid you're thinking of asking the ministry to assign soldiers who are already spread thin."

"Ask for help, Valor," Sush insisted. "Ask those who already have the skill. We'll get our people to train with the archers we'll be bringing back. In the meantime, we get someone else to protect us."

Valor looked at her like she'd grown a second head. "And who is this someone else you're referring to?"

"The lycans and werewolves," Sush said with utmost certainty.

Kenji choked on air from pure shock. His profuse coughing bounced off the walls of Valor's office, and no one judged him. It was a justified response.

Patterson's eyes bulged from their sockets as he turned to Sush at what he saw as an absurd suggestion.

Valor was utterly lost for words, standing so still that he could pass as a statue.

Taking advantage of the silence, Sush continued making her case, "They're trained. Properly trained. Many amongst them are seasoned fighters. They can do it, Valor. Ask them for help."

When Valor finally snapped out of his daze, he harrumphed and came up with the best excuse he could think of. "Just because they can, it doesn't mean they will, Alagumalai. Our species haven't seen eye to eye for generations, and you're the last person who needs reminding that the tension has only worsened recently."

Not backing down, Sush argued, "We've been giving them everything they want. We've been cooperating, and the execution of the terms in the treaty is smoother than any one of us can expect. We may not be in the kingdom's best books, but our present cooperation offers us a good enough standing to ask for their assistance."

Valor took a wary sideway glance at the duke, who was looking through his cluttered cabinets, when the commander questioned, "And you're saying all of this while *he* is here?"

Greg scoffed. As if he weren't listening. "Obviously." He reached to a random folder—the thickest one—and pulled it out, eyes going down the Contents page. When he urged Sush to let him dig through the physical archives, he'd never imagined being able to do it in front of Valor, which only meant one thing—there was nothing valuable here.

Patterson looked between Greg and Sush before offering his opinion, "Commander, perhaps . . . circumstances have changed enough for the kingdom to take a request like that seriously."

Valor caught the chief chameleon's sights. He was not deaf to the rumors circulating about the duke fancying the most difficult and terrifying person in the headquarters either. If Valor was being honest, it was the second reason he'd defended her from Ferdinand. The last thing he needed was for the duke to fly off the handle about her dismissal and create another mess that would take another four months to clean up. The first reason for defending Alagumalai was—as much as he hated to admit—she was, at present, irreplaceable.

As Greg placed the folder back in its place, he turned and stole a quick glance of a still-serious Sush and a reluctant Valor as the commander heaved a defeated sigh. "I'll have to run it through Ferdinand," the old man murmured.

Sush firmly said, "Tell him it's either taking a chance on the kingdom's forces or his own soldiers. Remind him what happened in the east and our recent disaster in the west. See if the soldiers are up for something like this."

Valor's head gave a slow shake like it was a plan that was never going to be approved by a minister who wasn't the strongest advocate for humanizing creatures he saw as animals.

So Valor wasn't surprised when Ferdinand gave a flat "no" through his secretary, but when Valor elaborated on the available options and their situation, there was a pause before the secretary said he'd call back. Within ten minutes, the call returned with a grudging "okay."

The kingdom was contacted, and warriors were promptly deployed to human territory as selected archers were called back to manage things at the headquarters. To Valor's and Ferdinand's dread, the kingdom's willingness to provide assistance on short notice only meant they had to extend a personal courtesy to convey the highest gratitude that neither of them could summon.

CHAPTER 42

The hunter-lycan gala was an annual affair, attended by the highest officials from both sides. Xandar and Lucy attended every alternate year, taking turns with Christian and Annie. Although it took place under the guise of an event to raise funds for equipment and manpower to train new recruits and solidify the public image that everything was well and good with the neighboring kingdom, the attendees knew full well it was a show. Behind the cameras and smiles, both species had still been keeping to themselves to a significant extent.

It had been exactly three days since the call was made and the lycans and wolves had begun standing guard. Because of the "generous contribution from the kingdom" the media reported, Ferdinand—who attended once every three to four years—had to show his face at the gala this year despite having already attended the previous year.

The stench of the animals was just awful, the minister thought as he stepped through the doors, despite the empty smile that he wore so well. His gaze swept the place before Valor came forward to greet him. The commander nodded to his left, gesturing toward the smiling queen chatting with an archer and the brooding king with a hand around her waist—half listening, half assessing the increasingly crowded room, nodding at acquaintances and curious faces, glaring at ones staring hungrily at his mate.

"They'd expect a personal thanks," Valor noted the obvious.

Ferdinand released a subtle exasperated sigh, dragged his feet, and held his smile as he approached the lycan rulers, internally cursing the unwanted baggage that his position came with.

The king noticed him first, who returned the minister's feigned welcoming gaze with a less welcoming one of his own as his lips made the lightest contact with the queen's temple before the couple's eyes glazed over. Lucy's smile withered when she wrapped up her conversation with the archer, who noticed her boss and boss's boss striding over and quickly excused herself.

"Your Majesties, so good of you to join us," Ferdinand began.

Lucy mirrored his empty smile. "Good of you, too, Minister."

It was as if Ferdinand's and Valor's presence had alerted the rulers' allies. Toby, Ella, Phelton, and Greg stood close by, far enough not to be intrusive but near enough to defend the royal couple if and when needed.

Ferdinand looked past the queen's shade regarding his infrequent attendance at the annual event and proceeded to get his words out so he could call it a night, "On behalf of the government and the hunters, allow me to convey our most sincere thanks for the warriors offered to secure our borders. I assure you, their presence is merely temporary, and we are more than happy to discuss a way to repay this debt."

"In that case," Lucy began, which brought a look out of the minister, his deputy, and the commander, a look that said, "Oh no." Those last few words were merely meant to convey an empty promise, a well-rehearsed political line that was never meant to be taken literally. The queen obviously knew this and clearly didn't care when she continued with a snarl, "Make sure you're doing everything within reach and beyond to find the culprit. We offered two hundred warriors. We expect to get two hundred in return."

Nodding in comprehension but with zero empathy, Ferdinand replied, "I feel you, Your Majesty. They will be cared for as if they were our own."

Xandar's face grew darker, and his tone grew firm, "If that's the treatment our people will be getting from you, we're insisting on greater care and more substantial hastening on the part of the ministry and the rest of the government. The ministry *and* the rest of the government, Ferdinand. Not just the hunters. The last thing we want is to have you *care* for our people the way you do yours, seeing that security structures weren't even disclosed to the ones managing security."

Xandar was referring to the metal walls that concealed the archers' floors, which ended up trapping everyone. They were built long before this generation but were never utilized, which was why no present-day hunter knew about them and no precautionary measures were taken to install an escape route in case their own people were trapped. They were lucky that the codes to remove the walls were the same as the codes to access the emergency doors on the archers' floors.

Ferdinand nodded once more, and his voice lost strength and smile lost stamina. "That was a very grave error on our part, I admit."

"Admission is crucial but insufficient, Minister," Lucy noted, swallowing back another snarl. She still couldn't get over the fact that so many hunters were sacrificed. She had paused for quite awhile in pure shock the other day when Greg linked her with the news. Those weren't her people, but she still felt something heavy pulling her to the ground as she imagined the countless families that would be mourning their losses. That night, after putting the pups into bed with Xandar, she sat in his lap for about an hour. Neither one of them said anything as they allowed their sorrow to flow through each other.

Now, taking a step toward the minister and commander, Lucy warned, "If any of our warriors acquire as much as a scratch, know that the two of you will receive a similar laceration: across the face, along the neck, through the heart, whichever is appropriate depending on the severity of their injuries. Is that clear?"

"Yes, Your Majesty," Ferdinand's and Valor's joint response came out in an unexpected synchronicity that a bystander would have interpreted as a declaration of subordination, out of instinct if not out of fear.

The two men exchanged disapproving glances before Ferdinand forced another smile. "Your Majesties, I can assure you we take the attack very seriously. The lives lost won't be forgotten, and it serves as a reminder to keep our defenders informed. The motion on compensating the affected families will be tabled tomorrow—the very first thing on our agenda. And the second issue is with regard to the borders. The entire day is dedicated to keeping the hunters and your people safe."

Xandar used this opportunity to deliver a reminder, "We look forward to receiving the details of the discussion."

Ferdinand's brows knitted and forehead creased, failing to understand. As Greg scoffed darkly from the side, Valor murmured to the minister, "Clause 10.1 in the agreement, Minister—the kingdom is entitled to the minutes of every discussion and decision involving hunters."

"Ah," Ferdinand noted like he'd forgotten and then just remembered such a bullshit clause. Still, he turned back to the rulers, uttering, "Our people will send you a copy as soon as possible."

Lucy knew this game. "Minister, I'm inclined to remind you that—per the treaty—nothing should be redacted. And the details should reach us within twenty-four hours post-discussion, in case those particular details slipped your mind."

Although Ferdinand didn't appreciate being caught in his tactical maneuver to avoid having to divulge his country's affairs with the kingdom, he somehow managed to say, "I appreciate the reminder, Your Majesties. And many thanks for the aid provided."

He offered them an obligatory bow and left before more complaints followed while his deputy, Agu, stayed a few more moments to convey his own gratitude with much more sincerity than his superior.

Since that was over, Greg lifted his wrist to check the time, then extracted his phone and tapped a number on his speed dial with furrowed brows. At the second beep, he caught sight of a vision of beauty walking through the entrance. And his heart stopped.

CHAPTER 43

Sush was in an ash-gray dress that hung from her shoulders by thin straps. The length of her skin stretching from her neck, down her arms and hands was on full display. Her hair was loose from her usual ponytail, the pink headband no longer in sight, but her necklace still sat in its usual place.

She hadn't caught sight of Greg yet but felt a buzz in her purse, and her footsteps slowed as she dug through it. Her knitted brows eased into a soft line when she saw the caller ID. She swiped to answer as her head swung around, looking for him, which was when their eyes locked and the corner of her lips lifted naturally.

The background blurred away as they took steps toward each other, closing their distance. When they were six feet apart, a figure appeared from Sush's right, and a hand stopped her by her elbow. Sush's defenses took over, and she yanked her arm away, eyes taking a defensive turn before realizing the figure was Kenji, who raised both hands with an amused smile. "Woah, woah. Sush, it's just me."

"Oh, hi." Sush blinked the murderous glint away and offered a smile.

Greg appeared by her side, making a point to let the click of his shoes be heard in separate, distinct decibels.

Kenji didn't seem to get the go-away memo Greg was sending his way, which made the eastern octopus ask Sush, "How are you holding up?"

The duke didn't even bother acknowledging the eastern leader when he murmured under his breath, "How the fuck do you think she's holding up?"

As Kenji shot Greg a what-have-I-ever-done-to-you look, Sush's elbow delivered a soft nudge to Greg's side when she replied, "It's difficult. I'm sure you can relate."

Kenji's face morphed into embarrassed uneasiness. "I'm not sure if I can, to be honest. I was a mess after losing six. The one on this side . . . it was ho—"

"She gets it, Sophisticated," Greg interjected when he noticed Sush subtly stiffened at the reminder.

Kenji blinked in obliviousness. That wasn't his name, but it sounded like the duke was speaking to him. And judging by the tone, it wasn't a compliment. Before he could ask what it meant, not remembering his precise words during their first encounter, Sush spoke, "I appreciate the concern, Kenji. We'll just have to review the systems and rely on the lycans and wolves for now. Let's get everything fixed and scrutinized and pray . . ." her eyes darted to Valor and Ferdinand hanging around the other higher-ups ". . . that certain people won't be screwing us up anymore."

Kenji and Greg followed her gaze as the latter scoffed.

Turning back to Sush, Kenji shook his head in disgust and disappointment when he whispered, "I hated that it happened. But I'm glad their attention is now diverted away from me and toward covering their own asses."

"Tell me about it," Sush murmured in agreement. "The only thing that would make this night better would be someone throwing shade at them without consequences."

Greg's lips stretched into a smile as his hand reached for her lower back. "Oh, someone already did. And it was very entertaining."

"I fully agree," Kenji offered, beaming until the duke looked at him like he wasn't asked for his opinion, so he harrumphed and added, "I was . . . happening to get drinks when I overheard their conversation with the royal couple. Anyway, uh . . . I'm going to just . . . disappear. Have a good evening."

Finally, Greg thought.

As Kenji left to mingle with other octopuses, Sush turned to Greg. "Was it the fox? I mean, the queen? Did you have it recorded? A voice recording at least?"

Greg blinked at the first nickname he'd heard from her. "The fox?"

Sush didn't even look sheepish when she defended, "You have to admit the queen is crafty, even before she was crowned."

"Well, she does have a lot to protect, so that's probably a prerequisite trait. Many of us from the kingdom are like that. You're like that, too, if you haven't noticed."

Waving a hand, Sush readily admitted, "I know. It's probably why between me and her have an unspoken love-hate relationship."

"Interesting," Greg noted. He didn't know there was a bond between the women before tonight, though the queen did speak very highly of Sush when the four-month negotiation commenced. He'd always thought it was one-sided.

"So I assume you *don't* have a recording?" Sush asked, already dejected.

His smile returned, and unfiltered amusement lit his face. "I apologize. I didn't think of doing that at the time." The curl of his lips flattened when he asked, "What took you so long to get here, by the way?" The question didn't come out as judgmental; it only amplified concern.

"Is it bad to say I didn't want to come?" Sush replied with a smirk.

Chuckling briefly, he ventured, "And what would you rather be doing?"

No one had ever asked her that. Whenever she honestly said that she didn't want to be where she was, the listener would normally ask her to lighten up or keep an open mind, saying that she'd have fun if she let herself enjoy the event. The thing is, even when the events were not horrible, they were not her ideal way to spend her precious hours. She and social events had never been a good fit.

Giving Greg's question some thought, she ultimately said, "Well, before I stepped in through those doors, I was thinking of heading to the park for a nice stroll. Or over to the archery range to shoot a few arrows, but I'd have to pay the premium rate since it's late evening. And the place would normally be too crowded at this time to be any fun. Or I could have an early night. Haven't had that in weeks." Staring into space, she concluded, "Actually, the last one was the most appealing—an early night."

"Was?" Greg questioned in a whisper, taking a small step closer to not just look at her but also feel her.

There was no denying it—the pull was there, the pull he'd been feeling since the second week. Her smell, he concluded, was her natural scent. The low voltage passing from her back to his hand that traveled through his body and invaded every cell and vein didn't stem from surface attraction. It was something deeper.

He didn't know if this was how a second mate bond was supposed to feel—milder than the first. And he realized that, even if it was, he didn't mind. Even if it was, he felt blessed.

His heart beat for this second chance in ways that it never did for his first, especially when his first had only been a champion in offering heated sex and sultry looks and touches in exchange for his heart, the most vulnerable parts of his soul, and access to the people in his life. Hardly a fair trade.

Sush wasn't asking for anything but gave him so much more: intriguing conversations, amusing comebacks, glimpses into her innovative mind, her temper, and her vulnerability. He doubted she let anyone see the fear and dismay she showed him in his car the other day, or the sudden shock and anxiety that lasted for mere seconds when they were trapped in the elevator.

She was his, he was sure. He had never been more sure of anything else in his life.

Sush saw it in his eyes—the yearning to hear her next words, the hopeful glint giving away the fact that he'd already had a good guess of how her dread over the gala changed within minutes if not seconds.

It was him. She knew it was him. He probably knew it too. The way he looked at her when she entered—mouth agape, eyes zoned in. Desire wasn't just written all over his face; it oozed from his being even from a distance, calling out to her to take notice. It was like she was the only one in the room, the only one that mattered.

And she liked it. More than like—she loved it. She loved that he only saw her the way she only saw him.

Her heart implored her to speak, yet one thing—one dreaded thing—now held her words back: the fact that she didn't know whether he'd still see her this way, want her this way if he knew the extent of what she was up to.

Tell him, her naive heart whispered.

He's different. He'll understand, the stupid, illogical part of her soul chimed.

There's a risk: a risk of losing him, a risk of him seeing you differently, her cautious brain echoed. Finally, a part of herself that she could agree with.

Greg's throat bobbed, eyes dimmed from her silence as he took her hands. "Are you alright? You don't have to tell me if you don't want to, you should know that." He wanted her to, yearned for her to, but not until she wanted to, not until she was ready to.

A booming voice from the speakers took their attention from each other as everyone turned to the source—a beaming woman in a glorious red gown.

CHAPTER 44

The woman in red stood on the steps, introducing herself as the wife of the minister of defense, Larissa Ferdinand, and—as if on cue—Ferdinand beamed emptily as his wife of fair skin and dark hair with winged eyeliner brought the room back to herself.

Flashing those pearly-white teeth with a depth of smile that mirrored her husband's, she began, "On behalf of the ministry, I'd like to thank all of you for attending this year. Yes, that includes my own husband."

Barks of laughter followed as Ferdinand feigned embarrassment.

By Sush's ear, Greg muttered, "Can they get any more perfect for each other?"

Her finger came up subtly. "You haven't seen everything yet. Keep watching."

"Goddess help me," he murmured.

Sush reached to her side for a glass, handing it to him, which he accepted without thought when she said, "I'm no goddess, but that should help a bit."

A soft chuckle left him, and he pulled her closer, letting their bodies touch and their warmth meet, the trail of electricity spread through them both.

Larissa's voice continued echoing through the hall, "For those wondering why I was late," she sighed dramatically, "unlike the men in this room, we ladies have to actually make sure the kids are looked after before we leave the house."

As some laughter came from the crowd to get the men in the room flustered, Sush murmured in Greg's direction as he sipped on the drink, "They have two maids: one for the house, one for their two kids. Full time. Mrs. Ferdinand came into the headquarters once talked about her children, and mistakenly said her younger one was Alexis the entire day when his name is actually Alvise."

Greg snorted into the wine and unintentionally drew attention to himself.

As he attempted to suppress the coughs, Sush plucked the glass off his fingers. "Alright, that was a bad idea."

Her words lifted his lips even when he was still muffling out the coughs.

When he finally got a hold of himself, he skimmed the room to find all eyes on him, but his gaze only lingered only on those who mattered: his mavericks' concerned stares, his cousin's disapproving scowl, his queen's knowing smile as her eyes flickered between him and Sush, the octopuses' puzzled looks, and Larissa Ferdinand's quizzical surprise that—to Greg's own surprise—looked genuine.

Clearing his throat, his confident voice projected, "Please accept my humble apologies, Mrs. Ferdinand. Very rude for me to be sipping on a drink during your speech."

Forcing a smile and not appreciating the interruption because she'd rehearsed for her speech to go smoothly, Larissa replied, "Having heard about you, Your Grace, I suppose I shouldn't expect anything more. As I was saying . . ."

Many lycans' eyes—including the queen's—welcomed shades of onyx at that remark as growls bubbled up their throats.

Greg wasn't going to throw shade, but since the Red Devil had served from her court, he figured it'd be rude not to return the ball, especially when he knew he could deliver a smash. "You were talking about your children, Mrs. Ferdinand. What are their names, if I may ask?"

Sush's head swung to him, and her eyes looked like they could set him on fire.

The hunters either stood very still or nudged one another, as if asking whether he knew about the inside joke. No one had outright told the minister's wife she'd gotten the name wrong on that day, but they imagined she'd discovered it somehow.

Larissa's demeanor morphed from one of quizzical surprise to angered humiliation that lasted a brief moment, confirming she did eventually find out about her blunder. "I'm afraid, for the children's safety, I'm unable to divulge their names in a public setting, Your Grace, as my husband frequently reminds me."

"Ah, of course. How ignorant of me to have asked. My apologies, Mrs. Ferdinand."

Larissa nodded uneasily, turned to look elsewhere, and droned on about how grateful they were to be living in a time of peace and harmony, conveniently failing to mention the murders in the east, the death of Catrine Carter, and the recent massacre in the west.

Sush refused to hand Greg back the glass, holding it away when he tried to reach for it.

At the end of Larissa's speech and during the obligatory applause that followed, Greg finally got back his drink when he murmured, "Maybe she's forgotten both children's names today."

Narrowing her eyes at him, she hissed, "I'm convinced you're trying to get me suspended or fired."

"They won't touch you," he insisted in a low tone, as if promising death if they did.

"That doesn't mean they can't make my life difficult, Greg. Honestly, what were you thinking?"

Chastened now, he said, "I was planning to die of boredom with the rest of the audience, so the impromptu conversation with the Red Devil really was unintended . . . and admittedly, at your expense. I would apologize, but I fully comprehend that an apology is far from sufficient."

Her eyes trained on him, her hard gaze holding his soft, remorseful ones, and she heaved a defeated sigh and uttered, "Next time you want to burn someone with an inside joke, do it far away from me so it doesn't look like you heard it from me."

"Duly noted. I'll stand next to Valor or Patterson in the future."

"Good," she mused, sipping on her drink.

"And now"—Larissa's voice pierced through the speakers again. A glint in her eye looked genuine but not encouraging. If anything, those gray eyes looked scheming, even from afar—"in the spirit of diplomacy—between the government and ministry, and that of our neighboring species—let us join hands and share the dance floor. And since the ongoing treaty is only going so well thanks to the chief octopus from our side and the leader of the mavericks from the kingdom, I'd say that it's only apt for them to lead the way, wouldn't you?"

Greg did not see the point in that whole thing. The Red Devil was basically asking him and Sush to dance. He would've asked her himself. Why was that conniving gleam dancing in the woman's eyes? It only made his animal want to scratch out her eyeballs.

As he turned to Sush, ready to murmur something to berate Larissa Ferdinand, he realized he wasn't the devil's target, Sush was.

CHAPTER 45

His octopus's usually confident frame and posture now shrunk like she was trying to keep to herself as her eyes—though pinned on Larissa Ferdinand in shock—amplified a need to leave.

Greg's own eyes turned onyx, and he shot the Ferdinands a glare—which neither of them noticed—before he positioned himself in front of the only one in the room who mattered, blocking her view of the sharks out to gobble her, though he couldn't understand how or why yet.

His hand reached for her face, cupping her cheek, and his voice came in an assuring whisper, "Sush, this is not an obligation. No one is going to die if you refuse. And you're not a politician. You can refuse."

His large frame shadowing hers offered her cover, made her feel protected, encouraged her to loosen, allowing her to come back from her shrunken posture. "I . . . haven't had good experiences dancing," she blurted. "The one time I was on the dance floor, I, uh . . . I was being spun around too much, too fast, and I . . . threw up all over the place and on two people, and then I . . . slipped and fell into my own vomit. It was embarrassing. Everyone here knows. I've never been on a dance floor since."

"So that's the game she's playing," Greg muttered, head angling to his side, about to shoot the Red Devil with his most murderous glare and even fire a growl.

But before he could, Sush's grip on the lapel of his coat held him back. "Wait." He did, knowing where his priorities lay, knowing it was with her. He'd think of something for the Red Devil later.

"Can you dance?" she asked.

His brows rose. "I can. What are y—"

"Let's do this. Go easy on the spinning."

"Sush," he stopped her by her waist. "You don't have to do this just to prove it to her. She's a devil, for Goddess's sake."

"It's not about proving it to her." The fierce glint, the sure voice—the ones that made him listen—now continued ringing through his ears. "It's about proving to myself that no one can use that incident against me again after tonight."

His heart swelled at her insistence, lips curled up at her courage. Stepping back and offering her a proper bow and an outstretched hand like a gentleman, he uttered, "Then allow this professional to show you how proper dancing doesn't induce nausea."

His boastful line brought out her smile, and she whispered, "Show-off."

Greg was glad to see his efforts to distract her were working to a certain extent, but the moment they were on the dance floor, she stiffened, taking breaths that gave away her anxiety about having so many eyes on them.

As Greg guided one of her hands to his shoulder and took the other in his, his free hand resting on her waist, he murmured, "At any time you want to stop, we stop, and we'll try again if you want to, okay?"

She nodded, forcing a smile. The music began, and they started slow. From the way Sush tried to keep track of every part of her that moved when they began, Greg gathered she wasn't one who enjoyed expressing herself with her body, but as they swayed, he felt her leaning into the idea, leaning into him, trusting him and relinquishing control. Greg gradually increased the pacing as she loosened.

Sush forbade herself from looking anywhere else, focusing on his eyes—the way his gaze shielded her from the stares, from the murmurs that she wasn't hearing because her attention was only on Greg and on not messing up.

"Ready?" Greg whispered.

And she knew what he meant. The quicker they got through this, the less anxious she'd be waiting for it to come. So she nodded, bracing herself.

Greg drew their joined hands up and sent her into a graceful pirouette, bringing her back into him, which was when a relieved smile played on her lips and she uttered, "That was actually alright. Better than alright, even."

His own anxiousness vaporized with those words, and he beamed, lighting up by seeing her light up. "I'm betting your previous dance partner was an amateur."

"A humble one though," she pointed out.

Spinning her around for the second time, he then responded, "With that kind of skill, he had no choice *but* to be humble."

She chuckled, all fear forgotten, anxiety washed away. She didn't even notice the unnerving stares anymore.

And the Red Devil just had to ruin their moment by speaking through the microphone again, in an annoying high-pitched cheery voice that carried a tinge of jealousy when it echoed, "Well, would you look at that, ladies and gentlemen—the *show* that no one expected!"

It would have passed off as an encouraging statement if the tone didn't carry the scorn that it did.

The spite of this woman knew no limits, Greg deduced. This wasn't a show. It was a special moment he was sharing with the one he intended to make his.

Sush heard Larissa, heard the jab in those words, and chose not to care, reminding herself she didn't need to care. She'd overcome her fear of putting herself on the dance floor and actually dancing in public tonight. That itself was something not even the worst people in the room could take away from her.

Greg, on the other hand, was born not to turn the other cheek, so his mental gears spun, thinking of a sardonic comeback.

But someone beat him to it.

CHAPTER 46

"Come, darling." The queen's voice, loud and jubilant, filled with just the right level of hypocrisy and a shard of scorn, sucked all attention away from the Red Devil. Hands gently tugging her husband's bicep with a mischievous smile, Lucy announced, "It's time to join the show: this ministerial-organized circus."

The human ministers flinched, Ferdinand included—a sight witnessed by the majority of the room. The Ferdinands' forced smiles withered. The only difference was that Larissa's smile withered under the spotlight, her mask falling a little too long.

With bright eyes and a broad smile, Xandar bowed low and offered his wife his hand like he was still courting her, knowing the game she was playing as he responded with a glint in his eye that matched hers, "Yes, wouldn't want to disappoint the ringmasters. I mean, government ministers."

"What a careless blunder, my love," Lucy playfully reprimanded.

Placing a kiss on her hand before pulling her in, he uttered loud enough for everyone to hear as they continued putting on their own show, "Forgive me, my little freesia. I hope you understand that animals take a little more time to keep up."

As Lucy chuckled, Toby—who stood nearer to the Ferdinands—offered Ella his hand and chimed, "Something to look forward to reading in the news tomorrow."

Ella placed her hand into his and built on his efforts. "I wonder if someone has to step down after this."

Her husband shrugged. "Eh, we'll know by the end of the week. Not our problem. We're just here to perform."

As the hunters themselves randomly paired up and joined the show, effectively making a statement that they sided with the chief octopus over the minister's wife—with even Agu offering his hand to a random huntress and everyone beginning to fill up the dance floor—Ferdinand snatched the microphone from his wife and signaled for the music to stop. If the king's and queen's words got out—words implying that there had been disrespect initiated by his own wife—Ferdinand would be submitting his resignation within the next forty-eight hours.

Apologetic and directed to the lycan rulers, Ferdinand eked out a smile and said, "Your Majesties, there appears to be a misunderstanding. I'm quite sure what my lovely wife meant was . . . it's wonderful to see our species interacting. In harmony."

"What a lovely set of words from your lovely wife in the lovely tone she found appropriate to use," Lucy replied, not even needing the microphone to be heard or make the minister and his wife cower from a distance.

Ferdinand chuckled awkwardly. Lonelily. After clearing his throat twice while trying not to crumble under the queen's glare and the king's scowl, the old man uttered, "On behalf of my wife, I apologize, Your Majesties." Turning to Greg, he continued, "Your Grace." Seeing Greg's opening mouth and his hand that never left the octopus's waist, Ferdinand quickly added, "And you, too, Alagumalai."

Wow, that was a first, Sush thought. She didn't care if this was a show anymore. She liked being in it, loving how it was playing out.

Ferdinand handed the microphone back to his wife, gripping her arm and muttering something into her ear with a sternness that only she could hear.

The Red Devil's chest heaved as her eyes closed, and when they reopened, the pair stared at each other like it was agreed how much was at stake before Larissa turned back to the crowd with feigned remorse. "Your Grace, Ms. Alagumalai, my poor choice of words was . . . uncalled for." Shooting her husband a microsecond-long look at the last two words he insisted she used, she then continued with her empty smile, "The night is to celebrate peace. It always has been. Never was it a show of performance."

"Oh, that's a relief." Lucy continued with a smile challenging Larissa's own. "And when are we going to see you on the dance floor celebrating peace with us, Larissa? Or are government ministers and their spouses exempted from having to participate in performances that they force others into?"

All eyes pinned on the woman in red, and not in a good way. Amongst each other, the hunters were taking bets. Half said that Larissa would give a half-believable excuse to wriggle out of having to dance; the other half said she'd be obliged to put on a performance. Since the kingdom had just offered their help, refusing the queen wouldn't look good in a political sense.

Ferdinand snatched the microphone back from his wife's hands, not trusting her to utter a politically safe sentence without going through his filter. "We support no form of coercion, but we do support our allegiance, Your Majesties. My wife and I will be joining everyone in the center shortly."

The minister then offered his wife his hand, which she accepted with a forced smile.

Interesting, many in the room thought as the hunters who lost the bet groaned.

While leading the way, Ferdinand mindlessly slammed the microphone into a random man's chest, thinking it was someone who'd take care of it. The problem arose when this random man was Giovanni Patterson, who didn't appreciate being treated like a punching bag, even if it was just one punch by a microphone that didn't feel like a punch.

First, his name had to be on the accountability paper of Catrine Carter's death that he felt he had no fault in causing. Then, he lost six chameleons to metal walls and a poison that the minister and commander conveniently never mentioned. Now, as chief chameleon, he was being treated like someone Ferdinand could just dump things onto?

Oh, no, no, no. Call him petty, but that was the last straw. Even ass-kissing has its limits.

Patterson tossed the microphone to the person in charge and took brusque steps toward the Ferdinands, motioning his clueless deputy to join him. The chief chameleon brought himself before Larissa, bringing her hand to his lips and brushing a kiss, all while looking at her with a coy smile he mastered years ago.

Larissa, though briefly shocked, seemed to be enjoying the attention.

Right before Ferdinand spoke, Patterson's deputy, Mary Brown, joined them—vaguely guessing what she was going to be asked to do, already dreading it.

Patterson beamed brightly, hiding the offense he took with Ferdinand treating him like a random servant, and suggested with a diplomatic smile, "Since Mrs. Ferdinand has said this is a night to celebrate not just our relationship with the neighboring species but also between the ministry and hunters, how about we see that our dance partners reflect that notion, Minister?"

Patterson knew the last thing the minister wanted was to be dragged onto the dance floor, which would stop him from leaving earlier than he wanted to, so this was exactly what Patterson was giving him. If he kept the minister's wife throughout the night, the minister himself would be forced to stay for that long as well.

Petty. Pointless in the larger scheme of things. But effective nonetheless.

Mary Brown didn't blink when Patterson whispered into her ear, "I'm cashing in the debt you owe me. I entertained the duke last time. It's your turn to entertain the minister."

With that, her lips curled into a practiced smile as her chief pulled away and instructed audibly, "Go easy on the minister, Brown. He may be a little rusty."

His deputy turned to Ferdinand, gracious and ready. "Nothing I can't handle, I'm sure."

Ferdinand knew better than to refuse, especially after the way this man—whose name he couldn't recall—phrased things the way he did.

Guiding Larissa away as the music began, Patterson behaved as if he was on an assignment, speaking alluringly, "I'm sorry to have stolen you from your husband, Mrs. Ferdinand. I can tell I'm a far cry from the minister as a partner."

To his surprise, which he successfully kept to himself, Larissa's hands boldly slid up his muscular chest and rested around his collar when she whispered, "Don't sell yourself short, handsome."

He recognized the look in her eye from his years as a chameleon, and he had to admit it was a development he hadn't seen coming.

###

The sight of Patterson and Larissa was too much for Greg to refrain from speaking, making him murmur by Sush's temple, "What is he up to?"

Sush followed his gaze, then shrugged as her head leaned into him while they swayed to the slow melody. "To hell if I know what goes through his mind."

Greg's eyes returned to her, hand reaching for her chin, bringing her face up, gazing into her eyes. "I hope you know what goes through my mind."

One brow lifted, and she taunted, "I thought we've established we're both not mind readers."

Lips twitching, he uttered, "Reading is specific. Knowing requires only the outlines of our thoughts—the general things our minds breeze through every day."

"And I'm supposed to know the general things your mind breezes through every day? Do you know mine?"

His lips lifted higher. "Work, rest, archery, and—I'm venturing—your late family."

Failing to find a loophole since it was meant to be "general things," she gave a brief shake of her head and muttered, "I set the bar too low."

He chuckled, the deep rumble from his chest vibrating through her fingers, sending the electrifying charge into her own heart. "Your turn, Sush." What went through his mind every day? "Take a guess," he purred.

"Your sweetheart."

"Mm."

"The mavericks."

"Right."

"Anything to do with work."

"That's a given."

"Ways to kill Valor and Ferdinand, I hope?"

"Not at present, but if you like, I could—"

"Don't. It was a joke."

"Hm." He swayed them to a stop, hands still on her back, above her hips, when he brought their faces closer and whispered, "You're forgetting someone very important."

"Another sweetheart?" she teased, yearning to know the answer her heart already knew yet still skittish about admitting it to herself.

His gaze dropped to her lips, and he swallowed, then meeting her eyes once more. "If that's what you'd like to call yourself, I'm more than happy to oblige."

Their noses touched in an affectionate tap, their eyelids fell to make way for a moment that was better felt than seen, and the surface of their lips met in a featherlight touch. Breaths mingled, and Greg's lips were closing in before Sush pulled away, hesitance dawning on her, needing him to know something before they took things further.

"Sush?" his hands clasped both sides of her face, concern laced in his voice and etched on his arched brows.

She didn't know how to start, where to start. There were so many people in this room, with many pretending not to look while really looking. It didn't make this an ideal place to talk.

"Sush, are you alright? Do you need something to eat?"

Just then, a cheery voice chimed from their side that echoed, "Aww, look at you two."

CHAPTER 47

"My queen. Cousin," Greg acknowledged, bringing himself next to Sush, facing the royal couple.

"Your Majesties," Sush greeted with a bow and curtsy.

Lucy's brow lifted at the title and formality, which she and Xandar returned before the queen said, "Honestly, Sush. You've been calling me Paw for years. This isn't an email. It's either Paw or Lucy, especially now that we're technically closer through a . . ." she glimpsed at the duke and said, ". . . family member. Actually, I'd prefer Lucy."

The hint wasn't even subtle.

That was when Greg had an epiphany—the queen never allowed Izabella to address her like a friend. The one time Izabella had tried, using her shortened name, the queen diplomatically put it to a stop by saying she was more comfortable with the title for the time being. It was an awkward exchange considering the queen had always been more comfortable with anything but titles, Xandar having to fill the sudden silence by saying that they should get to the food before things got cold when everything had *just* been served. The last server hadn't even left the room yet.

Izabella bounced back, didn't make a fuss. And Greg assumed the queen had simply warmed up to her position—and maybe she had—never thinking her name-over-title preference hadn't changed.

He himself was given the permission to address her by name—several times. Tried it on his tongue once and never went back, finding it inappropriate and disrespectful. Lucy went so far as to say he was like Blackfur in that sense—a psychological maneuver to get the dukes to drop her title since they repelled sharing any similarity with one another. But because Greg knew the game she was playing, evident from the glint in her eye in those times, he simply said the heed to title was something the majority of the kingdom shared, not just him and the other duke, then tried not to look too amused at her frustration that his cousin eventually had to cool off.

His gaze now fell on Sush, her silence pulling him back to the present.

Although Xandar and Lucy had expected Sush to laugh a little, or at least smile, grope for words for a moment, accept or politely decline addressing the queen so casually, or, better yet, be her complete self and say something audacious, the chief octopus was—to everyone's concern—lost for words.

"Sush, are you alright? Is he treating you well?" Lucy didn't wait for her response before turning to Greg and questioning more defensively, "Are you treating her well?"

Greg's mouth opened when Sush finally spoke, "It's not him. Really. I'm just . . . shocked. And my brain hasn't been at its most optimum these past few days, given the circumstances. I think I'll stick to Paw for now"—since she wasn't sure where this thing with the duke was going yet—"and maybe transition into your first name if and when the time comes."

"Of course," Lucy muttered, perplexed by Sush's demeanor.

The queen had read their body language from a distance and now again up close. There was undeniable attraction yet hesitant reciprocation at Sush's end. Lucy and Xandar had been discussing the possible reasons behind Greg still not feeling a mate bond despite having moved on from Izabella, despite already being attracted to Sush when they cliqued in so many ways, and now, looking at them together, she had her answer.

Turning to her husband, she mused, "The Ydaer effect might cover hunters too. Who knew? I always thought it only applied to our species."

"First time for everything, my little freesia. And Ydaer did say it was about the mate bond in general, not one confined to our species, so it does make sense," Xandar responded with a similar intrigue behind his eyes, along with a soft smile—one reserved only for his wife and pups.

Sush blinked, coming back to herself when she turned to Greg and asked, "The what effect?"

Lucy, satisfied that she'd successfully planted another seed into Greg's mind, offered the huntress a smile and said, "Do let us know if you need anything else, Sush."

The queen excused herself, letting her king lead her to the drinks and food.

Greg fell into deep thought. Sush extracted her phone and googled "Edear effect" as Greg closed in on her ear and muttered, "Y-d-a-e-r."

"What type of word is that?" Sush complained in a whisper as she typed it out, skimming through a few summarized definitions before making sense of the queen's words from earlier. That bloody fox was a fucking mind reader.

"Is it true?" Greg asked when she'd stopped scrolling, drawing her eyes to his. "Is there something holding you back?"

Sush sighed and tossed the phone back into her purse as she murmured, "Sort of. And it's quite . . . layered."

"Indulge me." All this time, he assumed he'd been the one holding them back. But now that he thought about it, he recalled the times she pulled back—all the times that required words. Her body responded to his as his did to hers, but were their minds headed in the same direction? The fact that they weren't bonded crossed his mind before, but he didn't care. He didn't think the absence of the bond could be from the Ydaer effect. On *her* end.

Who had she not moved on from? Mr. Sophisticated? Another man from her past? Had Greg just been someone she clung onto while she hunted for the one she truly wanted? Or worse—a vessel to make a former lover jealous this whole time?

He'd given his heart and let his head take the backseat once, and it ended worse than bad. He wasn't making the same mistake again.

When Sush said nothing for a few moments, gathering her thoughts, his hand left her back as he created a distance—one they both dreaded as he said, "If you're not ready, or if this isn't what you want, tell me now. My days of fooling around are long behind me. I thought I was building something permanent with you. After my former mate, I thought I didn't want that anymore, until I met you." The warmth in her chest blossomed, but it came as quickly as it left when he continued, "If you don't feel the same, we end things here. We move on. No hard feelings. But I need to know where you stand in this. It's only fair to us both."

"It's not about not feeling the same!" Sush spat without thought in an angered whisper like it should have been obvious.

Her hasty reply shocked herself and softened Greg, who closed the space once more and asked, almost begging, "Then what is it?"

Her eyes darted around the room, taking note of the curious glances and quiet chatter. Facing Greg once more, she knew she'd hidden the truth—the depth of who she was—for long enough. It was either tell him, taking a chance that he'd be okay with her plans and where she came from along with where she was going, or lose him entirely. "Can we go somewhere quieter?"

She felt sheltered and safer with him now, but there was still a risk of eavesdropping that she'd prefer to remove.

Sliding his hand into hers, Greg pulled her away from prying eyes and uttered a deep but gentle, "Come."

CHAPTER 48

At the balcony that Greg emptied—he literally stepped into the space and said, "Out. All of you."—he guided Sush to the far end, away from the light and noise from the inside, glared at the slowpokes taking their time to disappear, linked two mavericks to stand by the balcony entrance to stop anyone else from entering, and then gave his full attention to his octopus.

Sush had been mentally rehearsing how to start when they were on their way here, but she knew the lengthy story she hoped he was prepared to hear would still come out unstructured. "Before we get into . . . the layers, I need to know two things: one, your stance on marriage and, two, whether kids is something you're looking for."

Unfazed, Greg replied, "I'll start with the first: I don't give a fuck about marriage, but I do want my mate and I to mark each other."

"So civil partnership isn't a problem with you?" Sush questioned, growing hopeful.

"Those are just labels to me," he said truthfully, never seeing the difference because—unlike in some parts of the human world—there really was no difference between the two in the kingdom. Both involved two people. Both involved signing a certificate. Both may or may not have a ceremony. Benefits and aid were provided to both with mirroring terms. Greg wasn't the only one who saw marriage and civil partnership as merely different labels. The law did too.

Greg went on, "At the end of the day, it's whether my soul and hers are entwined in a bond that's meant to last for eternity."

"Okay," she nodded. "And . . . children?" She was much more pessimistic about this part. Given Greg's relationship with his niece, it was hard to imagine he didn't want pups of his own, so she was utterly surprised by the words that came next without hesitation.

"Offspring had never been on my list. Being who I was, I never saw myself as a parent. I'd love to have them with my mate if she wants one . . . or a few, preferably not more than half a dozen—it'd be difficult to monitor their movements—but having them is not a must for me. Never has been. And frankly, I'm more than happy with Enora for that kind of company and happiness."

Wow. This was easier than Sush had anticipated. Blinking in disbelief, she admitted, "Same here. I don't have an issue with kids, but I never pictured myself as a mother, something that some people still find hard to understand." Taking a deep inhale, she continued, "Okay. Since we're on the same page in those regards, I should tell you why I'm here with the hunters, and where I'm going. This is going to be . . . a very long story."

"Good thing we've got time." He came closer in a way that was telling her he wanted to know, even if they took all night, even if it took all week.

She nodded and began, "So . . . I wasn't born a huntress. I only got my mark when I was eighteen, after the last of my relatives died."

This was unusual. Late bloomers didn't exist amongst hunters. You were either one or you weren't. You couldn't just be one midway because marks didn't appear midway. It was the reason some hunter couples gave away their children at birth if the infant bore no mark. It was disgraceful for two hunters to birth a Liability. Marriages had broken down because of it—because suspicions and questions of adultery were brought into question. Even when paternity tests were done and the DNA confirmed, some children may still be given up for adoption and divorce was considered because of some superstitious belief that they couldn't produce a hunter due to the fact that they "weren't the best fit for one another."

Sush's case was different. She was born a Liability. A Liability was supposed to live and die as a Liability. No exceptions.

"How did you do it?" Greg asked, curiosity channeling through his voice.

"I don't know," she whispered, lost. But then she frantically retracted, "Wait, that's not completely true. I mean . . ." she sighed, shutting her eyes against the cold night air, hating to sound scattered. The last time she was like this was when she lost her uncle, which felt like a lifetime ago.

Greg's thumb drew slow circles on the back of her hand. "Take your time."

It didn't make her feel any better. Sush felt that she'd already taken her time. She knew how she felt about him. She knew how she was when she was with him. She knew she wanted more with him, and had always ended up smiling to herself when she knew he wanted it too. But she also knew she was the one who'd held them back, because of a side of herself that she'd gotten used to hiding from everyone.

Letting his touch guide her back, she continued, "I don't have concrete facts or any . . . certainty of how the mark ended up on my nape, but I suspect it's from . . . trauma."

A pocket of silence followed before Greg's voice—careful and crestfallen—echoed, "I'm sorry."

Sush held up a hand. "No, you don't get it yet. It wasn't from the trauma of losing my family. That was . . . worse than horrible, but before they passed, my uncle decided that I was old enough to know . . . or that I should know my mother . . . didn't just die." Her eyes met his, and she disclosed, "She was murdered."

Greg's brows shot to his hair. His animal sat so still. And they both stopped breathing. When he finally blinked, he only uttered three words—low and homicidal, "Who did it?"

One of her shoulders lifted and fell back, her head gave a slight shake, and her lips pulled into a grim line. "I wish I knew. I wish I had a name. A short answer. But I don't. When I was ten, the last time I saw my mother, I stayed the night at my aunt's place when my mother was supposed to meet him—my birth father. And she never came back. She told my aunt and uncle that she was going to tell my father of my existence, to insist that he start taking responsibility for me."

His brows furrowed, recalling her personal details that were kept with Human Resources. "I thought your father died in an accident."

"The name on file was my stepfather. He came into the picture when I was four and died when I was seven. Abusive as hell in the years he was married to Mom. I was so glad the truck ran over him that I smiled in my sleep for a whole month after he died."

Explains her aversion to marriage, Greg thought.

Drawing a breath into her lungs, more for courage than for air, her fingers fiddled with the locket before gripping it tight, clutching onto it like she wouldn't survive the next minute without doing so. Taking a shaky breath, she undid her necklace and unclasped the locket, holding it his way in one hand as she murmured, "This is her." As Greg came closer to take a look, she continued in a whisper, "That old headband I wear every day? It was the last thing she bought for me. It was too big for me at that age, but I loved it so much that Mom said I could always wait till I was older to wear it. I've worn it every day since I got it and even wore it to bed in the months after she disappeared."

Greg's sights committed the woman in the black-and-white photo to memory, which wasn't an arduous task to begin with. Holding Sush closer, he uttered, "You look just like her."

Sush managed a small smile. "My aunt used to say that." Holding it for a moment longer, she then gently brought both sides of the locket to a shut, clenching it in her palm as she continued, "When Mom didn't come back, my uncle and aunt contacted the police, and after three weeks of investigation, they found her . . . remains . . . in a jungle . . ." Her nose siphoned a sharp inhale as her eyes closed again, letting the tears burn behind the closed lids when she muttered, "Remains from an explosion."

Greg's thumb had stopped stroking her. He'd seen and done a lot of ugly things in his life, but even this shook him. His eyes darkened into a furious shade of onyx. His shoulders stiffened. He was going to kill someone, and it was going to be his best work yet. It was going to be slow and painful, and end with a finale as grand as that explosion.

"But then, something weird happened," Sush proceeded, putting his murder plan to a pause to fully focus on her. "The investigations for the ones behind the explosion just . . . stopped."

Greg's brows furrowed. Deep.

Fuck killing someone. He was going to kill more than one. He was going to kill them all.

"The reason?" Sush scoffed. "They couldn't find anything leading them to any perpetrator. You know, it would've been believable if the police didn't suddenly get swapped with hunters. The policemen leading the first team were dismissed from the force and—two months later—were deported. I tried looking them up, thinking they may have answers, or clues at the very least, but I never found them. To the government and the police, it was a closed case within a year. To my relatives, it was an enigma that they hoped would be resolved, but it never was in their lifetime. And to me—" her free hand wrapped around the cold metal railing, heating it up by sheer aggravation of the injustice that tainted her memory and dictated the course of her life "—to me, I know that, if I want to find the truth, to excavate it from however deep it's been buried, I have to do it myself."

Taking comfort in his touch that—in its own way—told her she wasn't alone before bringing her eyes up to his, she explained, "My mark appeared the moment I decided I didn't want to accept what was done to my mother, to me. I doubt she was perfect, but detonating her took things too far. There are more civil ways to handle things. Also, this is probably a good time to mention that my mark has an anomaly."

She turned, her back facing Greg as she held her hair to one side.

Greg came closer, peering at the gray mark of an octopus with . . . five limbs.

"No other octopus, past and present, had less or more than eight limbs. Believe it or not, this was the anomaly that held me back in terms of rank all those years." She let a moment of silence pass, giving Greg time to study the mark before she said, "The original plan was to hone my hacking skills enough to get into the archives of hunters headquarters. But when I met Kenji as an engineer and we started dating, he eventually saw the mark two weeks later and found out what I was, basically like him, and he introduced me to the hunters' world. I saw a better way to find the truth. I was assessed, and the assessors figured I was defective in some way. Some still do. Others just say it's because I'm the product of Liabilities. By the way, the name of my mother on file? I changed her first name in every registration system connecting me to her, to keep suspicions at bay."

Staring at her mark and swallowing a lump in his throat, he asked, "May I?"

With a slight shrug, she muttered, "Of course."

His fingers gently traced the mark, conveying the shape to memory—the low voltage of electricity felt a little higher this time. Unbeknownst to him, Sush felt something, too—a spark, a charge, one she'd never felt with anyone else, one that traveled through her heart and set the butterflies in her stomach free while also depositing a pleasurable warmth there.

Clearing her throat in a way that made his fingers pause, she uttered, "That's not all of it yet, Greg. There's still one more thing."

He turned her around gingerly, eyes fixed on hers. "I'm listening."

CHAPTER 49

He wasn't just listening. He was absorbing, taking in every word like she was preaching a sermon imparted by the Goddess. The intensity in his eyes radiated his need to know. The range of emotions—from anger to sorrow—marring his face showed that he wasn't just listening, he was connecting with her, *feeling* these things with her, and it was that very action that drew her physically closer to him, because emotionally, she was already attached.

Her throat flexed a hard swallow, and she threw out the biggest confession of the night, "I'm not with the hunters because I want to be." Admitting it to herself, in her head, was one thing. Confessing to someone out loud, someone she hadn't known very long, was foreign and unnerving. "I'm here because I'm convinced there's something in their systems that'll lead me to the truth on the night my mother was murdered. I've been looking for years. I'm sure it won't be something obvious, but I know there's something—a link, a clue that I'm not seeing yet. Remember the files from the east? The one on an explosion of a huntress?"

Greg's heart stopped beating, but Sush went on, "It wasn't a case on my mother, but the modus operandi is creepily similar. I have a lead, and I think I'm getting close." Eyes trailing to his throat, she said, "I'm not here to serve or to protect, Greg. I'm not here because I can or want to help. I'm here to draw blood, for revenge. After I've gotten what I want, I'm leaving, putting all that—the murder, the psychoticness of the plot, the hunters—I'm putting it all behind me and moving on."

Greg didn't look surprised, and she didn't know why she expected him to be. He was a firm believer in revenge as well, evident from the executions. Perhaps it took a bloodthirsty creature to appreciate another bloodthirsty creature.

His hand, rough and warm, reached to cup her cheek when he questioned in a wary baritone, "Are you sure about that, Sush? Are you sure that's what you want?"

She knew this was coming. The doubts, the sheer lack of morality in the whole thing, the fact that she wouldn't be the better person if she trailed down this route.

The fact is: She didn't care about being the better person. If better people lost the ones they loved in the most horrible way imaginable, then she was more than fine with being the worst person. Besides, if one adopted a different perspective, they'd see she was technically ridding the world of dangerous people who'd continue harming others like her mother if Sush herself didn't follow through with her plan to end them. She didn't have to be the better person; she needed to be the person that ended those who took the lives of others.

Sush reluctantly removed his hand from her face. Her eyes darted to his shoulder as her insides began twisting, mourning for having to lose him too. In a weakened voice, she said, "I'm not changing my mind, Greg. I deserve to know the truth. And if there's a cover-up, those behind it sh—"

His grip tightened around her fingers when he interjected, "I don't disagree. In fact, I fully support it. And I'm certain I just fell even more in love with you because of it. What I meant was . . ." as Sush held her breath, he continued in a firm whisper of disbelief, "are you sure you're not here because you want to serve and protect? Perhaps I read you wrong, but you seem to love it in the trenches. The way you get lost in your work is something many creatures fail to find or follow through with in their lifetimes. You clearly don't like people like Valor, Patterson, and a few of those incompetent fools, but you seem to love what you do. You seem to always enter a different universe when you work. Did I read you wrong?"

She'd long known he was checking her out, feeling his eyes linger on her and never seeing those lilac orbs travel to anyone else the same way. But the fact that he read her—and read her accurately—brought out her vulnerable side that she'd never shown to anyone since her late family. It never felt safe to be vulnerable with anyone. Not until him. He might not have known her as well as her family did yet, but it was clear he wanted to.

In a whisper, she admitted, "No, you didn't read me wrong. But—" she sighed "—I don't see how I can keep being there after I've drawn blood. If the murder has been buried this deep, someone powerful is involved, and to topple a person like that would trigger a lot of hunters, if not the government itself. I already have people wanting me suspended—or worse, removed—for the executions I purportedly let happen. This plan to fulfill my own interest? It's going to be ten times worse."

Greg's teeth gritted at the suggestion that someone would want to hurt her, that someone *dared think* about doing such a thing. "There are ways to get around those things, Sush. There are methods to get what you want and get rid of the people against it. Murder itself is an option." In fact, he was already curating the steps for it.

Eyeing him a glare, she declared, "I don't want to draw any more blood than necessary. Murders aside, I wouldn't want to be working in a place that sees me as a traitor. Besides, I'm not out of options. You read my profile. I have a degree and a good enough track record in the non-hunter world to start again somewhere."

Greg sighed, knowing her well enough to know the look in her eye when she wasn't going to change her mind. Slowly, he lifted her hands, watching himself stroke her fingers, getting lost in the motion as frustration creased his forehead. Then, his voice came in a low murmur, "If that is what you choose, if that is what makes you happy, then I don't see why you shouldn't do it."

Happy? Ha. "Not all of us have the luxury to be happy, Greg," she remarked with a smirk that carried evident loss—an emotion that she hid well before tonight.

His jaw clamped taut, heart ached at the thought that she wasn't fully happy. Someone like her deserved all the happiness the world could offer, maybe even more. Knowing better than to disagree, which would push someone of her character away, he decided to simply say, "Maybe, but all of us do have the power to sabotage whatever little we have of it."

There was a pause, a quietness between them, allowing Sush to ponder before he added, "I'm sure you thought this through long before we met. I'm sure you know what you want. And you've clearly shown that you're more than capable of getting anything. At the end of your venture, all I want is for you to be somewhere without ever needing to leave, somewhere you're safe and happy, somewhere that allows you to escape into your universe when you work."

That made her think. Really think. She'd worked in a notable company in the non-hunter world, but she wouldn't say she was happy there. Everything was so rigid and controlled, especially if one was new. Plans were handed out. Innovation was only welcomed if it coincided with the project and research at hand, and it was always about what the market wanted.

Sush didn't give a damn about the market. But she did give a damn about security and everything it took to perfect it, if not improve it. Admittedly, her mother's disappearance and the subsequent discovery of the murder had been a strong motivator behind the direction she'd wanted to take her skills, but the point remained: security, weapons, defenses—they fascinated her. These were the things that brought her soul to life, that launched her from reality and into the universe Greg had apparently caught her in.

He was right. She loved it in the trenches. And although she'd been mentally preparing herself to ultimately let go of it, a part of her was still holding on to the thread of hope that she wouldn't have to. On her best days, she even wondered whether she should just stall the plan or give it up entirely to keep working there. But then she recalled where she was, who she was amongst—the people who had a hand in burying the truth, and she brought herself back on track.

"I won't change my mind," Sush said, firm and sure. "I won't stop until I know what happened, why it happened, and finish off those who made it happen."

A smile cracked on his lips as he brought her closer. "I know. And I hope you know you're not doing this alone. We'll get to the bottom of things together."

It wasn't just gratitude that coursed through her veins, but happiness as well. His words, though delivered in a monotone, touched her heart in more ways than one. His eyes conveyed more emotion than any intonation ever could.

In the midst of her enjoying the silence between them, Greg's eyes went to the springs of her hair, the curls that captivated him every single day, that he only touched when they were close to kissing the other day. Without the pink headband to overshadow them, they looked all the more whole and perfect, especially on her, especially with those eyes.

His fingers reached out, threading through her hair, and he couldn't help but smirk when Sush released a sigh, leaning into his hand that ultimately found her cheek. His thumb traced her lower lip, the yearning from the elevator the other day and the dance floor just minutes ago rekindled, the urge coming back ravenous and ferocious—a hunger she matched judging by the way her pupils dilated and her breath shallowed even though they hadn't even done anything.

Her hand slid up his shoulder as her body glued to his, eliciting his growl as blood shot to his groin before he pressed her against the wall, hand behind her head to shield her skull. The move sent her arousal spiraling free in the space between them, making her want to submit, which she instinctively did when he captured her lips, melting into him as he pressed his mouth deep onto hers. His cocky smirk lifted his lips when she moaned, creating the opening he was waiting for as his tongue plunged in without permission, and he explored, tasting her and stroking her tongue slowly, lovingly, drawing out her whimper, bringing another snarl out of him. She felt him pressed against her thigh—hardness to softness—as her fingers raked through his hair.

Rough hands glided up her arms before they pinned her wrists above her head. Leaving one hand there, Greg's tongue went deeper into her mouth as his free hand trailed back down her bare arm, leaving a searing trail in its wake. He reached her waist before moving quickly to her butt, where he squeezed forcefully, famishedly.

Another gust of air left Sush. Her body arched toward him, relishing in the scorching sensation his palm left on her butt, which moved up her back and finally to her breast. The strong, calloused hand kneaded the softness, and fingers and thumb fiddled with its peak, pinching it to bring her impossibly closer, intensifying his need for him, coaxing her to relinquish control. He felt it was only fair, since his need for her had long been anything but controllable.

When her tongue retreated and she backed away, a fierce growl of protest left the depths of his lungs.

He was far from done.

Instead of looking afraid, she looked softened, flushed as her chest rose and fell. Her heart beneath his palm cupping her breast pounded in trepidation with the quickened breaths. Her eyes drifted from his mouth to his nose, then to his eyes—which looked like he was ruminating on something that matched the very thing she had in mind.

With a conspiratorial smile, she whispered, "Want to get out of here?"

CHAPTER 50

In the bedroom of the diplomatic residence, Greg pushed her up against a wall, mouth sucking and teeth nibbling on her cheek, jaw, and neck as his hands roamed her body, bolder than before, committing each curve to memory.

Her moans came out louder as his mouth trailed down her cleavage and then snuck underneath the garment and padding stitched to the fabric before his tongue greeted her peak with a wet, seductive stroke.

She groaned, eyes rolling back and hands clinging onto his hair for support when her legs gave way. Her underwear was already drenched as heat radiated in waves from her body, need coursing through her veins and making her lower region throb.

"You should know," he began in a low rumble before kissing her breast and continuing, "I'm anything but gentle when it comes to this." With that, he took a nipple between his teeth and bit, and a precious whimper escaped her lips. "It won't be an amateur performance of sucking and kissing. And there won't be whispers of sweet nothings." He went to her other breast, making her back arch before he proceeded to utter, "You'll be bitten, slammed, and spanked, and you *will* scream."

The visual sent Sush on an all-time high. Her arousal filling the room beseeched his animal to pounce, but his human preferred dragging this out, wanting to hear her beg before giving himself to her.

Leaving a wet trail all the way up to her neck, he bit on her earlobe and said, "I won't go slow once we start. And you won't get the respect you got from me in the trenches. I may be at your mercy out there, but here—within these walls," he scoffed, darkly and alluringly, "I will make you *submit.* I will make you *bend*. And I will make you *beg* me to fill you up until you can't *breathe*."

Sush sighed, already surrendering.

Submission had always seemed daunting. It meant giving in, relinquishing all control, trusting the one leading completely. Since Sush had never managed to trust anyone fully, she'd never relinquished control, never given in. It never felt safe to submit.

With Greg, though, it was different. Especially after the way he'd shielded her in the elevator that almost crashed, especially after witnessing the lengths he'd go to protect his family, especially after their heated stares and conversations in recent weeks. Submitting to him didn't just feel right; it made her feel safe, and it made her feel free.

An arrogant smirk tipped the corners of Greg's lips when he peeled the thin straps off her arms, letting the dress pool around her legs before creating a small space between them, hands on both sides of her bare waist as he admired the feast before his darkening eyes. The delicious view got his animal even more impatient, wanting nothing more than to lunge, to bury deep inside her at that very second. But his human remained adamant about savoring every moment, and his lustful eyes trailed to the set of breasts, the bare skin that made his chest rise and fall.

In the midst of his heaving, her hands trailed to her underwear, slowly tugging at the waistband. She enjoyed the way his eyes darkened further as she slid the last garment down inch by torturous inch. A growl left Greg's lips when the masterpiece of brown flesh was now bare and in all its glory before him once the last impediment was on the floor.

Peeling her off the wall, he took his time circling her like a predator would its prey, the features of her body imprinted in his mind. Her skin glowed beneath the dim lights. Her perky ass was a real tease, and those long legs . . . Goddess, he could picture himself licking the mile. And those rising and falling bosoms would fit perfectly into his mouth, hardened nipples that he was going to enjoy nibbling and pulling.

He paused behind Sush, one hand spread on her abdomen as the other reached for her hand, guiding the slender fingers to his zipper, making her breath hitch. They pulled it down together, and Greg unbuckled his belt before his pants joined her dress on the floor. She felt him through his underwear.

Stiff. Hot. Large.

As his hand found her breast once more, he brought her face to the side and took her lips in a devouring kiss, tongue invading her mouth fervently, like he was determined to leave his mark there. Her fingers sneakily trailed up his waistband, giving it a tug, trying to pull down the garment until she figured it was easier to pull him out.

The moment her hand snuck in, a low, alluring growl echoed from his mouth into hers as he gave her breast a merciless squeeze before pinching the nipple and hearing her moan. Her hand found what it was groping for, and she gently brought it out. But before she could go any further, he held her wrist, bringing her hand away, pressing his steel hard-on against the arc of her butt and hearing her sigh.

His lips came to her neck, relishing in the rapid flutter of her pulse beneath his mouth. His deep voice penetrated through the small space between them, "I don't know how you did this in the past, but here's how I'm going to do it." His fingertips trailed down her bare arm, leaving hundreds of goosebumps in their wake. "First, I'm going to choke you with my cock. Then, I'm going to eat you out. After that, I'm going to pound into you so hard you come out shattered and nothing less than a mess. And we're not leaving this room until you can't remember your name." His hand ventured to her ass, cupping it and gripping it fiercely, bringing her close as she gasped when he asked, "Are you amenable to that, my octopus?"

The lust in his eyes, possessiveness in his words, and dominance of his aura sent her further to the edge. Another sigh left her when she leaned into him, pressing herself into his erection when she breathlessly replied, "Yes."

In a more serious tone by her ear, with his nose buried in her curls, he murmured, "At any time any of it gets too much, double tap me anywhere. Is that understood?"

She mm-ed, no longer able to speak.

Holding her by her abdomen and gluing her back to his front, he parted her thighs, sliding his fingers through her slippery folds as he hummed in approval of her wetness. Her body quivered, and his fingers were drenched, her cunt clenched around them as his other hand held her up by her throat.

Slipping his fingers out of her folds, eventually getting her whimpers of protests that sent more blood to his groin, he brought the wetness to his mouth, licking the taste off his fingers and humming by her ear. "I hope you know what you've just agreed to, my huntress. You've awakened this beast before today, and you've baited it tonight. Now, there's no turning back. Get on your knees."

She sank to the floor, so willingly that his chest constricted as his cock throbbed. Her hands worked fast in pulling his underwear all the way down. His hand fisted her hair and tugged it back. Her eyes bulged at his upright shaft, mesmerized by its length and girth. Before he could instruct her to open her mouth, she brought herself to the tip, her tongue toying with the fluid there, the sensation making him groan as a hot shudder rippled through him.

After her first leisurely lick of his length from the base to the tip, he slipped the head into her waiting mouth, letting her push herself deeper until he was completely buried. "Holy fuck," he cursed, not recalling being this responsive this soon, not even when he had his first blowjob. Either he was slipping, or his octopus knew how to take him in a way that no other woman ever did.

She started slowly, then gradually increased her pace, building up a rhythm that had her head bobbing in enthusiasm. The vibrations from her ensuing moans shot up his spine, and he thrust into her until the only sounds in the room were his ragged breaths and the gurgles leaving her throat.

He pounded into her so forcefully that he expected her to double tap, but she never did, not even when her eyes watered. In fact, when he slowed down out of concern for her, her moans almost sounded like protests as her head bobbed more fervently to keep their pace, and he was more than happy to cooperate, speeding up from there.

At his climax, his body stilled as his viselike grip on her hair locked her head to his cock, shooting his load into her mouth, hearing her moan in satisfaction as his orgasm burned through him, feral and heated. The sensation coursed through her as if his pleasure was her own, and she sucked him gently to the end of it.

"Open your mouth," he ordered, lifting her chin. "I want to see it."

She complied, and his primitive snarl that followed traveled through her like a pleasurable wave. Strong finger pads massaged the back of her neck as she swallowed. His thumb captured her jaw, not roughly like she expected, but carefully, gingerly, affectionately. His eyes stayed on her, gazing at her like she'd just given him the world.

This part of the experience was new to him. He couldn't for the life of him remember wanting to see his own cum in a woman's mouth, and he'd never massaged any of their necks to ease the downflow or paused to caress a face.

So much for not being gentle.

Hoisting Sush up when he met her lust-filled eyes, he tossed her on the bed face-up and instructed, "Legs. Spread. Now."

She complied, her legs parted to reveal the throbbing region as the scent of her arousal saturated the air while Greg removed his shirt. Her body heated further at the sight of his sculpted physique, one that would put models to shame.

Each block of muscle was as distinct as it was symmetrical with its counterpart, the muscles' allure only shadowed by the chest hair that mostly gathered in the upper area.

Forget models, Greg's body would even make Greek gods envious.

Greg's smirk boasted how much he was enjoying the attention—her attention. And the scent of her intensifying arousal was as intoxicating as it was consuming.

He spread her thighs even wider to an angle Sush didn't think she was capable of reaching, and his face buried itself at the source of her arousal. She moaned the loudest that night when his hot tongue flicked through her folds. Her legs weakened from his toying around with the layers and the bump of her clit. And that was just the test run, a taste of what he could give her.

As his tongue left and she desperately tried to find it again, he held her by her thighs, leaving wet kisses along the valley between her legs and cunt, then asking in a voice thick as gravel, "Do you want me to eat you out, my octopus?"

"Yes," came her breathless answer, fingers digging into his hair, more than ready to take whatever he was about to give her.

Two of his fingers plunged into her entrance, getting her first of many screams for the night.

As he worked up a rhythm, he asked, "Do you want me to make you cum?"

"Yes."

Rewarding her with an increased pace as a steady stream of moans echoed off the walls, he questioned in a warning, "Will you let anyone else eat you out? Will you let someone other than me make you moan and scream?"

"N-No."

"Is that hesitance I hear, my huntress?" Greg's fingers continued at a punishing pace, eliciting more screams and moans, making it hard for her to speak, to think. "Answer me," he demanded, knowing full well that what he'd termed as hesitance was nothing more than a temporary impairment of her speech as she writhed in pleasure under his control.

"No. I . . . oh . . . mm . . . I won't."

"You won't *what*?" he pressed without compunction.

"I won't let . . . ohh . . . I won't let anyone else do this. Mmm. Only you. Please." The last word came out so labored with the torture of waiting that Greg gave into his urge to bring ecstasy to her.

His mouth went back to her clit, alternating between torturously slow licks and exhilarating fast ones. He and his animal were starving for her, feasting on her like a man possessed. His fingers dug into her flesh to hold her still. When his mouth found the spot that had her pushing herself against him, he held her in place and gently took her clit between his teeth. His tongue flicked over the sensitive nub, and her screams echoed off the walls when she exploded.

Greg groaned, savoring her taste, lapping up every drop as she trembled beneath his touch. When the last of the delectable fluid was gone, he licked the area like he was asking for more, though he was forced to come to terms with the fact that he'd devoured it all a little too quickly.

"That was one fantastic appetizer, my love."

When she caught her breath, her head lifted to look at him, her face flushed from her orgasm as euphoric eyes shone when she said, "Glad to hear this isn't the end. I was beginning to grow concerned with your stamina when you stop doing anything."

He flipped her over with an enticing growl, turned on by the challenge as he spanked her left butt, then her right, drawing out her screams before the yelps melted into moans as she brought herself up by pushing her knees into the mattress, inching her butt closer to him.

As his hands grip the reddened flesh, he uttered, "Trust me, baby. I'm not the one you should be worried about."

He grabbed a silver-foiled packet from the drawer—a supply he had just stocked up after meeting this delicious thing—slid the rubber on, and glided his shaft into her without warning, stretching her walls as she released another scream at his sheer size while he grunted at her tightness.

She felt him in her stomach and, for a moment, wondered if she'd be able to breathe. But the pain, as Sush discovered, was brief. The following sensation was one of fullness, completeness. She'd admit, when she sucked on him, she didn't know if he'd fit. But now, she smiled to herself that he did. He fit perfectly.

Greg pulled out a little only to begin pounding into her hard and fast, riding her like he was in a race and he was determined to come out a champion.

Conversation and verbal teasing ceased. More moans and grunts followed as he slammed into her with a pace that Sush wasn't familiar with because this was her first experience with a lycan, and not just any lycan, but one of the fastest of their kind. She should have been worried for herself, but she didn't have the mental space for that at the moment.

True to his word, she couldn't even remember her name. She was riding her waves of pleasure that were at an all-time high, knowing that she'd give anything to make it go on forever, resisting the urge to explode—twice—just so she could make it last.

"You sly creature." Greg caught her resistance, and she could almost picture him smirking, which he was—in amusement and with a determination that accepted her challenge. Hands cupping her breasts and toying with her nipples, he uttered, "Two can play at this game. Let's see if you'll be able to do that one more time."

And she tried to, very hard. But between his quickened pounding, breast kneading, nipple pinching, and alluring voice whispering into her ear—how bare she was beneath him, how she was at his mercy, how his cock was buried deep within her, and how he was stretching her over and over—his hand fisted her hair and tugged, and she crumbled within seconds, clenching around him as he stiffened in her, grunting as their orgasms ripped through them like a raging cyclone.

His body fell next to hers. Their eyes locked as labored breaths slowed, coming down from their high.

Her hand reached for his face, which softened under her touch. Her fingers traced his brows, the area under his eyes, the crook of his nose, and the curve of his lips, where his mouth snatched her thumb, savoring her taste on the small structure, drawing out her beatific smile.

Letting go of her thumb and kissing it lightly, he pushed himself up, hovering over her. "Looks like I'll have to get you extra coffee tomorrow if you plan on getting through the day."

"It sounds like you're suggesting I won't be able to make it through the day." With a smirk that attempted to match his cockiness, she questioned, "Do you think this is the most vigorous exercise I've done on a weeknight?"

Greg's lilac eyes turned a deep onyx as his growl reverberated through her ears, jostling her heart that didn't just beat for herself anymore—it beat for him too. Smiling broadly and leaving a light kiss on his lips, she confessed, "I was going to say this has been the most vigorous exercise I've done on any night, not just a weeknight." She pecked another kiss on his chin before she whispered, "Thank you."

The onyx faded as his lessening scowl and brightening face promised something—punishment. Reaching for another silver-foiled pack, he tore it off and slid on the next condom, snarling, "You're going to regret pulling my leg."

"Am I?" she challenged with a gleam in her eye.

He thrust into her in one fell swoop, making her back arch toward him as she gasped, eyes rolling back. He smirked at how powerful her reaction made him feel. He leaned by her ear and whispered, "I guess we'll see."

It was a long night, different from all his others, different from all of hers too. She moaned at the building pressure, squirmed when he identified her sensitive regions, and begged when he slowed down just to hear her breathless plea.

This time, it wasn't her who was holding back. It was him, letting her teeter on the edge for too long before the final plea tore him from within and his animal made him cave, giving their all to watch her shatter beneath him as he shot hot liquid into the rubber buried deep inside her, the surge of electrifying pleasure coursing through him and leaving a mark on his soul. There was no way he'd be able to give her up now even if he wanted to.

Why he had settled with performing intercourse with anyone else before Sush, he didn't know. Sex with this gorgeous, ravishing octopus was beyond perfection.

Their lips met, and they devoured each other until they were ready for the next round, working their way around and learning each other's bodies deep into the night, falling asleep only when Sush could no longer move.

As Greg held her in his chest, his hand went for her thighs, massaging them to ease the soreness that he hoped—for her sake—wouldn't affect her in the morning. But the thought of her walking or looking different the next day because of him, because of everything they'd done tonight, tipped his lips, and he planted a kiss on her forehead, letting her soft breathing guide him to his own slumber.

CHAPTER 51

The next day did not start with good news, nor did it progress with any. Abbott and his deputy were dead, as were many others who had been exposed to the poison. Only three of the sixteen archers survived the coma, with the doctors reporting that the survivors' ability to make a full recovery remained uncertain; thus they were under strict monitoring. Hazel survived, but her condition remained under supervision as well. And she was awake for not more than four hours a day, as were the three archers. Even during their short hours awake, they weren't lucid enough to recall the events from the other day.

The next chief archer had to be appointed, but the discussion and vote wouldn't be for another week, so Valor was chief in name, and Sush and Patterson were co-chiefs behind the scenes. Everyone, including the entire defense ministry, knew this.

"Fucking assholes," Greg cursed, not bothering to tone it down when she gave him the news after returning from the noble leader's office.

Flatly, she replied, "Yes, always have been and always will be. Now get off my chair, Greg. This is my desk."

Smirking at her feistiness, he leaned into her seat and swiveled for a bit, refusing to budge. "Having trouble standing already? It's barely noon."

With a hand buckled at her hip, she retorted, "If anything, I'm having trouble with your self-inflation."

A slow smile spread across his lips before he stood and sauntered to her. Hand clutching her elbow, his mouth closed in on her ear, and he questioned in his deep voice, "Are you?"

His breath coasted across her ear and trickled down her neck, sending a rush of heat spiking through her core. It was insane how two words that were completely unrelated to anything sexual were able to set her ablaze and send her arousal spiraling free.

Not bothering to keep his knowledge to himself this time, especially not after their magical night, he took a deep, animalistic, audible inhale, the smile morphing into an arrogant smirk when he muttered, "If that's the case, I'd say you have an appetite for trouble."

With that, his hand left her elbow, fingers brushing across her skin as he left her station.

Just like that.

He'd turned her on, getting her hot and bothered, and left, letting her deal with her flushed face on her own. The mavericks around her were already trying very hard not to look at her in case their taunting smiles revealed their ability to detect her arousal as well.

Sush sank into her chair as business-like as possible, trying to cool herself off before her prying colleagues tossed questions that she didn't know how to answer without smiling like a lunatic.

Her body was sore as hell, but it did get a little better after the warm bath Greg prepared and soaked her in that morning, then massaged her thighs with the little knowledge he absorbed from the Internet while waiting for the tub to fill.

She could walk normally, for the most part. But she'd already been getting questions about her looks, about whether she had changed anything. She hadn't, but she hadn't yet realized the glow that she now carried. Her scowl was replaced with either a flat line or a slight smile, even when she wasn't around Greg. The stern energy remained, but anyone could feel it was less malicious.

They had witnessed her behavioral change at gradual paces, especially after interacting with the duke in the past weeks. When they saw her leave with the duke the previous night, as subtle as the two had tried to be, many wondered if the duke would be so kind as to extend his stay to keep their chief—whom they feared but respected more than Valor himself—as she was now, less daunting.

When she had sat long enough with the paperwork, she left her desk and made her way to the test lab, checking on the progress of the bulletproof bodysuits they were improving on, retractable laser blades to escape confinement, and also safety goggles and masks that every hunter would eventually be mandated to carry around.

The blades, goggles, and masks were a new plan, implemented after the western massacre. The idea was for hunters to shield their senses with the goggles and masks in the presence of zahar while using the blade to cut their way out to safety.

Kenji joined her as they discussed probable complications and brainstormed improvements with the rest of the team.

Greg kept his eye on them, making sure Mr. Sophisticated was staying in his lane and wasn't trying to take the one that was his to claim.

###

In the lab, Kenji had been avoiding Greg's glare, yet their eyes still met. Three times.

Carefully approaching Sush, who had her back against the duke as she ran through the specifications, Kenji kept a safe distance from her and whispered, "Sush, I know we don't owe each other anything, but if you could get your boyfriend to ease on the scowling, I'd owe you."

Sush's brows knitted, head pivoted to him, and eyes blinked in confusion. Then she turned just in time to see Greg's lips tilt into a seductive smirk directed at her. She quickly twisted back to Kenji before being sucked into those lilac eyes.

But right before she got any words out, Kenji spoke, "Don't believe that smile, Sush. He's been giving me the exact opposite the whole morning. I didn't even do anything."

She shrugged and directed her attention back to her tablet. "He knows we dated."

Whisper yelling in panic, he hissed in betrayal, "Why would you tell him that?"

"I didn't. He figured it out himself. But I didn't deny it, so . . . yeah, he knows."

"He knows something that happened eons ago! People move on. What is his problem?"

"Relax, Kenji. The jealousy trait is imprinted in that species' DNA. For all we know, he'd still be like this even if we didn't date. I mean, have you seen his cousin?"

"Don't remind me." Kenji shuddered. "I met the king once before the queen came into the picture. My voice cracked midway when I was greeting him, and it came out sounding like a squeak. I've never greeted him after that. Stayed far away and avoided him at all costs. My brain may be at its best with systems and screens and in underground labs, but I'd take working overtime over meeting the king again."

Sush's tapping and scrolling halted, then turned to him and questioned with a smile that was paving the way to a laugh when she asked, "Squeaked?"

"Alright, now you're just being mean," Kenji noted with narrowed eyes. "The point is, as much as I enjoyed the king putting Patterson in his place when the jaw-incision tale spread to the east, I've done nothing to be at the receiving end of this . . . barbaric wrath." Casting a wary glance at Greg, Kenji murmured, "God, he looks like he's about to pounce." His head swung to Sush. "Has he pounced before? Are these walls thick enough to stop lycans? We should look into modifying the thickness of the glass, for our safety."

"You actually squeaked." Sush chuckled, still stuck on that topic when her sights returned to the device.

"Oh, fuck. Now you've done it," Kenji cursed when what seemed like a gust of wind whooshed from the other end of the trench.

"What?" Sush asked just as the monitor at the entrance beeped and the glass door opened.

In walked the devil himself as Kenji muttered, "Of course. Who needs him to break the glass when he's been given civilized access. God, I can't wait to head back to the east."

With those words, he promptly excused himself as Greg took large strides toward Sush, eyeing her with partially onyx orbs when she noted pointedly, "You're scaring him."

Greg's scowl pulled into an arrogant smirk. "Good. That's the idea."

His hand slid across the small of her back and landed on her waist, trailing to her hip as he offered Kenji another glower when he happened to look, which was when Sush whispered, "He's not doing anything, Greg. Take a chill pill."

As if to make a declaration that everyone at the gala the previous night was well aware of, Greg left a statement kiss on her temple. Positioning his mouth directly at her ear, he murmured, "If Sophisticated does anything, or tries to, he's going to be castrated and buried six feet underground. Alive. And if *you* showed the mildest interest, I'm going to tie you to my bed and fuck you in every hole until he's erased from your system. When we aren't fucking, I'll let you handle octopus matters with one hand untied, but I'll be monitoring your server. Very, very closely. Is that understood, my huntress?"

As sick as it was, Sush found herself wanting to be tied to his bed and fucked in every hole until everything was flushed out of her system. He'd already fucked her in every hole the previous night, without the tying part. She wondered if it'd be better with her hands tied. The image conjured up from his words sent a thrill up her spine, and she tried her best to control it this time as Greg's nose stayed close to her hair, challenging her ability to focus, to think of saying anything but yes.

Grabbing onto a single thread of thought within her reach, her eyes that had been glued to her device gave her an idea to deflect just so she wouldn't end up flushed in a room full of people. Clearing her throat, she actually sounded matter-of-fact when she asked, "One question: How am I going to run tests from there?"

That caught him off guard, turning his homicidal intentions to logical contemplation. His eyes skimmed the room they were in, sighing to himself, knowing he'd be damned if he took this from her. Eventually meeting her waiting gaze, he vouched, "I'll think of something." Voice taking a defensive edge, he continued, "I look forward to hearing about Sophisticated's joke at lunch. We'll see if his sense of humor will end up getting him killed."

Shaking her head and returning her sights to her device, she murmured, "Demented animal."

Greg scoffed, dark and alluring, just the way she liked it. "I'm surprised it took you this long to come to that conclusion. See you in a bit. Let me know if you need more coffee or food."

She mm-ed lightly, affectionately, before Greg made his way out, and she swore she saw—from the corner of her eye—Kenji loosening in relief when the door closed behind the duke.

CHAPTER 52

Seated side by side at a circular lunch table that they weren't sharing with anyone else, Sush disclosed Kenji's joke in hushed tones, and Greg decided the wimpy eastern octopus was humorous enough to not get himself killed. This time.

Fear his cousin? Please. That softie's rules were so much less rigid and so much more standard and boring than Greg's own ever had been.

Sush promptly added, "I'm only telling you this to come clean. Don't spread this around. For all I know, he either told me that in confidence or during a temporary lapse of judgment."

"Well, that's *his* mistake, isn't it?" Greg smirked, practically inviting her strong kick to his leg, at which time the tilt of his lips drew higher when his breath glided across her ear as he purred, "I see you're regaining your strength. Looks like we can look forward to an eventful night."

"Is that all you think about?" Sush reprimanded in a whisper, not admitting to herself that it was all she thought about whenever she wasn't working and her mind was left to wander.

"Oh, I think of other things too. Things that would speed up your recovery from a busy night for us to keep having busy nights."

"Hm," she hummed, as if impressed. "And what did you find?"

His hand on her thigh climbed up her waist, skating across her back, fingertips skimming up her side when he muttered, "There are certain things that I leave to showing, not telling."

"Like your temper when I speak to the opposite sex?" she deflected before her own restraint disappeared.

His lips twitched. "Let's not dismantle the honesty we've built by succumbing to hyperbole, my huntress."

Swallowing the chicken sandwich faster just to be able to deliver a retort a few seconds earlier, she fired back, "How is it hyperbole when you literally said you'd shoot Agu *and* threatened to bury Kenji alive?"

"First of all, I implied that *you'd* shoot him. Not me. I could do it, too, if you allowed me. And second, I'm not like that with every man. I wouldn't mind if you spent hours with your noble leader, your co-chief archer, or many of your baby octopuses."

Her eyes narrowed. "Baby octopuses?"

"Your subordinates."

"I know. They're not babies."

"I'm well aware. Some of their competency just makes them look like they are, I must say."

Bringing her mug to her lips, she murmured, "Demented and arrogant. Impatient and presumptuous even."

"Afraid so," Greg readily admitted. "You've got the worst member of the family, Sush. Probably the worst in the kingdom. Luck has definitely not been on your side."

Eyeing him in amusement, she uttered, "You've got the most overbearing, demanding, obtrusive, and dishonorable member amongst the hunters, one who's here for herself and not the entity. I wouldn't say you've been blessed either."

Chuckling lightly, he brought her hand to his lips. His breath fanned across her skin when he uttered, "If this is who I get from being cursed, I'll never ask to be blessed."

The declaration rang through their ears, its meaning easily understood. When he was "blessed" with the mate bond, he became bonded with a monster that was using him to get to the most important person in his life. The experience didn't destroy him only because he was determined to destroy her and everyone she was connected to first.

Although Sush didn't leave the most memorable first impression—didn't seem to carry a light that made creatures gravitate to her at first blush, her light shone when she began speaking, and it blinded the room when her mind worked, when she worked. Her light parted the darkness in any room, and it was this very element that made people remember her.

Greg learned quickly that he wasn't satisfied with just being acquainted with her skills anymore. He was obsessed with cataloging every way her brow could arch, the rhythm of her chewing that would give him a clue of what she was eating, the sound of footsteps that echoed off the floor differently depending on whether she was thinking while sauntering, pacing in frustration, or just striding across the room to get something.

Even having that set of knowledge now, he felt it wasn't enough. He loved that he could read her mood based on her quirks, but he wanted to *feel* her. He wanted every sliver of emotion running through her veins and every gentle nudge to her heart to be tangible to him. Only to him.

He wanted to mark her.

CHAPTER 53

In the evening, the official training of the chameleons and octopuses in preparation for them to replace the archers at the borders began. They used the simulator in teams of ten—the maximum number of archers stationed at a particular location. They would gauge their competencies from there, forming a baseline, and would eventually work their way down to three—the minimum number of any given team standing guard.

Greg was in the control room behind Patterson, Sush, and a recently called-back Millicent who'd been at her post for two days before the massacre had happened. Their eyes trained on the chameleons armed with guns and knives in the simulator, dodging and running.

One of them couldn't run fast enough along the running belt that made up the floor, and slammed against the simulator wall. A team of octopuses went next, and their performance wasn't much different. At the end of the session, the unspoken consensus was that they had a long way to go.

Most hunters began to wonder whether their commander and defense minister had to swallow further pride when an extension of the lycans' help was ultimately needed.

Valor lingered around for a bit, saw the first few teams, and decided he'd seen enough, telling Patterson and Sush that they needed to "find a way for everyone to pick up archer skills quickly."

Sush feigned ignorance and asked if he'd like to give a demonstration, given that he was an archer himself. Valor harrumphed and muttered something about needing to update the defense ministry about their "progress" and disappeared.

In his absence, Patterson uttered, "He'd probably hand in his resignation before stepping foot in the simulator, especially since we'd be out here watching him."

An upward curl tipped the corner of Greg's lips. "Something we can both agree on."

Though less daunted by the duke, Patterson's anxiety with how far his chameleons and Sush's octopuses had to go only allowed him to manage a shake of his head as he left the room to give pointers from everyone who'd watched them to those who'd just completed the simulation . Millicent and Jason didn't hold back the criticism, nor did Sush and Patterson, but one person did.

Greg didn't say a word throughout the process, simply leaning against the back wall and watching, ears catching the comments made in the background.

Sush's scribbles were pages long now, and Patterson looked five years older just by glancing at the sheer thickness of it, hoping she wouldn't reach the end of the notebook by the end of the day.

As they paused for a break and Sush flipped through the pages, she realized something. Her head turned, eyes meeting the lilac pair, and her brows rose. "Is there a reason you haven't said anything?"

They were alone. The rest had gone for a breather.

Greg's stationary posture had his left arm stretched across his chest and his right elbow resting on the horizontal plane created by the left, fingers resting on his chin and covering his lips like he was physically stopping any words from spilling out.

"Just say it," she said, exhaustion evident from her face and voice.

Greg detached himself from the wall, approaching her. His hands reached the back of her shoulders, and his thumbs worked their way along her tensed muscles as he reluctantly murmured, "You're not all ready."

"Obviously," Sush huffed, though finding relief in his caress.

That was until he said, "I doubt any of you can be within the next year."

"Wait, what?" Her head spun too fast, and the sensation of what felt like a snapped vein at her nape had her cursing as she winced.

A sharp breath of air left Greg's nostrils as his animal reprimanded him, blaming him for her brief anguish. His thumbs shifted their attention along her nape, looking for the tightness before smoothening it out. "That was my fault. I apologize."

"No," she began, forefinger lifted. "Your fault was not speaking up when the rest of us were firing insults."

"Comments."

"Offensive comments—insults. Come on, tell me. I never thought you'd need permission to speak." She spun herself around in her swivel chair to face him, making his hands that were at her nape hang midair before they fell to his side.

His lilac eyes went to the simulator, and he said, "Well, first, their physiques are off. That's why at least one on each team got thrown at the wall. I'm surprised there weren't more. Another thing is the simulation itself. Sush, they're not very . . . practical."

Her head tilted, eyes enlarged and shone to comprehend. "Meaning?"

His hand reached for her face, thumb trailing down her jaw. "The simulation is training them to fight off thugs that come in a gang of five to ten, or lycans and wolves in some instances. That's not the immediate enemy. The immediate enemy either operates alone or is a team that only uses a single member to intrude. It's an enemy who knows your systems and inventories. If you and Patterson intend to get them and yourselves ready, perhaps energy should be directed toward how the hunters should retreat or—even better—attack their single assailant who can kill them with nothing more than having access to the hunters' sprinklers system or knowing that metal walls could encase an entire floor. I understand this is the standard training procedure of the archers, but without the eastern and western threats neutralized, training the chameleons and octopuses like archers will only kill them the way the archers had been killed. Consider narrowing the scope of training for now. You can start all this . . ." he waved at the empty simulator ". . . step-by-step, tedious, all-encompassing archer training when you have time to spare. I wouldn't recommend it at present."

As she took in his words, pondering hard on the things she would recommend discarding, the familiar warm and callous hand cupped her cheek, lifting her face. Guilt impaired his features, his stomach knotted as his brows drew together, lips downturned as his thumb traced the length of her jaw once more when he said, "I should have phrased that with less . . . judgment."

Sush blinked, not knowing what the hell he meant. The confusion was quickly replaced with a flare of irritation. "Greg, we were all judging. We've phrased things more harshly than you did. Safety before diplomacy. I honestly feel like strangling you for keeping that to yourself. The logic is so obvious. We should have seen it. And you didn't say anything when we didn't see it!"

"Hm." His face softened, a ghost of a smile coming up as his fingertips trailed down her neck, his thumb tracing the middle of her throat. "Are you really going to *strangle* me for the misalignment in our critical vigor?"

"Are you admitting it's your fault, that you weren't being hard enough on us, on me?" she challenged. Her tone and the glint in her eye sent blood straight to his groin.

He smirked, his grip tightening around her neck. "Was I not being hard enough on you?"

His thumb traced her lower lip, edging toward the middle, coaxing her lips to part, which they did. Her tongue glided across his thumb. The mere sight of it darkened his eyes, and the sensation elicited his growl. He leaned in and smashed his lips on hers, savoring her taste, drowning in her moans as a hand palmed her breast and the other rested on her nape to angle her head.

As the aroma of her need took over the room and her mouth left his for air, he sucked on her neck, murmuring against her skin, "I thought I could wait until tonight." That made two of them. "But I need you clenching around my cock. Now."

"What happens if I say no?" Sush whispered breathlessly.

Pulling away from her neck, taking his warmth and kisses with him, he leveled his eyes with her, seeing the hunger and need that mirrored his own when he uttered, "Then you're to be blamed for our miseries."

A taunting smirk lifted her lips. "Denying accountability?"

"Warning you of the consequences."

"Sounds dire."

"It is."

"Better safe than sorry, then."

CHAPTER 54

Greg scooped her from the chair and fastened her legs around his hips as his hands on her butt pinned her to him, bringing her to the wall, where he locked the door and was immensely grateful for the lack of cameras in this room as she began grinding his steel-hard rod.

He held her still so he didn't cum before he wanted to—before she did—as his fingers and thumb moved skillfully along her shirt, unbuttoning from the top. Her black lace bra got him even more aroused. He never thought he had a thing for lace lingerie.

And he didn't. Not until they were on her.

Undoing the front clasp, he devoured her softness, and his tongue toyed with the hardened peak as she gasped, jerked, and moaned. Her fingers in his hair pulled at his locks at delicious intervals.

His hand headed south, undoing the top button and dragging the zip down at a slow, torturous pace, so much so that Sush whimpered and shifted in protest. But Greg held her still, gluing her to the wall as he took his time with the zipper, even though all he wanted was to rip it off. The wafting scent from her wetness got stronger with each lowered inch, and when the matching black lace underwear was revealed, Greg broke away from her breasts to admire the thin, see-through fabric against her skin.

Sexy as hell.

The only thing that made it better was that it was drenched. Palming the area and feeling it throb against his hand, his mouth dropped to hers again as he gave the needy area a few strokes, finger lifting the hem and teasing the part of her that felt empty and needed something to fill it.

His lips skated against hers when he whispered, "I'll get you new ones."

"New wha—" she gasped as her eyes bulged wide, shock taking over her face as the sound of torn fabric bounced off the walls, the cold air making the bareness shrink. In a frantic whisper, she exclaimed, "I don't pack extra lingerie to work, Greg. What if I get my clothes dirty?"

As Greg stuffed the torn underwear into his back pocket, the obnoxious smirk played on his lips. "Your clothes will be fine. I promise to lap up every single drop of juice you give me." The drawn-out manner he uttered the second half of the sentence sent a rush of heat back down there, quickly working up the moisture again.

Greg continued, "And don't worry about walking around like this. Those who can smell it will know who you belong to."

Before she could argue, his lips were back on hers, breathing her in, taking her logic and rationality with him as his fingers filled her space in one swift motion and thumb massaged her clit. His fingers were fine, but they weren't enough. They weren't . . . big enough.

Her hands around his neck traveled fast to his pants, and he sucked on her neck as she undid the belt, the hook, and then the zipper. The bulging hardness under her palm had her moaning with need, and he snarled, "Take it out."

Groping her way to the waistband, she finally found her way in. A thrill shot up her spine when the shaft twitched under her touch. Her feet worked to get rid of his pants, which Greg only let fall after he'd gotten out the condom he kept in the back pocket for emergencies.

Taking the silver pack from him, she leisurely extracted the part of him she wanted like she was drawing it out, inviting it to the room, feeling the girth from the base all the way to the top that was coated with precum, her hand swirling at the moisture as he grunted and growled low enough for her to hear.

His reaction lifted her lips, knowing that she'd awakened his animalistic urges. He didn't just make her feel desired, he made her feel powerful. The way she slid the rubber on was so painfully slow that it was obvious she had already begun playing with fire—his fire.

Greg had had enough of waiting. The next few things happened so fast that Sush didn't even have time to process before it happened: him bringing her hands above her head, his shaft thrusting into her in one go, and the pumping beginning hard and fast, his balls slapping her flesh as his girth stretched her walls with each bittersweet thrust.

"So fucking tight," Greg uttered through the pounding. "Do you like this, my octopus? Do you like me stretching your tight little cunt?"

"Mm. Yes. Oh!"

"Has anyone stretched you like this?"

"No."

"Who's the only one who can stretch you like this?"

Despite knowing that it was his ego that was begging to be stroked, she was too near her high to disappoint him. "You. Only you."

"That's right. As a reward for your lack of hesitance today, how about we take it to the next level?"

"The next l—" Her screams cut her sentence off midway as Greg utilized his animal's speed to increase the pace, a pace that Sush had never—in her wildest dreams—thought existed.

"How does it feel?" he asked, despite having just watched her eyes roll back, her head fall backward, and her body arch toward him, giving him closer access to her set of breasts that bounced to his thrusts, like even they submitted to his claim over her.

When she only murmured unintelligibly, he toned down the pace and was immediately met with her eyes amplifying loss, the movement of her butt protesting the decreased pace. When he increased it again but kept it controlled, knowing that Sush was aware he could go faster, he demanded, "Answer me: How does it feel?"

The fullness of him was addicting, and she knew that after him, she couldn't hope to climb to her peak on her own. "Like heaven. It feels like heaven."

Greg beamed through ragged breaths, rewarding her with the acceleration she needed, shooting her to her climax as she clenched around him. Their sweat-dotted bodies were flush against each other, and she felt him pulse, spurt after spurt, shooting into the condom. His breathing was labored, his face resting in the crook of her neck, indulging in her scent.

Bringing his forehead to hers, his breath tickled her lips when he whispered, "You feel like heaven to my hell."

Ironically, she felt it was the opposite: that he was heaven to her hell.

CHAPTER 55

In the midst of brainstorming with Patterson, Millicent, and Jason, Greg excused himself from Sush's side with a light kiss to her temple when he received a link from Nash Beaufort.

'Your Grace, I hope I'm not interrupting.'

'If you were, I would have blocked you out. What is it, Nash?'

'This is about the inventory of poisons you requested a few days back.'

The poison room on the archers' floor had been infiltrated and destroyed, most poisons in the inventory gone, and their supplier was facing a shortage, so Greg offered to help stock them back, sending the list of substances that the hunters needed to Nash. *'Don't tell me you don't have enough in stock.'*

'No, no. I'm not an amateur, Your Grace. But I did notice something peculiar, though let me first say this is purely speculation. The, uh... poisons that you requested ... there happens to be a combination that enables the production of zahar.'

Shock rained over Greg, making him pause before responding, *'Repeat and elaborate.'*

'Zahar isn't a . . . how do I say this . . . a genesis of usual chemicals. It's synthesized with the combination of brodifacoum, difenacoum, bromadiolone, and flocoumafen—all of which were listed in your request. So the synthesis starts with ten milliliters of br—'

'Skip the process, Nash.'

'Right. In essence, those four are capable of being lethal on their own—with the right conditions, of course. Zahar can easily be made with these by anyone who knows how to operate the Internet.'

'So that's why we hit dead ends at the zahar trail after the eastern attack. It wasn't zahar that was bought. It was the other four that made it.'

Nash pointed out the more pressing issue, *'And it means the culprit looms within the hunters' circle, Your Grace. No one else would know what they have in storage, I hope?'*

'I hope so as well. Anything of concern in the list of purchasers for the four poisons to make zahar?'

'Well, yes and no. No, because the types of buyers have always been consistent. Yes, because I'm not sure whether the hunters use our supply through a middleman or have a supplier of their own. I'm not familiar with human territory, Your Grace. Should I have someone contact my purchasers to see whether they've sold the products and, if so, to whom?'

'That would be helpful . . . though tedious.'

'I'm open to suggestions, Your Grace.'

'So am I. Unfortunately, I can't think of anything at the moment.' A low chuckle came from Nash's side as a guilty smile tipped Greg's lips. He thought for a moment, finger tapping his chin before he linked, *'I recall you have logos at the bottom of vials and flasks . . . but repackaging would cut off that trace like a thirty-sixth-hour mark on scent sprays.'*

'Indeed. Shall I await further instructions or execute while waiting, Your Grace?'

'Execute. The hunters are now more vulnerable than ever. The last thing we need is an enemy strengthening their base here and affecting our territory later in the future.'

'I'll see to it that it's done. Is there anything else, Your Grace?'

'Not at the moment. Thank you for the update, Nash.'

He ended the link, eyes staring into space.

"Hey," came a soft hush. A hand fell on his shoulder. Though absolutely no force was physically applied, the touch itself commanded he turn to face her. "Who was it? What happened?"

Noting that they weren't alone, he brushed a kiss across her cheek to murmur, "Nash. Tell you later."

###

After wrapping up, Greg drove her home and filled her in on Nash's update on the way.

In her apartment, with Greg taking up more space than Sush herself ever had, Sush was mindlessly stuffing clothes into the opened suitcase on her bed as they discussed whether the poisons they ordered were capable of producing anything else lethal. Sush stalked into the bathroom to get the toiletries as she began tossing ideas of creating a raincoat that would repel poison.

In her absence, Greg got a better look at his surroundings, not having her to distract him and suck his attention like a vortex. There was a tablet on the nightstand, along with an alarm clock. He then peeked into a pulled-out drawer revealing underwear of dark tones, smiling to himself, knowing that he now had one in his pocket. As Sush blabbered on, his fingers ran through the fabric of black, gray, green, and blue tenderly, and that was when he noticed something pink.

A brighter shade of pink than her headband.

Curious and uncouth, he extracted it, which was when Sush emerged, stuffing the toiletries in the bag, seemingly unfazed that Greg was holding the very thing she hid in her lingerie drawer. "Hey, give me that drawer, will you?"

"What is this?" Greg's face snapped to her, brows knitted, accusations written all over his face.

Her arranging of the items in the suitcase halted. Her spine straightened when a hand fastened at her hip as her eyes narrowed. "You've never seen a vibrator before? Really?"

He had hoped it was something *disguised* as a vibrator. Hell, he didn't care if it was a gun. Anything but a fucking vibrator! "Why the fuck do you still have this?"

"Like any normal creature, I have urges. Drawer, Greg. Now."

As Greg pulled out the wooden drawer and tossed it on the bed, the hand holding the vibrator crushed the device and snapped it in two before he tossed it into the trash.

Sush's packing paused at the snap. Their eyes locked as Greg's fiery gaze penetrated into her part shocked, part annoyed one when he declared, "You don't need it."

"You do realize we only began fucking yesterday, right?"

Holding her gaze, he plodded to her with downturned lips, hand reaching around her back, and brought her front flush against his. "We didn't just fuck, Sush. We made love. There's a difference. The only things you've been fucking are that thing and anyone that came before me. Are we on the same page?"

A shade of disbelief entered her eyes. "You're saying you've never made love to anyone before me?"

They both knew he was in love with Izabella—deeply in love, so it was impossible that he hadn't made love to her. But it was only at this moment he realized he hadn't thought about his former mate sexually in months, since finding out about her betrayal. And he hadn't thought about that woman at all the moment he laid eyes on his octopus on the day of the executions.

It was as if Sush erased the remnants of Izabella from his intimate life with her presence, even before their heated sessions the previous night. Whenever Izabella came to mind now, his brain went along the lines of declaring her as a danger, slut, and hell-qualified bitch. He was no longer attracted to her in the ways he once was.

His throat worked and darkened eyes softened, hand reaching to trace the curve of Sush's ear. "I would've forgotten had you not reminded me." His thumb trailing along her jawline stopped at her chin. "Please don't remind me about it. You have a way of making other creatures forgettable. Let's keep it that way."

In a whisper that was initially meant to be a scream, softened by his gaze and words, she hissed, "Then don't remind me about mine either. God, you lycans! No, wait. Maybe it's just you."

"Maybe," Greg murmured with a slight crook of his lips before letting her get back to packing as she murmured something about him not just being demented, but also temperamental and possessive—like an animal.

Greg's lycan, who listened to the murmuring complaints with a leisurely wagging tail, simply nodded in agreement at the labels. Unlike his cousins, he didn't mind having more than a few flaws. If the flaws had gotten him this far, and gotten him to her, they weren't really flaws to begin with, were they?

His line of thinking was confirmed when Sush—while slamming the suitcase shut, used the noise from the zipper to block out a low-volume grumble that sounded like, "Crazy how I'm still falling for you even with all of that."

Greg's biting of his bottom lip did nothing to hide the increasing radiance and smile spreading across his face. Despite her tone, his brain interpreted her words to be an affectionate embrace that was so warm and promising.

When the zipper got stuck and Sush groaned in annoyance, huffing a breath from the exertion, Greg snuck a kiss to her lips and said, "I love you too."

She was left stunned, and the apples of her cheeks flushed crimson.

He used the momentary silence to help with her zipper, working it a few inches back and pressing the top of the suitcase down, then pulling the zip seamlessly to the end. Lifting it off the bed with one hand, he asked, "Is that everything?"

"Uh . . ." She shook herself out of her daze and skimmed her room, grabbing another bag that stored her archery bow. "Yeah, that's everything."

They were two steps out the door when Greg snatched her bag from her, making her mutter, "Deranged but gentlemanly."

"As gentlemanly as anyone who'd go through your underwear drawer."

She scoffed, a smile lifting her lips. "It's not as if I'm not going to do the same at your place later."

In the car, Greg began, "It's the end of the week tomorrow. I'm headed back to the kingdom."

"Yeah, I know," she said, forcing a smile even though her chest dreaded the thought.

His hand reached for hers, bringing their eyes to meet when he said, "I'd like you to come with me. Do you want to come?"

She blinked. "What?"

"There's a family event of sorts next week. Would you like to come with me? It's time you meet everyone. It's time you meet *her*."

Sush's eyes bulged wide. "Her? You're sure?"

CHAPTER 56

Greg wasn't sure. He was definitely sure how he felt about Sush, but he wasn't sure if those feelings would be accepted by his little sweetheart. Still, he wanted to give this a chance.

Sush was more nervous about meeting the pup than she was about meeting the other octopuses on her first day as a hunter in training. She had unpacked her clothes and went through her options so long that she and Greg didn't have time for sex.

Greg was on his routine call with Enora as he watched Sush swap one shirt for another on the bed, ponder, then swap the pants for another pair of pants. Brows arched deep like she was trying to crack a code, she then brought the shoes she intended to wear and placed them at the foot of the bed, then swapped the shirt again.

Enora excitedly told Greg that she wanted to share a secret with him the next day. At the end of briefing her uncle on how her day went, she then asked about his day, and he had to clear his throat before admitting he was bringing someone to her archery competition.

The mood shift was quick; silence permeated the line until Greg asked if she was alright. Sounding like she was on the verge of tears, Enora asked if he'd "found" Ugly Deli and was bringing back that woman.

Restraining himself from saying that Ugly Deli was most likely next to the thrown-out teddy bear in some dump site, or had already gone through the recycling and come out as a new product, Greg fervently denied that Izabella was ever coming back. Again. He made a mental note to ask the queen for the appropriate age to explain death to the pup.

Though sounding less upset, Enora was nonetheless skeptical. Her earlier eagerness to see him the next day was now fogged with conflict. And it was the first time Lucy didn't have to remind her about needing to hang up for bedtime. She tried to sound normal when she bid her uncle goodnight, but a pup's acting could only go so far.

Greg linked the queen right after, practically confessing to upsetting Enora. Lucy assured him that she and Xandar would take care of it.

At the dining table, Enora numbly welcomed the apple-and-pomegranate-flavored ice cream her father was bringing to her mouth as she sat on his lap, eyes downcast, placing her tiny hands on Xandar's much larger one holding her as her mind wandered.

Her parents repeatedly told her that it wasn't going to be Izabella and suggested she might feel differently about her uncle's mystery guest.

Ken climbed out of bed when he found the lights of the corridor still on and followed the scent of his mother to the kitchen. His eyes zoned in on the ice cream going into his sister's mouth, feeling something akin to injustice and abandonment until his mother's voice rang through his ears, "Chocolate chip and walnut, Muffin?"

Ken beamed at his pet name born out of his mother's severe muffin cravings when she carried him and Enora, leaving the other less severe craving/nickname—Cookie—for Enora.

"Yes please, Mommy." He grinned and dawdled across the room as Lucy got out the tub of Ken's favorite ice cream, getting a scoop and putting it into a bowl before seating him on her lap as he took the wooden spoon and rushed through the cold, creamy dessert.

Reida came next, frightened by the thunder that came out of nowhere outside her window before rain fell. The eldest princess would normally go to her parents' room and climb on her father's side of the bed if she needed to feel safe, but like her brother, her nose led her to the kitchen. Xandar got out the peppermint and blueberry tub, repeating the process in another bowl, planting his eldest on the other side of his lap, holding his girls like a proud father.

The pups rambled on about school and classmates when Enora murmured that their uncle was bringing a stranger. Reida choked, and Ken dropped his spoon. A modicum of relief entered the youngest pup's eyes when her siblings shared her pessimism, her mother getting her sister a glass of water. Only when the choking stopped did the room mellow from its panicked state.

Before any debate, discussion, or argument could unfold, Xandar hastily placed Enora on his shoulders, put Reida on her feet, and dropped the empty bowls into the sink. He specifically asked Lucy to leave them, saying he'd clean them up in the morning. Then he said to their pups, "It's late. Time for bed. We have a big day tomorrow." Looking up, he held his youngest's gaze when he asked, "Don't we, Cookie?"

Enora mm-ed and managed a smile, eyes droopy as her head leaned into her father's hair when he took her and Reida to bed.

Ken stayed behind to wipe the ice cream stains with Lucy, then admired the clean floor with a proud smile as his mother washed the bowls and spoons. He held her hand afterward as she flipped off the lights and walked him to his room, tucking him into bed and kissing him goodnight again, then leaving when his father's figure appeared at the door.

###

The skepticism remained even in the morning. The pups began wondering what Sush would look like, whether she'd be as creepy as "that woman," and whether her fingers would be as cold.

Lucy sighed, meeting Xandar's concerned gaze, and instead of telling her children to "be nice" like she did with Izabella, she said, "Be honest with your uncle about his guest, but also remember to be fair and be kind."

"Yes, Mommy," the pups chorused, albeit reluctantly.

If Enora had it her way, she wouldn't want to meet anyone new at all. So when she saw her uncle at the kindergarten archery range with a brown-skinned woman, she surprised herself when curiosity flickered through her in a way that never did with Ugly Deli.

Her uncle's open arms and squatted posture brought a smile to her face as she ran and hopped into his embrace, hands wrapped around his neck as he lifted her off the ground.

Sush's anxiety was reduced by the sight before her—of a man normally so brooding and cold now breaking into a smile as he pressed a kiss to the little girl's hair while asking the pup in a conspiratorial whisper, "What's the secret, sweetheart? I couldn't sleep last night thinking about it."

CHAPTER 57

Enora grinned, showing her incomplete set of teeth when her arms shot to the sky. "Lionel MacDonald changed schools! Yay!"

"Enora, pipe down," Lucy reprimanded, trying not to make eye contact with any parents looking at her daughter either in bewilderment due to their unfamiliarity with her classmate's name, or in amusement because their own pup had been victims to Lionel's misbehavior as well.

Another pup not far away even threw his own arms up in the air and exclaimed, "Yay!" at Enora's announcement, even though he'd already celebrated the day before when their class was told the news. Only then did Lucy have the courage to meet the other set of parents' sheepish gazes and smiles.

"Hello, Sush. Glad you could make it," Lucy welcomed her with a smile, needing a desperate change of subject before her pup got carried away.

"Lucy, hi." Sush pushed a smile that hopefully matched hers.

The utterance of her first name was a very specific declaration, and the queen's mouth gaped for a moment before it morphed into a smile when her eyes locked with Greg's smiling ones.

Turning to Xandar, Christian, and Annie, Sush greeted, "Your Majesty. Your Graces." The three greeted her with warm smiles.

"Blackfurs," Greg uttered their way with a curt nod, to which Annie responded with a cordial lift of her lips and Christian with a similar nod without a word, lips pulled back down into a tight line.

Alissa, Desmond, Hailey, and Ivory were there, too, carefully stepping into the circle, greeting their boss and acknowledging what many of their colleagues in hunters headquarters suspected would be the new duchess who—in their comrades' words—was less pretentious, more daunting, more intelligent, and easier to read.

Enora stole everyone's attention when she asked, "Is this your new fwiend, Uncle Gweg?"

Bringing her closer to Sush, he kept his anxiety to himself when he introduced them, "Yes, her name's Sush."

Enora's head cocked. "Like Japanwese food?"

It was on the tip of his tongue to say Sush tasted better than any food, and he had to physically swallow before replying, "Well, almost. And you want to know something else, sweetheart?"

Her eyes stayed on Sush when she hummed, "Mm-hm?"

"She shoots arrows too," Greg whispered like it was a secret shared only with her.

Enora's head spun to him, and he could see a whole galaxy of stars behind the lilac orbs when she asked excitedly, "Weally?"

"Yeah, ask her." His chin gestured Sush's way, bringing Enora even closer when his niece looked like she was trying to climb over him to get a better look at his octopus.

The girl's face leveled with the woman's. Enora blinked a few times, studying Sush just as she scrutinized any stranger on a first meeting, conveying the woman's features to memory, forgetting that she was supposed to ask her a question. Then, her small hand reached out and gingerly landed on Sush's nose before the pup beamed and said, "You're pwetty."

Sush's brows shot to her hair. She couldn't remember the last time someone said she was pretty. People normally told her she was smart, accomplished, efficient, bossy, overbearing, or stubborn. Creative, sometimes—when it came to invention and innovation. But never pretty. Especially not from children. In fact, the other adults frequently told her she had a daunting presence, as much as she tried to be friendly with kids. Eventually, she gave up trying at all.

She liked this girl already.

Lips cracking into a surprised smile, Sush said, "Thank you, Enora. Your uncle was right about you being a sweetheart. But he didn't tell me about Lionel MacDonald. Who's he?"

Greg did tell her. But he left out the pup's name when he shared the tale, using what he thought was a suitable nickname, so before Enora could reply, he explained, "It's the bastard—the one wh—"

"Greg. Claw," Lucy snarled.

Realizing his tongue had slipped, he almost cursed, "Oh f—," promptly substituting it with, "Oh great."

As he swallowed and met the queen's fiery gaze, his cousin promptly took a step back with a proud smile and crossed his arms as if he was giving his wife free rein to pounce.

In Greg's arms, Enora asked innocently, "What's *bastard*, Uncle Gweg?"

On Xandar's sides, Reida and Ken tugged his pants and asked him the same question, as did Lewis and Ianne with Annie and Christian, at which time Xandar fibbed and told the pups that he'd never heard that word before in his life, adding that Greg would be the best person to explain what it was, seeing that he used it.

Christian merely told his children, "What your uncle just said." He thumb-pointed to Xandar, internally grateful for not needing to be the one to explain, and simply piggybacked on his cousin's lie.

All eyes fell on Greg.

Greg returned his sights to the pure little thing in his arms, not knowing how to explain because his mind had frozen. So many things to teach her, yet so many things couldn't be taught yet. Now with the queen's glare burning through his skin, he wondered if his days of imparting knowledge to the pup were numbered.

A cheery voice came from the speakers, asking the participants to meet under the red-and-yellow tent for a short briefing. Enora's eyes bulged wide, and a sense of urgency took over her when she wriggled in her uncle's hold and patted his shoulder, demanding him to put her down.

He set her on her feet, and Enora started to flee when Lucy promptly stopped her, holding her by her arms, and told her she wasn't allowed to use that word, making her promise to never use it.

In a hurry to get to the briefing, Enora mindlessly nodded and was only freed from her mother's hold after Lucy had kissed her good luck. In her little white shoes, Enora followed the yellow arrows guiding the pups to the field for the briefing. Her family watched her speed with the other participants to the tent, forming a line with two teachers, one of whom was Hailey, doing a head-count in front.

All eyes returned to Greg. The appearance of Alpha Juan and his family, along with the former alpha and luna—Ken and Janice—gave the impression that Lucy had backup, though her family had no idea what was going on. The old man turned to his son-in-law, a silent demand of an immediate explanation for his daughter's readiness to kill, and Xandar obediently linked him, making the scowling old man break into a light chuckle as he shared the knowledge with his mate, who was less impressed—a reaction that had her husband chuckling more.

The noise in the background couldn't even penetrate the silent atmosphere. And the duke came up with the first excuse he could think of. "On the bright side, my queen, it isn't anyone's first word."

A chuckle bubbled up Xandar's throat, but he bit back, struggling to hold back the laughter and smile. His amusement was not shared by Lucy, who huffed between angry breaths, "You . . . have no idea . . . how long it took to undo that. You're *lucky* we have too many witnesses right now."

"I am grateful, my queen. And I do apologize . . . In my defense, that pup didn't deserve any name other than the one that just slipped."

"That. Is *not* a defense," Lucy noted pointedly, then added, "Though you'd be happy to know he was actually expelled."

"Really?" Greg questioned. The stars in his eyes matched his niece's from earlier.

"Don't push it," Lucy reprimanded, disapproving the shine in his eyes that her own husband had the night before, despite the slight lift of her own lips. "The pup exhausted all three warnings and was expelled. That's the end of it."

Glancing at Sush, who was finding Greg's interaction with Lucy more entertaining than daunting, the queen composed herself and said they should head for their seats. They did so, offering her Blue Crescent family a hug when she turned around.

Following the royals at their heels who held each of their pups' hands on one side and their mates' on the other, Sush murmured Greg's way, "She's right, you know?"

"About what?" His hand left her back, and his fingers slid between hers.

Cherishing the warmth and strength from his callous palm, she answered, "You're lucky there are too many witnesses here for her to murder you."

CHAPTER 58

Ken was on Lucy's lap when she chatted with Liam, her favorite nephew. He was already nine years old and picking up math and science taken by twelve-year-olds but struggling in general studies. Since he spent most of his time in the scientific realm, he always failed to allocate enough time to keep up with the happenings of the kingdom.

He only got a decent grade because his father was alpha and mother a luna and minister. Conversation on the kingdom's affairs and those of the pack was normal at home, which was apparently enough for him to pass but never enough to score. He didn't mind it, nor did his parents or favorite aunt, though his grandmother—ever the perfectionist and high achiever even at her current age—did suggest he try allocating more time for the subject. Liam tried it for three days before calling it quits and returning to the numbers and equations that put the shine in his eyes and made him lose track of time.

Reida sat between him and Ianne as the two girls listened to Liam with deep interest, being science and math geeks themselves. When Liam talked about the cardiovascular or respiratory systems of any species, Reida's ears perked, and when he talked about the pollination and certain flora's ability to self-fertilize, Ianne didn't blink. But when he began rambling about the solar system with brighter eyes and more elaborate hand gestures, the girls turned back to each other and did a recap of everything they'd just learned from him.

The trio was close, so much so that whenever Reida informed Ianne she and her family were visiting Blue Crescent, Ianne would beg her parents to let her tag along. Together, the three would conduct experiments behind the packhouse, in Liam's room, in the basement, or at the sink. The last one had Hale and Lucy scraping off some glittery, blue thing from the sink's surface for half an hour. Juan even had to have the piping below the sink changed because of it, while Xandar had to make a call for certain underground piping in the pack to be replaced when the same blue substance got stuck and inhibited the waterway. The adults then told the pups to pick another place next time.

Some experiments were successful, but most weren't. Even so, the trio always had fun. They always did something fresh, saw something new, and learned something different.

Ciera—one of the pups Juan and Hale had adopted—was now in her late teens and loved chatting with Christian about economics. The duke was more than happy to share what he knew and how he thought things through, even lending her books and recommending podcasts and courses she may be interested in. When she asked for a tertiary program recommendation, the duke was steadfast in suggesting Helm University. He then paused before telling her to check the programs in the vampire community first—being an option that the students of his generation never had.

Another three of Juan's and Hale's sons who were more interested in business, and another daughter who immersed herself in history, always fought for Xandar's attention, asking questions and getting intrigued or mind blown by answers and explanations. Before they began, the boys and girl normally flipped a coin to see whether their conversation with Uncle Xandar should start with business or history. To the boys' annoyance, the girl seemed to have some kind of luck in the coin flip more often than they liked, and it didn't matter how many times they swapped the coin.

Little Ken, despite being on his mother's lap, paid full attention whenever his father explored tales of history and explained the aftermath of each event to his maternal cousins, thinking to himself that these were far better than bedtime stories and definitely beat the nursery rhymes and pesky tongue twisters in kindergarten.

By far, the only quiet one was Lewis Blackfur, whose eyes never left Sush. Sush was speaking to Ken, Janice, Juan, and Hale about her work—the retired and present lunas curious about how they nominated and appointed their superiors, and the retired and present alphas interested in the gadgets and systems the hunters had come up with in recent years.

Greg gazed at her with pride as she explained the repertoire eloquently, and the energy that radiated off her when she spoke had his lycan cooing.

When Sush's gaze tore away from the elderly couple and locked with the pup's, Lewis cocked his head as if pondering a curious equation on the board. Head pivoted to his mother, he whispered something. Annie's eyes flickered to Sush before the chief saw the duchess turn to her son with a proud smile as she encouraged, "Go on. Ask first, okay?"

Lewis nodded obediently and made his way from the far end of the bench.

It was only when he got up that Sush spotted the camera in his hands hanging from his neck by a dark gray strap as he sauntered past the adults, toward her.

When he'd finally reached her, Greg's left brow lifted in a way like he was asking the pup why he was there. The dukes were placed at opposite ends for a reason—to stay at opposite ends.

Not even noticing Greg, Lewis timidly asked, "Can I take a photo of you, Sushi?"

Not minding the slight error in her name since it came from a child, she said, "Uh . . . sure. Right here?"

Lewis nodded, more confidently as he stepped back and looked through the lenses. Dissatisfied, he stepped forward and asked if she could sit with her shoulders back—the way he saw her when she was speaking to the alphas and lunas behind her. Lewis then asked Greg—nicely—whether he would be so kind as to move out of the frame while he took his shot.

Irritation at the pup's audacity flickered through Greg, but Sush got him to move from his seat, eager to please the pup. Greg stood to the side and waited with crossed arms.

Lewis took two shots, checked, and took another two. He then smiled at the results and moseyed to her as she moved back to her space and Lewis climbed up and took Greg's seat, showing Sush his shots when he said, "You're bweautiful. See, you have a nice nose." She'd been here for less than an hour and she'd been called pretty *and* beautiful *and* been told she had a nice nose. She liked it here a lot. And Sush might have been biased, but Lewis was the cutest little boy she'd ever seen, and the way he leaned into her side made her heart melt in a way that she didn't think was possible.

When Lewis began swinging his legs, it was clear he wasn't going to move, and Greg instinctively shot Blackfur a glare.

Christian, who caught the scowl by accident, paused midsentence in his conversation with Ciera, brows furrowed as he leaned back to see what the issue was. He made a mental note to buy his son whatever he wanted the next time they went to a toy store, before turning back to Greg with a you-deserve-it smirk, which had Greg heaving a long exhale. Turning back to the pup with the camera, Greg thought to himself that if he didn't have a Blackfur he hated most, he did now.

Not having the heart to ask Lewis to leave, Sush invited the boy to sit on her lap. At the same time, Annie noticed the stolen seat, making her push her husband further down the bench with her ass as the duchess prompted everyone else to move toward her to recreate the other duke's lost seat.

Nodding to the duchess with gratitude and residual guilt, Greg sank into the empty spot. He was very tempted to sweep Little Blackfur off the bench with one hand now that the entitled little brat had planted himself between him and his huntress.

Lewis was practically showing Sush his entire portfolio from the camera, explaining where he took each one, telling her which landscape she'd look good in—which was most if not all of them.

The speakers sounded again, and the participants finally emerged from the red-and-yellow tent.

CHAPTER 59

The crowd howled in short, repeated intervals, offering the pups a boost of encouragement as they took their positions several feet away from the designated target boards, Enora's head swung to find her family, lips breaking into a grin before her sights found Greg, and she gave him a wave.

Greg waved back, a proud smile stretched across his face when he murmured, "Shoot them dead, sweetheart."

From his side, Sush questioned, "Isn't it *knock them dead*?"

Eyes never taken off Enora while she took her position with the other pups, he responded, "No, this isn't about impressing anyone. It's about literally shooting down the competition."

Sush took note of the pups aiming for the target board instead of each other, which came as a relief. "I may be new here, but I don't think that's how it's going to go."

"It'd be a lot more interesting if it were. But the bast—" Greg cleared his throat when he remembered Little Blackfur was still with them and continued, "But the one who should be placed at the target board has already been expelled so finding a suitable target would be a problem."

Behind him, Juan offered, "Lucy mentioned Lionel is now in Connard, the kindergarten nea—"

Smack!

Hale delivered a slap to his biceps and reprimanded, "Don't give him any ideas."

Juan's hand snuck behind her and went to her waist as he pulled her to himself. "It's not as if he wasn't going to find out anyway."

Greg liked Juan that way, not the goody-two-shoes Blackfur was, though still not sadistic enough for his taste. He watched his sweetheart's first arrow fly and the orange tip came between the innermost and second innermost dot as a teacher came to see where the tip landed more on before writing the score on the board. Greg then waited for her to turn and lock eyes with him as she did an excited jump before turning back to the front, which was when Greg turned to Juan just slightly—not wanting to miss a thing on the field—and said, "I appreciate the intel, Alpha. It cuts short the hunting time."

Hale glowered at her husband, and as Juan stroked her side to smother her anger and disapproval, Juan uttered meekly but affectionately, "Baby, he's just saying that. We've known him for years. He's not going to do anything."

Though offended, Greg chose to say nothing, understanding the alpha had a pissed-off luna to calm, something that probably took precedence over the probable murder of a pup he didn't care for, that no one in the family cared for.

Despite the luna's assault, Sush found herself leaning into the warmth of the dynamic not just between the couple, but between the couple with Greg as well—the level of confidence that was there and the degree of trust placed on Greg's restraint.

In the trenches, apart from the mavericks and herself, Greg made himself seem so untouchable. Some hunters even dubbed him as a lone lycan, the only one at the top of his self-created pyramid. But she realized that he had more family than he'd let on. A real family, not one for publicity. He hadn't shut up about his sweetheart, but Sush wished he hadn't shut up about the rest of the family, too, or at least had brought them up.

She overheard bits of the conversations between the more grown-up pups and the adults, stole glimpses at their interaction, and was attracted by the vibrancy and warmth radiating from each creature. It was so different from the way the royal family members carried themselves in interspecies mediations and meetings—always cold and deathly. Sush counted herself lucky they were less—much less—malicious with her, even before Greg came into the picture.

She watched Greg watch Enora, and fell in love with another part of him that no one beyond his circle would have known existed—his love and attention for a pup that wasn't even his. It was beautiful. Sush turned back to the field just in time to see Enora's next arrow fly and hit the bullseye, and a loud cheer came from everyone in their section—herself included—as the other pups shot to their feet and punched to the sky in celebration.

Greg snuck a hand across the bench to reach for hers when he said, "It's her first perfect shot from that distance."

Enora was so happy that she squealed for a second, then kept the excitement to herself when it was time to fire the next arrow, vaguely remembering her parents' words about being graceful with a triumph and a good sport with a defeat. As the next arrow fell more to the second innermost circle than the innermost, she huffed and concentrated on her final shot, taking her time to get the precision right, blocking out the noise around her.

Her brows arched, sweaty hair stuck onto her forehead, eyes focused—the same look Greg had as his phone wallpaper. Lewis got off the bench and moved as near to the edge as possible, with Sush's eyes going between him and Enora, undecided on where to look as the boy took several shots of his cousin, but waiting for the one shot that he felt mattered most.

The other participants had fired their arrows by then. If there were cheers and shouts of encouragement, Enora didn't hear them. When her hands steadied, she let go, holding her breath as the arrow left her grip and landed—edge-to-edge—on the innermost circle, inciting another loud cheer from behind her.

Lewis's fast hands worked his way with the camera, making sure he was quick enough in getting pictures of Enora leaping and then waving at her favorite uncle, Uncle Greg, who was glowing with nothing short of pride, and the way his family members' faces lit up.

Dawdling back to Sush, Lewis showed her the shots.

###

Over lunch at tables and chairs set up on the freshly manicured lawn behind the kindergarten, Lewis climbed into the seat between his mother and Sush, asking the latter which of the almost-same pictures she liked more, and they'd discuss the details of each one before Lewis decided on which to discard.

The sight warmed Annie and Christian. Their son got along well enough with the rest of the family, but he didn't have someone he particularly cliqued with. Ianne had had Reida since the day they could recognize scents. And although Lewis got along with his sister and cousins alright, he never really gravitated toward them. Seeing him with Sush now, it was evident he'd found his person.

CHAPTER 60

After the meal, the families strolled around the greenery of small trees and flower beds, mingling with other families and teachers. Pups either left their parents' side to play with their friends or were clung to tightly by their respective parents as their teacher spilled every detail of their grades and behavior in class. Some grinned with pride, while others hid behind their parents' legs, which were as good of hiding spot as having none.

Little Ken was well-loved in terms of character and behavior, but could use some help in sports.

Reida and Ianne were a lovable pair, mostly due to their inquisitive nature, but their chatter during lessons was incredibly hard to stop. The teachers—especially the science teacher—appreciated that their chats were about the scrawls of facts and processes on the board, but he made it a point to note that he'd appreciate it more if their discussion didn't come when he was still talking and trying to get the pups to pay attention.

Lewis was adored by many but remained an enigma to some—he was too quiet. Several teachers were concerned about this and his tendency to keep to himself, even during recess.

Enora didn't know about her siblings and cousins, but she was beyond relieved her teachers hadn't said anything too bad about her. However, that was only because—unlike with her cousins and siblings—her teachers had to call her parents every few weeks (or days) when she was caught doing something she shouldn't be doing. The feedback was already given through those phone calls, so there wasn't anything new to add.

Grateful that her archery win wasn't dampened by the impromptu feedback session, she capitalized on the positive mood and asked her parents if she could go to the pond with Greg and Sush later that evening. When the "of course" came from her mother's lips and her father gently brushed her hair as a sign of acquiescence, the pup leaped into the air in excitement and then ran over to Uncle Greg two feet away to tell him.

Lewis wasn't far, and he heard this. With a frantic tug on his mother's skirt, he said, "Mommy, I wanna go to the pond too." He didn't even know which pond he was talking about, but he knew he wanted to go.

Annie was hesitant, not because of Sush or Greg, but because her husband had issues with Greg, justifiably so. Turning to her husband, she linked, *'This is Lewis coming out of his shell, Christian. He's never asked to go out before. He could start taking pictures that are not within the confines of home.'*

'We could always take him to a few places for that during the weekends, my duchess,' Christian answered briskly, reluctant to let his pup anywhere close to Greg. He may as well throw his son into a tank of sharks . . . Scratch that. Lewis would most likely be *safer* if he was tossed into a tank of sharks. Who knew what Greg would do?

Annie tried again. *'He wants to go because Sush is going, Christian. You know that.'*

Facing his wife with a deep frown, his hushed link echoed, *'Annie . . . It's dangerous.* He's *dangerous.'*

Granted, Greg had never hurt the Paw-Claws, who he stood by and protected over and over again, but that didn't mean the same courtesy was extended to the Blackfurs. They couldn't stand each other with their moral compasses not always pointing in the same direction. They may have been civil in recent years, but civility didn't connote unbridled trust. What if Greg did something to Lewis?

'We could go with them,' Annie suggested, placing her hand over his, her thumb grazing his knuckles as the tension in his body loosened under her touch, the stubborn glint of onyx in his eyes fading away.

Accidentally catching his son's pleading gaze ping-ponging between him and Annie, he released a conflicted sigh. He cast a glance at Greg, who was updating Lucy and Xandar about the hunters while Sush let Enora drag her around as the pup pointed to various parts of the kindergarten and told her where the classrooms, playrooms, lunch room, teacher's lounge, and restrooms were, and also where she hid when she shot Lionel MacDonald with her classmate's crossbow.

Christian remained pessimistic. He knew Sush, but what degree of power did she have in her relationship with Greg?

Flickering his gaze back to the other duke, who now had one hand in his pocket in a serious pose, Christian responded to his wife, *'I doubt he'd say yes to that. It's his and Enora's bonding session, and now with Sush—for them to warm up to each other, though I doubt Enora needs any coaxing.'*

'If Greg says we can tag along, would you be okay with Lewis going?'

Christian instinctively met his son's gaze again. The boy seemed to have deduced that it was his father's permission that remained pending, which made him say, "I pwomise to clean up my toys before bed next time, Daddy. Can I go to the pond with Sushi?"

Well, when he put it that way . . . it actually sounded like a good deal. Lewis normally played before bed, and although he cleaned up the toys on some nights, he'd actually fall asleep amongst them on most nights, so the mess would be there the next day to be cleaned up by their housekeeper, Mrs. Clifford, or by Christian and Annie themselves.

Leveling himself with his pup, Christian ruffled the boy's hair and said, "Let's go ask Uncle Greg."

Lewis's anxious face lit up, and he made a dash toward Greg, surprising his parents with his speed, making Christian ask Annie, "Could he always run *that* fast? He always takes forever to come in from the garden for dinner."

Lucy was saying something about having to be careful when Lewis boldly stepped next to Greg, pulled at his pants, and asked if he could join him, Sush, and Enora at the pond.

Xandar's brows shot to his hair.

The words that Lucy was going to say drifted from her brain, no longer retrievable.

Greg began suspecting he was in a dream. That or Little Blackfur had run up to the wrong creature.

Eyes finding the other duke, Christian's face was equal parts disgruntled and reluctant when he uttered with visible difficulty, "May we join the three of you? Annie and I will be out of your hair—just watching."

And we'll be witnesses if you get our son poisoned or murdered, Greg added in his own mind since he doubted Blackfur knew about his no-violence-against-pups code.

After the longest five-second deliberation, Greg turned, and his face softened when he called out, "Sweetheart."

Enora paused her tour guiding and pulled Sush along as she sauntered back toward Greg, eyes widening in curiosity.

Getting down on one knee, Greg explained, "Lewis wants to come with us. What do you think? Should we get more bread for the pond later?"

Enora's eyes sparkled when she turned to her cousin. "You feed duckies too?"

Lewis's eyes were on Sush until Enora's question came. Embarrassed to admit he'd never fed ducks before, he simply leaned into what he thought was the right answer. "Um . . . yes?"

"Yay!" Enora then turned back to Greg. "We need more bwead later, Uncle Gweg."

Her uncle beamed as Lewis did a subtle leap of happiness, but the pup blushed when he met Sush's smiling eyes.

###

By the pond, each pup held a brown paper bag with stale bread. Lewis sat on Sush's lap after seeing Enora falling naturally into Greg's.

Christian and Annie sat at one of the two benches nearby, eyes pinned on the pups at the pond.

Greg found the stares invasive, but Enora didn't seem to mind, nor did Sush, who was helping Lewis tear up the bread into smaller pieces. Since his niece and octopus were fine, Greg made no comment and concentrated on not letting Enora assault the ducks instead, which proved to be a not-so-tedious task this time around. Perhaps her archery win got her to show mercy on the animals.

"Do you feed duckies often, Sushi?" Enora piped, pivoting to her after hurling another piece near the fourth duckling that was too slow to get any bread when the other three gobbled the food first.

"Not really," Sush answered honestly. The last time she fed anything—a duck in the pond, a fish in an aquarium at a friend's place—she was no older than ten. "I forgot how much fun it was."

Enora's head cocked. "What do you do for fun, Sushi?"

Sush's lips parted, but she abruptly stopped herself from saying that her job and the ongoing concerns in hunters headquarters provided little time for rest, let alone fun, and chose to say, "Well, I either go to the park for a walk or to the archery range for a few hours."

Enora's lilac orbs shimmered in excitement. "You go to the park too?" Gaze shooting to her uncle, the pup eagerly chimed, "Uncle Gweg, Sushi goes to the park like us. But we never see her. We can go to the park with Sushi next time."

In Enora's mind, there was only one park in existence—the one Greg and her parents always brought her to. "Lewis, you wanna come to the park next time? We can see birds' nests!" she asked even before Greg said a word in response, omitting that "seeing birds' nests" meant shooting them off the trees.

Lewis's eyes lit up for a moment, then dimmed again when he cast a wary glance at his parents. "I'll have to ask Daddy."

Sush's heart sank when Lewis's face fell. Gently brushing the boy's hair, she reassured, "As long as you put away your toys before bed like you promised, I'm sure your daddy will let you come."

The boy brightened a little with that reassurance and the soothing sound of Sush's voice. After finishing up throwing his share of the bread, he stood and got to work with his camera, taking pictures of the pond, trees, Greg, and Enora, and many pictures of Sush—on the boulder, under the tree, near a duck when a duck waddled toward them.

Just as he did at the kindergarten, Lewis showed Sush the pictures he'd taken, then reorganized the ones from the archery competition, separating them from those taken on his first trip to the pond.

Greg, whenever Enora didn't need his attention, took peeks at Little Blackfur's shots. When Lewis was sorting out the pictures from the competition, the duke realized—in dismay—that he wanted a few of them, especially the one with Enora concentrating. He'd tell anyone that it *wasn't* the same as the one he had on his phone, even though his sweetheart's posture and the competitive glint in her eyes were indistinguishable.

Now, the only problem was that he had to ask. A Blackfur.

CHAPTER 61

"It must have taken a lot out of you," Sush taunted with a smirk when they were in the car after bidding the Blackfurs goodbye and dropping off Enora at the royal residence, promising to pick her up for ice cream and a trip to the park next time.

"It did. I felt like I gave an arm," Greg replied, recalling the way he had to lower himself to Little Blackfur's level, swallow a sigh, hold back his dislike for the pup for stealing his seat, and ask whether he could have the photos he wanted. All without scaring the child. And all this hassle could have been avoided had Sush simply asked on his behalf, which she didn't.

What made it worse was when she said that it was unlike him to hide from a challenge. His plan B was to wait for the photos to circulate within the family and then get them from the queen, but after what Sush said, it would just seem like he was running away from someone whose height didn't even reach his thigh.

Scoffing in amusement, Sush replied, "I think you'll find the arm you lost was your pride. I wouldn't worry about it not growing back. Lycans possess superior healing abilities, after all." Greg made a sound, eliciting her chuckles, before she reached over to his thigh. "You did good. Lewis seemed to be okay with you."

Before her hand retracted, Greg grabbed hold of it. His fingers laced between hers, and his grip tightened in a way that forbade her hand from leaving when he murmured, "You're going to pay for that snark."

As much as the thought excited her, she had the urge to point out, "I doubt asking you to give away your arm of pride changed anything we're going to do in the bedroom. Besides, Lewis is sweet. You know, I thought I understood the extent of your love for Enora at first, but I realized I didn't. It isn't just a bond. It's also . . . a promise . . . to celebrate who she is, be there for the moments, protect her, and decimate everything that could hurt her. I think I feel the same way with Lewis."

The last line made Greg choke on air, and he had to pull over just to get his situation under control. He held his chest and coughed profusely as a very frantic Sush unbuckled her seatbelt and leaned over. She held their joined hands to his chest and angled him forward, letting him cough out the sensation while she waited in wide-eyed dismay, worry flitting across her eyes.

When the coughs finally stopped and he took in lungfuls of air, his forehead rested on the steering wheel, his eyes shut when he thought about what she'd said. After her interaction with the boy, it wasn't a surprise to hear that she liked the pup. But to hear that she had developed something for Little Blackfur the way he had for Enora, his whole body went into shock.

Eyes still shut and breathing steadied, he murmured, "Can't you pick another pup? The other princess and prince are still available."

When she didn't answer, he looked to his side just in time to see her irritation. "Next time, I'll let you choke to death."

"You're picking Little Blackfur over me?"

Entertaining his petty argument, she responded, "Lewis is cute and sweet. And he doesn't ask me to pick someone else."

"Good looks and a lack of demands are hardly a foundation for a healthy, long-term relationship." He straightened and began to carefully put the car back into drive.

"And what, pray tell, is a foundation to a healthy, long-term relationship?"

"My moral compass is skewed to a certain extent, so don't take what I have as the rule—frank communication, conscious commitment, and wild sex." The directness got her tongue-tied, and he took advantage of her speechlessness. "Little Blackfur doesn't even have ten thousand words in his vocabulary to communicate with you, let alone communicate frankly."

Despite his emphasis on the first thing on the listed criteria, Sush was mind-boggled with the last one, leading her to say, "You do know I was talking about platonic love, right?"

"Fine. Drop the sex. It's still not healthy. Communication and commitment—conscious commitment—are paramount."

"You're not being fair to him. How many words does Enora know?"

"By next week, I'm going to make sure it's at least ten thousand and one. And let's not forget she's younger."

"Still, what does she know about conscious commitment?"

"That she chooses to look at me every time her arrow hits the target board and not at any other uncle."

"That's subconscious."

"It was a conscious choice."

"Why are we fighting about this?"

"Of all the pups here and the children available in human territory, you had to bond with a Blackfur."

"What's wrong with them? They're good people. Annie is particularly sweet. I can see where Lewis gets his charm from."

Murmuring to himself, he said, "Goddess, this has been a trap by the divine all along. Making me fall for someone who got herself attached to a Blackfur."

"I know. What a nightmare," Sush said monotonously, taking out the vibrating phone from her pocket with an incoming call from Kenji.

"Yeah?" she began, placing him on speaker.

"Sush, we've got a weird lead on Monica Upshaw's location."

"Weird how?"

"It's a message passed on from one retired hunter to another until it eventually reached one of my eastern octopuses who is nearing retirement. And the message—if it has been passed on without mistakes—said that Monica has been in touch with you."

There was a pause, and then her ears heated when she exclaimed, "I haven't seen that woman in months!" She'd been doing everything within her power to track down Upshaw—from cornering Valor at the cafeteria to forcing an appointment at the defense ministry, and they all seemed content with keeping Upshaw's location to themselves.

Now the subject herself claims she'd been *in touch*? With *Sush*? The audacity of that archer!

"Remember I said *if it had been passed on without mistakes*," Kenji reminded. "I find it weird too."

"Track down the line of messengers," she growled.

"I have. Having Manickam send them over. You should receive it right about . . . now."

Sush felt her phone vibrate, noted the email that came in with a list of names, and continued, "Thank you, Kenji. Does the first messenger know where she is?"

"No. The last contact with Upshaw was weeks ago, when the message was sent."

"Location?"

There were murmurs in the background after which Kenji uttered, "A night market five kilometers off eastern headquarters." Only hunters who had to travel to work would stay within that radius, prompting Kenji to say, "I . . . don't recall seeing a western profile being sent over."

"I don't recall sending a western profile over."

"Ah. So we're both lost. Good to know. I should probably check with Asahi to see if there've been any archer assignments involving western hunters that I wasn't informed about."

"Yes, please do that."

"I'll keep you posted."

"Thanks, Kenji."

A long pocket of silence followed. Sush's mind went to the various things that could have already happened while the message was being transmitted.

Greg's voice brought her back when he asked the question blaring through both their minds, "Do you think she's dead?"

Sush's head did a half nod then a half shake, undecided. "Yes . . . no. Maybe? I don't know. Catrine Carter's death went by ten hours before anyone found her. Monica Upshaw has been unreachable and untraceable for weeks."

There was something Kenji said about Upshaw that Sush just couldn't let go of: They'd been in touch? What did that even mean?

CHAPTER 62

Days after Kenji's update, Sush was no closer to figuring out the last time she had been in touch with Upshaw, and Asahi pointedly told the eastern leader that despite the eastern attacks—which he was still blaming Kenji and his octopuses for—he would never stoop below professionalism and hunter hierarchy. That assertion was entirely believable because Asahi had never broken a single rule in his career—be it something as serious as committing treachery or as trivial as abiding by lunch hour to the dot.

That brought them back to the lead itself: What did Upshaw mean? When did she and Sush last meet?

It was probably when Upshaw was still in the western headquarters, and the exchange was either in a queue during lunch at the cafeteria or when they brushed past each other on the archer's floor when their practice sessions coincided.

In both scenarios, they wouldn't have even spared each other a nod or greeting. Did that count as *being in touch*?

"What's on your mind?" Greg's drawl brushed against her skin in a sensual caress, tugging the contemplative haze away from her eyes. The soft dip in his voice echoed curiosity, patience, and concern, lilac eyes focused and waiting.

Sush heaved a steady exhale, unsure whether the sudden malfunctioning of her mental faculties was the result of the still-unsolvable Upshaw puzzle or the attentive gaze of the man before her. "Upshaw," she eventually uttered. "I can't even remember the last time I spoke to her . . . or saw her."

Now that she was plucked from her restless pondering, Sush tried to concentrate on her surroundings, which was what she was supposed to be doing in the first place. It was her patrol team's turn to stand guard in place of the fallen archers.

The presence of the lycan warriors lifted a huge burden off the hunters' shoulders, but it didn't seem right to only have them patrolling the borders since it was technically not their problem, so the octopuses and chameleons took shifts on a rotation basis on top of their respective duties.

Greg didn't need to be there, but he'd rather not stay at headquarters and wonder whether his octopus was safe for each minute he couldn't see her but knew she was exposed to direct danger. He would say she could take care of herself, but when poison was in the picture, no one could take care of themselves, not even the lycans.

Nothing had been happening for the past three hours and forty-three minutes, so everything was pleasantly dull as fuck. He noticed Sush zoning out every few minutes, but her last space out had been the longest—a full five minutes. He ditched his post and approached her, and he was certain she didn't even sense him coming.

Upshaw.

That *was* a mystery worth losing focus over.

"You'll figure it out," he reassured with a level of certainty that she wasn't able to relate to at the moment. "I normally wouldn't tell you what to do, but if you could keep your head out of the clouds for another—" he checked his watch "—twelve minutes, I'll cover your archery range entrance fee for the next two months."

Her lips quirked into a smirk. "Bribing me so that I'll keep *myself* alive?"

"Yes."

"How does that make any sense?"

Despite their proximity, he stood closer. The tip of his shoes met hers, and his presence engulfed her in a protective embrace. He didn't even have to touch her for her to feel touched. The way his gaze seared into hers put a stop to her breathing but ramped up her heart rate—a contradictory bodily response that only made sense when she was around him.

"It makes sense," he uttered, "because I plan to keep you." His eyes steadily dropped to her shoulder, and the back of his forefinger trailed down the length of her arm when he continued in a seductive whisper, "For a *very* long time."

His touch left a pleasurable sensation—one that had her begging for more.

The corner of his lips lifted when he leaned in as his mouth hovered above her ear. "Your desire smells delightful, my octo—"

A snap of what sounded like a broken branch made heads whip at the ordinary-looking trees as everyone's attention snapped that way, weapons clicked and ready to fire, including Sush's.

Greg's claws extended on instinct, as did those of the other lycans.

But when they were greeted by nothing more than a gentle gust of wind and an eerie silence, Sush began taking steps forward, ready to investigate.

Greg retracted his claws and pulled her back by her elbow, holding her by her shoulders. She then found herself looking into a pair of onyx eyes as his growl came out in a low warning, "Don't. Even think about it."

Before she could argue, the next few snaps came in speedy successions, but the sounds grew fainter, like whoever it was was making their escape.

Two of the three lycan warriors on guard charged into the forest with Greg as Sush and Manikam struggled to keep up. The two remaining hunters and a lycan warrior stayed behind.

Greg's superior speed enabled him to beat everyone and—with the assurance that Sush was lagging with the other hunter, momentarily out of harm's way—he found himself tracking down a scent that smelled . . . human.

Had they unintentionally scared some random human exploring the forest?

It took Greg point two seconds to eliminate that thought. No random human would be exploring the borders of territories when there was nothing to explore in the first place. The trees here weren't rare, and there weren't any unique or exotic species living amongst the greenery either, so no curious minds would ever find themselves here.

If it was law enforcement from the neighboring species—the vampires—there wouldn't have been the need to run. The empire would have known by now that the kingdom and hunters were working together. The bloodsuckers weren't *that* ignorant or inefficient.

The scent trail was getting stronger, and Greg's ears began picking up the sounds of panted breaths. He was close. And there was more than one of them.

When three men came into view, the lycans surrounded them, snarling in warning as Greg assessed them with more curiosity and disdain than defensiveness. The way the men were holding and aiming their guns showed that they were practiced shooters, and the way they were huddled—back to back—against each other while casting one another panicked, sideway glances showed that whatever plan they were executing, they did not take into account the presence of three lycans, or any lycans at all.

Sure, this wasn't the most well-guarded part of the territory, but it wasn't *unguarded*. A minimum of two hunters and a maximum of three would always be on patrol.

As the thumping of Sush's and Manikam's footsteps drew nearer, one of the three intruders fired at Greg while his comrades discharged their weapons at the other two lycans, all three of whom dodged the bullets and—as soon as they regained their balance—charged forward with ferocious snarls.

What the lycans didn't expect was witnessing the intruders slit their own throats and collapse to the ground, gurgling their own blood. Their widened eyes of anguish gradually turned blank just as Sush and Manikam arrived.

Greg heaved a frustrated sigh. The shots fired at them were a distraction, not an attack.

"Search them," Sush ordered calmly as she knelt in the dirt and her hands began rummaging through the corpse nearest to her with Manikam while the others did the same for the other two corpses.

In a zipped compartment within the dead men's pockets, they discovered vials of brownish-gray powder. Each intruder was carrying ten vials apiece. Manikam extracted the hunters' drug tester—a rectangular device with nothing more than a screen. Upon turning it on, he sprinkled some of the vial's contents onto the screen, which scanned the product from top to bottom.

After measuring the weight, it briefly loaded before displaying the name of the substance—maruntu.

"So that's why rehab facilities are still getting maruntu addicts," Manickam murmured to himself, moderately paralyzed at the results.

Maruntu was a drug that was banned over two decades ago. Even so, the number of addicts for this feel-good substance had been increasing bit by bit over the years. Traffickers were hard to find and even harder to convict, and the source was never near being found.

Was *this* the source? If it was, which patrol team had let the traffickers through? Hunters were rotated every three weeks until the western massacre turned everyone's schedule upside down.

Every three weeks . . . Sush sighed to herself. The fixed schedule was too routine—too predictable. The traffickers may have tracked the archers' rotations and knew which ones would let them pass and which wouldn't. And someone must have forgotten to let these intruders know about the changed routine.

But that also meant Sush had a lead on possible moles amongst the hunters. She would have known whose turn it was to patrol today, had the massacre not happened, as soon as she checked the archives, but the issue would be *proving* those hunters were moles, now that their evidence—the traffickers themselves—were dead and couldn't be brought in for interrogation. Without evidence, Valor wouldn't even consider suspending them, especially now that they were low on archers as it was.

"We'll have to submit a report to the ministry," Sush decided. "With any luck, these three may have been arrested for trafficking before, and the police might have more information about who they are, so we can find out who they're linked to and who we should be looking for next."

From her side, Greg uttered, "It probably isn't as tedious as it sounds, Sush. Look." He gestured at a body he had turned over.

On the corpse's nape, there sat a mark of a chameleon.

They flipped over the other two, and they bore the chameleon marks as well. These were thugs. Which was odd. Neither Sush nor Manikam had seen these faces before, so they either left the hunters before Sush and Manikam joined, or they never joined the hunters in the first place.

Who were these chameleons? And who were they working with?

CHAPTER 63

"Oh! Oh!" The moans came in successive streams. Her smooth, straight hair was now sprawled on the quaking bed as the largest shaft she'd ever had filled her in ways that sent her to her climax quick, and the most gorgeous man she'd ever seen pumped into her like a deranged animal. His blue eyes carried the primitive glint—a hunger, a yearning, a desire—one that she hadn't seen in her own husband's eyes in decades.

The moment her body arched and her walls clenched around him with a scream, his own body stilled as he grunted, cumming inside her, shooting deep.

Without a condom.

She'd insisted.

And although Patterson's standard practice was to never fuck without one, Larissa Ferdinand had taken the trouble to show him her successful tubal ligation procedure that Patterson had confirmed with his own resources. And besides, if the report was fake and the woman got pregnant, it'd only get more amusing.

For him, that is. Definitely not for the minister.

Her slender fingers trailed from his broad shoulders down to his six-pack, taking her time tracing each hard, distinct block, licking her lips as Patterson pulled out of her. He was about to get off when her hands reached for his nape, pulling him down for their lips to crash, her perfectly manicured fingernails dug into his skin to hold him in place.

This part, he didn't really enjoy. With anyone, really. But it was, unfortunately, necessary in any . . . assignments of this nature, even this particular unauthorized assignment that he had given himself the green light to execute.

Rage and pettiness combined were capable of motivating one to follow through on some of the most . . . innovative things, he deduced.

While waiting for the ordeal of her tongue ransacking his mouth to pass, Patterson wondered whether that was why Sush had a reputation for raging and—when it came to the hunters—she seemed to be so obsessed with the most minute details that it often came off as being petty. That was, of course, until it didn't—when the dismissal of details resulted in failed experiments, delayed success in devices, and, more recently, death.

Perhaps it was time to take a leaf out of his colleague's book and embrace the rage and pettiness within himself. Pettiness, he could master. Rage would be challenging. Patterson didn't have the preference or fuel for that much anger.

When the very obviously sexually deprived woman below him finally released her hold over his mouth, he tried to slip off but her hand on his neck wasn't letting him go.

Good God, what now?

"What's the rush, handsome?"

Mental muscle memory built from seduction assignments got him answering, "Well, for one, it's almost eight, so the nannies are probably coming back soon with your kids."

She rolled her eyes. "Those two are on my payroll. And they signed an NDA. With me, not my husband, so they can't say a word."

Displaying the smirk that made ladies swoon, he praised, "Perks of being a lawyer."

"Partner, handsome." Her finger ran along his bare chest when she added, "I run my own firm, let's not forget."

As if he could. As if anyone in society could. The Ferdinands were known to the public as the power couple that many aspired to emulate. It was *the* main factor that kept Ferdinand in office for so long and kept Larissa's firm business and book sales as lucrative as they had become. The passion between them died an eternity ago. Their children, aged eight and ten, were supposed to be the ember that rekindled the spark, but they only came with more problems rather than being a solution—the solution.

Even so, the Ferdinands still seemed to be going strong in the eyes of anyone who couldn't see through the walls of their house and the veils of their pretenses. Because if there was one thing the couple was good at, it was keeping up appearances. The marriage was kept on paper for the benefit of themselves, if not for their children—who knew Daddy as a man they saw once a day at the breakfast table, and Mommy as the pretty woman who spent the morning getting dressed, telling the maids which food needed tweaking and how they didn't clean a particular corner of the house, and was the one who reminded them—even as children—to always smile because outward appearances mattered.

"How could I ever forget?" Patterson mused, and tried to get off but was pulled back. Again.

She stole another kiss, then another, and another.

This is getting exhausting, he thought.

Hand threading through her hair before cupping her cheek, he pulled away and held her face at a distance as she took bated breaths, using that time to utter, "Nannies and kids aside, your husband should be back in less than an hour. I don't want to have to climb out of the window to make an escape."

As he finally got off and began gathering his clothes and then pulling up his pants, Larissa scoffed. Darkly. Scornfully. "He wouldn't do anything. We came to terms that—no matter what—we'd be stuck with each other for all eternity."

"For better or worse," he chimed, which elicited another scoff from her. As Patterson zipped himself up, getting his shirt, he remarked sardonically, "You definitely sound happy about it."

Pushing herself off the bed, her gray eyes stared into space, and she released another scoff, mindlessly grabbing her silk robe and fastening the sash. Right before Patterson was about to take his leave, she said, "I want to show you something."

It took everything in him not to groan when she looped her hand under his arm. If this was another piece of see-through lingerie that another woman wanted to show him because they bought it for him, he'd be requesting a few days off work to cleanse his mind if not his eyes, though he doubted Valor and Sush would approve it, given their current circumstances.

Why was it said to be bought *for* him when they were the ones who'd eventually be wearing it? When he fucked, he liked his women fully bare, so he truly didn't see the point in all the lace and thin fabrics that had less material but was more expensive than a handkerchief. Honestly, just use two handkerchiefs—one for the top, one for the bottom. It wouldn't make a difference to him once they were scattered on the floor.

To his surprise, she wasn't leading him to her wardrobe. They exited the bedroom, sauntered down the corridor, and came to the room right at the end, opening up to her pale green-themed home office with a large desk and high bookshelves, a round mandala carpet in the middle, and two large windows where light spilled in.

Larissa went to her desk, reached for her over-congested pencil holder, and poured everything out before her fingers parted the stationery and finally found a silver key. Pulling out the second drawer on her right, she took out a small, wooden box, and slipped the key into the keyhole, twisting as the lid opened with a click. She then handed Patterson the whole box.

Brows furrowed, confusion marring his face, Patterson warily accepted the wooden thing and found not used underwear—thank God—but stacks of folded papers. Some had been crunched up and subsequently smoothed out before being folded methodically like the rest.

He selected one at random, picking a white sheet from the middle, not knowing what he was looking for at first as he skimmed down the tiny, faded blue ink words, but when one particular line caught his attention, his breathing hitched. He should have known. In fact, some part of him already knew, despite the lack of proof . . . until now.

He dug out a second sheet and found another line that he recognized. On the third sheet, there were three such lines.

"He won't touch you or me," Larissa said softly, eyes amplifying certainty and defeat as she leaned into her swivel chair. "He won't touch us, even if he sees you here. Because I have evidence. And those are only the physical copies."

CHAPTER 64

Sush, Patterson, and Greg paced down the white-tiled floors and past the sea of green patients dotted only by the white beds and doctors and nurses in white.

Valor received word from the hospital that Hazel had been lucid for a good two hours a day since three days ago, and sent the two chiefs to ask about the events leading up to the incident the other day, about whether there was a system error and who she saw behind the computers. Several octopuses and chameleons had already interviewed the rest, but since this was Hazel—the deputy octopus—Valor insisted the chiefs went.

Hazel was in green like the others, back against the bed frame cushioned by a pillow. She looked pale and her eyes were dull. The usual jubilant shine was no longer in sight as she stared out the window. The moment she heard footsteps approaching, her head swung, and her droopy eyes locked with her colleagues, lips tipped into a lazy smile. "Hey, guys."

"Hi, Hazel," Sush began, standing by her bed. "How do you feel?"

Hazel shrugged. "Lucky," she murmured, almost inaudibly, her smile already withering.

Patterson shifted uneasily and pushed a smile. "The doctors say you're recovering well."

Eyes flickering to him, she merely mused, "Yeah, I hear that every day in the short time I'm able to stay awake." They weren't used to this version of her—this melancholic version. The vibrancy seemed to have been poisoned and died with the archers. "They said it was zahar?" she asked, more to make conversation than to know the answer.

"It was," Sush confirmed. Her deputy's demeanor—weak and depressed—made her wonder whether the things Greg found on Hazel were true, whether Hazel actually owned an encrypted phone and really did send those coded messages. Sush didn't doubt Greg or Jade, but what if someone had planted the evidence on Hazel? Or what if Hazel had stolen the encrypted phone to conduct her own investigations on the matter? Looking at her now, it was difficult to see she had initiated any of this. Hazel seemed as shaken as anyone would be. Clearing her throat, Sush began, "Haze, I don't mean to be an ass, but we're here on Valor's instructions to ask about what you remember from that day."

Hazel's eyes trained on Sush, taking a moment to ponder before her small smile came back into place. "Then Valor's the ass." The ladies chuckled briefly—treasuring the brief moment of familiarity and closeness they shared in the trenches for years. Hazel then looked at her fingers, counting that there were ten because she couldn't even count to four before dozing off on the first day she woke up.

When the deputy was ready, Sush hit the record button on her phone, and Hazel began, "What I remember was . . . I went up for my weekly training. I was with Joshua. We were talking about how hot Baxter was." Sush's brows shot up at the candidness. Maybe the poison hadn't washed a lot of Hazel away, and the chief had to will her brows back to their resting position as Hazel continued, "We were . . . waiting for our turn for the . . . simulator." She yawned. "Then, the, uh . . . you know the generators make a sound?"

"Yeah?"

Hazel continued, "The buzzing stopped. The place went dark, and I heard those sharp sliding sounds. The emergency lights came on, so we could see, and we saw we were trapped. All the doors just . . . disappeared, and practically everything else was shut down. Then I heard something hit the floor . . . like a clang, and I think someone screamed, or it could have been a few people, or it could've been me, I don't know. And then I woke up here. And that's it. That's all I remember."

When Hazel didn't say more in the next three seconds, Greg questioned, "Do you remember the color of the emergency lights, Deputy?"

"Uh . . . white, why?"

"How far would you say you were from the nearest metal wall?"

"Six feet, I guess?"

"And the clang, what did it sound like?"

Hazel blinked like she was fighting the fog. "Uh . . . like something being thrown on the floor."

"Take a guess of the material."

"Aluminum, I think? I'm not sure."

Greg continued, "After the clang, did you hear anything before the screams?"

Hazel thought hard, the veins on her temple getting more distinct. "I think I did . . . something whooshing out, like a gas leak."

Beneath his hand covering his mouth, Greg's lips tipped just the slightest. Hazel, having to use her full mental faculties on the questions that were being posed, hadn't noticed the way Sush blinked before her eyes shifted and she began staring into space at her final answer.

Patterson said nothing, fearing a wrong move or word would demolish the duke's momentum and the chief octopus's train of thought. They bid Hazel goodbye, and Sush channeled every bit of hypocrisy she had within her being—which was not a lot but hopefully enough—when she offered Hazel a hug and asked her to rest well.

Trotting out of the hospital and to the parking lot, Patterson decided he'd had enough of the silence. "Sush, I hope you know by now that under any normal circumstance, I wouldn't give a damn about what you discovered in a room, but the fact that my chameleons were involved makes this my business, not just yours. What happened there?"

Sush turned to him—judgment written all over her face—when she questioned, "The can was thrown at the innermost corner. The mavericks monitoring Hazel after she fainted and carried her out said she was near the entrance. How would she have heard the gas coming out of the can from the other side of the archers' floor?"

Greg's hand slid to her lower back when he added, "Not even every one of my mavericks heard the gas, even with their animal senses. Out of the four near the deputy, only one *thought* he heard it. The others didn't."

"She was lying," Patterson murmured to himself, then locked gaze with Sush again. "I'm not defending her, but . . . what is she getting out of this? The poison has clearly affected her. She could have died. If she's part of this new . . ." he couldn't believe he was saying it; it hadn't even been a year since the last one occurred ". . . conspiracy, how is she alright with putting her life on the line for it?"

Unbeknownst to them, at a small window high up in the hospital floors, Hazel, who stood on the toilet tank in the empty patient restroom, was watching their little meeting, and although she couldn't see their facial expressions from afar, the way Patterson's arms went across his chest was a dead giveaway that the talk was serious business. That, along with the fact that her chief didn't crack a lame joke or drop some kind of sarcastic remark before leaving, told Hazel that she was short on time.

Her fingers moved to feel the flat-shaped device tucked in the raised edge of the right side of her bra, confirming it was still there since her mother's visit a few days ago, and she knew it was time to use it.

CHAPTER 65

Valor defended Hazel when Sush and Patterson played the recording and then disclosed their suspicions of her. The commander insisted the deputy chief octopus had only ever been loyal to the hunters and would be the last person to lie or betray them. Refusing to authorize an immediate freeze over her access to the headquarters files and confiscation of her weapons, Valor "suggested" they look further into the matter and find "more plausible leads."

Not even Patterson, who'd been in the commander's good books, could say anything to change his mind.

After that unsuccessful discussion, Greg brought Sush to the archery range, telling her she deserved some time off, which she wholly disagreed with at first, until—with a mischievous expression—he asked, "Are you sure you're not in the mood? I checked the range schedule: It's helium balloons day. Any particular face you want to see there?"

That did it. The next thing she knew, she was giving him directions to a longer route with less traffic, and they arrived at their destination earlier than they would have had they followed the direct route.

Greg parked and got out her bow from his boot, making her eye him in suspicion. Unfazed, he explained, "I picked it up around four."

Realization dawned on her. "That's where you went? You said you were picking something up from the residence."

Greg's brows furrowed. He took a look at the bow in his hand and said, "This *is* from the residence, and I'm assuming this—" he held the bow a little higher "—qualifies as being *something*."

"I thought you meant *your* thing." Sush's eyes narrowed, and she took the bow from him.

Before Greg paid the premium rate as Sush queued for arrows on the other side, he asked the man at the counter about the deluxe option being advertised on the wall in big yellow font against a blood-red, multi-limb star. The enthusiastic man in a white cap explained the deluxe rate offered a range that had more space and was less crowded and had light snacks along with alcohol. "Still balloon targets?" Greg asked.

"Yes, of course, sir."

"Perfect. I'll take that rate for two," he said before handing over his card.

After Greg had gotten the passes from the smiling vendor, he led Sush through the doorway with a hand on her back, but just as she was about to make a right down her usual route, he redirected her, hauling her to the left. "White Cap said it's this way."

"It's usually that way," Sush argued, but followed nonetheless.

The moment she saw a canopy with a crowd of less than fifteen instead of more than thirty, with target segments demarcated by buntings of yellow flags, each segment for each archer three times the size of the ones she was used to seeing, and a table with pastries and sandwiches, along with a section for alcohol, her surprised gaze took a fierce twist when her head turned toward Greg, who merely scanned the food options and said, "Oh, look. They have cream puffs. How many would you like?"

Battling an eye twitch, Sush whisper-yelled, "This isn't the premium package!"

"Thankfully. You were right about the crowd. Imagine the noise and sweat stench." He made a look of disgust before his hand left her back as he grabbed a plate, placed two cream puffs into it, saw something green, leaned in for a whiff, and then turned back to her and asked, "Do you only take matcha cupcakes or matcha anything, by the way?"

Sush was about to scream at him for changing the subject, but the flames slowly died off when her heart told her why he was doing this, and her soul yearned to be closer to him because he was doing this. Sighing in defeat, she responded, "Matcha anything."

He placed two green-colored cream tarts on the plate, then moved down the table. "Bagels?"

"Yes, please."

"How many?"

"One."

"Cream cheese, or homemade peanut butter and granola?"

"The latter."

When he reached the end, he asked, "Anything else I haven't taken that you'd like to have?"

"I think I'll eat those on the plate first."

Going over and taking the filled plate from him, she used the opportunity to leave a kiss on his cheek—one that stunned him. Her hand fell on his bicep when she gazed into his eyes and muttered, "Thank you."

A dazed smile lifted his lips, and he stole a quick kiss from her lips. "Those two words are appreciated but unnecessary, my octopus. I *need* you to be happy. Go pick a table. I'll join you in a bit."

"Wait," Sush glanced at her plate. "We're not sharing?"

Picking up a new plate and placing an archery-bow-shaped butter cookie onto it before taking a sandwich of each type, he replied, "We could if you want to. We'd get to try each of everything that way. Go pick a table. I'll come with the remaining options."

Sush picked a white table and sat, refusing to touch her food until Greg arrived, even when her stomach growled at the sight of the peanut butter and granola just waiting to be spread on her bagel. When he came with two more plates, they dug in. The moment the bagel with her thick-layered spread hit her taste buds, sparks erupted in her being at the impeccable flavor as her toes curled, and she spoke between moans, "Whoever made the spread deserves a place in heaven. God! Here, try some."

She brought the bagel to Greg's lips, offering him the unbitten part, but he leaned in and bit off from where she did, taking the pastry and light brown spread topped with nuts and seeds into his mouth, licking off the excess from the corner of his lips as he chewed. Washing it down with the wine, he concurred, "Definitely the second most delicious thing I've eaten."

No words needed to be said for them to know what Greg found most delicious, especially when his eyes conveyed it with the way he looked at Sush with that brief glint.

Their moment was only interrupted by loud cheers from the other side after a few balloons popped.

CHAPTER 66

Six! That's a new record," one of them said.

"He's the best of the best. What d'you expect?" another praised.

It was easy to see that the group of three men and two women were at a corporate gathering, and the one who was being bombarded with praises looked like he had everyone under his thumb as he beamed and began his story—probably not for the first time—of how archery was a skill that had been in his family for generations, his grandfather being one of the best in the country and once best in the world, so "he supposed" he inherited the skill in some way, never needing to put in that much effort to be good at it, at one point saying that he might have even been better than a professional hunter, which prompted more ass-kissing from the over-agreeable people around him.

Lilac eyes of mischief locked with Sush's smiling, dark orbs when Greg asked, "What's your record?"

He was sure she was better.

"Twenty," she replied, a smirk slowly forming along her lips when she was getting an idea of where he was going with things.

His brows did not raise in surprise, but his lips tilted with pride and arrogance. "How about you show these ignorant amateurs how a *real* hunter shoots, my love."

Putting away the half-eaten matcha tart and downing half her glass, a competitive tug of her lips beamed with the acceptance of a challenge as she picked up her bow and arrows before striding out of the canopy.

Greg's eyes followed her every move as he swirled the drink in his hand from where he sat.

Sush took her position fifty-four yards away from a wooden crate that was placed under another canopy that was much higher than the one they were under. Plucking out one arrow from the quiver, she fastened it on her bow. When she was ready, her foot stepped on the red button on the ground, at which time the wooden crate opened to release balloons of all colors. Once a balloon disappeared under the dome cap, it was a lost target. She had one minute to shoot as many as she could.

Her arrows came out in ones for the first three shots, before they came out in twos. Gasps and oohs came from behind her, but those murmurs and subsequent cheers were ones that Sush could neither hear nor see as she continued firing, shooting Valor, Ferdinand, Hazel, and Valor again and again until her time was up.

The shot counter who stood at the midpoint between the balloon canopy and customers' canopy wrote a two-digit number on a board and held it up.

Greg rose from his seat and clapped, shouting, "Fantastically done, my love. That's a new record!"

His enthusiasm was strongly shared by the other shooters who did not belong with the corporate group, all of whom shot up from their seats and clapped as well, men and women alike. Some cheered with fists punching the air, and one even screamed and applauded her feat next to the corporate group on purpose.

Thirty-nine balloons really was a new record. And she'd give full credit to her rage, but she had to admit—halfway through—she wasn't even thinking about the people she hated and the ones she wanted to kill. She just wanted to be here, in the moment, to have a little fun. The first half of the arrows must have brought her anger to the balloons because she had mellowed out by the second half.

Turning to Greg with a mildly embarrassed smile at the way he was flaunting her skill, calling her his love, she couldn't help the heat that surged to her cheeks as he lifted his glass and tipped it her way, which drew an even brighter smile out of her.

Striding back to him like she was taking a jog home, her home, they stole a kiss before he congratulated her again—this time with more happiness than haughtiness. They spent the next couple of hours there, not knowing when the corporate group left as faces came and went in the small crowd around them, a few dropping by to commend Sush's skill before leaving, saying they hoped to meet her again.

"The deluxe package offers great perks," Greg noted after the third one came with praise before leaving. His smile hadn't fallen since she put down the half-eaten tart to break her own record.

Eyeing him in askance, she mused, "And I suspect one of those perks is getting to show off?"

Unabashed, he lifted his glass, clinked it with hers, and replied, "Without a doubt."

Sipping on their drinks, they spent a few quiet moments just being with each other. Greg then noticed Sush's sights flickered to her bow and stayed there for longer than a few moments, contemplation whirling in her eyes, a small smile playing on her lips.

Reaching over, his fingers came between hers, feeling the higher voltage course through him when he gently asked, "What is it?"

Sush came out of her thoughts, smiling broader, letting the sides of her fingers brush against his, indulging in the feeling, in the electrifying rush, before she nodded at her bow. "It belonged to my uncle."

Greg's brows rose, his eyes darting to the curved piece of wood, thanking Goddess he'd been careful with it. There was no replacing something like this. The almost imperceptible tug of his hand brought his sights back to her, and she continued, "They were Liabilities and had no connection to the hunters whatsoever, but archery was a family hobby. Holidays when he was a kid meant men at archery ranges and women gossiping at the snack tables. It was a different time. I'm the first girl he taught and the first female in my family to know how to shoot."

His face softened, smile widened. "They would be proud of you."

She scoffed. "I'm not too sure about that." Taking another sip, she explained, "They've always been big on forgiveness. That's where we're not alike, despite our shared blood."

Choosing his next words carefully, he ultimately said, "You don't have to be like them for them to be proud of you, Sush. I'd say it's impossible not to be proud of the strides you've made in your life. As for that . . . particular venture, you're not really doing it for them, are you? You're doing it for yourself."

"Yes," she admitted in a whisper.

"Then does it matter whether they'd be proud of that segment of your life? If you're proud of yourself for going down that route looking for answers, why give a fuck about what anyone thinks?"

"That's what I tell myself on most days," Sush replied. "But on some days, I wonder if it'll even be worth it, whether more harm will come from knowing the truth than not knowing."

"Crossing the line or staring at it forever," he hummed.

"Yeah."

"Has there ever been a line you just stared at and never crossed?" he questioned, though already knowing the answer.

She smiled. "No."

His thumb brushed her fingers, soothing her as best as he could. "We're finding those answers, and we won't rest until we do."

She gazed at their joined hands, letting happiness engulf her at how lucky she was to have met him, to clique with him, to be able to argue and still laugh with him. "I don't think I tell you this enough, Greg, but having you around just . . . makes things easier, better. Be it complaining or laughing, I know I have you to turn to, to do all those things with me, without judgment. I mean, you can be a complete asshole at times, but even then . . . I know I can trust you. With anything."

Greg's lycan rolled over and cooed as his human fought back tears, understanding it as an elaborate version of three simple but powerful words, which he was more than happy to say in return after pressing a deep kiss onto her hand: "I love you too."

They stayed for a few more minutes before leaving in better spirits than when they arrived. In the car, he held onto her hand on his lap, replaying her words over and over again, failing to comprehend how someone like him had gotten a creature this impeccable.

CHAPTER 67

Back in the diplomatic residence, Greg parked and they unbuckled their seatbelts. He had already detected a faint whiff of her arousal on their way back, and smiled to himself knowing that—despite the hours at work and at the range—his octopus still had energy for an eventful night.

Placing a quick kiss on Sush's hand before letting it go, he was about to turn off the ignition—at which time the doors would automatically open—when Sush lunged at him from her seat and crashed her lips onto his before he could take out the key.

Shocked and disorientated, it took him a moment before he began properly savoring the feeling of her tongue in his mouth as he brought her onto his lap, letting her legs spread across his waist as he held her by her hips. When he had gotten his vehicle fully tinted windows, the consideration was one of privacy for himself and safety for his nieces and nephew, not pleasure.

In this moment, having her devouring him like a starved animal, he knew he had gotten a great return on his investment.

When she had to let go for air, her fingers worked quickly down the buttons of his shirt, and he asked in concern, "Would you prefer a bed?"

He could carry her if she didn't want to walk. He wasn't exactly skilled at maneuvering around in a car for this particular activity, wasn't sure if he'd be able to satiate her by doing it here.

Sush pulled his shirt open and ran a hand up his torso, hearing him groan as he hardened beneath her, and she leaned her forehead against his, uttering in a seductive whisper, "I'd prefer you in me, filling me up, making me scream."

Those words painted a visual that had Greg tossing out the last shred of logic and rationality left in him as he emitted a growl of hunger. His hand came down hard on her ass, earning him her scream before whimpers took over when he gave the heated flesh a merciless squeeze and brought their mouths back together.

His hands trailed up her body and paused at her sides, thumbs grazing over her breasts and toying with her hardened nipples beneath her shirt and bra, drawing out her moans as his hands snuck down to the hem of her blouse, fingers sneaking underneath, relishing in the heat of her skin as her butt moved in a way that further stimulated his groin.

He pulled the blouse over her head and dropped it on the side somewhere as his darkened eyes feasted on her bosoms held by a navy-blue bra. A low rumble reverberated from the depths of his lungs, and eyes trained on her, he ordered, "Take it off."

Her lips tipped as her hands worked their way around the clasp, releasing it as Greg watched the way the garment loosened and fell off her shoulders. The strap had only come off one arm when Greg's mouth latched onto her left breast. One hand held her in place, and the other yanked the bra off her other arm and tossed it aside, letting her moans and whimpers consume his mind as he took the other breast and worked his way around the button of her pants.

He jabbed a button to give them more leg room, and the last of her clothes were slowly peeled away as he rid himself of his shirt and undid his pants for her to bring out his shaft that stood at attention at her command.

Grinning at his tool as he slid on a condom, she then leaned over his shoulder and grazed her lower region along his shaft. Greg moaned at the moistness coating his length, and she continued stroking him like this, never making a move to put him into herself—teasing him.

A snarl left him, and he held her bum in place, muttering, "Enough games, my octopus."

He slid himself into her and got her second scream for the night, pumping violently to get the continuous stream of moans and pleas that made him feral and drove him insane. The way she said his name—out of breath and with undeniable need—got him spanking her rounded ass and driving into her harder and faster. At their climax, they jerked and could see nothing but stars for the next few seconds, hearing each other's ragged breaths, euphoria washing over them like a city-clearing tsunami.

Concerned that they wouldn't be satiated? What was he thinking? That was fucking perfect.

He used to think car sex was not what it was made out to be, having tried it twice in his much younger days before calling it quits when both ended up unsatisfying. It was never the issue with the setting; it was always the creature he did it with. How could he not have known?

She was nibbling his neck in a way that got his lycan rolling over and cooing, then made her way to his chin and lips, where they shared a few quick, brief kisses before he pulled her body back to admire her disheveled hair, the orgasmic glow on her face, and the shine in her eyes that reflected his own. His hand trailed up her front, feeling her bareness—the smoothness of her skin, the small globes of her breasts. Then he reached for her face, where he pulled her in for another kiss before asking, "Shall we continue here or make our way inside, my love?"

There was a consensus in the way they locked eyes, the urge to explore, so they did another round in the driver's seat, with her back against his front as he pounded forcefully while his fingers swirled mercilessly around her folds that got her screaming and him grunting in no time at all.

Only after that did they dress each other and make their way inside, continuing their fun in the bedroom.

They tried their hand at slow and gentle sex before deciding the style and pace didn't suit them and went on their wild and fast rides again to hit the intensities of their passion multiple times over before calling it a night.

There on the bed, lying in each other's arms, there was an unspoken understanding, an undousable fire of hope, that tomorrow would be better, that they'd get up the next day, make love, go to work, and deal with anything that came their way. Together.

But optimism could only take one so far, and it wasn't enough to prepare them for the news that hit the hunters the next day.

CHAPTER 68

Monica Upshaw was dead.

Her body was found by two lycans patrolling from a distance, who detected her scent but didn't think much about it at first before realizing—after an hour—that the scent had neither faded nor gotten stronger, and it carried the familiar smell of blood. As they followed the trail, they discovered the huntress, hair sprawled on the ground, eyes wide but empty, with a number of slashes at her neck.

Word arrived at hunters headquarters from the defense ministry, and Valor demanded Sush, Patterson, Kenji, and the newly-appointed chief archer, Millicent, be at his office two hours before their usual 9:00 a.m.

Greg did *not* appreciate having to skip a love-making session because of the defense ministry's recklessness in losing yet another huntress. And he much less appreciated that Sush had to start off her morning being upset upon receiving the news, as much as she tried to hide it.

Honestly, could those idiots do anything?

In Valor's office, Greg made himself comfortable on the couch, one leg folded with the ankle resting on the opposite knee. But his collected posture was not shared by the hunters in the room: Kenji had a few strands of hair that went out of place, Patterson looked deep in thought, Valor looked like he was about to deliver news on yet another death, and Sush looked a few years older within hours.

Heaving a frustrated sigh, the duke questioned, "Are the defense ministers invisible?"

Valor harrumphed, noting the sarcasm. "They have given their orders, Your Grace, and since the Upshaw death has attracted the media, the ministers are occupied with having to put out the fire."

"How very sympathizing," Greg replied monotonously with onyx eyes and a scowl. "Though since they possess no skills in ensuring something as basic as safety, I doubt they're capable of smothering any kind of flames."

A hand reached for his, the touch delivering a charge through him, drawing back his rage, and he held back his next words.

Sush turned to the commander. "This is on them, Valor. I've done everything I could to ensure Upshaw's safety. The ministry screwed up. Don't expect me to handle the media."

"You're not," Valor began.

Kenji's and Patterson's heads bobbed up. If Sush wasn't helping to control the issue, who was? They begged the gods of heaven and hell that it wouldn't be them.

The commander cleared his throat, glanced uneasily at Greg, and announced in a somber murmur, "The ministry has decided that—until investigations are complete—your involvement pertaining to any issue concerning the hunters shall cease, Alagumalai."

"WHAT?" Kenji and Patterson barked as Millicent exclaimed, "NO!"

Greg growled and was about to pounce from his seat had Sush not held him back by his arm.

Eyes trained on Valor, Sush questioned as calmly as she could, despite the fire in her eyes, "And the reason for my suspension?"

"They suspect you were involved," Valor admitted, resigned.

Kenji hissed, "That's ridiculous! There's a higher probability of Ferdinand executing such a thing than any of us in this room!"

Valor's gaze flitted to him, still looking at the eastern leader in disdain. "I'd be careful of what I say if I w—"

"What's the point?" Patterson exclaimed, shocking the room. "What's the point of us being careful when the ministry has recklessly sent two of our own, given us no access, no information, then later, news reaches us when they're found dead! This isn't the hunters' fault, Commander. And accountability should be taken by the ministry, not us, especially not the chief octopus."

Kenji added, "How was her suspension even a solution? Who the hell do you expect to fill her shoes pending the investigation?"

"The deputy has been certified to be fit enough fo—"

Greg snapped, "The Traffic Cone? She can't stay awake for more than five hours a day and you expect her to run the system? Have y—"

"Six hours, Your Grace, as of this morning," Valor corrected.

"Hazel's not fit enough for this, Valor," Patterson argued. "It'll do more harm than good. Why do they even suspect Sush is involved in anything?"

Valor shifted in his seat, ran his hand over his balding head, and cleared his throat twice before he shared, "Upshaw's last known location is Itam, and her last form of communication was made through a message sent to the ministry three days ago, begging the ministry to get Alagumalai to 'stop it.' Only no one knows what *it* is."

"I . . ." Sush began, taking heavy breaths. The fuel in every part of her had been set on fire with those words, and her entire being was preparing to explode. Her voice came out in a hauntingly low whisper ". . . have not even been able to contact her in weeks. Every single fucking attempt was blocked. By the ministry. By Ferdinand. And by YOU."

Kenji questioned like he was interrogating, "What were the other messages?"

"We are not privy to that."

Greg berated, "So you're suspending the hunters' greatest asset, opening yourselves to vulnerability based on a message completely taken out of context?"

Being more cautious with his words with the duke, Valor uttered, "Things may work differently in the kingdom, Your Grace. But over here, we are bound to the commands of the defense ministry. I have tried to argue for Alagumalai to be retained, but the message, on top of the fact that she survived the supposed elevator crash the day we lost our archers, has not put her in a good light."

"Spare us the bull, Valor." Greg leaned in. "It has not put *you* in a good light, and it's definitely raining shit on the ministry now, nothing less than what you all deserve. And you and your superiors must have a penchant for disaster because if things are on fire now, it's only going to get worse without her here."

"Greg, it's fine. That'll do," Sush uttered.

Head swinging to her, and with controlled anger, he argued, "It is definitely *not* fine. And this—you not being here—it won't do. Carter's and Upshaw's deaths happened when you had no access to them. Imagine what will happen to the rest of them once you relinquish access entirely."

From his peripheral vision, he sighted Sophisticated staring into space, murmuring to himself like he was delivering a prophecy. "We're all going to die.

If the mystery killer doesn't finish us off, the lycans and wolves will. If not them, then maybe the vampires. We're all going to die."

Holding Greg's gaze, Sush insisted, "It's not a dismissal. It's a suspension. We'll wait it out."

Greg's adamance and momentary disbelief urged him to fight her, but that was when he caught something in her eye—a glint, a signal. She could still find the culprit without being chief. All she needed was an encrypted laptop. Greg himself still had access to files and everything else pertaining to the hunters. She would still have access—through him.

"There's one more thing I should mention," Valor declared, pulling the attention of the room back to himself.

Valor braced himself for the most explosive outburst yet. "In light of recent developments in Alagumalai's . . . relationship with His Grace, the kingdom's access to anything pertaining to the hunters sh—"

"Finish that sentence and you'll die," Greg snarled. "The treaty clearly states the kingdom would be given at least a seven-day notice before our involvement can cease."

"I was getting there, Your Grace," Valor hummed. "The kingdom is being notified as we speak."

"By whom? Ferdinand's secretary?"

"By the deputy defense minister himself. We're expecting the kingdom's immediate demand for a meeting to renegotiate the terms. You see, some in the ministry suspect that the lycans who found Upshaw were the ones wh—"

"I dare you to finish that sentence," Greg growled, rage rolling off his being like a heatwave even though the lycan warriors weren't his people. "And I dare you to say that to the queen."

Valor shifted again, sweat beading on his forehead, before proceeding to get the last of the message out, "Until the meeting with the defense ministry concludes with the lycan rulers, your access will be confined to information pertaining only to the hunters, meaning should something on file link to the defense ministry, even something as vague as a footnote, you and the mavericks are barred from looking through it for now."

Kenji's eyes bulged. "Commander, this is the time to *share* more information, not withhold it. Our numbers have dwindled, and the ministry is demanding we further dwindle them by kicking out the lycans? How is it that you weren't able to argue in our favor?"

"We are dependent on the ministry for all our resources, Suzuki. I can and have argued, but if they insist on us pulling the plug on anything, we are obliged to pull it."

Patterson was beginning to get a migraine. "Valor, let me get this straight: The defense ministry suspends the main brain of the hunters and cuts off the mavericks who have been the reason some archers, chameleons, and octopuses are still alive after the zahar massacre, and the ministry's strategy now is to continue keeping us in the dark while someone who can't stay conscious for more than six hours takes the reins of all systems, which essentially includes our lives?"

Valor sighed, resigned. "It's a matter of perspective, Patterson."

"But that's essentially the plan?"

"Afraid so."

"Then it's settled," Patterson declared, rising to his feet. "I'm handing in my resignation."

"As am I," Kenji said.

Millicent uttered, "I suddenly don't feel fit to lead the archers anymore."

"No," Sush commanded. "You three are staying."

"What?" Patterson hissed, face morphed into disgust.

"Why?" Kenji whined.

Patterson continued, "There are other ways to kill us, Sush. I don't want to die this way."

"You're not going to die," Sush noted pointedly, eyes narrowed.

Her curt dismissal of his concern sent him further to the edge of a temper he didn't even know he had. "You won't be here. You have no way of knowing that!"

Millicent interjected, "Yeah, Sush, not that I don't trust you, but in this case," she thumb-pointed at Patterson, "I'm taking his side."

With a stern gaze, Sush insisted, "Running away is not going to keep anyone alive."

Kenji was the first to throw those words under the bus. "That makes no sense. Once we resign, many others will follow suit. We'll all be alive."

Sush argued, "Whoever the killer is, he or she wants our defenses compromised—targeting the archers, now having the lycans dismissed. It's not a coincidence. Each of us in this room knows more than the rest." She glanced at Patterson, who sank back into his seat, and Sush continued, "If they suspect we know something that they'd prefer to never surface, they will come after us—every one of us—meaning we need to get to them first." Turning to Valor, she asked, "Did the ministry say whether the lycans were able to sniff out Upshaw's trail from where her body was found?"

"I'm not allowed to further discuss anything with you, Alagumalai. But . . . even if I am, I'll tell you that particular information is being marked as confidential."

"Fan-fucking-tastic," Patterson cursed in a murmur, staring out the window.

In a low, apologetic tone, Valor turned to Sush and said, "You may collect your personal items within the next hour. After that, you cannot step foot on these premises until you've been cleared in black and white. I'm sorry, Alagumalai."

"Sorry our ass," Greg shot back. As his nostrils flared and Valor began turning white under his onyx glare, Greg's claws swiftly extended and dug into the armrest. The only thing holding him from going old school on the commander was Sush frantically muttering for him to calm down and telling him that killing Valor was going to do more harm than good, which Greg wasn't sure he quite agreed with.

Despite that, his claws reluctantly retracted as the seconds passed with Sush's voice, and he took a deep inhale as commanded by the siren he had for a lover. Eyes still glued to the commander, Greg's mouth opened—ready to deliver the most destructive retort to make the noble leader squirm when Lucy's link came in. *'Greg.'*

Greg's mouth closed—the link taking priority. *'My queen.'*

'How is she?'

'Less enraged than I am.'

'Mm. We just got on the jet and are on our way. Xandar is getting our pilot to delay the journey by an hour. At the ministry, we'll be able to hold them for another hour. Two, tops. Take everything you need until then.'

'They've already blocked us from government-related files, my queen. We can still hack into many things, bu—'

'Xandar and I have just removed that hurdle. Took us all morning. There's no evidence linking our warriors to the killing. Agu cracked and mentioned there were two soldiers nearer to Upshaw than our warriors were at her time of death, so if our people are suspects, so are theirs. They couldn't insist on keeping lycans as suspects because it rings diplomacy alarm bells. The media would have a field day, and the government would have an even bigger mess to clean up. Now that their national security excuse is demolished, the treaty remains valid and enforceable. Your access to everything persists until the end of our meeting with the ministry, which would most likely end with a momentary suspension of our demands. Hack and break into everything until then.'

'As you wish, my queen . . . and thank you.'

'Take care of each other. I'll link you again later.'

When his eyes cleared, he simply informed Valor, "There has been a recent development regarding my accessibility. Give your superiors a call."

Without waiting for a response, he rose from his seat, offering Sush his hand out of instinct, which she accepted without thought. They left Valor's office, but not before Sush and Kenji exchanged a look, one that they shared many years ago, one that conveyed they had each other's back.

As the two strode down the corridor, Greg linked his mavericks. *'We're being kicked out and we're short on time. Take every single thing that'll be inaccessible once we leave. We have less than three hours. Step on things.'*

'Yes, Your Grace.'

By the time his eyes cleared, they were on the ground floor, walking through the reception area, the sound of heels clicking against the floor.

"The first mind-link—was it the fox?" Sush asked.

Greg nodded. "She's concerned about you."

"I'm alright," she said, though her voice already seemed weakened when it wasn't even 9:00 a.m. yet.

Sush had no personal items to collect. Everything she did here, everything she deemed personal, couldn't be taken with her: her plans, her inventions, her sketches. These were things that belonged to the headquarters.

When they were several steps away from the glass-door entrance, something glaring came through the entrance. And it wasn't the sun.

CHAPTER 69

The doors parted to both sides as Hazel sauntered into the welcome lounge, orange hair pulled up in a high ponytail with eyes that shone with health, thanks to the antidote tucked in her bra.

Her pink lips curled into the congenial smile Sush so often saw, but there was a glint—a flicker of knowingness in those eyes she used to trust so much—and Sush wondered if the glint had always been there, or had it just revealed itself now?

Hazel skipped at her last step and hopped in front of Sush, saluting. "Reporting for duty, Chief!"

She never saluted, not even as a joke. And the slight over-emphasis of her title was a dead—but intentional—giveaway.

Cutting the crap and getting to the point, Sush said, "Whatever it is, Hazel, we'll find out. And we won't rest until we do."

The glint from before got slightly more visible. The tilt of her lips no longer carried warmth because it felt like the mask hiding that sly grin was being peeled back.

The most satisfying thing for Hazel was that it was being peeled back by herself, on her terms. In a voice that did not match her demeanor—one that her gossipy self always used, one that most found welcoming, she said, "I hope so, Chief. I don't know what we'll do without you. We need all the help we can get to find the culprits."

A deep rumble of a suppressed growl came from Greg, which was where Hazel's sights went next, and she revealed more masked layers. Pride exuded from her being at her success in bamboozling the sharpest tool in the lycan shed.

Her late best friend was right—the duke wasn't as brilliant as they made him out to be.

After giving him a moment to see the real her, her layers came back on. "Your Grace, how have you been? Oh, it's so nice to see you taking care of Sush. I knew there was a spark between you two! You're both so cute together, like a big ball of love just waiting to *explode* into little love fragments for the babies."

Sush's chest began rising and falling more prominently. Her eyes didn't just emanate betrayal and determination, but anger as well. "You know about it," Sush muttered, realization dawning on her. The word *explode* wasn't used by accident. When Hazel took off her mask for another two long seconds, Sush got her answer: Hazel knew something about the explosion that took her mother away.

The deputy chuckled lightheartedly and replied, "Our tenure forces us to know a lot of things, Sush. You gotta be more specific."

"My mother," Sush spat in a low utterance through gritted teeth and burning eyes.

Hazel shrugged. "I haven't met her, but I'm sure she's nice."

"She's dead, Hazel. She's been dead for years."

"Oh, I'm sorry." Hazel feigned devastation.

"No." Sush took a step forward like she was going to tear out Hazel's throat. "You knew she was dead. You've known it for years. You never let it slip. You've even told people on my behalf when they asked, back when we were trainees. You know more than you're letting on. What else do you know?" Sush demanded, voice raising with each word. She might have gotten better at keeping her cool when it came to other things, but she was nowhere near calm when her mother was brought up.

Unaffected by her chief's murderous energy since she carried her own, Hazel pursed her lips and shrugged again. "Sorry I can't be of help. Maybe try asking your Pop? Oh, wait. You don't know who he is. Maybe revisit your time with your mother? Get some clues or something? Funny thing about parents though: They try to hide so much from us kids, but there are just some things that cannot be hidden, you know? Things in plain sight." On that note, she turned to her watch with an arm that was raised unnecessarily higher than usual—above eye level—when she said, "Welp, I gotta go. Got systems and files to look through, and I only have six hours. I'll call to check up on you later. Safe drive back!"

She sauntered away and hopped into an empty elevator, commenting in passing, "Whoo, sure miss *this* elevator." That was the recently repaired and replaced elevator that Sush and Greg were stuck in, the one that could've taken Sush's life had Greg not been there.

Sadistic bitch, Sush thought.

A tug at her waist made her stop trying to burn the elevator with her glare, and the deep voice that was now her source of comfort reverberated through her ears, "Let's head back. We'll start cracking her riddles and take things from there."

Letting him drag her away, Sush couldn't deny the heaviness that set foot in her heart. She took a good look around, not knowing whether she'd ever again see the walls that needed a new coat of paint and the desks that had lost their shine over the years. Her ears perked at the sound of aged air conditioners, recording the low hum and saving it, in case she didn't get to hear it again. The moment she took her first step out, she broke from within.

For so many years, this place had been home. She had arrived with an agenda, jumped through hoops with only one goal in mind, and it wasn't a noble one. But somewhere along the way, she must have gotten so enraptured with the work, seen the potential and tested the possibilities, that she began putting not just her mind but her soul into everything she did. Funny how it took this experience—one that could snatch all this away from her in the next few hours or weeks—to make her realize how cruel fate could still be despite the scars that tainted one's past: Her passion lay in a place run by people who had taken her mother.

Her eyes burned with tears, and she refused to reach for them until she was in the car. She picked up the pace, and Greg kept up without issues, his thumb on her waist drawing circles, aware that it wasn't helping much but not knowing what else to offer her but his silence until they were in his vehicle.

About ten steps away, Greg slid his free hand into his pants pocket, only to realize he didn't have the keys. Heaving a frustrated exhale at himself while pulling Sush to a halt when they were two steps away from the car, he had her face him, and she'd already begun rubbing her tears on one side when Greg's gentle stroke reached for the stream on the other. "Sush, she and everyone else involved will pay for this, I promise you. And now, for my embarrassing confession—I think I dropped my keys in Valor's office. Can you wait here while I go get them? It'll take less than a minute."

He could speed using the emergency stairs; it would beat waiting for the elevator.

"No, I . . ." her eyes went back to the building ". . . I want to wait inside." She'd get to see, smell, and hear everything one more time.

"Come." His hand returned to her back, and they took about twenty steps before a forceful impact threw them far from the parking lot and toward the lounge, with Sush securely held in Greg's embrace as his back faced the source of the impact. The deafening blast banged their eardrums, and the accompanied seismic waves reverberated through their heads, making it hard to get up.

Greg turned Sush to face him, thumbs brushing over her face to feel for any scratches as her features scrunched in discomfort. "Sush, are you okay? Can you hear me?" he hollered in wide-eyed franticness. "Sush!" He gave her a gentle shake.

Sush delivered weakened punches to his arms as she groaned, "My hearing is fine. Stop . . . shaking me, Greg. God!"

"Oh, thank goddess," he breathed, and pulled her back into his chest, planting a kiss on the top of her head as he apologized, hiding her from the hunters who'd just arrived for work and were rushing toward them, some of whom had already called the emergency line.

Patterson and Kenji arrived, took in the scene, and shared horrified gazes with everyone on site.

Greg finally turned around to assess the damage. His car was gone—combusted parts of it fell all over the place, radiant flames of orange and yellow attracted an audience, especially when some of the exploded parts fell on both hunters and mavericks screaming for help. The mavericks got out quicker, jumped around shouting curses and trying to shake off the scalds and burns while waiting for themselves to heal as the unaffected ones went to the hunters, shifted and burned their hands to lift the parts just to get them out.

Greg's onyx eyes scanned his surroundings, and when he looked toward the sixth-floor window, he locked eyes with a very displeased Traffic Cone watching with crossed arms, whose hair morbidly matched the flames of the crime scene.

As Greg reminded himself to reward Desmond for telling him ten times over to never get a keyless car, he swore to Goddess and Satan that he was going to make the Traffic Cone's death his most legendary kill yet.

CHAPTER 70

Patterson was in Ferdinand's residence again for another session to satiate Larissa. He'd initially planned to only do it so he could leak this affair, but now he came with something else in mind—wanting to find out if Larissa knew anything else about Catrine Carter, perhaps even Monica Upshaw and the recent attacks on hunters headquarters.

What he couldn't comprehend was what the perpetrator could hope to gain from these strikes. The hunters were a large part of the defense systems too. Soldiers alone weren't enough. Why did it feel like they were being exterminated? There were no casualties from the parking lot explosion, fortunately. The most severe injury was a third-degree burn that had been treated with a positive prospect of recovery.

And the situation got really suspenseful when the media caught the fire because some witnesses nearby reported hearing the explosion. When the reports and headlines circulated, speculations went two ways: Some thought someone sought to murder the duke after the brutal execution of many high-ranking hunters; others opined the duke himself had planted the bomb in his car to kill the hunters within reach along with the chief octopus as revenge for the Delilah conspiracy, weakening the hunters' mechanics by annihilating the main brain behind their day-to-day operations and killing himself because he never got over the heartbreak.

Public opinion from the kingdom and human territories seemed skewed toward the former, most finding it difficult to believe that the duke would detonate his own car if he'd really wanted to annihilate the hunters. The bomb would've had a better chance of accomplishing that if it had been installed within the headquarters itself.

So bad light was now projected on the hunters. Again.

And thanks to that development, the kingdom's access to the hunters' systems remained intact, which meant Greg and the mavericks weren't being kicked out, much to the hunters' relief. They could use the help and protection in case another attack occurred.

As an added problem, the lycan rulers now demanded the defense ministry hand over every single piece of information the government had on file and in their physical archives, access to their defense systems and troops, and every password within the system. The attempted assassination of the duke had been their main point of argument.

From what Patterson had been told, the kingdom's defense minister very crudely said that the human government had displayed—over and over again in the span of weeks—that it was incapable of cracking its own cases and protecting its own people. This gave the kingdom no choice but to interfere to secure the safety of the mavericks and the duke. The queen added that if such a failure had come from their side to the hunters' detriment, the hunters would've already declared war. The king finished off by declaring that he would wage war if their demands had not been met by the end of the day, and so followed a very interesting next few hours.

Passwords were surrendered, and non-physical documents were shared. Physical documents were being photocopied the entire day until some machines broke down. The kingdom's defense minister verified passwords while the queen herself checked the first three stacks of photocopied documents, making sure none had been redacted before giving her people the nod to take them away.

Kenji and Patterson secretly celebrated the defense ministry being stepped on for once, but knew the battle against an unknown enemy was far from over, which led Patterson to disclose to the eastern leader of his involvement with Ferdinand's wife.

Kenji only got three words of protest out before Patterson asked whether he wanted to continue living in fear of another attack or perhaps take his place to fuck some information out of the woman.

With that, Kenji surrendered and claimed that Patterson's self-authorized plan was—in a technical sense—still authorized.

For the first time, Patterson called to ask Larissa if he could come over, when she normally extended the invitation. He was shocked to see the defense minister's car in the driveway and was about to leave when Larissa opened the door wide and waved him in.

Deciding to just play it by ear if he ran into the minister, Patterson entered through the doors with an external confidence and courage that did not reflect the anxiety spiraling within his being telling him to turn around and run while he still could.

Upon stepping foot into the house, he heard some shouting and instantly recognized it as Ferdinand's voice, hollering, "I DON'T CARE THAT HE'S IN A MEETING! TELL THE PRESIDENT WE NEED TO MEET TO DISCUSS WHAT TO DO WI—"

The shouting was muffled after Larissa signaled one of her two maids to shut the door before leading Patterson by his hand to the bedroom, locking the door behind them.

As she undid her robe at an unhurried pace with the intention of seducing Patterson in stages, not knowing he was far from affected after the years of successful assignments under his belt and the fact that he'd seen her body at least six times before.

Still, he let her have her fun, seeing her drop her robe before stepping to him and removing his coat when she purred, "Long day?"

"More like a long few weeks."

Larissa smiled sadly. "I heard. He's in his home office in case the lycans decide to pay a sudden visit to the defense ministry."

"Hiding away," Patterson summarized.

Larissa mm-ed, beginning to unbutton his shirt as she swayed her butt when Patterson's hands went to her waist and slowly trailed down the curves. When her fingers reached the third button, she said, "Despite what the public thinks, he's actually a coward."

"I know from experiencing it first hand," Patterson noted in amusement.

Larissa shook her head with an empty smile—in disappointment and disgust—at the man she had chosen to be her spouse. "Same here."

He scoffed. "And what has he done to you? Make you take the blame for a family accident?"

The unbuttoning stopped, her eyes delved into deep contemplation, and her chest began to rise and fall at the thoughts invading her mind.

Patterson was *not* going to ask if she was okay. In a previous visit, she stayed silent for quite a while before showing him the receipts in her home office—the receipts that confirmed Catrine Carter's grand transformation was in large part thanks to her affair with Minister Ferdinand when the figures there matched the withdrawals from a ghost account that was set up by Ferdinand's former secretary. Larissa's silence now only meant there was more information, and Patterson braced himself for intel about Monica Upshaw.

If only he knew Larissa was thinking about someone else, someone long before Upshaw, someone who even preceded Catrine Carter.

Her pondering continued as her fingers worked through the last of the buttons and peeled his shirt away. She was hesitating, he could see, even as she worked on his belt.

To offer her the dash of motivation she needed to open up, Patterson's fingertips made the lightest trail from her waist to her back, then down to her bum before his large hands cupped both butt cheeks, bringing her closer as their eyes met, hers with desire and his with well-practiced hunger. He just had to think of a woman who truly turned him on, who he truly wanted to drill into to get his shaft to stand the way it did when Larissa freed it from his underwear.

Her slender fingers wrapped around his girth and stroked along the length, at which time he released another practiced grunt when he squeezed her butt to elicit her gasp and moan. She brought their faces closer, their lips inches apart, when Patterson said, "Something's on your mind."

"It's not important," she said meekly.

Patterson didn't care if it wasn't important to her, but he'd like to be the judge of whether it was important to him and the hunters.

Pressing his lips onto hers as his fingers threaded through her hair, he elicited a stream of moans as his hands went to her thighs and lifted her up, bringing her against the wall as he hooked her legs around his ass, building up the tension before he brusquely pulled away, feigning annoyance when he said, "Larissa, something's wrong. Your body's not responding the same way. Tell me, what is it?"

It was a lie, but he'd tried it a few times when sniffing out intel, and—nine out of ten attempts—it worked, so he prayed this was not the one time that it wouldn't.

Larissa's brows knitted, confusion flitting across her face. Her whole body was already sizzling at the sight of him; her mouth watered with need, her lower region was moist and throbbing, ready to take him. "What do you mean?"

"You know what I mean," he continued his line of bull.

"I *am* responding to you."

"But not in the same way," he insisted, tone taking a fiercer turn. "We've fucked six times, Larissa. I know what I'm talking about. I know when there's a difference in enthusiasm."

Pulling him closer by his nape, she whispered in a desperate plea, "I want this. I want you."

"That may be true, but until you get whatever you were thinking about off your chest, it's going to impede our fun. And I, for one, am not settling for anything less than the happiest ending."

His next move was a gamble. He unbuckled her legs and set her on her feet, which was when Larissa caved and said, "Wait."

He paused, let the internal waves of relief wash over him, and waited with a grim expression.

Larissa sighed, reaching over to smoothen his arched brows and trace his frown. She swallowed and began, "It was something that happened over twenty years ago—in his first affair."

Further perplexity marred his features. So they weren't going to talk about Monica Upshaw?

Swallowing a lump in her throat, Larissa continued, "The woman he slept with birthed a child, and she came to him asking for financial support a few years after the child was born. And . . . I found out about the affair after it ended, but I didn't know who the woman was, not until that day, so when she left . . . I . . ." She averted his gaze, then with nothing but vulnerability, she pleaded, "You have to promise me you'll still look at me the same way after everything I'm about to tell you."

That he'd look at her as nothing more than a vehicle to drive Ferdinand toward the tainted segments of political history and force the minister into resignation once this affair was out? Yes, Patterson was quite sure he'd look at Larissa Ferdinand exactly the same way. "I promise."

She nodded and forced a meek, grateful smile, which fell instantly when she explained, "I called Valor that night, asking for a few hunters and . . . I lied to him that my husband was preoccupied with a government crisis and I was conveying orders on his behalf, then . . . lied again that the woman my husband slept with was disguised as a waitress but was capable of the highest level of danger." Swallowing another lump, she whispered, "I demanded they put an end to her, somewhere deep in a forest where her body could never be found."

Patterson blinked and had to remind himself why he was here. "And I presume you succeeded?"

"Of course," she said numbly, without a smile or a frown, but there was something in her eyes—the residual cut of betrayal. "I specifically ordered Valor to have the hunters end her by explosive means."

Patterson willed his mind to keep working, to keep going because this was not the time to freeze, not in front of a murderer, and definitely not while he was naked. Clearing his throat, he spoke like he was reciting something from a manual, "Hunters don't keep explosives in their inventory."

"They don't store them in the headquarters, and only a select few know about the supply. I don't know if it still exists today, but it did over two decades ago."

"And putting a bullet to the victim's head, then using acid afterward to remove traces of the corpse has never crossed your mind, I presume?"

"It has." She bit her lip, tears of rage burning in her eyes. "But it was too simple. Too easy. And let me remind you that she was never the victim. I was and still am." Her voice radiated infuriation, and her eyes exuded unregretful vindictiveness when she spat, "That woman was the beginning of the breakdown of my marriage, my once perfect life. She deserved a much more brutal end than the one I gave her. Looking back, I should have ordered them to skin her alive before having her detonated."

Patterson thought back to the minister's conversation he overheard earlier. "Was that the issue with Ferdinand on the phone? A two-decade-old problem now resurfacing?"

"No. That's another thing. You see, after my . . . unauthorized order, not only was I banned from making security calls entirely, but I was also forced to stand by and watch my husband hop from one affair to another without being able to say a word, all because he would end my career, my reputation as well as those of my family's by exposing what I did to his first mistress. When the storm of that affair and my . . . unauthorized instructions passed and we tried to make it work, have our own kids and try to leave the past behind, we only came to realize that we would never work, and his affairs started again."

In a lowered voice, hushed like a secret, Patterson questioned, "The Carter and Upshaw deaths. Were you . . ."

She shook her head. "I no longer have the means or access to the professionals to accomplish such a feat, but I'd be lying if I didn't say I'm happy they're dead. My husband has had a penchant for huntresses in recent years, probably because they're young and most have an almost perfect body from your profession's need to work out. He was so terrified of what I'd do to his subsequent mistresses that he hired professionals to keep them safe. Can you believe that? Hiring people to keep his mistresses safe from his own wife. And the stupidest part of his whole plan is that he thinks I don't know. He hasn't told me about the current crisis, but if I were to guess, I'd say his hired professionals screwed up."

"Clearly," he murmured, doing a quick mental recap. "You mention the first mistress had a child."

Larissa bit one side of her bottom lip, admitting, "Yes. And one of your colleagues carries eerily similar features to that woman."

No length of tenure and experience could keep him composed when his eyes widened in genuine shock. "Who?"

CHAPTER 71

In the trenches, Kenji put on a numb exterior—one he wore every day as the head of the eastern octopuses. It was the best way he knew of to withstand the stress that came with the job. And in recent weeks, he'd been under a lot of stress. His vulnerable side had only ever been shown to the people he trusted, which were not many to begin with. And this arrangement worked well enough for him to never contemplate changing.

His numbness projected a firm and tough exterior, one that had always been responded to with efficiency and near-perfect delivery of tasks from his subordinates. Like Sush, he wasn't liked by many, but was well respected by most.

When he was not checking or correcting the western octopuses' work, he hung around the mavericks since he didn't know which hunter to trust, seeing that Hazel was friendly with everyone.

As he was minding his own business in the test lab, the scanner beeped, and in walked Satan's daughter in her impeccable disguise. "Yo! What are you up to?"

He used to be okay with Hazel—didn't like her but didn't hate her either. But after Patterson shared his knowledge about the lie from the hospital, Kenji grew wary. "Test runs," he answered curtly, continuing tapping on his device and watching the simulation unfold, taking notes on parts that required tweaking.

"You haven't been avoiding me, have you?" she asked, undeterred by his indifference, pushing herself up to sit on the empty spot of the table.

Judgment creased his forehead. He refused to meet her gaze as he said pointedly, "You do know test run tables are meant for equipment, right?"

"Ugh, you and Sush are so alike," Hazel groaned and got off.

Kenji had to admit that was true. They were quite alike. It was how they cliqued in the first place, at one time even thinking they shared something more when time showed that they didn't. They were friends—good friends, even, but there was nothing beyond platonic love.

"How do you even do it though? Be okay with her being with someone else?" Hazel piped.

"By being an adult."

"Meaning?"

"Having the sense to remember why it didn't work and the maturity to move on and be happy for myself and for others."

"Even an ex. Wow."

Kenji offered no response, wanting to ask her to leave, but not being able to since she was technically his boss for the time being. When could he return to the east already?

"You're not gonna ask how I'm doing?"

"You seem better than fine. You'll probably last more than six hours."

"Exactly what I told the docs! But they said not to push it. *Leave by the fifth hour*, they all said like I didn't hear it the first time."

Kenji mm-ed. For once, he would've preferred sharing a room with the duke than with Hazel. At least he wouldn't be having mindless conversations with a suspected murderer. The fact that she was still here was a joke to the defense mechanics. She should have at least been suspended, he felt.

"Is this because I'm taking Sush's place? Is that why you're like this?"

"I'm always like this, Hazel. Stop making a fuss."

"You're not like this with Sush."

"You're not Sush."

"Is it because you're only nice to the chief and I'm not one?"

Kenji exhaled hard, eyes shut and neck angled for him to face the ceiling like he was sending a desperate plea to the deity. Any deity. "Hazel," he began, voice low. "I'm working. We're all working. You should be working too."

"You're an ass," Hazel remarked, striding toward the exit while adding in a sing-song voice, "Don't say I didn't try to be your friend."

"Wouldn't dream of it," he muttered. Before learning about her lie, Kenji wouldn't have given Hazel's words another thought. But as she left the room, Kenji's mind wandered.

She was moving about exceptionally well for a person who had been exposed to zahar. The others like her were still stuck at home and worked from home a few hours every day.

Waiting to be left alone in his cubicle, Kenji then waited for Hazel to leave the floor entirely before using his personal tablet to hack into the hospital records. He managed to hack into their systems but—for some reason—hit a wall when he sought to open Hazel's profile, a wall that he didn't immediately know how to break through. And it was strange that there weren't similar walls with the other patients' profiles.

"Yo," the voice from behind him made him jump out of his seat and reflexively let his device fall face down onto the table with a loud thud, garnering attention that he didn't want from the octopuses around him.

Jade seemed unfazed. Kenji wasn't the first hunter he'd unintentionally spooked. "Need some help with that?"

Kenji blinked. "Do you know how?"

Plucking the tablet out of Kenji's hold, Jade casually said, "Maybe. Maybe not. Let's see." He extracted a thumb drive–looking gadget from his pocket, inserted it into the multipurpose jack below the home screen button, returned to the wall Kenji had hit, and tapped in a few digits, and the impediment disappeared as Jade handed him back the device.

"H-How . . ." Kenji accepted the tablet, but his eyes stayed on the gadget that went back into Jade's pocket. Pointing at his pocket, the eastern octopus asked, "Where can I get that, and how much does it cost?"

Jade's lips tugged up. "We made it, and it's not for sale."

"Oh."

"But," Jade continued, giving him a firm pat on the back. "If you're nice to the duke, he might make an exception."

"Ah." Kenji was sure that was never going to happen. "I'll just be content marveling at it from afar."

Jade chuckled as Kenji swiped down the hospital records, and they skimmed through them together, brows furrowing deeper with each paragraph. Each *edited* paragraph.

"Man, this bitch got skills," Jade chimed.

"Or the money and network to buy such skills. We have to warn them," Kenji murmured, his mind bringing in something Hazel said earlier—*"Don't say I didn't try to be your friend"*—it felt like a warning of sorts. Most likely another attack. He just didn't know what it was going to be.

CHAPTER 72

At the diplomatic residence, Sush was on a high stool at the kitchen counter, scrolling through the eastern files that had been opened before the archer massacre for the umpteenth time. She and Greg agreed there wasn't a pattern when they discussed it, but what if they'd missed something?

She lost count of the number of times she tried Ctrl + F and typed in "hyena," "owl," and "rat" and found nothing.

"Eat, please," Greg urged, and left a light kiss on her temple after placing a takeaway box of pasta in front of her as he got into the seat next to hers, removing the laptop from beneath her fingers and setting it to the side, placing it next to his own.

Sush heaved an exhausted sigh and rubbed away the stinging sensation from her strained eyes before lifting the ready cutlery and spearing into the meatball. As she munched, she asked, "Found anything on the ones whose throats were slit?"

"Yes, fortunately. All of them have some form of experience in hacking into the most sophisticated systems." As Greg sliced through the lamb, imagining it was Valor's and Ferdinand's flesh, he continued, "The first octopus, Porsha Delaware, was a coding prodigy and once hacked into a toy company to get her brother a building block set for his birthday that their family couldn't afford."

"Champion of a sister," Sush mused, subconsciously raising her half-filled mug like she was toasting to the feat.

Despite being equally impressed, Greg continued monotonously, "She impressed the state so much that they dropped charges, gave their family another few sets of toys, and gave Delaware a fully-funded education until she graduated and joined the hunters. But she was kept at the innovation side of things, never system codes."

"I wish I met her," Sush commented, then slurped on her pasta.

"Didn't think you had a penchant for toys," Greg taunted in feigned ignorance with the same flat tone but with a slight tilt of his lips, inciting her annoyance. She nudged his side with her elbow, drawing a bigger smile from him.

Melting at the lift of his lips, she replied, "Why wouldn't I? I plan to get Lewis something anyway."

Greg was careful enough to not choke this time, and deduced his best way forward was to just move on—to change the subject. But the best way wasn't normally the fun way, so he refused to drop the matter. "Unlike the Delawares, the Blackfurs are nowhere near the edge of poverty. The little seat stealer doesn't need more toys."

"Do you know anything about kids his age? There'll never be enough toys. Has Enora ever had enough weapons?"

"That's different," he defended, raising his forefinger like she normally did. "She's training to defend herself when she grows up."

"Shooting a bastard with a crossbow is an offense, not defense."

"Using offense is a defense. And one can never wield too many weapons."

"Those are toys, too, Greg," Sush noted with narrowed eyes.

"Toys that have better applications in the real world. You're a huntress. You know that."

Shaking her head with a smile, conveniently choosing not to mention that the hunters of today used guns and other heavy machinery, never crossbows or arrows, she then prompted, "Who's next after Porsha Delaware?"

"The twins—Regina and Austin Chen. Chameleons. At seventeen, they created a system that hacked into any hacker's account when one invaded their private files, sending over a computer virus to wipe out the hacker's hardware completely."

"Nice."

"There's nothing to show that they utilized those skills when they joined the hunters, seeing that they were chameleons."

"That's a waste."

"My thoughts exactly. And the final one: Shahrul Ibrahim from the east—wiretapped his teacher's phone at the age of twelve after being verbally abused in class. He later released a recording of some very explicit content."

"Of?"

"That teacher and his mistress. Word spread throughout their region. The two were forced to resign."

"Wow, a legend of an octopus right there." Closing the empty box, she piped, "They were all precocious hackers and privacy invaders . . . which means they invaded the privacy of someone who had the resources to remove them. Could the mavericks find anything? Any particular person they've all pissed off?"

"I haven't told them yet. Thought I'd run it through you first."

Brows shooting to her hair, she said, "The mavericks are under your command."

"And the hunters' archives—which are all that I've been digging through—are under yours. I don't have sole jurisdiction here." He stood, grabbed her empty box and his own, and headed for the trash.

Her brows furrowed. "You've never needed my permission before deploying your people before."

The corner of his mouth quirked in a way that made her insides flutter. He came back over with eyes fixed on hers, leaning forward to press a kiss to her shoulder, murmuring, "I wonder what changed."

When their faces leveled, she stole a kiss from his lips, forgetting about her suspension and everything else for a few moments, feeling the warmth of his lips, tasting the saltiness in his mouth, getting lost in the dance between their tongues as her hands trailed all over him while his hands groped every part of her. Their touches were filled with a different kind of need—not the primal, lusting kind, but the kind where two souls yearned for the deep connection they could only find in each other.

It took a long moment before they came down from their high, coming back from the fantasy where it was only the two of them, then reluctantly left each other's embrace—but not each other's side—and got back to work.

In the following hours, as Greg checked in with the mavericks in the trenches, Sush went through the eastern documents.

Then she remembered something: There was a formatting issue when she first opened these files. Her mind came to a standstill for a minute or two. Then, deciding to backtrack her edits and remove each one, she again scrutinized the sections she'd changed. That was when she saw it—not a pattern, but a message.

"Greg!" she hollered, too shocked to get up.

Greg sped from the study, immediately dropping his link with Jade and Ella, appearing by Sush's side within the next second. "What happened?" he asked, frantic, skimming her—twice—and being relieved to find no injuries.

"I found this," she uttered, voice lowered, stunned, as she angled the laptop toward him.

He positioned the laptop back in front of her as he stood directly behind her, and his breath fanned the crown of her head when he tried to see what she saw. Sush leaned into him as she waited, drowning in the heat radiating from his body, taking comfort in his scent, and cherishing the safety that came with the way his body shielded hers.

Greg's eyes on her desktop popped from one minimized screen to the next, going through all seven of them and starting again.

The first file, Ferdinand's name was bolded.

The second, Jagah—the remote location where Catrine Carter was sent to and subsequently found dead in—was in a smaller-sized font for some reason. The change was so minute that it was almost imperceptible at a cursory glance.

The third was a page that specified the hunters involved in the task, and the word "Robinson" had a double spacing between each letter, and—coincidentally or not coincidentally—it was Hazel's family name.

The fourth, a three-line paragraph that was thought to be redacted for no reason, left only the words "premium," "lycan," and "blood" unredacted.

The fifth, the words "black market" was bolded the same way Ferdinand's name was.

The sixth, "Carter" was in the same smaller-sized font as "Jagah," though this Carter was another individual entirely—not Catrine Carter herself.

The seventh, the explosion file—there was nothing jarring within the document itself, but the jarring thing had already been identified earlier on: the fact that it was kept open the longest.

There wasn't a pattern. But there was a connection: Ferdinand and black market; Jagah and Catrine Carter; the Robinsons, which may or may not include Hazel's parents since the file was on a task that occurred during the retirees' tenure; premium lycan blood—Enora's blood, most likely because whispers in the underworld about the royal family's unusual ability to heal from poisons had circulated, as much as those who were loyal to the said family tried to stifle its circulation; and the explosion—vague, but not irrelevant—about his car, Sush's late mother, and the archer, Sakura Kondo, from many years ago.

"It wasn't a formatting issue," he muttered, almost to himself.

Sush had no response, and as Greg's hands wrapped around the balls of her shoulders, something else hit her and she turned frigid, which set off the panic button in Greg, too, when he gazed down and demanded, "What?"

Patting his chest in quick succession like she was hastening him, she said, "The footage of the eastern murders. The six archers with the culprit in the beanie. Where is it? I want it."

"You have it right here," he uttered steadily, as much as his heart was beating erratically inside.

He opened the file and pushed Play. Sush immediately paused the video when it reached the part where the culprit was facing—though not looking—at the camera. Zooming in, she groaned at the pixelated image, now blurred through enlargement.

"Patience, my octopus. Jade taught me this trick a while back." Greg used a program, clicked around here and there, and got the image to sharpen.

Sush knew those eyes. "Zoom out a little." Once he did, she stared at the screen with even larger eyes and hissed in a whisper, "Fuck. Me."

"I'd love to, but I hope you'll tell me what this means first."

"That's her!" Sush exclaimed like it was obvious, hand gesturing at the screen. "That's Monica Upshaw!"

The person in a beanie was—evidently—never a he and never a thug.

When Monica said she had been in touch with Sush, the chief octopus had expected it to be something more direct, but even she had to admit this was a sleek move to convey a message—a message that the archer most likely had conveyed at the expense of her own safety, resulting in her death. Someone must have found out and shut her up for good, and if the clues she left were to be believed, their answers lay in Ferdinand and the Robinsons.

CHAPTER 73

The doorbell jerked Sush out of her shock, and a deep sense of protectiveness took over Greg, who instructed, "Get your gun loaded and ready. Don't come out until I say otherwise."

Head whirled to him, she protested, "What? N—"

"*Don't* come out until I say otherwise," Greg repeated, his deepened voice and partially onyx eyes cutting her off sternly, though as gently as he could.

Greg strode away before she could argue and was relieved to hear her releasing the safety of her weapon. The moment Greg disappeared from the kitchen, Sush hopped off her seat and moved swiftly to the wall partitioning the kitchen from the living room, making sure she had a good angle to fire in case whoever was behind the door decided to attack.

Greg, however, blocked most of the door when he opened it, so she couldn't see who it was. He sighed, then impatiently said, "I don't recall organizing a bonding pity party."

"Your Grace, we came with important leads." Sush recognized it as Kenji's hushed voice.

We?

She came out of her hiding spot, approaching the door confidently as Greg replied, "There is something called conveying messages through texts or . . ."

"Greg, c'mon. Let them in," Sush urged, a hand on his bicep.

Greg heaved another sigh before turning to her and said, "What did I say about not coming out here until I say otherwise? What if they're here to kill you?"

Patterson's and Kenji's brows rose simultaneously. The chief chameleon blinked repeatedly and said, "Excuse me?"

Kenji followed suit. "We're not the ones prepared with a gun." His chin nodded at the weapon in Sush's hand.

Patterson's sights dropped there as well before meeting Sush's eyes with a narrowed set of his own. "Really, Sush? Really?"

"We weren't expecting company and took precautions when we heard the bell," Sush defended, then turned to Greg, once again urging, "Greg, let them in."

Greg turned to the men and put out a hand, demanding, "Weapons."

Patterson and Kenji surrendered their pistols, but right before they stepped through, Greg held a hand up, grabbed a dome-shaped gadget made to look like a keychain hung from the keyholder, and stuck the flat, adhesive side on the doorframe. "Metal detector," he explained, then stepped aside and waved them through, gesturing them to enter.

Patterson stepped through with no issues.

Kenji stayed outside, marveling at yet another thing he guessed wasn't for sale. "Why didn't you say that before you stuck it there? I'm wearing a belt and have coins in my wallet."

"Belt and wallet come through first then," Greg chimed, holding out his hand again, taking Kenji's wallet and belt as they came.

The midway line on the dome gadget glowed in faint yellow before it opened to both sides and fired a bullet, which—fortunately—shot directly at the opposite side of the doorframe, making a Kenji—who looked betrayed and frantic—whisper-yell, "What the fuck?"

As much as Greg wanted to remain serious, he couldn't help but feel amused. "It only fires in a straight line. If you're worried, you could always come through underneath it. The detector will still scan for metal, but it won't be able to kill you."

After Kenji patted himself, checking again that he had no metal on him, he lowered his head and entered below the invisible threshold that the gadget had set, relieved to see that it didn't go off.

"Congratulations, Sophisticated, you came out alive," Greg chimed as he extracted the dome from the wall and hung it back on the keyholder, shutting the door behind him.

As they made their way to the kitchen, Kenji wasn't even subtle in complaining to Sush that her boyfriend secretly wanted to kill him, which she denied, saying he'd kill whoever he wanted without waiting around for anyone to speculate, which didn't make the eastern octopus feel any safer.

Turning to Patterson, Kenji questioned, "How did your belt not set it off?"

"I'm not wearing one. Left it at the whore's house. I don't plan on going back for it." Patterson spared his colleagues the details of how Larissa wanted to "spice up" their session by having her hands tied to the bed frame and his belt tied over her mouth. When it was over and Larissa was about to slide the belt—infected with the dried-up bacteria from her mouth—through the first loop of his pants, he stopped her by her hand, whispering alluringly, "You keep it. For next time."

Though she seemed turned on, he was internally disgusted. He never wanted the belt back.

At the kitchen counter, they got into the high stools and spent the next hour exchanging information. Greg and Sush went first, Kenji next after they'd come down from the shock of the Monica Upshaw revelation, digesting the fact that she'd killed six of her fellow archers. Patterson, who went last, treaded carefully when he concluded by holding Sush's hard gaze with a wary one of his own. "She said the woman she killed looked a lot like . . . you."

In the pocket of silence, each dove into their thoughts.

Sush tried to think but suddenly didn't know how to.

Greg was momentarily shocked before his first meeting with Ferdinand flashed into mind and the befuddlement from the other day clicked—why he found the minister familiar yet unfamiliar at the same time—the slope of his nose and the thickness of his brows. He took another good look at Sush and ultimately realized—with dread—why that was.

Sush had inherited most of her mother's features, but she wasn't spared from inheriting parts of her father's face.

When Kenji was the first to get over the shock, he asked Patterson, "And you still slept with her despite that? After knowing she detonated someone?"

Patterson's eyes narrowed as he heaved a frustrated sigh that essentially conveyed, "Is that even the most important thing right now?"

Ignoring the two, Greg's hand found Sush's, his eyes laced with nothing but concern. "Sush, do you need a moment alone?"

Kenji and Patterson were about to get on their feet when she said, "No." Swallowing and averting her eyes from everyone, she said, "No, I don't. There's no way that's true. My mother isn't a . . . She would never . . ." Her head swung side to side, denial coursing through her body. But in that denial, a thorn of doubt grew. Her uncle had told her that her mother had fallen for "the wrong man." She'd assumed that meant falling for a man who neither wanted a child nor marital commitments. She'd never thought a wrong man could be loosely translated to mean an unavailable one.

A gnawing feeling spiraled in her gut, and heat rushed to her cheeks at what felt like shame, even though there was no concrete proof yet. In a whisper to herself, she questioned, "Would she?"

After another brief moment of silence, Greg gently lifted her chin and held her gaze, giving her a modicum of strength through his touch. "Sush, if you want to find out, we can. All it takes is a paternity test, but please know that who your mother was is not who you are, you hear me? Please."

"So you believe her. You believe the murderer," Sush deduced, her voice on the verge of breaking.

"Sush." Greg held her down by her elbows when he felt she was going to uproot herself from his hold, tears burning in her eyes in a way that was sending a twisting knife through his heart. His hands slid down her arms in a fruitless attempt to soothe her. Bringing her increasingly cold fingers to his lips, pressing a kiss, he uttered, "The Red Devil may be lying, or she may be telling the truth, in which case, it'll either simply be you sharing resemblance with a stranger she only saw once in her life or . . ."

". . . or my mother?" Sush finished. "You really think that's a possibility?"

Greg wanted to lie, wanted to say no just to please her, to calm her down even if it was only temporary, but he couldn't, not when he knew her, not when he knew she'd rather be gutted by the truth than be kissed by a lie. He stayed silent, knowing that she'd be able to extract her answer from it, which she did.

Looking away and biting the inner walls of her mouth, suppressing the shitstorm of emotions hailing inside, she reminded herself that Patterson's intel hadn't been confirmed, that it may not be true. If it was, then . . . then she'd deal with it when the time came.

Greg said nothing, eyes never leaving her, giving her time as his thumb stroked her hands, letting her know he was there, that he'd always be there.

When Sush came to terms with the fact that confirming the identity of her birth father was not the most important thing at the moment, she cleared her throat, wiping away a stray tear on her sleeve. Greg gently reached for the next one that came out before she turned back to the counter, staring at the marble surface, trying to sound strong when she said, "We should focus on exposing Hazel and getting to the root of the threats that've been hitting the hunters. How about we start with the retired Robinsons' current location?"

CHAPTER 74

On file, Hazel's parents were said to reside in their family holiday cottage in a quiet countryside. It would have passed off as an unsuspicious choice if that countryside hadn't been Itam—the very place where Monica Upshaw was found dead.

Upon hacking the Land Office's records, they also found that the Robinsons owned three other cottages in remote locations, one of them being Jagah, though the far end of Jagah from where Catrine Carter was later found.

After several mavericks confirmed the information, Greg mused, "Really confident or really idiotic to have the properties registered under their actual names."

"I'd say the former," Kenji offered numbly. "They probably got away with things before and didn't see the need to take such—" he waved at the screen "—tedious precautions."

"Over-confident idiots," Greg murmured.

Even if they were confident that they weren't going to get caught then, there was no guarantee that they wouldn't be exposed in the future. Changes in time, good practices, and leaders were factors that would always be beyond one's control, and precautions should have been taken even when times were good. Greg knew this from experience.

The more hilarious finding for the duke was that—with another few clicks—they pinpointed the retired Robinsons' most recent location in Itam, heightening suspicions that they really were behind the Monica Upshaw murder.

Why they'd done it remained the question. Was it because they had something against Ferdinand or the professionals he hired to keep his mistresses safe? Or were they commissioned by Larissa herself?

Patterson didn't think so. Larissa looked like she'd given up trying to go after all the women her husband was sleeping with.

The four of them in the kitchen contacted Millicent, who felt left out that she wasn't invited to what she'd gathered was an intel circle. They asked if she could get the archers stationed near all of the Robinsons' cottages to check if the places were occupied, with Greg insisting they took a few lycan warriors with them.

If the cottage had no signs of occupation in the next five hours, they were to leave and not bother trespassing. No one knew if the Robinsons had been careful enough to install security cameras around the properties, where the footage would be accessible through their phones or other devices from anywhere around the world.

Before Millicent deployed her troops, Patterson added—unnecessarily, in case the chief archer was hesitant—that since Millicent was chief, she didn't need authorization because self-authorization was apparently a form of authorization as well, a response that got a lot of narrowed eyes and judgmental looks around the kitchen counter, even from Millicent herself at her end of the line.

The newly minted chief didn't care if Valor or Ferdinand didn't authorize it. If Sush gave the green light, it was a go.

All that was left to do was wait and hope no casualties would be reported during the search for the psycho's parents.

At the three-hour mark, one of the teams reported that the lights in the house had just come on, and a man that matched the retired octopus's profile had come out and sat on the old wooden bench outside.

The location?

Itam.

"Over-confident idiots," Greg muttered again.

Linking the kingdom for backup of warriors and mavericks—with Lucy specifically informing Greg not to engage in any form of attack until they got there—the four in the kitchen then met Millicent at the hangar holding Greg's jet.

Prepared with the newly designed masks and goggles, plus a bulletproof bodysuit underneath, they kept reminding each other that they didn't know for sure whether the Robinsons were the actual culprits, though each found themselves unable to reach an alternative conclusion.

The issue arose as to how they'd bring in the retirees based on "reasonable grounds for suspicion" when none of them had been authorized by Valor to do that.

Sush flipped open her laptop and began forging an arrest warrant while Kenji worked on putting it into the system in case the Robinsons decided to check or call their daughter to have her do the checking.

They'd expected to only be confronting two Robinsons, so their plan became a little flimsy when their watchers reported that Hazel had just stepped foot into the perimeter. And she spooked them when the thin line of her lips curled into a sinister smirk despite not making eye contact with any of them.

"She's expecting us," Kenji uttered, exhaling like all hope was lost.

CHAPTER 75

The wooden cottage seemed normal enough from afar with its moldy brick walls, thatched roof, and casement windows. Narrow trees, bushes, and shrubs grew all around. Luscious grass covered the land, save for a stone path from the entrance door to the wooden gate.

The lights went off about thirty minutes before Greg, Sush, and the others arrived. The watchers reported that no one had come out. And everyone had been smart enough not to suggest that the Robinsons may be taking a nap since it had hardly been four hours since they were up. But the stillness was unsettling.

Greg grew impatient when nothing happened for the next thirty minutes, and ordered Baxter to send in a drone—one in the shape of a firefly that flew to the window, where its cameras caught nothing, then glided to the front door, sneaking in through the gap.

Despite the gloomy weather outside, it was still bright enough for the drone to spy without needing to turn on its torch. On every maverick's phone, they watched the footage live while the hunters who weren't keeping their eyes on their surroundings crowded around the mavericks.

The interior carried earthy tones—brown furniture, wool carpet, a stone fireplace with actual firewood, and pendant lights hung from the ceiling. A daffodil-yellow shawl was thrown over the edge of the couch littered with throw pillows of bright marigold. The coffee table had a tray of two teacups—one emptied and one half filled—and a white porcelain pot with printed pink peonies.

The drone flew closer to the ceiling, getting a bird's-eye view. Rows of framed photos sat on any flat surface that could hold one—the top of the fireplace, drawers, low cabinets.

Zoning in on the most cluttered surface—the chest of drawers—the drone landed and paused as the mavericks and hunters studied the photos. To everyone's surprise and bewilderment, none of the pictures were of the Robinsons. In fact, the people in the photos looked nothing like Robinsons.

There wasn't a common thread between them either. There were men and women of all colors, shapes, sizes, and attire.

When a picture of a man in a turban came into view, Sush instantly said, "Stop."

Baxter halted the drone.

"Do you know him?" Greg asked, hand on her shoulder.

Sush's brows furrowed deep, thinking hard. She knew him. She just didn't know where she knew him from. After a moment of silence, a bolt of recognition entered her eyes as she whispered like it was a secret, "He looks like one of those deported after the hunters took over investigating my mother's case. In fact, he looks like the one who *led* the investigation before he was dismissed."

"Is he the only familiar face so far?"

She mm-ed.

Greg nodded at Baxter to keep it going, and when there wasn't anyone else of interest, the drone flew over to the fireplace and continued its spying there. The first photo was strong enough to make many breaths hitch.

It was a face that had Baxter and the others whirling their heads toward Sush—a photo of a smiling woman who looked uncannily similar to the chief octopus. The dirty gold frame held a thin layer of dust, a sign that it was cleaned often though not often enough. On the lower right corner of the frame, there was a handwritten date in black, and Sush instantly recognized it as the date she and her relatives last saw her mother.

As the drone moved on to the next pictures, everyone tore their sights off Sush and reluctantly turned back to the screens. Only those who'd been privy to the eastern files recognized Porsha Delaware, Regina and Austin Chen, Shahrul Ibrahim, and Sakura Kondo. But gasps and murmurs soon spread amongst the hunters when the photos of the last three came into view—Catrine Carter, Monica Upshaw, and Sush herself. And while every frame had a date written at the right corner, the one with Sush's picture remained clear.

While Sush's mind ventured down the possible reasons the Robinsons wanted her dead—whether because she was getting close to discovering their crimes, simply because she was the daughter of one of their victims and was technically a living loose end, or something less aggressive like she had been appointed chief over their daughter who'd been deputy for years, Greg's darkened eyes and raging breaths radiated an anger that no one could match.

He instructed Baxter to scan the property for inhabitants, poisons, and explosives, finding nothing. The drone could detect that the air was clear of poisonous substances and that none of the cabinets and shelves held them, but that didn't mean there wouldn't be anything since the drone couldn't break through floorboards and feel through cushions for hidden poisons.

As the drone was being brought out, Greg uttered, "There must be a hidden room leading to an underground passageway. We should go in and have a look."

He meant the mavericks and lycan warriors, so when Sush rose from her squatting position, he held her by her waist with an unyielding grip that was more resolute than affectionate. "Where do you think you're going, my octopus?"

Her brows arched. "You said we're going in to have a look."

"I said *we*—" his hand gestured to himself and his fellow lycans "—are going in to have a look. You're not part of this club. Yet. I apologize for having to disappoint you, Sush, but you're staying until we've made sure that place is really poison-free."

"And what if it isn't?" Sush challenged, fixing him in an unwavering stare. "What if it isn't poison-free? What if there's oleander?" Despite her sharp tone, anyone could hear the worry in her voice even if they couldn't see it from her eyes.

Dodging her point on purpose, the duke simply replied, "Precisely. Which is why you and the other hunters should stay here for now." Leaving a quick kiss on her cheek, he attempted to wrap up the issue. "I'll update you once we'v—"

Eyes trained on him, she tapped on the communication device hooked at her ear, instructing the hunters, "Teams B and C, stay where you are. Don't engage until instructed. Team A, we're going in with the duke."

The leaders of each team responded, "Copy that, Chief."

As the mavericks tried not to smile or scoff at how little power their boss had over the chief, who was now smirking at him, Greg's brows furrowed just the slightest when he uttered in a dismayed whisper, "Why do you do this?"

"Do what? Not do as I'm told?"

"That's not what I meant and you know it."

"Just like you knew what my concern was when I brought up oleander."

"None of their victims were lycans, so I doubt they have oleander stored."

Jabbing his stone-hard chest with her finger, she refuted, "You have no way of knowing that, especially not when lycans have been curbing the last two attacks by getting the hunters out on time. Your species may have already created a big enough hurdle for them to take notice and put contingency plans in place."

In the pocket of silence that followed, with Greg scrambling his mind for a counter-argument, the firefly drone buzzed across the tense atmosphere and landed neatly back in Baxter's storage can.

Sush's firm voice permeated through the silence, "I've already given orders. We can either waste more time here, or we can check out the abode together."

At that line, Kenji rose and took the first step out, effectively signaling the rest of team A to follow suit.

Greg heaved a frustrated exhale, fingers sliding into Sush's as they barged toward the property together.

The hunters and mavericks circled the cottage, leaving no window or door unguarded.

Right before Greg touched the door handle, the wooden structure swung open from the inside, and they locked eyes with a sly smirking Traffic Cone, who cheerily chimed, "What took you guys so long? Have trouble finding the place?"

CHAPTER 76

Shocked. Spooked. Dubious.

Kenji was sure he was seeing a ghost.

Jade wondered if their drones had been hacked.

Baxter was recalling the last time he sent the drone for maintenance. How did it miss a human?

Patterson, Sush, and Greg knew the game was on.

Leaning against the doorframe with one hand holding her phone—screen facing Sush and the others that showed a big, bright, blinking orange button right in the middle that could activate Goddess knew what—Hazel began with the Chief Chameleon. "I always knew you had a thing for older women."

"Cut the crap, Hazel," he spat, not at all surprised by her knowledge.

"Who is that, my little hyena?" an unfamiliar feminine voice carrying a taunting ring came from inside.

Hazel kept her eyes on her colleagues, her smirk tilting higher when a flash of realization entered Sush's and Greg's eyes at her parents' pet name for her.

Hazel pulled the door back further to reveal her mother with lemon hair and marigold highlights, glasses that had medallion-yellow frames in the shape of a five-petal flower. She was knitting leisurely on the couch, and the daffodil shawl sprawled on the pillows before was now around her neck.

Her father, with short, combed-back caramel-brown hair that didn't look natural even from afar, beamed from behind the newspaper that was held upside down—most likely on purpose, looking more harmless than his wife.

At the door, their daughter chirped, "These are friends. You both remember, Sush, right?"

The couple's eyes hadn't left the suspended octopus since the door opened. Hazel's mother adjusted her lensless frames with a small smile that Sush once saw many, many years ago when she was invited to sit with them on a parent-trainee visit. "Ah, the Rat. You've grown! And looking more like your mother." She chuckled. "Good that you've been making better decisions than her though. I've always thought apples never fall far from the tree."

Although Greg and several others emitted warning growls, it took everything in Sush not to bark out questions when she had a strong feeling she wasn't going to like the answers.

The old man turned to his wife. "One who doesn't take after her mother could always take after her father, dear. This one may be leaning closer to the paternal tree."

"Oh, that's not fair, honey," she reprimanded, pausing the knitting like they were just spending a casual afternoon together. "They may have both found their ways to the defense sector, but Ferdinand never had the brains to cover his own arse with all those mistresses, let alone cover the arse of the country. God knows how many children he fathered, but this girl might be his most successful yet."

Deciding that she had heard enough, Sush suppressed the raging typhoon of resentment, unwantedness, and shame, and—through gritted teeth—warned, "You're surrounded and outnumbered. Surrender and we won't have to kill you."

The old couple burst into laughter like they'd just heard a joke. Mrs. Robinson even leaned forward to pour some tea. It was then that most of them saw a gun leaning against a throw pillow. Even with a gun, they were outnumbered, yet they seemed so calm about it.

Greg's restraint was hanging by a fine thread. The only thing stopping him was the damn button that matched Traffic Cone's hair. Despite not knowing what it did, Greg and his animal knew it was wiser to refrain from lunging until Hazel was fully distracted, which wasn't now.

Even if they got to the remote, there was no telling whether her parents had another one hidden somewhere that she'd be able to activate from a distance. He only hoped his people surrounding the property were already planting mini explosives to tear down the walls. The only problems with these mini versions they'd created was that they took time to set up. Their impact was limited to demolishing the building without affecting those outside, so the mavericks had to make sure the explosives were properly buried within the crevices of the walls.

Sush's voice, cold and calculated, rang through the air, "We've seen enough to know you and your family have something to do with the recent attacks, Hazel."

Hazel's head cocked when she said, "Well, that's offensive." There was a glint in her eye, the kind that admitted to a crime but was challenging her opponent, one that asked how far her interrogator would go to make her talk. The corner of her lips tilted higher. "It's offensive that you think we had *something* to do with the not-so-accidental accidents when we have *everything* to do with it."

Though unintended, several hunters amongst them took a step back.

"That's an admission," Kenji muttered to himself.

"No shit, genius," Hazel replied flatly, predatorial eyes never leaving her family's latest target, whose photo had a frame that remained dateless. "But I do admit I'm impressed with your speed this time, Chief. I was touched, though a little underwhelmed, when you never even suspected I was involved in the conspiracy with Izabella and the others. I mean, every other chief and deputy chief were involved . . . well, except for Abbott. We had to leave him out. Too straight an arrow. But the rest of us? We were a *great* team. Did you really think I was incapable of playing the game?" She chuckled. "And to top it off, you even threw my name in the hat when it came to appointing the next chief. Appealed when you'd been appointed instead." She shook her head, drawing immense satisfaction from how naive her leader had been. "And because of that, I thought it'd take you at least another week before you find your way to one of the Robinsons' humble abodes. Since I've had to rush back, there hasn't been a lot of time to clean up the place. I hope the dust wasn't too obstructive for the little bug you guys sent in."

"How did you even know we were coming?" Patterson questioned, brows furrowed, tone defensive.

Hazel asked. "Millicent really should have taken a few lessons on encrypting her devices, you know?"

Sush took over, "Since you're big on sharing and being honest today, let me ask you this: Why kill the people you killed?"

"Oh." Hazel's brows rose like she was reminded of something. "How rude of me not to explain. Your mother . . . it wasn't personal. It was a job. Valor got a call from Larissa Ferdinand, and then Valor called Mom and Dad here since they were the only octopuses with access to the type of . . . equipment requested, and—boom!—it happened."

Sush was about to lunge at Hazel at the unnecessary sound effect, but Greg held her back when Hazel's thumb got dangerously close to the button and the old woman's hand went around the grip of the gun, smile faltering just the slightest.

"As for the others," Hazel continued, "they were too snoopy. Delaware, the Chens, Ibrahim. All of them. They had one job—to be hunters and stay in their lane. But they just had to come across some shit on Ferdinand which—unfortunately—led the trace back to my parents, so Mom and Dad obviously had to get rid of them. And don't even get them started on Sakura Kondo." She shook her head and then rolled her eyes like something was bogus. "The lengths that little woman went to crack us down were psychotic. Did you know Mom was pregnant with me at that time? I mean, Kondo herself was pregnant, too, but that's beside the point. The point is, plotting with Dad to get rid of that nuisance of a Japanese flower did not help with the stress. We're lucky I came out healthy and well."

"Definitely not how I'd put it," Greg spat.

Ignoring him, Hazel tapped her phone on her chin like she was thinking, thumb staying a few inches near the button. "You know, Sush, you really should have taken a hint when your car was hijacked. That was a warning. But you obviously didn't listen. If you had, we wouldn't have had to do that whole thing with the elevator and the archers. It was so much work." Hazel sighed like she was getting exhausted just talking about it. A glint entered her eyes like she'd had an epiphany. "Come to think of it, you're rivaling Sakura Kondo in being a thorn in our side. Maybe anything Japanese related tends to be a nuisance, Sush. You're not of Japanese descent, obviously, but your name does resemble sushi. Then again, we only have you and Sakura so far, so we might need a larger sample before . . ."

Kenji stepped forward and snarled, "This. Ends. Here. Hazel. No more victims. You'll be lucky if you're ever allowed to see outside prison walls again."

"You sure about that?" Her thumb went that much closer to the button, and she relished the fear entering Kenji's eyes for the brief moment when he wasn't conscious of it.

Something still didn't click for Patterson. "And what do the Robinsons get out of this?"

Hazel's gaze pivoted to him, turning away from Sush and Greg, her face morphing into disgust at his lack of imagination. "Money for holiday trips and power over the defense minister to do whatever. Duh."

"Ferdinand knows you're behind the Delilah conspiracy?" Kenji questioned, eyes narrowing further.

"Why wouldn't he?" Hazel threw him another berating glare like he was too slow for her taste. "How do you think he's been maintaining his mistresses all these years? The black market pays a lot for access to human territories to sell and transport their products. And all Old Ferdy had to do was lower defenses. But his most daring venture definitely went sideways. Our family's mistake was to co-sign with him on a deal that he couldn't uphold, and we had to pay the thugs for the breach. Ferdy owes us a ton of money for that loss. We had to cut ties with him, obviously. The plan has been to take down his mistresses one by one every couple of weeks until he pays up. It really isn't that hard, seeing that we've been the ones protecting them. Spoiler alert, we're getting him kicked out of office pretty soon. Gonna circulate about how incompetent Old Ferdy has become with so many recent attacks. And our new ally, Joyce Clearwater, has promised to be a more cooperative new puppet. We'll still have to find a way to get what the thugs want to get back into their good books, of course, so not all is resolved yet."

"What do the thugs want?" Sush questioned in a snarl.

Shrugging like it was obvious, Hazel said, "What else? Royal lycan blood."

A thunderous growl that shook the walls came as fast as Hazel was knocked down, and the phone in her hand slipped before it was caught by Jade, who plugged in his gadget and shut the phone down entirely.

In Greg's defense, his animal made him pounce on the Traffic Cone before his human could rein in the beast.

CHAPTER 77

Several things happened within the next few seconds: a stone-faced Mrs. Robinson aiming at Greg and pulling the trigger to discharge the oleander bullet, Sush yelling at everyone to take cover while she herself attempted to pull Greg off Hazel, and Greg using Hazel as a human shield as the bullet scraped across her shoulder while he angled away before he saw Mr. Robinson aimed at Sush at the same time his claws scratched across Hazel's chest, tearing through her shirt and bulletproof vest underneath.

The initial plan was to kill the orange-headed nuisance as painfully as time allowed him to, and the smell of her blood had been a good start, but time clearly didn't offer him the luxury to do more at the moment. The gun aimed at his octopus took priority.

Greg wrapped his arms around Sush and rolled them out of the way as the bullet jammed through the door. On the ground outside, they overheard Hazel's mother apologizing frantically to her little hyena as her husband guided their daughter inside.

Mrs. Robinson—unsmiling and fuming murderously—stood by the door and aimed at Greg again before Kenji and Millicent shot her in the arm and hand while Patterson shot her in the chest. Her gun fell from her hand as blood splattered from her palm. She wobbled, but her chest was unscathed thanks to the vest. As Millicent aimed for Mrs. Robinson's head and fired, Mr. Robinson appeared just in time to haul his wife in, narrowly missing the bullet before slamming the door shut, at which time the little explosives that the mavericks had indeed planted around the property detonated while they fled and took cover.

When the walls crumbled, everyone's noses detected something. Some lycans began hearing it.

Gas.

Baxter cautiously linked, *'Boss, that smells like . . .'*

"MASKS AND GOGGLES ON! NOW!" Greg yelled when he, too, recognized it as zahar—and not a low concentration of it. Sush instructed all hunters to do the same and check that their skin wasn't exposed.

When the walls came down like wood raining inside the cottage, those surrounding the property waited for signs of life. And although nothing moved, no one was convinced that the Robinsons were dead. The hunters and mavericks began digging through the broken wood, yanking and throwing only to find furniture, fallen picture frames, and everything they'd seen through the drone's eye.

Foreheads creased as dissatisfaction tensed the quiet atmosphere. Their eyes searched until they landed on the fireplace. An empty fireplace. Without the firewood from before.

Ella tossed a teardrop-sized grenade toward the flat surface, and—after a brief blast—they discovered it opened into a tunnel large enough for any human to fit through. Baxter sent in his drone without being instructed while the rest of the warriors and mavericks who had dug deep enough through the wood and furniture now began tearing off the floorboards, scouring for anything that may be of use. The hunters pulled open drawers and patted through the cushions for the same reason.

The tunnel led to an underground passageway with a maglev train track. With a tap of a button, Baxter got the firefly drone to morph into a hummingbird, pushing its speed to the limit. On everyone's screens that had been split into two, the left side showed the map of their area from an aerial view, and the right displayed the image captured by the drone's eyes. Most held their breaths in pure awe at the escape route with impressive technological advancement under a region that seemed three decades behind, wondering how far it stretched.

In the quiet space, only a few heard Kenji ask in a whisper, "That won't run out of fuel, will it?"

"No," Baxter replied curtly, not having any surplus in his concentration to elaborate that the hummingbird could be pushed to its maximum speed for at least two hours before it faltered.

When a vessel finally came into view, Baxter tried his best to reach it—to latch the drone onto it. The adrenaline rushing through his veins and those of the others watching was momentarily interrupted by Ella, who was looking through the floorboards with the others, stiffly saying, "Boss, there's something ticking here. It's not a bomb, but it looks like it'll activate Lord knows what in less than two minutes. One forty-nine. One forty-eight. One . . ."

"JADE!" Greg called out. He handed his device playing out the hummingbird's journey to Sush and asked her to stay put and keep an eye on the lengthening route—a gentle but firm order that she didn't listen to as she followed him with eyes still glued to the screen. They joined Ella with Jade at the far corner of the demolished cottage, under the floorboards of kitchen cabinets.

While Jade carefully fiddled through the wires that were passed through holes that'd been drilled sideways underground, everyone contemplated where it could lead to. The moment Jade stiffened, Greg and the others stopped thinking when the top hacker muttered at the glowing numbers, "Please tell me there are no sprinklers on that field."

That line was enough to pull Sush's widened eyes off the screen and onto him.

Ulysa, who did a cursory search across the field with a few others, shut her eyes and heaved a sigh of despair. "Have to disappoint you, Jade. Good news is that we've taken some of their bowls here to cover the sprinklers. Bad news is that . . ."

". . . it'll corrode or break the material, and we don't know whether the sprinklers have been set to spurt people in the face. Yeah," Jade finished as his mind and hands got to work.

While silent curses flew and Jade examined the controls to see if there was anything he could do, Baxter yelled in excitement. "Boss, I got 'em! We're on the tube. Climbing to the front!"

"Once you're there, blow it up. We'll meet them at the end." Turning to his anxious hacker, he instructed, "Jade, leave it. There's no time and there's no need."

Sush instructed the hunters, "Stay off the field and head to the end of the tube."

They hopped into their vehicles hidden within the thick trees and sped to the location, hearing a blast and feeling the earth shake on the way as Baxter punched his fist in the air and chuckled like he'd just set a new high score on a video game.

Once they reached the site, witnessing the head of the tube protruding from the ground and windows broken, Greg ordered, "Search the forest. They couldn't have gone far."

The warriors and mavericks, who were either lycans or had the speed of a velox, sped without question. The remaining cavalry got back into their vehicles and sped.

As Sush headed back into her own ride, she ordered, "Team C, stay back and dig through the tube. Teams A and B, we're tailing the kingdom's forces."

"Copy that, Chief."

As she drove through the uneven terrain with Greg in the passenger's seat, they were forced to stop when a blast came from the front. The impact threw some of their own back as half-shifted lycans slammed into their comrades' windscreens and the vehicles were either pulled to an abrupt halt or swerved into trees.

"Looks like we'll have to proceed on foot," Greg murmured. Hand already on the door handle, he uttered, "Please wait here."

"Sure," Sush chimed, then got off at the same time he did.

He didn't even know why he bothered trying to get her to stay back when she clearly wasn't going to listen. But there was one thing he could do that she couldn't yet, and that was to speed ahead to check out the level of danger, maybe having time to speed back to lock her in her vehicle if it was too high a risk. So that was what he did—he fled before Sush got a word out.

He reached the source of the blast and expected to see Traffic Cone, Lemon Head, and Acorn, so the group of shifted rogues and ready proditors standing a few feet away came as a particular shock.

CHAPTER 78

Greg didn't recognize any of these faces. Who the fuck were they, and where did they come from?

His eyes glazed over, and he linked the mavericks who hadn't arrived, *'Do not let any hunters enter the field.'*

'As you wish, Your Grace,' they chimed.

His octopus was going to kill him, but he'd deal with that later. This set of rogues could kill three hunters at once if they were trained, which he hoped they weren't.

'Greg!' Lucy broke into his mind with a deafening snarl. *'Itam's reception is already bad as it is, so why the HELL were you blocking out links?'*

He didn't realize that he was. But between watching the drone in the cottage, listening to nonsense from the Robinsons, making sure Sush wasn't shot, wondering what the ticking thing under the kitchen cabinet was for, mentally formulating backup plans during the ride to the end of the tube trail, and contemplating how to end the Robinsons' lives, he may have unintentionally kept people out of his mind.

Taking in the growling creatures before him as his people gathered by his side, Greg replied, *'I'm about to be fully occupied very soon, my queen. How about a different question for now?'*

'It's already starting, isn't it?' she responded almost monotonously, but he'd known her long enough to know her worry had removed the earlier anger, and her perturbation was escalating. There was just that slight pitch in her voice that made all the difference—one only her allies and friends could hear.

Not wanting to express his shock, he casually uttered, *'Well, if you mean a battle with rogues I've never seen, along with proditors I didn't expect meeting, then, yes, my queen. I probably have thirty seconds before someone lunges. I hope none of the bloodsuckers are manipulation freaks.'*

'And Sush?'

'Some of our own are holding her and the rest of the hunters back.'

'Don't know how long that will last.'

That wasn't encouraging. *'Then we have to finish this quickly. How did you know, by the way?'*

'Margaret.' Of course. His guess was Tristan, but who needed his people to report when the rulers had a clairvoyant wolf as a handy contact. *'We landed ten minutes ago and will be joining you shortly.'*

'What did the fortune-teller see?' Greg asked, though he wasn't sure he wanted to know.

'Everything we're going to stop,' she uttered firmly before dropping the link.

The fact that she didn't want to tell him about the maggot's psychic vision was not a good sign, but if there was one thing he'd learned as the leader of rogues, it was to never consider negotiating when there was a chance of winning. And with backup coming, he was sure they'd be winning, hopefully at no cost on their end.

A voice boomed from the back, "KILL THEM ALL!" And many recognized it was Mr. Robinson, though none could see him.

Great. Now he had to plow through a team of strangers to reach the psychotic family.

Their opponents pounced with unsynchronized growls, three coming for Greg himself. They clearly knew who the leader was, and Greg didn't know whether it was the misfortune of being the largest in his group or being the only one to radiate the aura of a royal.

Shifting and charging forward, he came head-to-head with the first one, which was an easy kill: claws through her throat and body flung at one of her two friends. The second was more agile, but not more agile than the queen—fortunately for Greg, who'd been undergoing one-on-one training sessions with her once a week for the past three years.

As he dodged two punches before delivering his own blow to the opponent's gut, considering and concluding he was not being manipulated to fight thin air or kill his own people, he began wondering how the Robinsons planned to win this. Everyone on his side had been trained under the best fighters for years. Their opponents were clearly not. While the third attacker sped to him, Greg still had time to look around and could see everyone was faring well, yet the queen's link still lingered.

The maggot's fortune-telling had been accurate in the times she had visions. Could this be the first time she was wrong?

As the thought came, so did a gunshot, quickly followed by another and another and another. The first bullet—to Greg's surprise—went to his opponent's body, making it slump onto him. Greg narrowly missed the second bullet aimed at his head. The third scraped his neck before he began using his opponent's body as a shield as he linked everyone to fall back, all using the trees for cover.

The small wound at his neck wasn't healing, and he realized in dismay that it must have been oleander. He took a look at the corpse he had dragged with him for cover, realizing these rogues must have been double-crossed.

Of course the Robinsons would have thugs on the battleground despite the risks. It wasn't just rogues and proditors anymore, apparently.

Greg may not have even brought a knife to this gunfight, but he did bring a few other things.

Checking that his people and the warriors had taken cover or were close to doing so, he carefully reached for his torn-up pants and dug out a cookie-shaped explosive that functioned akin to a military squib. It was small, but it would still create significant damage. He'd heard the way his cousin and cousin-in-law called his little sweetheart, and felt this suited her—an explosive little cookie.

Tossing it at their opponents, he retained another gunshot wound on his arm before the space in front of them blew up, tossing their enemies in all directions. The unluckiest ones were flung their way and met their demise when the warriors or mavericks killed them.

Greg and his people wasted no time charging forward before the dust had completely settled, getting to as many thugs as they could first. Those thrown at trees by the impact were getting up and advancing toward them.

One, though shifted, found a gun on the ground near where he had landed and was about to pull the trigger on Greg before multiple firing of another weapon from a distance threw the rogue off balance, at which time Ella—who was nearer to the rogue—impaled her claws through his gut before she broke his neck.

Greg already knew who was behind the multiple firing. Her pull was magnetic, despite the way her glare was burning through his skin as she fired another four bullets somewhere next to him, where another body fell.

Who was supposed to hold her back again?

It was then that Vix linked, *'Boss! The chief is on the loose!'*

'Yeah, I can see that.'

'And it isn't just her!'

'Might as well join us here yourselves, then. We need reinforcements.'

It was like he'd just given permission to let out a pack of starved animals, and the hunters weren't even animals.

While shots were being fired, Sush and Greg dodged attacks and took steps closer toward one another with each kill. She'd never met his animal before this day, yet she could still tell it was him by the look of his eyes and the way he looked at her. As magnificent as his animal was, Sush reminded herself that there was no time to gawk in awe because she was insistent on being mad at him.

When their opponents had gained sudden ammunition, he pulled Sush into himself as they hid behind a tree.

Despite their situation, he shifted back and calmly said, "I was just trying to keep you safe."

The blood on his neck got her attention. Reaching to feel it and seeing him wince, realizing it was his blood and a wound he clearly wasn't healing from, she snapped, "Sure, by narrowly dodging a bullet—an oleander bullet—and almost dying from another bullet."

Thinking about how she had shown up to the battlefield and practically saved his life, a smile crept up his lips. "Thank you for that, by the way."

Sush's eyes continued raging before a large figure appearing by their side pulled her attention. She reflexively fired at the rogue lycan's chest as Greg shifted once more to bring their opponent to the ground, at which time a bullet scraped his chin and one landed neatly on his arm. Another bullet scraped across Sush's cheek. They pulled each other back behind the tree.

Greg didn't make a big deal of his own injury as his hand went back to her cheek, releasing a low, furious snarl, at which time she uttered, "I'm fine." She then began firing at their opponents, noticing faces she could have sworn she'd seen before, killing three before she ran out of bullets and cussed.

Turning her attention back to Greg for a moment, her blood ran cold at the sight of the way he was slumped against the tree and his eyes were going through brief flickers of daze. "Greg? Greg, stay with me."

Greg was willing himself and his animal to do just that, to hang on because she was still in danger. They couldn't leave her like this.

Harnessing the strength he had, he linked the mavericks and warriors, *'How many more are there?'*

'Can't tell, Boss.'

'The Robinsons?'

'Can't see 'em yet. And bad news: The hunters are running out of ammunition.'

'Yeah, I can tell.'

Shifting back, he pulled Sush onto his lap, eyeing her with conspicuous fatigue and dead seriousness. "Get the hunters to fall back."

"What? No."

"Sush, without ammunition, the hunters are defenseless."

Adamant, she argued, "You and the others aren't exactly armed against those psychos either."

"Sush, please," he pleaded, looking into her eyes, trying to reach into her soul. "I need you to be safe."

Pinning him with an equally uncompromising stare, she uttered, "Guess it won't take much for you to understand that I need you to be just as safe."

That didn't do. He needed to get her out of there. "The queen linked earlier, right before the battle. They're on their way. The hunters can fall back. We'll be fine."

Nostrils flared, she snapped, "Then how about you let me do my job until they get here."

In an incoming message from Millicent, the chief archer said, "Sush, the mavericks and warriors are asking us to fall back. Many of them are injured, but they insist on staying behind."

"And the hunters with you?" Sush queried.

"Slight injuries but nothing fatal. Is it just me, or have our opponents been targeting the kingdom's forces in particular? My team got a clean shot of more than twenty because the shooters were focusing on the mavericks."

Kenji agreed, "It's not just you. My aim has never been good unless the targets were static, but I've already shot five and killed three in that five. We're running low on bullets, and the mavericks are trying to get us to leave, too, but none of us hunters want to, so what do I tell them?"

Eyeing Greg like she was speaking to him as well, Sush ordered sternly, "Tell them we don't work for them and won't take orders from them. Keep an eye on their situation, and don't let any of them go to sleep. Drag them away with you if you have to leave."

"Copy that," they chimed.

Right after her instructions had been conveyed, two rogues—one wolf and one lycan—appeared, one on each side.

Greg's animal managed to push forward right before the rogue lycan, with an arrogant smirk, began wrestling with him. If Greg had his full strength like before, tossing the rogue would've been a piece of cake. But it was proving to be a challenge now.

The rogue wolf caged Sush, and she fell flat on her back. She was going to hit its face with her gun, but the rogue knocked it out of her hand before she could. She was instinctively backing away, hands ruffling over the leaves and branches, all the time thinking about only one thing—she needed a weapon, a weapon, a weapon.

Right before the rogue's canines went for her neck, she picked the first thing she felt off the ground—a branch? The five-limbed-octopus mark on her nape glowed in gold as her eyes developed rims of the same color before she jammed the branch through the creature's jaw.

She was shocked for two reasons: one, that the branch didn't break; two, the part that went through the wolf's jaw and protruded right behind its nose had a tip of an arrow.

There were arrows on the ground this whole time?

CHAPTER 79

As the rogue wolf howled in pain and fury, leaping around and shaking his head, trying to get the arrow out but obviously unable to, another one lunged at Sush while her hands groped around for another branch. This one went through the rogue lycan's throat. She rolled away and saw that the tip protruding from the fallen creature's nape also had a pointed tip of an arrow.

It was Greg's snarl—when he pushed his opponent down with every bit of strength he could muster—that pulled Sush's attention away from the rogues she'd killed without fully comprehending how. Greg was too caught up in snapping the neck of the one below him to notice another rogue lycan lunging at him from behind, claws out and ready.

Sush picked out another random branch without so much as a look and used her full body weight to knock the rogue away from Greg, which wasn't very far to begin with, given the brawniness of their species. She slit the branch-turned-arrow through the creature's neck.

Unrelenting, the rogue managed to cut across her thigh with its claws before she made her escape with a groan, trying to muffle the pain as Greg came over to break off the rogue's hand—its claws still protruded—and jam it into the creature's chest, just above his heart, offering him a slow death.

As Greg pulled himself over to examine Sush's injury, a mix of anger and confusion set in him—fury for failing to keep her safe, and confusion at her wound exuding a blue liquid instead of the usual red when it came to blood. The next thing his vision caught was something glimmering in faint gold at her side, under her hand. He neither moved nor spoke while witnessing a normal branch extending into something long and sharp.

A javelin?

When his animal looked to her face for answers, he found her golden-rimmed eyes glaring at something behind him, and before he knew what was happening, the javelin she had created flew and struck the proditor that was coming at him and ultimately fell on the lower part of his body as he released a grunt at the weight.

"Oh, God. I am so sorry, Greg," said Sush frantically, leaning over to push her latest victim off him.

With his state weakened from oleander and the force exerted to end his opponent, his animal retreated, and his human came into view, huffing with a smile. Even his dirt-filled face and tired eyes didn't take away the pride he had for his octopus's unique ability.

"My dear," he grunted as the numbness from the oleander began destabilizing him with each passing second, as much as he tried to hide it from her. Her eyes were trailing to the gray lines on his arm before he brought her gaze back to his, saying, "If you have to apologize for saving my life, I'm not treating you very well. Where and when did you learn to turn branches into weapons, by the way?"

Blinking like she didn't understand him, she pivoted her sights to the branch below her hand and saw it turn into an arrow, witnessing the transformation herself for the first time. "I . . . don't know how I'm doing this."

Chuckling lightly at her discombobulation, Greg was as happy for her as Sush was confused. But a sudden firing from his right had him hauling her under him to fully shield her with his body. The bullet Hazel had fired at her chief ricocheted off the tree trunk before a second bullet came their way when Sush—out of pure instinct—stretched out an arm from under Greg's cage and brushed the leaves on the ground into the air, making a circular shield appear right before their eyes, and that was the exact thing the second bullet ricocheted off.

Across the space, Kenji exclaimed with excitement that resembled that of a person who'd just witnessed magic, "How did you do that?"

The next bullet from Hazel was aimed at the eastern octopus's arm, but his suddenly improved reflexes enabled him to dodge the bullet before one of his team members hauled him back behind a tree. While Millicent was reprimanding him for his recklessness, Kenji couldn't shake off the feeling that it wasn't his brain that had made him lean away. It was as if his arm knew it was in danger and pulled itself away. When they said that one's hands, arms, or legs developed minds of their own, he didn't think they meant it literally.

Before he could contemplate further, his dominant right hand—which had clearly developed a mind of its own since Kenji had planned to stay low as Millicent ordered—tightened its grip around the trigger and pulled him to lean over the trunk to fire a bullet, which missed Hazel, while the thugs on her side began firing at him and the ones he was with.

As he hid behind the tree once more, he came to terms with the fact that whatever the new reflex was, it arrived after he saw Sush's trick with the shield, and the reflex was apparently shared with Hazel since she dodged his bullet the same way he dodged hers.

As more shots were fired his way, Millicent yelled, "Well done, Einstein!"

"It wasn't me!" Kenji argued, his left hand pointed at the guilty right hand as an explanation to a narrow-eyed Millicent before the continuous firing blocked out their conversation.

Millicent and her archers aimed at the thugs, rogues, and proditors surrounding and protecting Hazel, taking them out one at a time and realizing that—unlike before—they couldn't seem to miss their targets now. Every bullet struck. Even when they thought their targets would move and they'd miss, they didn't miss even if their targets moved by those few inches.

Unbeknownst to them, when Sush's survival instincts peaked and her eyes turned gold, she awakened an ancient power of the hunter breed—one that no hunter knew about since the first and only generation of power-imbued hunters were decimated in the first interspecies war millennia ago. While the octopuses now had better reflexes and their limbs—like the limbs of the underwater creature itself—had minds of their own, an archers' weapons never missed their target, which posed a problem to those on Sush's side as well, seeing that some of the thugs were archers by birth.

Millicent, noticing this change that she didn't yet understand, now gave new orders. Half of the archers were to deal with Hazel's seemingly endless flow of protectors while the remaining half, including herself, fired at their opponents bullets—as unrealistic as it sounded. But when it was actually done, it awed every archer and continuously shocked some others that none of them seemed to be missing a single shot. Bullets clashed and were thrown off course, angering their opponents, who were also running out of ammunition and would have to rely on brute force soon.

As for the chameleons, when someone asked Patterson how he'd managed to paint himself in the midst of battle to match the tree he was using as cover, he gaped at his camouflaged body before looking around and found fellow chameleons blending into their surroundings as well—some aware of it and some not. One *idiot* was even standing out in the open, near a puddle, frozen and awestruck by what she was seeing.

Heaving a frustrated exhale, the chief chameleon tapped on his communication device and bluntly said, "Anna, if you don't take cover right now, I'll shoot you myself." At that order, Anna snapped out of it and ran to the nearest tree, alerting their conspicuously surprised enemies when she'd suddenly moved. Some would later argue that she would've been just fine even if she hadn't moved for the rest of the battle.

Hazel turned her attention back to the chief octopus, who was getting annoyingly hard to kill, thinking the shield that came out of nowhere must have been a cool magic trick that she'd never bothered sharing. The ones on her side were given explicit instructions not to kill these two. They were her targets, her trophies. She released another two shots at the shield, stepping closer each time before she fired at Greg's exposed leg.

Once. Twice.

As Greg groaned while trying to drag back his leg, he muttered, "Fucking Traffic Cone."

Sush's hands searched for another branch and—with more anxiety than confidence—turned it into another javelin when she pushed Greg off and threw it blindly over the shield. Hazel leaned away just in time to see it fly past her chest, but right before she turned back toward her targets, a bullet scraped across her chin and Kenji cursed his latest miss while a trail of blue flowed from the minor wound of Hazel's face.

Mr. Robinson had seen the assault on his poor little hyena, and he loaded his gun, aiming at Kenji. But right before the bullet was discharged, something lunged at him, holding him to the ground. It weighed a ton, and when the old man's eyes met an onyx glare that was coupled with the snarl of the lycan king, his face paled.

Several fired at the king, and although the archers on Millicent's side shot a few bullets out of the way, some still landed on Xandar's neck, arm, and leg. Unaffected, Xandar merely scowled at the source of assault and released an enraged, thunderous growl that shook the earth and rattled leaves as the oleander bullets fell off his body while his wounds healed within seconds.

"FALL BACK!" someone yelled as the surviving rogues, proditors, and thugs retreated at the speed of a strong breeze. They didn't see the point in ingesting the shell since their profession kept them within human territory—one where none of them expected to meet any lycan ruler.

Xandar tossed Mr. Robinson at a tree near Kenji, making the hunter jump before the king said, "All yours."

Kenji took a quick glance from a groaning Mr. Robinson, who may have broken more than a few bones, then back at Xandar before he offered a confused, awkward bow. "Th-Thank you, Your Majesty." At least he didn't squeak this time, he thought, but his right hand smacked his forehead like it thought Kenji had just embarrassed himself. Kenji found himself looking at that hand and uttering, "Oh, like you could've done any better."

"FALL BACK! FALL BACK!" the warning ensued.

But it was too late. Xandar had emitted his Authority and compelled every rogue to drop their weapons and sink to the ground on both knees with their backs bent forward and heads leaned so low their necks and spines were on the verge of breaking.

His wife arrived a few moments later, panting heavily from the sprint.

Lucy took in the scene of blood, weakened hunters, and her injured subjects. Her chest rose and fell as her nostrils flared and ears heated. Her onyx eyes glowered at the retreating figures now at a distance as she snarled, "Fucking. BASTARDS!"

Eyes turning blue, she reached for every single rogue and compelled them to turn back.

The rogues' limbs halted, turned, and began heading in the direction of the pull, their brains engaged in a losing battle when their autonomy was no longer theirs, covering the distance they'd just made from the battleground.

They stood before their queen like loyal soldiers and knelt to her like devoted subjects as their king joined them by her side, the power and rage emanating from their beings overwhelming and undeniable. The rogues' animals whimpered before their rulers, pleading for mercy.

Lucy's wrath forced their animals back in, revealing their humans as she delivered a chilling promise, "I'm going to break you . . ." her fingers twisted inward, slowly cutting off their air supply as their necks stretched, their eyes rolling back as they faced the sky ". . . each one of you . . ." most were already gasping for air ". . . very, very slowly."

"Oh dear Lord."

The familiar voice from behind softened Lucy as she released her compulsion strangulating the rogues but still kept them rooted to the ground when she turned and offered the vampire empress and her party a small smile. "Pelly."

"Aunt Lucy, Uncle Xandar," Pelly greeted as Octavia, Rafael, and Amber offered brief waves or nods, all sheepish that they couldn't get here sooner.

Wasting no more time, Pelly expanded her Authority up ahead the way Lucy did earlier, hauling back the creatures under her command.

The proditors thought they were getting away until they, too, were forced to return against their will, trotting toward a source they didn't know of yet, though many of them had a good guess of what it was, or rather, who it was.

CHAPTER 80

Within a minute, the proditors were before the very person they'd only heard about and never wanted to meet. Their empress's scowl had some of them fidgeting when she uttered, "The fact that any of you tried to run is deeply, deeply insulting."

She entered their minds all at once, took out the most fearful thing in their mental archive, and manipulated them to see it in its full force for a moment before the proditors each paled, shuddered, and—one by one—dropped unconscious.

Lucy turned back to her own hostages, and she questioned, "The thugs—where are they running to?"

"Six miles north, Your Majesty," they disclosed in unison.

Upon hearing that, Millicent raced back in the direction of their vehicles as she yelled, "Thank you, Your Majesty!"

On the ground, as soon as his cousin and cousin-in-law had entered the field, Greg allowed his weakened state to be revealed, and it wasn't looking good with his inability to push himself up and exhaustion so great that he was fighting to keep his eyes open as his hearing began receiving muffled sounds instead of clear words and voices. The gray on his body reflected the contamination of his blood, and the only thing guiding him was his sense of smell, allowing him to lean closer to the source of frangipanis and limes that made his suffering less tormenting.

Sush guided him to lay his head on her lap, and a doctor and two nurses—who'd arrived with the rest of the medical team—got the bullets out from Greg's body and worked on the blood transfusion while another nurse tended to

Sush's injuries. Sush's hands stayed on Greg's shoulders, shaking him every time his eyes were nearing to a close, but her sights kept flickering to the gray lines-turned-patches on his body that felt like they were strangling and suffocating her, forcing a layer of moisture to glaze her eyes.

How could the shield she'd created not be big enough to cover him completely?

She watched the medical personnel work and even asked whether Greg was going to be okay, whether they'd brought enough blood, whether they should do this in a more sanitary location so he wouldn't get an infection. The nurses and doctor answered every single question patiently, calmly, hoping to calm her too.

Only when Greg looked less dazed, the gray began fading, and the lines started receding did Sush release the breath she'd been holding onto and allow her lungs to replenish themselves, muffling out a sob that escaped her lips and letting the tears of relief fall into Greg's hair. Her arms wrapped around his shoulders in nothing short of immense gratitude for whatever power—probably the power of medicine—hadn't let his life slip away when they'd just found each other.

With his returning strength, Greg's unaffected hand reached for her arm, stroking it reassuringly, affectionately, and pressing a kiss there. He could sit like this in the dirt forever if it meant his head was resting on her lap, with her arms wrapped around his shoulders like they were now.

Sure, the receding numbness was a little uncomfortable and there might have been more than a few bugs on the ground that were crawling up his skin and then back down, but other than that, he'd never felt better.

The moment he heard Millicent thanking the queen for the location that probably hid another Robinson hideout, he gave Sush's arm a gentle squeeze, then tried to push himself up.

Since Greg hadn't gotten back enough strength yet, he was pressed back down by his octopus, whose teary eyes were now raging once more.

Before she got a word out, he calmly explained, "There's no better time to get your mother's killers than now, before the justice system and the whole defense circus get involved. Go."

"I'm not going anywhere," she insisted in a hushed whisper, adamantly holding him down, thankful he was still too weak to fight back.

The gray was still on his body, and the lines—though ebbing—were still visible. The color of his face hadn't fully returned. A partial recovery was not going to make her leave. She wanted to see every bit of intrusive color leave his skin before she'd let him leave her lap, and she was going to witness him stand and walk at least thirty steps before even considering looking—let alone going—somewhere else.

Befuddled, his brows furrowed when he reminded, "Sush, this is your chance. You've been waiting for this for more than a decade."

Her brain understood what he meant, but the yearning in her heart and soul to see him heal completely overpowered her need to draw blood. Hazel, Mrs. Robinson, and the escaped thugs could wait. There was something more crucial she wanted to see through, something more important than revenge.

The rage left her eyes, and her lips welcomed the softest smile as her thumb brushed across his bare skin in repeated motions when she whispered, "I wonder what changed."

Her declaration said more than anyone else knew, even more than she or Greg knew.

As her need for revenge no longer took the dominant spot in her being, the emotional block that was there disintegrated, and the mate bond from her end snapped into place, lining with Greg as he felt the sparks channeled through their touch surge at an intensity that made his animal howl like it had just discovered a gold mine.

Sush felt something too, a small spark, like stars glittering over her skin. She didn't know what it was, but it came right after her one-liner. It was as if her soul was being pulled into a safe haven, and she speculated whether this was how a human felt a mate bond—mild but present, noticeable when focused on.

Her question was answered when Greg's brightening eyes met hers, and the happiest smile stretched his lips when he uttered, "Mate."

As her lips at his temple curled into a smile, she whispered, "You don't really have a choice in that anymore, Greg. Not since that night on the balcony."

He chuckled lightly. "We're going to be stuck together for a very long time," he purred, drawing out a bigger smile from her, one that liquefied his heart.

Sush hadn't known yet that humans didn't feel a mate bond, that she only felt the glittering stars because hunters—with the awakened power—could now mildly detect and feel the connection.

"Hi, sorry to interrupt," Lucy came, Pelly and Xandar by her side. "Sush, this is Pelly, and she's saying that she can get the Forest of Oderem to haul the shelter up north back here within seconds. We understand this is the hunters' jurisdiction and teams have already been deployed, but would you like her to sort of . . . help shorten the travel distance?"

Woah, woah, woah. That was way too much information to process, even for Sush, whose eyes bulged wide.

First off, Pelly? Sush was fine if the empress was introduced as the empress. And shouldn't the empress appear a little less . . . friendly?

Second, the Forest of What-derem?

Third, it could . . . haul a hideout?

And she thought her weapon manufacturing from pieces of nature was great.

In the silence, Greg turned to Lucy to utter, "It's an honor for my presence to be acknowledged, my queen. And I'm recovering quite well, thank you for asking."

It was harmless sarcasm that they mutually understood, seeing that Lucy neither acknowledged him nor asked how he was to begin with, thus pulling Lucy's narrowed eyes to him. "I know you're not pretending this time, Greg, but you are clearly recovering with new blood and a second-chance mate. The ones who tried to kill you and her are now taking priority over your presence." Attention back on Sush, she added in all sincerity, "We won't do anything if you prefer we don't, Sush. You don't have to say yes."

Sush's mouth gaped, her mind going to a million places before she ultimately parroted, "H-Haul the shelter . . ." It sounded bizarre even when she said it. She expected someone to correct her, to tell her she'd misheard and repeat what was actually said. When they didn't, she simply uttered, "S-Sure, let's go with that."

Sush had no idea what she'd just agreed to, and she waited as Lucy and Pelly turned toward the targeted direction and Pelly's eyes and a streak of her hair glowed in bright, emerald green.

Nothing seemed to be happening yet, so Sush closed in on Greg's ear and whispered, "The forest of what again?"

"Oderem." He pushed himself up when he could feel all of his limbs and went on, "Temperamental forest from the vampire territory that casts voodoo spells, gives neck tattoos, and takes insults and insinuations very personally, so don't say anything offensive when it gets here."

Sush was certain fatigue was getting to her head and she was hearing everything wrong, so she replayed what she thought she'd heard—though still not making sense of anything—while helping him onto his feet, staying nearby, and reluctantly releasing her hands when the doctors said they wanted to see the duke moving about on his own.

He was fine, and Sush felt a huge weight being lifted off her shoulders, seeing him move as he normally did before he impatiently argued with the doctor in a low murmur about the extended reflex tests they wanted to conduct, which Greg personally found unnecessary.

Distant shouts, curses, screams, and something heavy being dragged back pulled everyone's sights to the source, and the first impression that the Forest of Oderem gave most hunters was that it loved making an entrance.

CHAPTER 81

Thick branches coiled around the waistlines of every thug who fled. Those who got a knife from their back pockets and stabbed the branch had another branch slap the blade away before their arms were restrained as well. Yellow flowers grew and exuded foul smells at their faces, making them curse and choke.

"You know . . . " Toby—all smiles for the first time in human territory—pulled Sush's attention away when he spoke to the queen ". . . call me crazy, but I kinda miss the forest."

Sush was so enthralled by the autonomy of something that was known to stay rooted that she didn't see Millicent, Kenji, and Patterson coming up to her when Patterson took bated breaths as he asked, "What. Is. That?"

Blinking while trying to look past the part of his body that matched the color of a car seat, Sush groped for the right words before ultimately saying, "I'm told it's called the Forest of Oderem."

Kenji questioned, "Why did we even bother driving? Did you know its roots practically made us turn back?" His right hand seemed restless, moving about frantically like it was trying to get a word in, so Kenji shoved it aside with his left as he chided in annoyance, "Oh, hush."

"What?" Sush's brows rose, not sure whether she was asking about him talking to his limb or the fact that roots had made the deployed troops turn back.

Millicent explained, "We were on our way up north. Then, these large roots started appearing out of nowhere like they were creating a barricade, and we were led back here."

"Was anyone hurt?" Sush asked.

Millicent gave a slight shake of her head. "Though we were a little . . . spooked." A stem grew from the ground next to Millicent, making her flinch, while a beige flower with red polka dots in its inner petals bloomed to steal the show.

As Greg joined them with an arm around Sush's shoulder, he nodded to the flower. "Speaking from observation, you're expected to pick it off the ground, Chief. It's befriending you. And the forest doesn't take rejection well."

A short distance away, Millicent witnessed the other duke of the kingdom doing just that with the exact same flower as the king gave him a pat on the back, biting back an amused smile that Millicent didn't quite understand.

Mind-boggled, Millicent turned to Sush, who gave a half-nod, half-shake of her head, signifying that it was up to her, and Millicent—mind completely blank—gently plucked it off the ground, then paused like she was waiting for a detonation that was never coming.

"Fucking sticks!" Hazel exclaimed and continued struggling. The branches around her waist tightened as three yellow flowers sprayed—not just foul odor but also pollen at her face, making her sneeze and choke.

"Told you," Greg whispered into Sush's ear. "Doesn't take insults well."

When Hazel thought the ordeal was over and began taking a lungful of air, the flowers sprayed into her airway. Her suffering continued until Pelly placed her hand on one of the branches nearby and gently told the forest, "That's enough."

Hazel took quick breaths as mucus flowed from her nostrils, and her eyes teared from coughing, eyeing Sush in nothing but pure rage—seeing her as a target missed, a task that she had failed, a trophy that she hadn't collected.

"What is this? Side project?" she exclaimed. "The defense ministry is going to have it easy dismissing you when they find out you have ties with a supernatural forest!"

A branch tapped on Pelly's back shoulder, making her look away before the yellow flowers sprayed Hazel in her face again when Sush remarked, "Sure. Because being dismissed is my main concern right now."

As Pelly looked back in confusion before realizing the forest's trick of making her look away just to get back at Hazel, she tapped her fingers on the branch and eyed it like she would a creature who'd pranked her.

"Fucking flowers!" Hazel hollered.

"Hazel," Sush began in a voice so low that it was almost a snarl. The betrayal didn't just cut deep. The wound from the cut flared when they found the cottage, the incineration heated her chest when her family confessed to murdering her mother, and the sheer anguish of trusting her, believing that she was a friend—for *years*—had left an indelible mark on her heart, in her mind. Challenging her deputy's glower with a fiercer one of her own, the gold rims in her eyes appeared when she said, "I could nail you to the ground and *choke* you for everything you did."

The muscles of Hazel's airway stopped working like she was being choked. Hazel's eyes grew wide, and she was willing herself to take in air—a forceful endeavor that was proving to be fruitless.

Sush hadn't realized what she was doing to Hazel yet and thought Hazel was just acting psychotic, so the chief octopus looked past her deputy's state and continued speaking, "Concocting zahar? Sabotaging our borders' defenses that we work so hard to make impenetrable? Wiping out the archers while killing the handful of chameleons and octopuses—our *friends*? The depth of shit you created for us gives me every reason to kill you in the slowest possible way. But since I'm not doing that yet, why don't you cherish the remnants of your luck in being kept alive and SHUT THE HELL UP!"

Hazel's lungs gratefully accepted air at the words *being kept alive*, and although she struggled in the forest's hold once more, she spat out words that no one could hear, not even herself. Mrs. Robinson watched her daughter in dismay, her own mouth blocked by a thick branch. Muffled sounds came out from the old woman until Sush unintentionally shut her up as well.

"Alright," Pelly began, waving through the air as the branch that had tapped her shoulder now extended in front of her like a table. Five flowers of different colors and patterns grew in place, attracting everyone when Pelly continued, "Sush, right? How do you want to deal with them? We have—" she began gesturing through the row of flora like they were items on sale in a market "—nasal infection, instant dehydration, internal bleeding, brain damage, and skin rash that'll spread to the internal organs within a month." When the only response Pelly got was a stunned Sush, the empress added, "Or just good old-fashioned strangulation by the forest, if you like."

"Uh . . ." Sush blinked, still processing the odd-looking flowers as the branch holding them left Pelly and came toward her, giving her a closer look at them.

Looking through the options over Sush's shoulder, Millicent began pondering before Sush did. "Probably not instant dehydration. Too easy," the chief archer deduced. The white flower with droplet-shaped petals dotted with blue wilted away.

Sush turned to Millicent, brows raising like she was asking, "You're actually thinking about this?"

Kenji seemed caught up in the options too. "Skin rash is interesting, though nasal infection would be good too. It'd be hard for them to keep that attitude when their airways are interfered with."

Patterson protested, "Why isn't anyone considering brain damage? The Robinsons' brains had been the very thing that caused us all that trouble. Even internal bleeding is a better option. Bleed their brains, for Christ's sake!"

In response, the blood-red flower with petals shaped like red blood cells bloomed bigger, taking up more space than its counterparts, luring them to choose it.

"How about—" Sush's voice, finally at her normal volume carrying the usual firmness, came as her hands rested gently on the branch at each end of the row of flowers "—we don't use these and just put our hostages to sleep for now?"

"WHAT?" her colleagues exclaimed, not ready to let go of the flowers.

It was taking every bit of restraint in Greg not to join them, willingly letting the sparks from the mate bond numb his disagreement, reminding him that he was on her side.

Patterson's eyes went to the flowers when he noted pointedly, "You seem to want the internal bleeding as much as I do, Sush."

"I don't."

"Then why are you waving to get our attention and pointing at that particular flower?"

It was only then Sush realized her dominant left hand was doing exactly that—waving to get attention and pointing fervently at the blood-red flora.

From the side, Kenji remarked, "It's weird, isn't it? I can't really control mine either."

Sush realized she could make it stop—with effort—but it was still struggling to make a point until her right hand slapped her left. And when the latter tried to point at the flower again, Sush instinctively glared at it and warned, "No."

Resigned, her left hand flopped like it was upset. Ignoring the oddity for now, she turned to her colleagues and explained, "I agree that the Robinsons and thugs should die, but looking at the long-term consequences of where that would leave us, I'd say they shouldn't die by our hands. Like it or not, they have a lot of evidence against themselves and the Ferdinands, and probably people we're not thinking of yet. Weeding out the Robinsons isn't enough. We need to pull out every last thorn in the system, and what they know can get us there."

"What makes you even think they'd talk?" Kenji groaned.

Flowers of transparent petals bloomed along the branch nearing Kenji, and Pelly explained their truth-telling element, which Greg confirmed was used on Izabella to extract the truth from her, so it worked on hunters as it did on their species.

Kenji turned to Sush like he was pleading. "Not even a little internal bleeding? A faint rash? For one short minute?"

With a conclusive tone and firm eyes, Sush uttered, "No."

At the side, Patterson muttered under his breath, "What a waste of fantastic resources." At that compliment, the beige flower with polka dots grew by his side, and—like Millicent—he politely picked it off the ground.

Turning back to Pelly, Sush said, "I like whatever you gave the proditors. What pollen was it?"

With a warm smile, Pelly casually replied, "Oh, that wasn't any pollen. I used their own fears against them and drove them into losing consciousness."

Patterson, Millicent, and Kenji saw that as a freaking genius alternative! They turned to the chief octopus once again, eyes practically begging her to say yes. The Robinsons' anatomy wouldn't be tampered with, so they wouldn't die, and any evidence they'd be able to produce could still be produced without health complications getting in the way.

Sush turned to the Robinsons, Hazel still making a fruitless attempt to loosen the branch, mouthing things no one could hear and taking breaths before repeating the process when the chief octopus finally said, "Yeah, if you could have them faint that way, it'd be great, Your Imperial Majesty."

Waving a hand, Her Imperial Majesty responded, "It's just Pelly, Sush. Just the three or all of them, by the way?"

Sush turned to her colleagues, who silently mouthed, "ALL!" before she conveyed their request.

"Raf! Some help!" Pelly hollered at her closest friend.

The empire's most powerful decipio entered their circle and offered everyone brief smiles before his friend explained the task at hand, "Faint through fear. You take those on the left; I'll take the right."

"Let's go. First one to wipe them out wins," Rafael mused with a playful smirk and a competitive glint in his eye, one that Pelly instantly matched as they began, with Octavia at the side shaking her head slowly with an amused lift of her lips.

The Robinsons' eyes and those of every thug around them turned dark green. Their eyes grew wide and faces morphed into nothing short of terror. Some began quivering at their lips, some chose to close their eyes, some shook their heads like it would shake away the nightmare conjured by the manipulation. Within a minute, every hostage had turned pale before surrendering consciousness.

Rafael won by a second and a half.

"That was actually quite satisfying," Kenji muttered to Patterson.

The chief chameleon rolled his eyes. "Would have preferred brain damage."

CHAPTER 82

After a very long day of surrendering the hostages to the police and making reports, submitting a public statement for the media to circulate throughout the kingdom, empire, and human territory in case someone did something to cover up the truth, everyone dragged their exhausted selves back home.

In the diplomatic residence, Sush was in sweatpants and one of Greg's shirts as they lay in bed. She lay on her side facing him, head resting on his arm, hand on his bare torso as Greg's fingers fiddled with her hair, relishing in the tiny sparks that dotted his fingers when he touched the strands. When he wanted to feel a higher charge, his fingers went to her shoulder, pulling up the sleeve to feel her bare skin, leaving goosebumps that his fingertips continued stroking through.

"Hey," she began in a whisper.

"Hm?" his face turned to her, lips touching her forehead, breathing her in.

"About . . . marking."

His fingers stopped. "What about it?" He prayed she wasn't going to negotiate out of this. Marking was one of the few things he would never think of compromising. In fact, it would raise suspicions if she didn't want to be marked.

"How does it work? When does it normally happen?" she asked.

The stiffness in his chest loosened, relief washing over him as he explained, "Our canines sink into each other's necks. If the books are right, there isn't a need to really think through the process. Our animal instincts just know."

"I'm not an animal," she murmured pointedly.

"Hunters and humans don't shift like us, yes. But after being marked, you're supposed to develop some animal senses and anatomy overnight, canines included."

Her brows furrowed. "Why do you say *supposed to* like it isn't certain?"

"Well, no human I know, have heard about, or have read about could fashion weapons out of leaves and branches, and I doubt their eyes strayed from their original color when they wielded any weapon."

Sush scoffed lightly, snuggling deeper into him, and Greg felt her lips on his chest curl into a smile which in turn tipped the edges of his mouth that was at her forehead. He held her closer and whispered, "As for when it normally happens, it's up to the pair. Some wait until they tie the knot. Some do it prior to that."

After a few quiet moments, she asked in a hushed tone, "So when are we doing it?"

"That's up to you," he said simply, pressing a light kiss to her head.

Her eyes narrowed. "Are you forgetting you're part of the equation that makes up a pair?"

"If I had it my way, I would've marked you on the first night I ate you out."

His admission made her eyes grow wide and her shoulders stiffen in surprise.

Greg's tone took a teasing edge when he said, "Why are you so shocked? Didn't I tell you you're the most delicious thing that ever touched my tastebuds?"

She smirked, matching his tone, "So that was the determining factor." Her left hand stood on the tips of its index and middle finger, walking along his chest like it was seducing him, leaving a tiny trail of sparks behind.

He flipped them over so she was on her back as he hovered above her. Their eyes locked when he brought her dominant hand to his lips for a kiss, making her two flirty fingers go limp as they swooned over the gesture when he declared, "You know it isn't. It's one of the factors, I admit, but not the determining one." His fingers threaded through her hair. "I'm not certain what the determining factor was or is, to be honest. Whether it was your wits, your brains, your temper, the way you use your hands and forefingers more often than anyone I know, the way you handle things, or the way you immerse yourself into the things you love . . . maybe it's all of those things. Maybe it isn't one thing about you that's distracted me these past few weeks. Maybe it's all of those things combined that's been pulling me back to you, no matter how far I go, because I've fallen for every piece that makes you who you are."

Saying that every word pulled at her heartstrings would be saying that her heart was held by strings. But it wasn't. She didn't know when, but she knew it had been some time that her heart had been held by him. And it had never felt better in the hands of anyone else. It had never felt safer and more protected with anyone else. For the first time in so long, it felt sheltered, happy, and loved—a combination of emotions that she thought only existed in someone else's life, never her own.

His face came close. Their breaths mingled. His lips stayed inches away from hers like he was challenging her to keep that distance, tempting her to give in.

And Sush knew that—for this particular temptation—she'd willingly give in, pulling his mouth in with hers, letting him take the lead in pressing her head into the pillow as she savored his taste, taking pleasure in the way his hand trailed down to grip her ass then squeeze the flesh at her thighs, then her waist before giving her breasts a rough kneading. She felt him smile as she moaned, and smiled to herself when he moaned.

When he had to release her for her to replenish her lungs, her hands clasped both sides of his face, refusing to let him move down her throat the way he usually did, keeping their eyes on each other as her chest rose and fell when she ultimately said, "I love you, Greg."

The broad stretch of his lips lit him up the way the moon shone in the night sky. His eyes held the stars that flickered as a layer of moisture formed over them when his forehead met hers. "I love you too, Sush. That's something that's never going to change."

"Then mark me," she whispered, eyes radiating nothing but certainty when she added, "Tonight."

He didn't think it was possible, but her request had just made him ten times happier. Leaving a quick kiss on her lips, he uttered, "With pleasure."

Sush didn't know what to expect and simply surrendered to the moment, feeling his lips leave a trail of kisses down her throat, then moving to the side of her neck. His warm tongue stroked her skin there seductively slowly, teasingly leisurely. She released a gasp and a drawn-out moan, which got louder when he began sucking on her skin and biting it gently, tenderizing the area. As his canines extended, he warned, "It'll hurt for a moment."

"Mm-hm."

After his nose gingerly nudged her earlobe one more time, his teeth sunk into her neck, and Sush yelped at the pain. Her fingers dug into the flesh of his back, nails piercing into his skin. Greg arched into her fingers, encouraging her to use him to cope with the anguish.

If she were to describe the marking, she'd say that it was like having two metal rods impaling her neck, though she'd never been impaled by metal on any part of her body. But the pain began receding as quickly as it came.

She felt his canines leaving her flesh, and as he lapped up the excess blood, something warm spread from the area where his mark now was, a feeling of closeness—one that felt like it was binding her soul to his, bringing them together in a way that could never be physically achieved.

What she wasn't ready for was the cyclone of emotions that followed: the intensified yearning, unassailable devotion, and aggressive love. He'd always been so controlled and composed. She knew he loved her, but she may have underestimated the depth and intensity of that love.

Greg sealed his work with a deep kiss on the red smear, drawing a moan out of Sush when sparks erupted from the area and shot throughout her body right down to her toes. As he brought their faces together once more, his smile grew wide with excessive pride as his possessive baritone reverberated through her ears when he declared, "Mine."

Sush chuckled with watery eyes as she cupped his cheek, and Greg stole another kiss from her lips before saying, "If the books are right, you're supposed to feel what I feel now. I'm not sure if you d—"

His words were cut short by her capturing his mouth, and he released a brief chuckle between their kisses. When Sush was forced to pull away for air, his lips stayed at the corner of her lips when he muttered, "I'll take that as a yes."

Pressing a kiss to her head and turning them over so that they lay in their original position—with her glued to his side, his fingers teased her with trail after trail of sparks as they glided up and down her arm. The tingles were stimulating at first, but as they prolonged, they also submerged her into a deep state of relaxation. The heaviness from the years of fatigue guided her into deep slumber, but not before her last bit of her consciousness caught Greg's crisp whisper echoing, "Sweet dreams, my octopus."

CHAPTER 83

Before her eyes opened the next morning, Sush's heightened sense of smell detected the distinct scent of musk and sandalwood wafting stronger than before from the creature lying next to her. Her eyelids slowly lifted as her vision adjusted to the darkness, and she was welcomed with a very clear view of the most gorgeous man in existence. She wondered if it was possible to find him more alluring simply from being able to smell him better now.

The tip of his lips quirked, lilac eyes gazing into hers.

He dozed off seconds after her the night before, and woke up just minutes before she did, using the time alone to watch her sleep, then watch her wake, which was better than watching the sunrise or sunset. He never understood the point in those. It was something that happened every day. Surely, at some point, anyone would get bored of it.

But watching someone he loved fall asleep like the fading colors of dusk and wake up like the soft but vibrant light of dawn, listening to her breaths that would put the hum of nature to shame, was the most wondrous experience that put him in a state of incomparable peace and happiness.

"Hey," she whispered with eyes half opened, voice slightly coarse from the night.

"Morning," he hummed, leaning in to kiss her lips.

Their foreheads met, and her eyes were now opened all the way. He smiled to himself at the sight of lilac rims creating circular edges around her irises. "Beautiful," he murmured.

Sush pecked a kiss on his chin, uttering, "Beautiful or not, you sealed your own fate after last night."

"Which brings us to our first task of the day." He scooped her up and placed her face down on top of him, holding her by her hips and back when he said, "Mark me."

"Hm," Sush feigned contemplation, elbow resting on his chest and hand holding her head up as she fibbed, "I'm not sure if I want to do it now."

Seeing through the game she'd started, a glint entered his eyes when he warned, "We can either do this the easy way or the hard way."

Her brows dipped in genuine confusion. "What's the hard way?"

His body responded before his words did, sending a rush of sexual hunger through their bond, knowing she'd be able to feel it if she didn't see it from his eyes first. The scent of his arousal was set free, an aroma that she could now detect, and it drew out her own arousal. The urge to taste her everywhere and drill himself into her fired through the mate bond, and she was finding it increasingly difficult not to give into her own urge to please him.

In the low voice that intensified her need for him, he crudely explained, "The hard way is to heat up every inch of you, target only your most sensitive regions at a pace that I already know by heart, and when you're close to your peak," His hand on her butt delivered a merciless squeeze, drawing a breathless sigh out of her as he continued, "I'll hold you there, and I won't let you get further until you've marked me. *That* is the hard way. You have two seconds to decide."

Sush wasn't sure whether it was the fog his words created, the arousing need she felt through the bond, or the way the threat sounded more like a reward that got her tongue-tied. Wherever her thoughts scattered, no decision came by the two-second mark.

"Have it your way then." Greg flipped them over with a zealous gleam in his eyes, taking her mouth first as he ripped her shirt from the middle and used the torn fabric to tie her wrists together, pinning them above her head as her back arched into him.

Pressing her back down with his weight and drawing her out of breath in less than a minute, his mouth then ventured to her throat, sucking and nibbling on the part just above her collarbone, biting in parts that drew out her whimpers as his hands worked their magic down her body.

Bringing himself up to offer her a full view of his body, which her eyes devoured despite the many times she'd seen it, Greg switched things up when he lifted her legs and removed her sweatpants at a torturously slow pace, eliciting her groans of protests as she tried to kick them off faster. Once the lower body garment was on the floor, his eyes stayed locked with hers as his tongue started at the heel of her foot, slowly gliding up to her toe and sucking on each one slowly, leisurely, making her breathing hitch, her lower region wet with need.

A trail of kisses followed from her foot up the length of her leg. Extra attention was given to her knee, then her thigh, where he focused fully on the heated skin of the inner region as she spread her legs wider even before he reached the part of her that throbbed so hard, waiting for him to fill the emptiness.

An arrogant smirk played on his lips as he followed the delicious smell wafting in the air to its source, blowing a gust of air just to watch her body quiver.

"Greg," she sighed his name like only he could give her the air she needed.

"Hm?" he hummed, feigning ignorance.

Looking at her from where he was, his tongue licked up the wetness in repeated strokes of the number eight—the very move that always had her moaning the loudest, which she did this time as well, and the sound was killing him.

"Please," she whispered in a breathless plea.

Resisting her wasn't easy for him either. His shaft had already stiffened from the moment she'd issued the challenge. His animal had been telling him to pounce and pound, but his human remained patient, playing the long game, unwilling to go further until he was wearing her mark.

Climbing up for their faces to meet, his thumb circled her nipple, which made her sink further into submission when he asked, "Something you want, my dear?"

His hardened tool pressed on her wetness through his pants, and although it only got more difficult to resist plunging into her, he persisted, trying to convince himself that she wasn't going to last much longer, though on a deeper level, he wondered if he was going to last any longer.

The moment he pinched her nipple with just the right amount of pressure, making her back arch, she whispered, "I need you. In me. Now. *Please.*"

Leaning close to her mouth, the tip of his tongue glazed over her lips, and he pulled back right before she took his lips. Confusion entered her need-filled eyes, and he placed a kiss on her nose, declaring, "I need to be in you, too, my love. But I want to feel you when I do it this time. It's either we both feel each other or nothing at all. So how about you rethink y—"

Before Greg finished, the binds on her wrists were ripped apart as she flipped them over with a strength and speed acquired overnight, taking his breath away. He didn't even have time to process the change in position before he felt her head buried at the crook of his neck with relentless strokes from her tongue and suctions from her mouth, emanating a hunger that had him moaning as his hands on her hips kneaded the flesh.

Sush didn't know who had written the books on marking, but the authors were right. There really wasn't a need to think. Her body just knew. She knew instinctively where her mark was supposed to go and the way she should tenderize the area. When she was ready, her mouth closed in, making Greg hold his breath and his hands kneading her hips come to an anxious pause.

The moment her canines sunk into his flesh, he released a loud groan of satisfaction like he'd just overcome an insurmountable challenge.

When the new set of canines retracted and Sush licked away the excess blood, Greg was bombarded with an intensity of desire that rivaled his own, a level of certainty that he easily matched, a degree of hope and happiness that brought moisture into his eyes, and a vigor of love that he could never imagine receiving in this lifetime or the next.

Sush sealed her work with a kiss the same way he did the previous night. Hovering above his face, her lips stretched broadly as she followed the mild animal instincts now within her, proclaiming, "Mine."

One of his hands glided up her back and rested at her nape, bringing her down for their lips to crash, repeating whispers of "I love you" between each brush.

Thinking to herself that she'd let him stall them long enough, she worked her way to his jaw, then his neck, quickly learning that the fresh mark was now the most sensitive region. She peppered kisses down his chest before sitting on her knees, got rid of his pants, and finally got to see his erection.

Bringing her mouth to the tip, her tongue glazed the surface as he grunted, and she slipped him into her mouth so swiftly that he moaned, "Fuck."

He reached over to take her hair and held it to the side as her head bobbed up and down his length. The sight was breathtaking, the pace was perfect, and it didn't take long before he came in her mouth with a grunt, shooting down her throat as she moaned with him, her mouth easing on the strokes, guiding him back from his high.

He pulled her next to him, bringing her face-down on the bed as he climbed behind her, hands prompting her to support herself by her knees. Slipping a condom on, he then thrust into her all at once, and moans of pleasure escaped, the space in her finally being filled and him being the one to fill it. He went harder and faster than he did in all their previous times now that he had acquired a new level of speed from being marked and she had the traits of a lycan to cope with the pressure and pace.

Any thorns of concern that grew were brusquely plucked away by her moaning and repeated urging for him to go even harder and faster in a way that even challenged his own speed and strength.

Moments away from her peak, she whimpered and muttered, "Please, please, please."

With a resounding growl, his hand on her waist moved to her abdomen as he gradually angled her upward while he continued pumping, holding her flush against his chest and biting on her mark, feeling her core clench around him as she screamed when he grunted and stiffened. Their orgasms rippled through their bond as Sush melted into his embrace while they took bated breaths, feeling light. Satiated. Happy.

While they were enjoying the nice, quiet moment together, his animal just had to ruin things by demanding his human ask their mate whether he could have a go with her. His human refused, saying she was worn out as it was, and they regulated their time for sex in the morning because they still had to work throughout the day. But his starved animal insisted he ask, wanting to hear the refusal from her lips before agreeing to drop the matter.

Clearing his throat, he began, "Sush, forgive the excessive entitlement of what I'm about to say, but my lycan is asking . . . if he can fuck you."

Her relaxed posture turned frigid, and his animal braced himself for a no, already swallowing a sad whimper and turning away with slumped shoulders. But when Sush turned to his human with shining eyes, the beast held on to a modicum of hope.

And when she asked, "Is he as good as you are?" he howled, insanely loudly, almost deafening his human and breaking their shared eardrums.

An amused but arrogant smile tipped Greg's lips. "I doubt it." His answer drew an instant growl from the animal as he continued, "He'll try, but don't be too hard on him if he doesn't meet your expectations, hm?"

His beast was going berserk now, fighting for dominance, trying to push his human to the back.

Sush reached for his cheek, gazing into his eyes that were in alternating shades now, and she knew she was seeing his beast at the flickering intervals. Bringing their lips close, her lids fell halfway when she whispered, "I just need him to be hard on me."

Those words gave his animal the boost he needed to push his human away and come forward. The straighter posture, the sudden flexing of his shoulders, and the way his hands on her abdomen and shoulder gripped her firmer and tighter told her she was now in the presence of his beast, who emitted a low snarl as his dark, hungry eyes zoned in on her like a predator would its prey.

Not knowing where to begin when it came to making love with his animal, she let her instincts guide her, leaning into his hold as her voice came out in a submissive purr, "Your Grace."

The erotic ring she brought to his title boosted his already inflated ego, and he flipped her around, pressing her back down against the mattress and pinning her wrists to the headboard, plunging into her and snarling in satisfaction when she gasped and moaned in ecstasy. His prolonged starvation and thirst for her had him going all out, getting her core to tense around him as he stiffened and grunted from his release in less than a minute.

The animal rested his forehead on hers as they came down from their high, cooing to her, not knowing another way to express how much he loved her, a gesture that she understood, seeing it from the affection in his eyes, feeling him through their bond. Her lips touched his in a quick peck, and his mouth took hers in a greedy kiss.

Even after the kiss, the beast refused to return control, savoring the moment with his mate, taking her two more times—from the side, then back—before lowering himself to rest on her front.

Head on her chest, he listened to the thumping cadence of her heart.

So beautiful. So perfect. And all his.

It took some time before his human regained control, at which time he pushed himself up and prompted, "Well?"

Knowing exactly what he wanted to ask, Sush's eyes narrowed. "Really?"

"I want to know, and I have a feeling he does too."

"It's not a competition, and you're both equally good."

"You're worried about hurting his feelings, aren't you?" Greg mused, ignoring the pouncing animal in his head.

"I'll say this," Sush began, putting his animal's protest to a stop, "he may *look* more egotistical, but I have a feeling you're the one with the greater ego."

As his animal celebrated the win, his human cut the victory short by uttering, "If a greater ego equates to better performance, I'll happily take it."

"You and your need to win," she reprimanded, brows arching as annoyance set in.

He grinned, gently nudging the tip of her nose, confessing, "Me and my need to please. To please *you*. I love you."

Those words softened her entirely, vaporizing the annoyance, and she didn't even need to think before responding, "I love you too."

CHAPTER 84

Back at work, many were pleased to learn that media scrutiny and public pressure were immense enough to force Ferdinand and Valor to take a temporary leave from office pending investigations of the reports made. Therefore, the two defense systems that human territory relied on now fell into the hands of the deputy defense minister, Agu, and for the hunters, the majority decided they wanted Sush. Sush received the same magnitude of support from the ministry, with Agu placing the discussion of lifting her suspension as the first thing on the agenda in the first meeting held without Ferdinand.

The second thing on the agenda was to officially remove the defense ministry's superiority over the hunters, letting them exist as a separate, independent entity, working with them as a partner rather than a subordinate. Agu's proposal was not well-received, and many suggested they wait for the charges against Ferdinand to be either dropped or pursued before voting on the matter.

At the end of the week, Greg and Sush returned to the kingdom. The first thing they did was get themselves registered as civil partners there after doing so in human territory several days prior. Sush wore a red-and-gold saree that once belonged to her aunt. The length of the silk garment was elaborately draped around her body, accentuating her figure, and Greg—who wore a complementary sherwani that was recently purchased—murmured, "Beautiful," into her ear no less than three times before they got their certificate, and many more times throughout the day.

After that was done, they arrived at the kindergarten to wait for the pups, standing amongst the crowd of parents, some of whom congratulated them on their union.

The entrance doors flung open, and the sea of pups trotted out. Greg's lips lifted higher when he spotted his little sweetheart sprinting toward him with a wide grin, leaping into his ready arms as she yelled his name. He scooped her up before her brother arrived a few seconds later, completely out of breath.

Weakling, Greg thought to himself, conveniently ignoring the fact that Enora had had more practice in outdoor activities and running away from trouble to attain the speed and stamina she now had. Greg ruffled the boy's hair as Ken gave Sush a shy wave. They were waiting for Reida when Enora said, "You smell diffewent, Uncle Gweg."

"Do I?" his brows rose, casting a knowing glance his mate's way.

Enora continued sniffing his hair and neck before she deduced, "Yeah, you smell . . ." she took another two whiffs and deduced ". . . nicer."

Sush snorted.

Greg pulled his favorite niece away from his shoulder, eyeing her when he asked, "Nicer? Didn't I smell nice before, sweetheart?"

Not seeing the implied insult in her statement and failing to understand how Greg didn't see what she said as a compliment, Enora simply blinked innocently and said, "You smelled nice befowe, but you smell nicer now." In her mind, he must have swapped shampoos or body wash the way she and her siblings did every few weeks after finishing a bottle.

"Hi, Sushi." Enora waved over his shoulder with a big smile.

Greg brought her closer to his mate, saying, "How about calling her Aunt Sush, sweetheart?"

"Weally?" The excitement in her voice was unparalleled. "Yay!" She stretched over and said, "You look pwetty, Aunty Sushi."

Sush got the cue to carry her, taking her from Greg and mouthing, "How?" because she'd never held a toddler. He helped adjust her arms and let Enora do the rest.

"Hm . . ." Enora sniffed. "You smell nice, Aunty Sushi. You smell a little bit like Uncle Gweg."

Glancing Greg's way and then back to Enora, Sush decided to have a little fun. "And who smells better, Enora? Uncle Greg or me?"

Enora sniffed her again, then shifted as Greg came closer for her to take another whiff before she delivered her verdict, "You smell nicer, Aunty Sushi. You smell like flowers."

Greg shot his narrowed eyes at Sush, linking, *'You did not just steal her away from me.'*

It wasn't her first experience with a mind-link, but the miraculousness of the instant mental messaging that her technical mind didn't quite understand yet still made her go speechless for a brief second every time before she ultimately replied, *'Relax, just because I smell better doesn't mean she'll love me more.'* As Enora continued sniffing, then resting her head on her aunt's shoulder and snuggling into her hold, Sush uttered, *'Or she might. Who knows?'*

"Alright, Aunt Sush is tired now. C'mon, sweetheart." Greg held out his hands, eager to steal her back, and Enora obediently leaned into his arms. There was something about her uncle's and parents' hold that always made her feel safe, and now she had Sush to add to that list, too.

"Sushi?" A small voice came from the ground, and Sush found herself gazing into the lilac eyes of another toddler, one she met in her last visit to the kingdom.

Squatting to level herself with Little Blackfur, her left hand gently ran through the boy's hair when she beamed. "Hello, Lewis. Had a good day?"

The boy's eyes dimmed. "No, not really."

"What happened?" Sush asked, concern filling her voice and emanating from her eyes as Lewis began telling her about him failing a math test and how he dropped his food at lunch when someone knocked into him, and how water spilled all over his painting just when he was about to finish so he had to start over.

Greg's eyes searched for the adult Blackfurs while the princess and Other Little Blackfur arrived, chatting non-stop.

Which irresponsible abominations would let their son suck away his octopus's attention like that? Greg would drag the Paw-Claws and leave, but it seemed a little mean, despite knowing the Blackfur children had security watching them from afar.

A car with a familiar plate pulled into a hasty park as Christian and Annie got out. The distant cousins' eyes instantly locked, and Greg's brows rose like he was asking for an explanation.

Christian took his little girl's bag off her shoulders before he did the same with his son. Ianne gave him a hug, at which time Christian held her close and explained to the other duke, "Quit judging us. Traffic was horrendous. The media practically made it impossible to leave government headquarters when they kept pressing for a statement about the hunters, which we've already given."

Greg replied monotonously, "And I suppose our cousin didn't use his Authority to clear the path?"

"He almost did, but the queen stopped him. And that's because it's not what the Authority is for, Greg. You should know that," Christian bit back before turning to the newest member of the family, failing to comprehend why the greatest hunter was settling for the dick of a creature when he pushed a polite smile and greeted, "Sush, nice to see you again."

"Your Graces," she greeted, looking up from Lewis and returning the gesture warmly.

Annie waved a hand, saying first names would do, and her husband gave a firm nod in agreement.

When it was time to say goodbye, Lewis refused to let go of Sush's hand, saying he hadn't told her everything yet, so—much to Greg's annoyance—Sush walked with the Blackfurs to their car as Lewis speedily updated her on the rest of the day and how things kept going wrong.

After giving Sush a hug and reluctantly waving goodbye as she made her way back to Greg's new car, where he was doing the usual headcount, now with Enora seated on Sush's lap, Lewis repeated the disaster of his day to his family like they hadn't heard it when he told Sush.

CHAPTER 85

In the following week, after returning from the kingdom, a paternity test was taken, and it confirmed Sush carried Ferdinand's genes—a fact that didn't surprise him but disgusted her. Of all the things she'd imagined her birth father to be, a defense minister that was the epitome of an irresponsible, disloyal, and unreliable hypocrite was not one of them.

Upon learning this, Sush sat on the couch and stared into space.

Greg came over soon after, placed her on his lap, and asked if she wanted to talk things through, preferred if he just held her and stayed silent, or simply wanted to be left alone for now, so he should go. At the mention of the last option, Sush grabbed onto his shirt—her action conveying that she did not want him to leave before her words did. She asked for the second option, and a very quiet stretch of two hours followed as she sorted through who her parents were.

She admitted she didn't fully know either of them, and perhaps never would. She sure wasn't interested in getting to know her biological father, but where did that leave her?

At that mental juncture, something Greg said from before played in her mind—about who her parents were having no bearing on who she was. She took a walk down memory lane—retrieving memories of being brought up by her uncle and aunt who loved her like she was their own, having worked her ass off in school and beaten all odds to complete her education, and having made memories with the people she loved or respected. She thought about the challenges she'd overcome—in her work and in life—most of the time with nothing more than sheer fucking will. There were bad days—lots of them, in fact—but even those storms had passed. She'd weathered every single one. Sometimes with support, sometimes without.

She thought about how far she'd come, from being orphaned to being a scholar, then an engineer, a huntress, a chief. She'd come far, and none of that had anything to do with the origins of her genes. She had something she was proud of, something she'd created—herself.

When her mental process came to an end, Greg was still holding her in his embrace and stroking her arm, neither bored nor frustrated. His emotions exuded patience with a tinge of concern, and a sliver of anxiety that he was trying very hard to keep to himself.

She left a kiss on his cheek, thanking him for doing this—for being there for her the way she needed him to. As his lips curled up, he murmured, "You needn't thank me for doing the bare minimum, my octopus. Thank *you* for telling me what you need."

Having processed the thoughts and emotions, she felt better—clear, emotionally stable, and at peace—ready to take on her new role amongst the hunters. And then came the drizzle before a quickly abating storm.

###

Questions of nepotism arose when it was reported that Sush had been sworn in as the new commander the moment charges against Valor were pursued, resulting in him losing the majority support of the hunters.

However, such skepticism was significantly reduced when many hunters—both on the job and several retirees—released independent statements and social media posts disclosing how Sush had been contributing from behind the scenes longer than anyone they knew and almost died on several occasions in her years of service. Some went so far as to disclose that Ferdinand had always voted against her when it came to promotions, appointments, and recommendations.

The months of trial that followed in human territory garnered universal attention, and many watched it live from wherever they lived. Some willingly woke up at ungodly hours just to see Ferdinand, Valor, and the Robinsons testify next to a potted plant of transparent-petaled flowers. Memes surfaced and circulated, labeling the flowers as the MVP of the courtroom saga.

It became something akin to a hit limited series on television, and the hunters tuned in to the daily episode like loyal fans. Patterson and Kenji chipped in to have large-screen TVs installed in their now-shared cafeteria in the newly built hunters headquarters. Everyone rushed for the best seats and watched it at lunch hour, either cheering or booing at testimonies like they were watching a football match.

But things took a melancholic turn when Ferdinand admitted to having fallen in love with Sush's mother at a point in time. They met at a bus stop, catching the same bus daily, and they eventually struck up a conversation. She was nineteen and didn't know who he was, not being one who was interested in politics. He only told her that he "worked for the government." Even so, the truth eventually came out when a fellow classmate who saw them together pointed out the resemblance he had to their defense minister, who was married. When she confronted Ferdinand about it, he panicked.

He apologized for lying to her and professed his love for her, promising her that he was already "thinking" about leaving his wife. Thinking about it wasn't enough, it seemed, and she made him choose there and then. He couldn't. He begged for more time. She gave him a week, and a week later, they met, with him proposing that they still see each other in private so he could keep his position in office, "to be able to provide for her with what I do best." Sush's mother called it off, and they didn't see each other until years later, when she turned up on his doorstep asking for child support for an infant he hadn't even been aware of. He didn't know Larissa had contacted Valor about the bombing until it was too late, and admitted to never making an effort to look for Sush, knowing the risks involved that would have led to career suicide.

Upon the close of arguments and testimonies, no one had their charges dropped.

The Robinson couple was sentenced to death for executing the long list of murders.

Larissa Ferdinand received the same sentencing, with the judges concluding that her act was strongly motivated by jealousy and anger, a fact that was cemented by the phone recording Patterson made of her confession the other day before they fucked, after which he testified against her on the stand, indifferent to her tears and scowl of betrayal she was throwing his way.

Hazel's lawyers somehow managed to successfully plead insanity on her behalf, thus bringing the charge of murder to the less serious one of voluntary manslaughter when the defense of diminished responsibility was accepted by the court. Her lawyers argued that being brought up by two parents who weren't in the right frame of mind, Hazel had developed certain levels of mental impairment—an assertion that was supported by clinical tests. They argued that contrary to her parents, who experienced a modicum of guilt in their first two murders, Hazel felt nothing after her first killings. Her parents were not insane when they committed the first murders, so the defense was not available to them, but their daughter had committed her killings with a mental impairment, so she qualified to have the defense applied to her. Nonunanimously persuaded, the court spared Hazel from the death sentence, but she would be kept behind bars for as long as it took for her to "recover."

Upon this pronouncement, hunters in the courtroom and beyond booed while wolves, lycans, and vampires snarled in protest.

Sush, despite sliding her hand into Greg's, found it difficult to calm him when she, too, was enraged by the decision.

At the other end of the same bench, everyone heard something wooden being broken as one of the three judges in front utilized the gavel to call for order and court decorum to be observed.

Lucy, while trying to calm her husband with one hand on his lap when his grip on her shoulder tightened, had her free hand holding onto the piece of wood she'd unintentionally broken off the bench when she was gripping it to cope with the anxiety. When Hazel's sentence was passed, Lucy closed her eyes and took a deep breath before releasing a drawn-out, frustrated exhale while amplifying a sense of control through the mate bond.

As the judge continued banging on the gavel and shouting for silence with less courage than the first time, Lucy shot her people around the courtroom a brief gaze—a silent command to rein in their emotions and beasts. This wasn't their territory. They had an image to uphold.

At their queen's silent command, they complied.

Seeing the kingdom's forces calming down, the vampires did the same.

Sush shot the hunters a similar look—one that reminded everyone they weren't in the headquarters cafeteria and conveyed a warning that they could be kicked out if they didn't pipe down. Although reluctant, the hunters silenced themselves as well—some with a groan.

Fortunately for everyone, the worst pronouncement had come to pass.

Hazel's conspirators within hunters headquarters, comprising two chameleons, two archers, and six octopuses, were sentenced to a thirty-five-year jail term.

Minister Ferdinand was sentenced to a lifetime behind bars for his involvement in the black market along with the fraudulent act of using a bank officer as a puppet to receive the tainted proceeds. This bank officer and another nine of his colleagues who made the transactions possible were bribed with ten percent of the proceeds to facilitate the minister's venture, thus they were subsequently convicted in separate trials.

The needle that broke society's back was Ferdinand's long line of affairs, plummeting his popularity overnight as his entire political party bore the brunt of the scandal. His former mistresses who hadn't been hunted down and slaughtered by the Robinsons either confirmed their involvement with the minister with pride like it was an accomplishment from their younger days or refused to speak to anyone about the past and went into hiding.

Needless to say, it wasn't long before an election was held and Agu was sworn in as the new defense minister. The first task he accomplished was to grant the hunters their independence, a motion that easily received majority support now that Ferdinand had been convicted.

Valor was sentenced to imprisonment for aiding and abetting the first of the Robinsons' murders and for omitting to report the crime as an officeholder. His sentencing got heavier when it was revealed that the former commander had been aware of the coded messages sent by Hazel through the encrypted phone to Ferdinand and himself but chose to do nothing. When the judge delivered the verdict, every hunter—even those who were supposed to be paying attention to their surroundings at the borders—leapt and cheered in undeterred jubilance.

By far, the lightest sentence went to Ferdinand's political rival—Joyce Clearwater. She was essentially given a hefty fine and seven years behind bars for agreeing to be the puppet for the Robinsons in exchange for a generous profit share from the black market, as long as the Robinsons could remove Ferdinand from office and rig the election to get her to take his place.

###

At the end of that momentous trial, Greg and Sush had a private candlelight dinner date in their newly purchased home, which had two extra bedrooms specifically allocated for Enora and Lewis whenever they wanted to spend a few nights there during the holidays. The property was situated within the kingdom but was only a twenty-minute drive to the newly built hunters headquarters, so Sush would see warriors and archers standing guard on her way to work every day.

Despite the disappointment in how things had ended with Hazel's case, Sush woke up with a smile every morning to admire the mark on her neck in the mirror and the other mark on her nape where the five-limbed octopus morphed into a crown with five spikes. At a cursory glance, the latter mark looked like a crown, but upon closer inspection, she could see that it was merely an evolved version of her five-limbed octopus, its limbs stretching further upward and covering part of its head.

As the new commander, she now had the abilities of a chameleon and archer as well, though her opinionated forelimbs were still her favorite part of herself. Having made peace with her past, she had no doubt that she was living the dream. She had a career she loved, a healthy professional circle, a mate that was a wild animal in bed and a complete gentleman whenever he wasn't getting her wet and making her beg and scream. An annoying gentleman sometimes . . . maybe a little arrogant, too, and he could occasionally be too demanding of their subordinates, but he made her smile nonetheless.

As their wine glasses tapped with a clink, Greg uttered, "I have to admit, nothing the Forest of Oderem could offer would top the months of public embarrassment and tainted legacies of the fallen heroes, save in the Traffic Cone's case. The forest could have done a better job with her."

Her lips quirked at the nickname—heroes. Scoffing, she tried not to let the Hazel debacle get to her like it still did whenever she thought about it, and chose to instead say, "Larissa's case came as a shock. I thought they'd let her off the hook like they did Hazel."

As Greg poured more wine into her glass, he uttered, "Traffic Cone is easily perceived as being mentally insane, even in court. That warning hazard can act. The Red Devil, on the other hand, looked normal, which was probably the issue."

Swirling her drink as Greg's fork pierced into his food, Sush said, "It doesn't really seem fair, does it—Larissa, I mean? The man cheats on his wife, she then resorts to act out of justifiable anger, and it's the wife who ends up with a death sentence?"

Greg responded nonchalantly, "Blame the justice system in human territory. Whips—that sometimes result in death—are issued here in the kingdom if affairs are ever brought to court."

Some of the wine Sush was pouring in through her lips slipped out, and she almost choked. "Seriously?" she asked while reaching to her mouth with the back of her hand.

Greg placed his cutlery back on the table and leaned over with his napkin to gently dab away the excess as he explained matter-of-factly, "Infidelity doesn't just disrespect one's marked mate; it disrespects our Goddess who bestowed the bond, so, yes, it's treated as a crime."

"Wow," she murmured, too shocked to speak any louder as Greg's hand and napkin left her face, but not before his thumb brushed across her chin and jaw in an affectionate graze.

As they returned to their meal, they went over their plans for the next day, being the start of their honeymoon. They agreed to postpone it until the trial was over, and now that it was, they were handing the reins to their subordinates—Sush to Millicent, Patterson, and Kenji; Greg to his top four—as they themselves took an extended leave from work.

The mavericks and hunters had been sharing everything since Sush and Agu took the helm of their respective departments, from knowledge in tech to sketches and prototypes—much to Kenji's excitement. As the new chief octopus, he was ecstatic to own some of the mavericks' gadgets, even working with Baxter and a few others over the phone to tweak and enhance the creations. He was also enjoying the fact that his hands could work on one thing while his mind thought through something else, a sentiment shared by many octopuses who had accepted their non-verbal but highly opinionated forelimbs.

Kenji used to think that he didn't have the mental capacity to multitask, but the new ability had proved him wrong. He was still based in the east, but continued working closely with the west, flying over once a month to check on the western octopuses' progress and aid in setbacks if Sush ever needed an extra brain and pair of hands.

The collaboration between hunters and the kingdom was revolutionary, and many celebrated the interspecies couple who couldn't care less about public support or lack thereof but appreciated the well wishes nonetheless.

While doing the dishes together, Sush and Greg brainstormed something that they had been building for Enora and Lewis because the pups were going to stay with them for a week during their two-month break from school. They went over the mechanics and necessary precautions over and over again, suggesting modifications to make sure everything would be safe yet fun, novel yet surmountable.

CHAPTER 86

A week after they'd returned from their honeymoon, the pups came over. Christian had been adamant about keeping his family away from Greg in the beginning, but it was difficult to keep his son away from Sush, so trust was built over time. In the first twenty times Sush and Greg brought Lewis to the park or pond when they took Enora, Christian and Annie went along, staying on the benches solely to observe, learning from there that their son had a knack for something other than his camera.

Unlike Ken, Lewis wasn't good with puzzles—wasn't patient enough—but he picked up using a slingshot quite quickly, shooting fake nests off high branches, even accidentally shooting Greg in his ass on his first try when Greg was placing the nests into trees. Lewis gasped and quickly hid the weapon behind his back the moment Greg turned around with a scowl, and Sush shielded the boy, blocking Greg's view of him and explaining to her mate that Lewis was practicing the pull, and the shot to his butt had been an honest accident.

Only after those observations did Christian and Annie feel better about letting Lewis go along without them, but only for an hour. And when things went well, their son coming back livelier after spending time outdoors, they allowed him more time with the Claws on the condition that Sush would always be there.

Greg took no umbrage in the condition. In fact, he respected Blackfur because of his continuous distrust of him. He himself would have never forgiven someone who'd poisoned his mate, even if it wasn't fatal, though it was amusing that the curse of his destined mate getting along with Little Blackfur was making them both suffer moments of awkwardness.

Greg took Enora's luggage and Sush took Lewis's as the pups embraced their parents and bid them goodbye for the week. After leaving their things in the designated rooms, they brought them to the new outdoor play site in their backyard.

Enora squealed in excitement, and Lewis's eyes widened in intrigue when their uncle and aunt told them they had a surprise. Greg opened the door to the back and checked that the invisible bulletproof walls were up three times before leading his sweetheart down the patio stairs. The little girl could not believe her eyes.

She scanned the archery range built and designed for a toddler, and her lilac orbs shone as her mouth gaped like she'd just discovered the secret at the end of the rainbow—and it was better than a pot of gold! In the field of green sat a huge train track with a blue toy train that held targets of different shapes and colors on each carriage, and when Greg turned the system on with his phone, the train began moving.

As Enora observed the moving train, an orange square target was shot, and her shocked eyes snapped to the source—from her side. She turned to see Lewis already holding a new slingshot as Sush guided him on estimating where to aim and how to wait before releasing.

"Sweetheart," Greg's voice brought her attention back to him, and she squealed and leaped when he handed her a brand-new bow and a quiver of arrows, even though she already had at least five sets at home. This one was different though. The brown bow and quiver had gold engravings of her name, and she took her time feeling the letters with her fingertips before throwing her arms around her uncle, exclaiming, "Thank you, Uncle Gweg!"

He chuckled, squeezing her in return and leaving a kiss in her hair. "You're very welcome, sweetheart. How about we give these a try?"

Upon releasing him, she brought the strap of the quiver over her head, and Greg adjusted it so it was secure on her back. Drawing an arrow out like a pro, she loaded the bow, aimed, waited for the train to get to where she wanted it to, and let the arrow fly. The rubber bullet landed on the far left of the target with a yellow bird.

After a few more shots, at which time it was getting too easy for both pups, Greg upped the speed without warning, and Lewis's perfect shot became a clear miss. The boy was enthralled by the zigzag route the train was now taking and the way it went up the hill that it didn't before! But Sush was clearly vexed by the missed shot, prompting her to yell, "Greg!"

Turning to her, he challenged with a smirk, "What? It's not a competition, is it?"

The glint in his eye did it for her, and she swore she was going to guide Lewis to beat Enora that very day, a quest that her mate saw clearly from her eyes and felt through their bond.

The day ended in a tie—much to Greg's and Sush's frustration and amusement—and the pups high-fived before being ushered in for a bath and dinner.

They did the balloon targets the next day, with Sush guiding Enora with her arrows and Greg doing the same for Little Blackfur with the slingshot. And although Greg and Sush had underwater targets planned for their third day, the pups insisted they wanted to do the train again, so that was what they did, moving the underwater one to the next day.

Both pups had to exert more force and ended up exhausting themselves earlier with the underwater targets in the mini pond. The seaweed blocking the targets was a nuisance at first, and the actual depth was difficult to estimate, but the pups got better with each try.

Between the banter, laughter, and watching their prodigies progress, Greg's and Sush's eyes always found their way back to each other. There was a deep sense of knowing that days like these were only the beginning, and the memories they'd make were only going to get better now that they had each other.

EPILOGUE

Xandar's jet landed next to the Forest of Oderem, and everyone trailed out to meet Pelly, Octavia, Rafael, and Amber.

The forest greeted them with the waft of freshly baked goods and a gentle breeze, growing pink and amber-colored flowers around Enora and bringing the butterflies that she always loved seeing. One landed on her nose, and Enora's hands were about to catch it when it flew away.

The breeze brought along dried leaves of different shapes, colors, and textures, raining them on Reida and Ianne, who collected them. The girls even brought a small sack to gather them after their first visit, always patting the branch that would magically extend toward them as a way of conveying their thanks.

Sush lay her eyes on the forest for the first time, feeling an undeniable closeness, an unexplained warmth, but she also felt a strong pull that did not just come from the forest. When the leaves had been properly sacked up, the vampires led the way. Every step they took was pulling Sush closer to the source of the magnetic haul, relaxing the tension of a rope she couldn't see being bound between her and wherever they were headed.

The moment a large castle came into view, her eyes bulged and her head cocked, brows furrowing deep, veins in her head almost popping from thinking hard.

A hand, calloused and warm, left her hand and grazed across her lower back, hooking at her waist, pulling her close. *'Everything alright?'* Greg linked.

'Have I . . . no, I'm sure I haven't. I've never been here.'

'You find it familiar too?'

Her head spun to him. *'You felt the same way on your first visit?'*

'No,' he admitted. *'But the queen did. As did the empress.'* After a moment of stunned silence, he added, *'After that day at the forest, when you turned pieces of nothing into weapons, I had a feeling you're one of them—one of the five.'*

"Five?" she asked aloud.

They entered the castle that was now used as a fortress for security—the one Greg spent two weeks setting up with the empire's forces. Trailing up the stairs had Sush's heart beating faster, and it wasn't because of the exercise.

Once the door opened, she let her instincts guide her around the empty room with a circular engraving on the floor, gravitating toward the sector with a carving of a bow. As she knelt at the edge, her hand reached to trace the shape, and she felt something—part filled and part empty. It took her a moment to realize the fullness was from Lucy's and Pelly's presence, and the emptiness was from the unoccupied parts of the circle.

Her fingertips traced the length and shape of the depression that made up the bow, which befuddled her at how perfectly it matched the one given to her by her uncle—one of the few things she had held onto for as long as she could remember.

There was a familiarity in this place, this room, this creepy circle that knew what her uncle's bow was like, and as her eyes turned gold, so did the carving.

AUTHOR'S NOTE

Dear readers,

We've come to the end of *The Indomitable Huntress & the Hardened Duke*. Please leave a review to share your thoughts!

When I started book one, I would have never thought this would be the direction I'd take in book three, especially not when I was writing the first chapters of my debut, but here we are.

I named the female lead Sushmita after my closest friend in the Sixth Form (she doesn't know yet), coupled with Alagumalai, which means "beautiful mountain" and is part of the name of my favorite English teacher (she doesn't know either). I almost chickened out and was going to use something generic, but the tale didn't carry the spark I wanted as I began writing, so I swapped it back.

I hope the male lead has been up to most of your standards. I understand many of us have had very high hopes for him since book one. Not sure if the hunger for him is satiated to a certain extent, but hopefully it's suppressed a lot more now that you know he's taken. XD

With the closing of this book comes a temporary closing of the adults' stories. In book four, the princess will come of age, and we'll meet someone new who'll be moving the series forward with her.

We will be seeing the adults again in the final book, but for now, the limelight will fall on the pups. I don't have a tentative publication date for book four yet, but I'll post an update on socials once I do. (Follow me!)

Per the usual way we part, I'll leave you with the thought I kept in the back of my mind for this tale: **It's not always easy to let go, but until we've**

unshackled ourselves from the chains of the past, we won't possess the eyes to see the wonders we desire or the heart to welcome a future we're craving for.

Thank you Stacey (@grammargal on Fiverr), for editing and proofreading every line and punctuation; Sam (@Psalmyy on Fiverr), for formatting this entire thing; and my cover designer, for the beautiful design concept.

Have a great rest of the day, and I hope to see all of you in book four!

Stina's Pen
AUTHOR

ABOUT THE AUTHOR

Stina's Pen is the pseudonym used by an author who writes to escape, sometimes even to manage her less-than-sunny days. She hopes to help readers take a vacation from their everyday lives and experience a whole new world.

When Stina isn't writing, she can be found reading anything that piques her interest, accidentally buying books on accidental visits to bookstores despite the shelves of unread novels at home. Always a daydreamer, she often fantasizes about what could unravel if something that didn't happen happened. She is also prone to buying stickers and washi tapes (by complete accident) and then wondering what to do with them.

With a goal of inspiring others and hoping they draw strength from her characters, she wishes to write in a way that makes everyone's days a little brighter, that allows them to appreciate who they are and fall in love with the magic they add into the world.

IG: @stinaspen
Facebook: Stina's Pen
TikTok: @stinaspen

Printed in Great Britain
by Amazon